FE 1 9

P9-CDA-455

A Deadly Divide

ALSO BY AUSMA ZEHANAT KHAN

ESA KHATTAK AND RACHEL GETTY MYSTERIES

A Dangerous Crossing
Among the Ruins
A Death in Sarajevo (a novella)
The Language of Secrets
The Unquiet Dead

THE KHORASAN ARCHIVES FANTASY NOVELS

The Black Khan
The Bloodprint

Ausma Zehanat Khan

A
Deadly
Divide

MINOTAUR BOOKS NEW YORK

This is a work of fiction. All of the characters, organizations, and events portrayed in this novel are either products of the author's imagination or are used fictitiously.

A DEADLY DIVIDE. Copyright © 2019 by Ausma Zehanat Khan. All rights reserved. Printed in the United States of America. For information, address St. Martin's Press, 175 Fifth Avenue, New York, N.Y. 10010.

www.minotaurbooks.com

The Library of Congress Cataloging-in-Publication Data is available upon request.

ISBN 978-1-250-29828-7 (hardcover)
ISBN 978-1-250-29830-0 (ebook)

Our books may be purchased in bulk for promotional, educational, or business use. Please contact your local bookseller or the Macmillan Corporate and Premium Sales Department at 1-800-221-7945, extension 5442, or by email at MacmillanSpecialMarkets@macmillan.com.

First Edition: February 2019

10 9 8 7 6 5 4 3 2 1

For Summer and Casim,
my chandni and
my chand ka tokra,
I pass the torch into your hands.

I learned that the Canadian government was going to take more refugees who couldn't go to the United States, and they were coming here. I saw that and I . . . lost my mind. I don't want us to become like Europe. I don't want them to kill my parents, my family. I had to do something. . . . It was something that tortured me.

—Alexandre Bissonnette, the shooter in the 2017 Québec mosque shooting

I do not know why I committed such a senseless act.

—Alexandre Bissonnette, Statement of Guilt, March 2018

A Deadly Divide

Prologue

The watcher followed Esa Khattak home, observing the detective in the dark. For all his skills and aptitude, Khattak didn't know. He'd never known that he was being followed because signs of pursuit had been cleverly disguised.

There had been moments when the temptation to leave a calling card had been nearly too much to resist. The furtive delight to be gained from witnessing Khattak's response. Of tasting his sudden panic at how close the threat had come.

But the watcher's patience was limitless. The moment to act would be soon. And when it came, it wouldn't be decided by a note left at Khattak's door. The endgame was playing out; the climax would be profound.

Just outside the door to his house, Khattak answered his phone.

He had seemed tired when he'd searched for his keys, but now his features softened, a smile curving his lips, as he set down his case at his side.

It would be the woman, then. The woman Khattak had left in Greece, the one he'd since come to love. The woman was intriguing because she mattered to him. Tracking her travels abroad had posed a new kind of challenge, but Khattak was, by far, the more riveting of the pair.

The watcher kept waiting for a misstep. For a sign that Khattak was someone other than he seemed. But his private face was not all that different from his public one, except where women were concerned.

That was when the detective finally let down his guard, just as he was doing now, laughing with the woman on the other end of the phone.

He was warm, expressive . . . perhaps even emotional.

Words not often used to describe Inspector Khattak.

But now there were next steps to be considered. Wait for Khattak to leave his house in the morning, or return to Greece to resume surveillance there? Or do neither of those things and head west to the home of Sergeant Rachel Getty, a woman of significance in Esa Khattak's life.

There were other possibilities, too. But these were the most compelling.

The strike, when it came, would be hard.

A moment of decision, now.

The watcher rubbed a cold steel weight with careful, clever hands. Paused for the space of a breath.

Then held it up to shoot.

1

Blood saturated the walls, the stink of it creeping into his nostrils. By any measure, the scene was sickening. It was more devastation at a single crime scene than Esa Khattak had ever witnessed. From the green tinge to Rachel's skin, he could see it was the same for her. Their eyes met across the hall, sharing the moment of horror. They'd been called at once and had arrived as quickly as possible after the shooting, a mere matter of hours.

Rachel was at the door canvasing the mosque's parking lot. Khattak had been permitted access to the narrow cordon set up by crime scene technicians in the midst of the dead. He wore a protective forensic suit, Superintendent Martine Killiam at his side. He photographed the scene methodically, finding it easier to deal with the sight of bodies through the distancing mechanism of his lens. He made the count to himself. Two bodies in the corner had fallen back against the small shelf of books. Two more were slumped sideways in the main prayer space, where the green and white carpeting was soaked through. Another body was pitched against the mihrab, its white robe spattered with starbursts of blood. The delicately tiled niche had been damaged by a spray of bullets, its shards scattered over the carpet. A tiny turquoise flower lay inches from Khattak's feet.

He turned in the opposite direction, to the scene he'd put off photographing to the end. Two bodies close enough to touch and farthest from the door, one huddled inside the protective embrace of the other. A father and his small son. The assailant had targeted both.

A small community, a small mosque, with seven dead in the prayer hall.

And there was one more. Killed in the small passageway that led from the imam's office to the main hall, this time by a single gunshot to the head, assailant and victim facing each other.

The man who Khattak presumed had shot them was sitting on a chair at the far end of the hallway, a semi-automatic weapon cradled in his lap. It was an AR-15. He was surrounded by Sûreté officers who spoke to him in French, patient with his bewilderment.

Khattak glanced at him once, a comprehensive glance. Long enough to see the small gold cross he wore on a chain at his neck. And to note the details of his clothing: A gray cardigan worn over a blue shirt. Black trousers and formal dress shoes, slightly scuffed at the toes. The man in the chair seemed slight and insignificant, his thin patch of hair compensated for by a full-grown beard, his eyes wide and dazed. His clothes, hands, and face were free of blood spatter, but his hands were locked around the weapon.

A powerfully built man with an air of command was speaking to the man with the gun in a surprisingly gentle voice, his tone respectful and kind. Esa couldn't make out his words, but after a few minutes the gun was released into the hands of the technicians. A moment later, the man in the chair was helped to his feet and escorted from the mosque through a side entrance.

Khattak turned to Killiam. The heat inside the mosque was stifling, yet he found his hands were cold. He put away his phone.

"No handcuffs?" he asked her, fighting the tremor in his voice.

Killiam shook her head. She'd made her own inventory of the scene, her sharp gray eyes missing nothing. She was wearing her dress uniform, the stripes at her shoulders indicative of her rank, and after a minute the man in charge of the scene nodded at her in acknowledgment. She nodded back.

Brusquely, she said to Khattak, "That's Christian Lemaire, a homicide detective with the SQ—the Sûreté du Québec. The man with the rifle is Étienne Roy; he's the priest at the local church. He holds a position of considerable influence. More than that, he is dear to the people of this town. They won't insult the church by cuffing him. My guess is Inspector Lemaire won't arrest him tonight."

Khattak glanced at her sharply. "He was found with the weapon in his hand."

"And what do you conclude from that?"

Khattak took a moment to think it through. Killiam had requested the presence of Community Policing detectives on-site for a reason. She'd accompanied him personally and not only because she expected Esa to do damage control in the small community that attended the mosque. Their relationship had progressed beyond that.

"He didn't look as though he'd ever held a gun in his hands. There's no blood trail leading from the prayer hall, his shoes are clean—and where's the gun?"

"Inspector Lemaire's team has confiscated it."

"I mean the gun used to kill the victim in the hallway. It wasn't the AR-15. From the exit wound, I'd say it was a handgun. Has it been recovered from the scene?"

Killiam looked at him approvingly. "No."

"So either there's a second shooter or the priest was not involved."

A new team had gathered at the entrance to the mosque. Lemaire went over to speak to them. Killiam straightened her jacket, speaking to Khattak in an undertone.

"Then why was the rifle in his hands?"

"Maybe the priest came to the mosque in the aftermath of the shooting. Perhaps he tried to help some of the victims. Or it could be he wrestled the rifle away from the assailant."

Killiam was watching Lemaire, a faint frown settling between her eyebrows.

"There's no evidence he did anything of the kind. And if he *was* engaged in a scuffle, why wasn't he shot?"

Lemaire looked back over his shoulder, fixing them with a penetrating glance.

Khattak didn't have the answer.

What he did have was questions raised by the way the priest had been dressed. He was about to raise this when Killiam swore under

her breath. Khattak followed her line of sight, to Lemaire and his efforts to coordinate the various branches of police insisting on access
to the scene. His voice cut cleanly across the clatter.

But it wasn't Lemaire who had drawn Killiam's attention.

In the flickering light cast by ambulances and police cars, a hastily
constructed platform had been arranged. A coterie of reporters were
gathered in a circle around a neatly dressed woman in her thirties.
Other press huddles had begun to form as well demanding the attention of local officials.

"We need to control how this shooting is covered from the outset."
Killiam sounded worried, a rare emotion for her.

"Lemaire should get out there, then," Khattak said.

But when Killiam glanced back at him, her gray eyes frankly assessing, he understood at last why he and Rachel had been allowed
access to the crime scene and, more important, why Community
Policing had been called to assist at this shooting at a mosque in
Québec.

She was expecting him to manage the public response to the crisis—
to give it the Community Policing Section's sanction. And to fulfill the
CPS mandate, which was to play a mediating role between minority
communities and law enforcement where violent crime had occurred.

But looking across at the gathering of reporters, he knew that nothing about the shooting would be easy to manage or suppress. Because
one of his chief adversaries was speaking even now.

2

WOLF ALLEGIANCE CHAT ROOM
[English-language page]

SUBJECT: MOSQUE SHOOTING
COMMENTS OPEN

WHITEVICTORY: TOO MANY ATTACKS BY "REFUGEES" THE GOVERNMENT LETS IN WITHOUT EXTREME VETTING. WE'RE FIGHTING BACK AND IT'S ABOUT TIME!!!!

NINEINCHNAILER: YEAH BUT I WANNA KNOW HOW THEY GOT THE AR-15.

FRENCHKISSER: AN ASSAULT RIFLE?

NINEINCHNAILER: JUST WHAT I HEARD SOMEWHERE.

FLAYALLTHEPLAYERS: WE HAVE TO PROTECT OURSELVES.

NOHA TEHERE: I THINK YOU MAY HAVE READ A DIFFERENT NEWS REPORT. THE PEOPLE *INSIDE* THE MOSQUE ARE THE ONES WHO NEED PROTECTION.

WHITEVICTORY: FUCK OFF, ALIZAH.

BROADSWORDBEN: I SECOND THAT.

NOHA TEHERE: THOUGHT THIS WAS AN OPEN FORUM. NICE TO HEAR FROM YOU AGAIN, BEN, BY THE WAY.

BROADSWORDBEN: SCREW THAT AND SCREW YOU. HOW THE FUCK DID THEY GET AN AR-15? THEY'RE ILLEGAL AS FUCK.

FRENCHKISSER: WHO CARES AS LONG AS THEY'RE USED TO FIGHT ISLAM.

NOHA TEHERE: YOU MIGHT CARE WHEN THERE ARE KIDS WITH GUNS IN THIS TOWN. ESPECIALLY SINCE THE GUNS BRING GANGS.

(continued...)

FRENCHKISSER: OTHER WAY AROUND. I'D RATHER HAVE GANGS THAN MOSLEMS. QUÉBEC IS GIVING YOU A MESSAGE. YOUR. NOT. WELCOME.

NOHA TEHERE: *YOU'RE*

NINEINCHNAILER: COPS HAVEN'T FIGURED OUT WHO DID IT, BUT THE FIRST THING YOU HERE IS "AREN'T WE ALL HUMAN?" AND "LOOK HOW PEACEFUL THEY ARE."

FLEURDELIS: DON'T KNOW HOW MANY THEY TOOK OUT BUT IT'S A START.

NINEINCHNAILER: ALLAHU SNACKBAR!!!

BROADSWORDBEN: ALLAH FUCKBAR!!!

NOHA TEHERE: DO YOU EVEN HEAR YOURSELVES? YOU'RE CHEERING ON MASS MURDER.

GOODGUYWITHAGUN: I CAN'T READ FRENCH. WHO THE HELL IS THE SHOOTER? AN ARAB OR SOME ANGRY QUÉBÉCOIS WHO'S HAD ENOUGH OF THIS SHIT?

NOHA TEHERE: YOU SHOULD MAYBE CHANGE YOUR USER ID.

GOODGUYWITHAGUN: MAYBE WHAT I SHOULD DO IS COME LOOKING FOR YOU.

NOHA TEHERE: YOU'D HAVE TO LEAVE YOUR MOTHER'S BASEMENT FIRST.

GOODGUYWITHAGUN: YOU TALK BIG BEHIND A SCREEN.

NOHA TEHERE: ALSO ON THE RADIO AND IN REAL LIFE.

GOODGUYWITHAGUN: GOOD TO KNOW WHERE I CAN FIND YOU.

NOHA TEHERE: OVERCOMPENSATE MUCH?

NINEINCHNAILER: I HEARD 4-5 MUSLIMS GOT SHOT.

FLAYALLTHEPLAYERS: NOT ENOUGH.

BROADSWORDBEN: IT'S NEVER ENOUGH, MAN. WE NEED A FUCKING CIVIL WAR. WE NEED TO EXTERMINATE THEM ALL.

FLEURDELIS: WHAT WE NEED IS BETTER AIM. HE MISSED LIKE 10-15 OTHERS.

NINEINCHNAILER: I SALUTE THE BROTHERS OF THE ALLEGIANCE WHO MADE THIS HAPPEN.

NOHA TEHERE: THE WOLF ALLEGIANCE?

BROADSWORDBEN: WHO ELSE HAS THE FUCKING BALLS?

NOHA TEHERE: THANKS FOR CLARIFYING. NOW I CAN REPORT YOU FOR INCITEMENT.

WHITEVICTORY: GET THE FUCK OUTTA HERE.

BROADSWORDBEN: GO DARK. EVERYONE GO DARK.

NOHA TEHERE: TURN OFF YOUR LAPTOPS, YOU MEAN. DON'T FORGET TO CLEAR YOUR HISTORIES.

BROADSWORDBEN: YOU'LL GET YOURS, BITCH.

NOHA TEHERE: PEOPLE LIKE YOU ARE THE REASON FOR THE SHOOTING AT THE MOSQUE.

BROADSWORDBEN: THANKS FOR GIVING ME THE CREDIT.

NOHA TEHERE: THOUGHT YOU WERE GOING DARK.

BROADSWORDBEN: WAIT UNTIL YOU FIGURE OUT JUST HOW DARK I AM.

3

Surrounded by the warmth of a sweltering summer night, Rachel Getty removed the jacket she'd thrown on when CPS had gotten the call. Though based in Toronto, Community Policing had national jurisdiction and had worked the Ontario townships in the past, but this was the first time they'd been summoned to Québec. The shooting at the mosque was a somber fit with their mandate.

They'd immediately flown to Ottawa to meet with Superintendent Killiam, then driven the short distance across the Québec border to this small town on the fringes of Gatineau Park. In daylight, under the warm wash of sunlight, the town's charm would have been apparent: Gabled houses and stone cottages jumbled together along narrow, cobblestoned streets. And at two opposite ends stationed on rolling green hills, the university and the church, the secular and sacred, each carving out a sphere of influence.

But somewhere between these stalwarts of tradition, a small, bright mosque had taken root, modestly asserting its presence and offering a promise of belonging to its small congregation. It was a newly renovated building, and the architect had given the mosque a distinctly French character—Rachel couldn't have said how, but she recognized it in the pattern of stone and the gallery of windows. Almost as an act of self-defense, the blue and white provincial flag of Québec flew from a staff in the parking lot. There was no accompanying Canadian flag, and no display of a crescent or a star. No exterior arches, no dome or minaret. A uniquely Québécois mosque? Or the sign of a community in hiding?

With the pavement bathed in the glow of police lights, and the yellow tape cordoning off the scene from onlookers who were arriving in increasing numbers, the town became like any other in Rachel's experience, its individuality flattened by the banality of procedure. She was no longer seeing shopfronts and cafés; she was checking lines of sight, modes of egress, suspicious faces in the crowd hovering too close to the cordon.

Her attention was caught by a woman motioning to a group of reporters. The woman brushed back her hair, straightened the lapels of her stylish coat, and readied herself to speak. She'd checked with Khattak, who'd told her that the woman who'd set up the press conference was Diana Shehadeh. She was the head of a civil liberties association, renamed and reconstituted after a smear campaign against an earlier iteration of the same group had rendered it defunct. The new organization she fronted would be busier than ever, now.

Before Shehadeh could speak, a giant of a man cut his way through the crowd and waved the reporters off. She recognized him as Inspector Christian Lemaire.

"We'll have news for you soon, but this isn't the moment, and this woman, whoever she is, is not authorized to give you information about a local crime scene."

A babble of voices erupted. Lemaire fixed them with an icy blue glare until they subsided, retreating to their vehicles to make contact with their desks. There was no story yet. But they knew there would be soon.

Khattak and Killiam cut across the parking lot, not to join the man who'd shut down the press conference, but to join the woman who was making a fuss over being silenced. Rachel continued to snap photographs of onlookers, of faces in the parking lot, of movement in and out of the mosque, trying to make herself useful until Khattak called her to his side. Technically, she was his junior at Community Policing, yet they most often worked collaboratively as partners.

An urgent conference was taking place between Khattak and the others. Rachel was so intent on it that she was taken by surprise when the tall man stalked over to her and grabbed her phone from her hand.

"Who the hell are you?"

Instantly antagonized by the kind of manner she detested, Rachel glared back at him coldly. Though his six-foot-plus frame was packed with muscle and his bright blue eyes were hostile, Lemaire didn't intimidate her. Far from it. She'd honed her skills as an officer facing down men like Lemaire. Men like her father, Don Getty.

Without a word, she removed her police ID from her bag and held it up under his nose. She was tall and strongly built herself; she didn't back up a single step.

"Community Policing?" His head swiveled in Khattak's direction; then his penetrating blue eyes were back on Rachel's face. "Who's he, then? God's gift to the SQ?"

Rachel looked Lemaire over. "What's the matter? Been hoarding that title to yourself?"

There was a short pause and then Lemaire laughed, emphasizing the crow's-feet at the corners of his eyes. He made the same survey of Rachel that she'd just made of him, taking note of the jacket she had folded over one arm.

"You don't like being stuffed into a suit any more than I do."

She supposed that was true. His jacket was straining the seams of his shoulders, and his tie had been yanked loose to hang around his collar.

She shrugged. "It's just another kind of uniform." After a moment, she added, "Inspector."

He made an impatient gesture, his eyes searching past her head, taking note of the growing chaos at the edges of the cordon.

"Call me Lemaire; everyone does." He pushed Rachel's phone back into her hand. "Never seen anything like this, though Christ knows we've been heading to this moment for a while." His eyes flicked across Rachel's face, making an assessment he didn't share. He nodded at the far edge of the parking lot where two trailers had been set up head to head, bracketed by ambulances. The blue and red lights cut across the parking lot, the sirens long since silenced.

"Incident room," he snapped. "Team meeting. Join us, Sergeant Getty."

He was scrupulously attentive to her rank considering he'd just told her to call him by his name. She wondered how much training he'd had to undergo when it came to interacting with women officers. She was also curious about his lack of an accent. He spoke like an Anglophone, but his name was distinctively French. Christian Lemaire. A bearish brute of a man with a weathered face and an undisciplined mane of hair, but one she would be wise not to underestimate. She followed him to the incident room, reserving judgment for the moment.

4

Christian Lemaire was a forceful presence on a unit bristling with egos. Within hours of the shooting, command of the operation had been assumed by the provincial Integrated National Security Enforcement Team known as INSET. Officers from other law enforcement agencies, including Rachel and Khattak from Community Policing, and members of the Sûreté, had now been seconded to INSET, to function as a single unit. In a room crowded with men jockeying for position, Killiam and Rachel were the only women.

Every woman who served in law enforcement was used to similar circumstances. Killiam took control of the room without noticeable effort, and when she was finished the officers in the room were taking notes. Her voice brisk, she laid out the operational procedures to be followed.

"What we must determine up front is whether we are investigating a mass shooting or conducting a counter-terrorism operation." She nodded at Lemaire. "Inspector Lemaire remains in command and all findings are to be channeled to me through him. Nothing gets leaked to the press, I repeat, nothing." She examined each face in the room. "We have had no issues with unreliable team members in English Canada; I expect no less from officers in Québec."

Well, Rachel thought, *that's one way of dealing with simmering Anglo-Francophone tensions. Dealing it a death blow at the start with a challenge to national pride.*

Killiam called Khattak and Rachel up to the front of the room and introduced them. Letting her glasses slip to the tip of her nose, she examined each man in the room, ending with Christian Lemaire.

"These Community Policing officers are here to deal with a community in grief and to head off an extremely volatile situation. You've seen Diana Shehadeh outside. She represents the Muslim Civil Liberties Union, and she will be waiting for us to make our first mistake. She'll try to control the narrative of this shooting, but our priority is to find out who is responsible and to hold them to account. Now." Killiam placed a firm hand on Rachel's shoulder. "Make no mistake. These are my officers. They represent *me*. Inspector Khattak is second-in-command, and he will be working closely with Inspector Lemaire. Any obstruction of his work or questioning of his loyalties will not be tolerated. Understand that this shooting is a crime *against* the Muslim community in Saint-Isidore-du-Lac; have I made myself clear?"

There was a rumble of assent.

Killiam turned the meeting over to Lemaire.

"I leave it in your capable hands." She pointed at Rachel. "Come with me."

Quashing her sense of alarm, Rachel followed Killiam to the exit.

"Are you taking me off this?" she asked when they were alone.

Like Killiam, she kept her back to the trailer and her gaze focused on the crowds. Family members were in the lot, their grief and heartbreak palpable. Rachel scanned the crowd. To the west of the parking lot a trio of young women dressed in identical trench coats pressed against the cordon. A pair of female officers held them back. Two of the young women were strikingly similar in appearance, with long fair hair and blue eyes. The third woman's hair was cut in choppy black waves that were subdued by a rhinestone headband.

Killiam cleared her throat. "Far from it, Sergeant Getty. I want you to monitor every aspect of the situation and report back to me. If there is insubordination of the kind Inspector Khattak faced over the case in Algonquin, I want to know it immediately. No incident is too small for you to bring to my attention. This is not a case where I expect either of you to fail."

"Understood, ma'am." Rachel tipped her head, considering. "Are you expecting trouble from Inspector Lemaire?"

"Not at all. I paired Khattak with Lemaire deliberately. I can't think of an officer in whom I have more faith."

Rachel was glad to hear it. It made a nice change from working under a cloud, even if she and Lemaire had gotten off to a bad start.

"That's not all, Sergeant Getty. I want you to report to me about Inspector Khattak."

Rachel frowned. "I'm not spying on Khattak for you."

Killiam's response was freezing. "I'm not asking you to. I'm asking you to consider whether this particular investigation may be more difficult than others assigned to your unit. More personal for Inspector Khattak. He would never ask to be reassigned." She sighed. "He treats each case like personal penance. If it seems to you to be weighing on him too deeply, that's something I want to know. We have plans for Khattak. We don't want to burn him out."

She didn't elaborate further and Rachel didn't dare ask. She was taken aback by the trust being placed in her and was eager to prove herself worthy of it. Seeing her commitment in her face, Killiam unbent to say, "Rachel. There may be some unexpected . . . unpleasantness . . . on this team. I know you've been there before, but as your superior officer, I'll treat any complaint you make with utmost seriousness. No matter who it's against."

A hesitant smile broke across Rachel's face. She'd never had a woman at her back.

"Thank you, ma'am; that means a lot." She glanced across at the crowd, some of whom were holding placards that featured appalling statements. "But that's not where I suspect most of the trouble will be."

5

ÉLISE DOUCET'S BLOG
[Translated from the French]

ÉLISE DOUCET
Montréal, Québec

To insist on a responsible immigration policy is not racist. We have a right to know who is coming here and what they stand for. Is it fair to bring people here and put them in detention centers at public expense when we can't even care for our own? There are people who need government services more than ever, the elderly, the disabled . . . meanwhile those who hate us come to live here on our dime.

Our government brings them and then tells us we must be the ones to adapt when they refuse to respect us. *They* must adapt to *us:* to our culture, our language, our values. Does saying this make me racist or does it make me a responsible citizen of Québec?

You asked about the Muslims. I am only against the extremists, the ones who hide their faces. I am not a radical. I am not for La Meute or the Sons of Odin or the Storm Alliance, though I do wish we could work together . . . maybe have a dialogue.

The people of Québec are always kind and generous. But when you make fools of us we get angry. And that's when we fight back.

COMMENTS:

CANDLELITVIGIL: 100% respect to you for your words. I am not racist either. I am someone who doesn't want to lose everything I love.

(continued...)

EDITH SAUCIER: I agree that we should not fight amongst ourselves. We need La Meute and Storm Alliance, and now that this has happened in Saint-Isidore, the Wolf Allegiance needs to start talking with them again. What is your position on the Wolves?

ÉLISE DOUCET: I am for whoever wants to work to build a better Québec.

EDITH SAUCIER: They are decent French boys who have been shamefully maligned.

ABEAUTIFULMERCY: Decent French girls, too.

ÉLISE DOUCET: In the new Québec, everyone's a racist.

CANDLELITVIGIL: We need to change that. We need to change the way they talk about us.

ABEAUTIFULMERCY: The change has already come.

6

The vast machinery of law enforcement was put to work. There were crime scene technicians on the scene, mortuary vans waiting to take bodies to the morgue, grief counselors keeping family members of those who hadn't returned home away from the scene using a wait-and-see vocabulary, senior officers conferring in government offices with local and provincial politicians, guards at the local station with strict instructions on the transfer of the priest Étienne Roy, others at the hospital with those who had been wounded in the shooting and taken away before Esa and Rachel's arrival, and armed guards outside the room of one victim in particular.

Killiam was dealing with politicians. Khattak and Rachel were en route to the hospital with Lemaire.

"There's more," Lemaire told them abruptly, leaning on his horn to clear the road ahead.

Rachel leaned forward in her seat. "More what?"

"There's another crime scene. Well, it's part of the same scene, but we cleared it before you got here. That's why the press arrived so quickly. That's why your friend Diana Shehadeh is here." He said this to Khattak, but the words didn't have the effect Rachel was anticipating; she thought Khattak might interpret them as an insult and choose to respond in kind. Instead, his face had gone pale—but then, he often made connections that weren't apparent to Rachel.

"The shooter began in the women's section?"

Lemaire turned left, his car slowing down on the long climb up the hill.

"How did you know that?" He made no effort to mask the unease in his voice.

"We were called to the scene because of our expertise."

Khattak's tone and words were neutral, but Rachel knew the undercurrents all too well.

"Yes, the women's section. It's in the basement. Four more bodies. We processed them first. They're already at the morgue."

"So the shooter came in the side entrance."

Khattak's voice had thickened slightly. He turned to look out the window.

"Back entrance. This is not the most enlightened community." Lemaire made no apology for his statement. When Khattak didn't react, neither did Rachel. She'd learned to hold her tongue, to wait for the opportune moment to speak. And she kept Martine Killiam's assessment of Lemaire in mind. She'd called him an excellent police officer, one of the best she knew. So Rachel would wait to see if that was true. She asked a different question, hoping to confound Lemaire's expectations.

"If the shooter hit the women's prayer area first, why didn't the men have enough time to escape?"

Lemaire drew into the hospital's parking lot. The receiving area was clogged with ambulances, their lurid lights flashing against the gray concrete. It struck Rachel that for a scene of such urgency and chaos there was a cathedral hush around events.

"Christ," Rachel whispered. "How many were wounded in the shooting?"

"Another dozen. The chief surgeon has warned us that many of them will die. You know what an assault rifle does to a person's body—the wounds are too severe. And to answer your other question, the basement is insulated. It has no windows, and the door and rafters are solid."

Khattak shook his head. "They would still have heard an assault rifle."

Lemaire's interest in Khattak sharpened.

"You're right," he said. "But each of the four women in the basement was killed execution-style. A single gunshot to the head."

"Back or front?" Khattak asked.

"Front. Just like the one in the upstairs hallway."

"It was personal, then. The shooter wanted to look them in the eye. Do you have anything else in terms of victim profile?"

Lemaire had locked his vehicle and they were headed to the hospital concourse, slipping past the cordon set up by team members to hold back nonessential personnel.

"Too soon. It's too soon for any of that. The women were different ages, different backgrounds. The only thing they have in common is that they all wore the veil."

"Head scarf or face veil?"

At the elevator, Lemaire paused to consider her. He didn't say, as she expected, *What difference does it make?* He rocked back on his heels in the lift.

"So that's why they called you. Because of the politics here."

"That's not an answer, sir."

"Lemaire," he reminded her. "I don't let anyone call me sir." He went on to answer her question. "We could see their faces, so I suppose they wore head scarves. Possibly that made them a target, or maybe they were just in the wrong place at the wrong time."

"No." Khattak's response was definitive. "A head scarf worn in the mosque doesn't necessarily translate into one worn outside the mosque. We'll need to check that out as it could speak to targeting. But execution-style killing is personal, regardless. We can assume the man in the hallway was killed in the same manner to buy the shooter . . . or shooters . . . time to use the assault rifle. Which brings us to the subject of your priest, a subject we need to discuss."

The elevator doors opened on to a scene of chaos. Though triage was still taking place in the emergency department, the surgical ward was packed with medical staff, police officers, and family members.

Lemaire cut the discussion short.

"You think this is a hate crime, eh?" There was something needling about his tone.

Khattak replied evenly, "I think it's an act of terror. That's why INSET is here."

Lemaire ran his hand over the bristles on his chin. He nodded at a passageway that led off the main reception area. At its end, four armed guards were stationed outside a door.

"What on earth—"

It was Rachel's turn to be cut off.

"We have a suspect under guard in a hospital room. He's being treated for shock." He shifted his body closer to Khattak, sizing him up head to head. "We caught him running from the mosque after police arrived at the scene and began lockdown. When we caught him, he had blood all over his clothes, and on his face and hands." He jabbed Khattak's chest with a finger. "If this was a hate crime, or an act of terrorism as you say, why was he shouting, 'Allahu Akbar'?"

Khattak took a step back. But he did so in a way that suggested nothing more than distaste at Lemaire's unwarranted encroachment.

"Who was he? Who did you arrest when it was your priest who was found with the rifle in his hands?"

"A young black man we've identified as Amadou Duchon."

"*You* identified him?"

Despite the press of people waiting to speak to him, Lemaire's attention focused on Khattak. "Fine, then. He identified himself to police."

Khattak was shaking his head. He pulled Lemaire a little aside.

"So you've arrested a young black man, while the priest you found with the weapon in his hands hasn't been processed or arrested?"

Lemaire fired up, at once. "There's no prejudice here. Not in my department. The boy ran, he was arrested." He caught the sharp edge of Khattak's smile, the instant of recognition, and his eyes flared in response. He nodded to himself, clasping his large hands together.

"All right. You've made your point, Inspector Khattak. I won't make assumptions about you, and you won't make them about the Sûreté du Québec." He glanced over at Rachel. "You should have warned me about your boss."

Rachel flashed him an insincere smile.

"The superintendent said you're good at what you do. I figured you'd find out for yourself."

Khattak interrupted. "Amadou Duchon. Where is he?"

Lemaire pointed to the door under guard. "He's been cautioned and interviewed."

"By you?" Khattak's eyebrows went up.

Lemaire looked wary. "Preliminary intake only."

"And did he confess?"

"No."

"Then I'd like to speak to him. Alone."

Khattak was heading toward the room under guard when a commotion broke out at the elevator. A young woman's voice called out Rachel's name.

Rachel turned at once. For a moment, memory slashed through her, sharp and sickening, of a beautiful, blank face on a table at the morgue.

The face looking back at her was just as beautiful but very much alive.

She hurried over to the elevator and clasped the young woman's hand urgently in her own.

"Alizah," she whispered, shaken by a surge of joy. Sometimes the past was less like a weapon that wounded you and more a harbor from pain.

She wasn't alone in feeling it. Alizah reached out and hugged her tightly. Then both women turned at the sound of Khattak's voice.

"Alizah," he echoed softly.

Alizah stood still, her arms dropping to her sides.

She tilted up her chin, eyeing Khattak with an expression Rachel couldn't interpret. Until she spoke, her voice rich with undertones of regret.

"I've missed you," she said to Khattak, as if the admission surprised her.

Khattak regarded her gravely, his green eyes steady on hers.

With a sigh of defeat, he said, "Not as much as I've missed you."

Then he seemed to remember where he was. "Give us a few moments," he said. "We're in the middle of something." He gestured at the reception desk and reluctantly she moved away.

When he would have headed off to Amadou Duchon's room,

Lemaire stepped into his path. Rachel's eyes widened at Lemaire's confrontational air.

"How do you know her?" he asked.

Something in Khattak's face softened.

"From a case some time ago in Waverley. From the murder of Miraj Siddiqui."

From his expression, it was clear Lemaire was familiar with the case. A young woman had been found murdered on the pier in the Ontario township of Waverley—a case that had made the national news as the first in a string of so-called honor killings.

Lemaire swore loudly in French. "You worked that case? Meaning you have a prior relationship?"

Khattak's eyes narrowed in suspicion. "I didn't know she was here. I haven't spoken to her in some time. How do *you* know her, Lemaire?"

"She's been a goddamned thorn in my side since the day she moved to this town. She's a graduate student at the Université Marchand. A *journalism* student. You watch her, Khattak. And I don't care what your relationship with her is, you don't tell her anything about Amadou Duchon."

He glanced back at the reception desk and groaned. Next to Alizah, a smartly dressed blond woman was waving to Lemaire from the other side of the corridor. He raised a hand in halfhearted greeting.

"*Merde.* She's already here."

The woman was so attractive that Rachel was taken aback by Lemaire's reaction.

"Who is she?"

"Isabelle Clément. Press liaison for the premier. He sends her to represent the province when matters like this occur. I'll need to speak to her." His eyes moved to Rachel's face. "Let me speak to her first; then I'll introduce you."

It would have been good to know how the premier of Québec was planning to spin this tragedy—as a premeditated hate crime or the act of a deranged lone wolf? But the players were just beginning to assemble, so Rachel agreed to wait.

7

Khattak didn't view Lemaire as a problem. Lemaire's posturing was standard; officers of different jurisdictions usually had different priorities when they were thrown together and expected to make it work. This was just the process of working out the kinks. Any judgment Khattak passed on Lemaire wouldn't happen until they'd mapped out preliminary work on the shooting—then the boundaries would be clear, along with any lines Lemaire was prepared to cross.

Until that happened, Khattak was trying to treat the crime scene like any other, though if he'd understood Lemaire correctly, the total number of dead would make the shooting the deadliest of its kind in the nation's history. And that it had happened inside a mosque by a man shouting, "God is greatest!" made no sense at all. The province of Québec had a unique relationship with its minority populations, a status enhanced by the province's distinctive cultural and linguistic heritage. And he knew whatever else happened during the course of their secondment to INSET, he and Rachel would be unraveling that relationship piece by piece.

Beginning with what had happened to Amadou Duchon.

Having seen him with Lemaire, the guards outside the room were prepared to wave Khattak through. Khattak showed them his ID; he wanted to be sure they checked that anyone who sought access to the room had the appropriate credentials. There were journalists waiting in the hospital concourse, and there might be a shooter at large who had specifically targeted worshipers at the mosque.

When he entered the room, Amadou was sitting propped up in his bed. He was dressed in a hospital gown that flapped loosely against his deep brown skin under an air-conditioning vent. His clothes were not in the room; one of his arms was handcuffed to the bed rail. At first he didn't appear to be injured, but when he shifted forward under the fluorescent lighting Khattak noticed the swelling along one cheekbone.

When he saw Khattak, he sat up straighter, brushing his free hand over his hair in a reflexive gesture.

"Alhamdulillah," he breathed. "You've come."

Khattak hooked a chair closer to the bed. One eyebrow raised, he asked, "You were expecting me? Does that mean you know who I am?"

"Alizah and I are friends; she told me you would come. She told me she knew you well. And I've been watching you on the news. We all have."

His eyes were fixed on Khattak, warm and liquid dark. He spoke with a Québécois accent tinged with West African overtones, his voice melodic and rich. Khattak couldn't pinpoint it, but he thought the young man's first name suggested a link to Gambia or Cameroon.

There was a glint of hope in his eyes, his wariness replaced by a frank expression of trust. And if Amadou Duchon trusted him before he'd begun his interview, it said a great deal about what Alizah must have told him about their past relationship. He wished he could extend that same trust in return, but he'd have to clear the ground first.

"Were you *expecting* an attack on the mosque, Amadou?"

Amadou blinked rapidly. "You can't think that's what I meant. You may not know what's been happening in Saint-Isidore, but you must know what it's been like here in Québec. An attack like this was only a matter of time."

Giant tears welled up in his eyes, spilling down his cheeks to disappear into the paper-thin neck of his gown. "I didn't think I'd be in the middle of it."

Khattak reached for Amadou's hand and squeezed it. He asked if he understood his rights and whether he wanted a lawyer.

Amadou gripped his hand with surprising force.

"Ya Allah," he said. "As God is my witness, I don't need one."

"But you *were* there?" Khattak prodded. "You saw the attack take place? Do you feel up to telling me about it?"

Amadou's head fell back against his pillow. He swallowed back a sob.

"I wasn't inside when it happened. I'd gone to the mosque to pray; then I planned to head back to campus. I was on my way when I remembered that I'd forgotten to speak to my friend Youssef about a meeting. I heard the sound of gunfire as I made the turn back to the mosque. I'm the one who called the police."

His breath was coming faster as he spoke. Khattak murmured a consolation to him in Arabic.

"Take your time; there's no rush."

"I parked and ran back in after I made the call. Maybe there was something I could do, so I made myself go in. There were so many bodies, so much blood. People were calling out, crying. I didn't know what to do, where to start; I helped those I could—and then I looked for Youssef."

"Where was Youssef?"

"In the main hall. Near Abubekr and his son, Adam. It was—they were—it was clear they were dead. Both of them. And Youssef had been shot, too. More than once." Amadou released Khattak's hand to gesture at his back. "Here. All over here. I had my kit. I did some preliminary treatment."

"Your kit?"

Amadou nodded vigorously. "I'm training to be a paramedic. So I worked on Youssef. I told him to hold on."

"But you weren't with Youssef when the ambulance arrived. Inspector Lemaire told me you were arrested running from the scene of the attack."

Amadou showed the whites of his eyes.

"My God, they'll say anything and expect you to believe it."

Khattak flinched a little and Amadou softened his tone.

"I was the only uninjured person inside the mosque. People were still alive and I didn't hear any sirens. I ran outside to flag down help.

I was calling out to the police, showing them where to go, when one of their officers tackled me. He brought me to the ground."

He showed Khattak his bruised cheek. "They did this to me while I was calling for help."

Exactly the scenario Khattak had feared. He leaned forward, watching Amadou intently.

"They said you were running from the scene shouting, 'Allahu Akbar!'"

Amadou closed his eyes.

"No, no," he said. "I cried out, 'Allahu Alam.' They just don't know the difference."

Because they couldn't imagine there *was* a difference, Khattak thought, any more than they could interpret all the nuances of meaning encompassed by a single phrase. It didn't make sense that a person would shout, *Allahu Akbar!* at the scene of a terror attack *against* a Muslim congregation. The way the phrase had been continually linked to terror was in distinct contrast to its daily importance in the lives of members of Amadou's faith. It could be used in any context—to witness an act of beauty, to marvel, to praise, to express gratitude or deepest joy. To use it to mark the murder of co-religionists was an act only thinkable to an extremist fringe. For members of the faith like Khattak, there was no phrase that offered more grace.

"Allahu Alam" meant only "God knows best."

In Amadou's case, it had served to warn of despair.

He didn't leap to Lemaire's conclusion that Amadou was guilty of mass murder. No weapon had been found on Amadou's body or in his car. He'd done what he could to help, risking his own life to save the life of his friend.

Khattak studied Amadou's smooth young face, the earnestness of his expression, the hair he wore closely shorn to the skull. The flimsiness of his hospital gown didn't diminish the elegance of his strong black body, too often seen as a threat. As witnessed by one simple fact.

Amadou had been roughed up, then handcuffed to a hospital bed, while the priest who had been found with a weapon at the crime scene had been graciously escorted from the mosque.

If word got out to Diana Shehadeh and the civil liberties group that she ran, the investigation would turn on its axis, evolving into something that would end up hindering their work. Yet Khattak knew he would have to speak to her and somehow warn her—try to bring her on board.

While watching out for Amadou.

"Amadou. When you made your way inside the mosque, did you see who opened fire?"

The young man squeezed his eyes shut. "If I had, he would be here instead of me."

"You didn't see anyone else enter the mosque after you did? Think carefully."

Amadou's eyes shot open. "Why? Who else was there?"

Khattak leaned in closer. "Just tell me." He was considering the nature of the shooting, the speed with which it had been carried out.

"No, no one."

"How many entrances are there to the mosque? Do you know it well enough to say?"

His head bobbed rapidly. "Sisters' entrance at the back. I just fixed the lights out there myself. Main entrance in front of the parking lot. And a small side door that leads to the office. That's the door the imam uses."

"Are any of the doors kept locked?"

"Not until late at night, after Isha prayer."

So the gunman could have come from any of three entrances, though the back entrance was the most likely in terms of how Lemaire had described the order of events. But what if there had been a second assailant? They knew there was another gun, a gun that was missing from the scene. Lemaire's men were conducting a perimeter search, but the mosque wasn't far from the lake that bordered the town or from the creek that fed into it. The search would take time, and in the end it might not prove conclusive.

And something else was bothering Khattak. He wondered if Rachel had caught it, too.

"When did you fix the lights at the sisters' entrance?"

Amadou turned his head. He was looking for something on the nightstand beside his bed. Whatever it was, it wasn't there.

"They took my phone? I could tell you from my calendar if you need an exact time, but it was sometime last night. Sometime after *maghrib*." His voice choked a little. "Almost the same time as . . . tonight."

No one was feeling the weight of it yet, Khattak knew. They were still in shock and would remain that way for some time—investigators, medical staff, family members . . . witnesses. He'd examined the scene thoroughly, seen the blood marks that desecrated a house of worship— a place of sanctuary—but he'd done so as a trained investigator, shutting everything else away. When he would pray, when he *could* pray, he'd think of what this meant.

Amadou was still speaking. "Alizah mentioned it two days ago, so I came prepared to fix the lights. I handle these kinds of jobs at the mosque."

"Officially?"

Amadou's smile was gentle. "*Non,* Inspector. Just as an act of service. I thought the lights needed to be changed because they'd gone out."

That prickle of warning stirred along Khattak's spine. "They hadn't?"

"They were smashed. That's when I realized why Alizah was worried."

Khattak left the young man with a few additional words of caution. Amadou needed a lawyer without further delay and shouldn't speak to the police again without one present. He was back to navigating a familiar set of tensions that came with the job he'd taken on, but in this case he didn't hesitate. He was disturbed by the instant focus on Amadou when there were other, more logical avenues to pursue. He hadn't ruled Amadou out as a suspect, but he was wary of a rush to judgment. He'd speak to Diana Shehadeh to ensure Amadou received fair treatment.

The entire team would be working around the clock for the next few days, following every lead, reconstructing the moments of the attack—

everything that had led up to it and everything that followed now. It was time for him to deal with what he'd been sent here to do.

He found Rachel in the hallway leaning against the wall as Lemaire spoke with the press liaison he had mentioned earlier. Rachel was watching them, but her presence wasn't intrusive. Her hair was combed into a ponytail, and her clothes were a mix of everyday and professional that let her melt into the background.

"Anything?" she asked at once.

Khattak shook his head. "It's not him."

"Sir." Her tone was chiding.

Khattak tried not to smile. He knew what she was warning him of, what she never failed to warn him of.

"Fine. I don't think Amadou Duchon is our man."

He summarized what he'd learned from Amadou, and Rachel's thick eyebrows climbed halfway up her forehead. She'd dumped her blazer on a nearby hospital bed, and now she rubbed her arms as she thought. Her ponytail swung over her shoulder as she flashed Lemaire a quick look. He was too far away to hear them.

Lowering her voice, she said, "Lends credence to the idea that the shooter entered from the back. The broken lights suggest recon to me. Someone knew they'd be entering the mosque from the back, so they knocked out the lights."

Khattak had considered this. "Amadou replaced them before the attack."

Rachel shrugged. "So they didn't have a chance to come back and do it again. But there's something else, sir. Something strange. Don't know if these guys have caught it yet, but if Amadou reentered the mosque to help the victims, that's who he sees inside, right?"

"Go on."

"Then he's back outside and he gets tackled to the ground. But even then, there's someone he doesn't see. Either inside or outside in the parking lot."

Khattak had known she would get there. The strange thing was that Lemaire hadn't. Or maybe there just hadn't been enough time for Lemaire to have told them everything he'd picked up. Lemaire had made a fair offer: withholding judgment at the outset of an investigation was necessary in any case.

He put a hand on Rachel's arm to silence her. Lemaire and the premier's press liaison were headed in their direction.

"Sir," Rachel whispered. "We need to figure out the timing of events here. When exactly Amadou went outside to flag down help, when he went back in, and so on."

"Why, specifically?"

"Because Amadou didn't mention seeing Étienne Roy. And if Amadou didn't see him, we need to know where Roy was when the shooting was taking place."

8

Isabelle Clément possessed the understated glamor and effortless chic that Rachel associated with Frenchwomen. She wore a dark plum dress that flattered her pale complexion and a pair of black heels that would have crippled Rachel in her job. She showed no sign of finding them difficult to manage. Her makeup was discreet, her ash-fair hair swept up neatly in a low chignon. Instead of a briefcase or a purse, she carried an electronic tablet. She was petite and very beautiful, with a mildly critical manner.

Lemaire introduced them, a glint of sardonic amusement in his eyes as he watched Rachel give the press liaison the once-over, smoothing a hand over her own blouse. Rachel ignored him. Another woman on the scene wasn't competition—she was a colleague of sorts.

And if it came to it, what the hell did Lemaire think she was in competition for? There was a crowing masculinity about the man that set Rachel's teeth on edge. She had found something like it in nearly all the men she had trained with, until she'd come to work for Khattak. Her instincts told her that Lemaire was a brute of a cop compared to Khattak, with his restraint, but she was annoyed with herself for wasting even a little of her time rising to his bait.

Clément didn't smile at either of them, and her response to Khattak wasn't what Rachel had learned to expect. Clément glanced at him, her attention briefly caught by the shadow of Khattak's dark beard; then her attention returned to the tablet she held in her hands. She seemed competent but worried.

"I've spoken to Inspector Lemaire. We've outlined the statement the premier is prepared to make."

Rachel shifted away from the wall. One of her strengths as Khattak's partner was to anticipate the questions he'd want to ask but make them seem like her own.

"Will you be naming Roy? Or Amadou Duchon?"

Clément gave a short, sharp shake of her head, her fingers sliding across the surface of the tablet. She pulled up a document on her screen.

"All the premier will be doing at this point is expressing condolences to the people of Saint-Isidore."

"Not to the congregation of the mosque, specifically?"

Clément looked up, giving Rachel her full attention. "Not yet. We need more time to work out precisely what to say. And it would help if we had all the facts at hand. The quicker you can deliver those, the clearer our statement will be."

Rachel noted the "our." A deliberate expression of the woman's political clout, letting them know her hands were on the reins. But as press liaison, she might be overstepping her role on the premier's team. From the curl of Lemaire's lip, it was possible he thought so, too. He winked at Rachel out of Clément's line of sight. She firmed her lips repressively, ignoring Lemaire's quick smile.

Khattak spoke up. "The premier is waiting to see if a member of the mosque community is responsible for the attack before extending his condolences."

The quietly delivered statement conveyed his anger nonetheless.

Clément put her tablet away. Her eyes flicked from Lemaire to Rachel to Khattak.

"When was the last time you visited Québec?" she asked him.

"I'm aware of the news," Khattak said. "It's necessary in my position."

"Whatever you've been following, if you haven't been here, you have no way of understanding the nature of our concerns. Not only does the premier have to manage Anglo-Francophone tensions; there's also the recurring problem of immigration. Any statement he makes must consider these angles."

Khattak's voice became even quieter.

"I didn't realize the premier considered immigration a problem. Or is it only a certain type of immigration?"

Rachel tried to make her face blank and failed. Khattak was never antagonistic; he rarely stated his positions in advance. Whatever mask he wore in order to do his job, he'd chosen to discard it now, yet perversely, his frankness seemed to reassure Clément. Perhaps she had been wondering how careful she needed to be about offending Khattak's sensibilities.

"Then you understand a little better than I thought." She didn't sigh. She was too chic and self-possessed for that. "But whatever you're thinking about this . . ."

Me, Rachel substituted for "this," a little world weary at the way it always came down to this. Women exerted themselves to make an impression on Khattak, whose dark good looks had derailed many a witness' powers of concentration. But Clément was a professional and, apart from that sidelong look at Khattak's smooth, dark beard, she had gathered herself quickly.

Her tone became oddly persuasive. "Superintendent Killiam assigned you here at the premier's request. Not to cover things up. Rather, to *expose* them."

"Why?" Rachel demanded. "What the hell's been happening here? No offense, but Saint-Isidore-du-Lac strikes me as somewhat of a backwater."

This was a harsh indictment given its proximity to Ottawa, the nation's capital, and its picturesque setting on the fringes of Gatineau.

Clément's smile was coolly ironic. "Maybe it is, Sergeant." She pressed the back of her neck with a delicate hand, and the loop of gold at her nape unwound, falling in disciplined waves. "But I think you may be unaware of the undercurrents this backwater has produced."

"Oh? How so?"

"The Codes of Conduct. Saint-Isidore-du-Lac was the second town to pass a Code, modeled on the one from Hérouxville. It banned certain . . . cultural . . . practices that were unwanted here."

Khattak's eyes slid to Rachel. The shooting at the mosque might be a hate crime, it might be a terrorist attack, but whatever else it was, it had just exposed an expanding rift in Québec.

"Why was a Code of Conduct necessary?" he asked. "Does the town view the community of congregants here as a threat?"

Clément avoided a direct answer. "The Code is about *Québécois* identity—it's meant to protect the values that Québécois hold dear."

Her eyes drifted drown the hospital corridor, and her smooth self-possession wavered. Nodding at the families of the victims of the shooting, she said, "These are not the values I mean."

Khattak didn't respond to this, but Rachel knew they were thinking the same thing.

The cultural fault lines in Québec had expanded from Codes of Conduct to encompass provincial hearings and then to the attempt to pass a Charter of Values for Québec. The 2013 legislation had mandated the uncovering of one's face when providing or receiving state services. It had also prohibited public-sector employees from wearing conspicuous religious symbols. Though Catholic symbols were considered a reflection of Québec's heritage, all others were banned. As a result, the new law had been roundly condemned on the grounds of freedom of religion. Yet though the Charter of Values failed to pass, iterations of it, such as Bill 62, had been revived and remained contentious.

But were they contentious enough to have been behind the shooting at the mosque?

9

One of Lemaire's officers called him away. Rachel caught the name Roy before the conversation was cut off. Lemaire gave her a look she couldn't read—assessing? Suspicious? Strangely calm?

"I'll be back, eh? Very soon."

It sounded like an apology, but Rachel couldn't think why this blue-eyed bear of a man would figure he owed her one. He was a homicide cop with the Sûreté. And God knew what Rachel was, a question she'd been asking herself since she and Khattak had returned from working a case in Greece. She'd needed time to reflect on her experiences during that case, where she'd ended a personal relationship that had never had the chance to blossom. She'd taken a break from her usual activities to take that time for herself—she hadn't hit the ice to play hockey in six weeks.

This new case was a good distraction. She might hate herself for thinking of a tragedy as a diversion, but she was honest enough to face the truth of her thoughts head on. She was trying to do what Khattak did, by insulating her thoughts.

She found herself speaking to Lemaire with some attempt at collegiality.

"We'll be speaking to Alizah Siddiqui. Just call us when you're done."

He paused at that, making a quick survey of the activity at the reception desk. Alizah wasn't alone. A group of young women stood close to her, but they weren't interacting with Alizah. The palest and youngest of the three was trying to get a nurse's attention.

Alizah squeezed the girl's arm. "I'll find out," she said crisply.

She caught up to Rachel's group. "Inspector Lemaire, what's the update on Youssef Soufiane? Chloé really needs to know." She gestured at the girl who was waiting at the desk.

Lemaire's dismissal wasn't unkind. It was resigned, as though he'd dealt with Alizah's persistence many times in the past. It made Rachel curious. How well did Alizah know the detective from the Sûreté?

"I'm sorry. That information is restricted to family."

Khattak pulled Lemaire aside to ask a question, while Alizah returned to speak to the young woman she'd called Chloé. When Khattak was free, Alizah joined them at the elevator.

"We need to talk," she told them. "I need to show you something important—something that's connected to what happened here tonight. I don't think it can wait."

"How long have you been in Saint-Isidore?" Khattak asked.

"A few years now." She explained that though she was registered at the university, she lived off campus in an apartment she shared, working year round in town. She knew the campus and community well.

"Let me show you the campus; then I'll tell you the rest."

At her urging, they left their car in the parking lot, skirting the group of reporters. A handful of streetlights illuminated the dark road, trailing away from the hospital up a hill. Alizah was leading them to the university perched at the top, its columns floating like sentinels against a midnight sky. Campus lights illuminated the grounds, thickly forested with maples, whose green leaves darkened to inky blackness as the night encroached. They crossed a bridge over a narrow creek that wound its way along the outskirts of the town.

For a moment, that sickening sense of nostalgia flared up in Rachel's thoughts. She was back at a pier looking out over White Pine Lake. A white gazebo stood on the opposite shore, and the space between Rachel and the shore was engulfed by sorrow and loss.

Miraj.

They hadn't been able to save Miraj, and she'd never expected to meet Alizah Siddiqui again.

She chanced a glance at Khattak and saw the same somber expression on his face. They should have returned to the mosque or, failing that, insisted on being present at Lemaire's interview of Étienne Roy—but Alizah's urgency about what she knew was compelling.

Rachel was quiet. The bridge gave her an excellent vantage point to view the layout of the town. She measured the distance from the university to the hospital, from the university to the mosque, from the mosque to the dignified church. The importance of the Catholic church had diminished over the decades—many in Québec now viewed it with open distrust. But that was not what Rachel had witnessed in the Sûreté officers' handling of Père Étienne. No, there had been a respect there that bordered on reverence.

Looking southward from the bridge, beyond the perimeter of the mosque, the streets of Saint-Isidore were empty save for patrol cars sweeping the dark with their lights. Isabelle Clément, the press liaison, must have made her statement by now, to keep the curious away. There might be a shooter at large. Nowhere was truly safe yet—which was why Rachel kept scanning the streets, watchful for signs of movement.

Lemaire hadn't seen fit to hold his own press conference yet, and she admitted that that was probably the right call. It was too soon to say anything that wouldn't raise more questions, so he was right to have his mind on the investigation. Catching the shooter was their top priority.

Rachel listened to Khattak's questions as they resumed walking, probing into why Alizah had chosen to come to Saint-Isidore and set down roots. There had always been a certain sympathy between Alizah and Khattak.

"Waverley became too small. After everything that happened to Miraj—the people who were involved. I couldn't look at them in the same way, and I wanted to talk about that."

Rachel was confused. "You wanted to talk about your sister's murder?"

"I wanted to talk about what happened in Waverley. Where fingers were pointed. *Why* they were pointed. I've never been able to forget. Since then, it's all become so much worse."

When she dipped her head low, shielding her face, Rachel was reminded of the girl she'd met in Waverley. Angry that no one apart from herself was willing to tell the truth.

From the beginning, the local police had dubbed Miraj Siddiqui's murder an honor killing. And that perception had colored everything about Miraj's life, as well as her unnatural death.

"Is that the reason you chose to study away from home?" Khattak asked.

Again, he perceived nuances that Rachel couldn't detect. When Alizah stopped to look at him, a sense of connection thrummed between them.

"It's Québec," she said simply. "And Saint-Isidore was quick to adopt a Code of Conduct. An important place for someone who's interested in politics and journalism. Because more than anything, this town is an emblem of what that code might become. What it *did* become," she finished bitterly. "But you'll see that for yourselves in a moment."

Khattak glanced down at Alizah's left hand.

"You didn't get engaged?" It was a question that arose from their history in Waverley.

Alizah pushed her thick, dark hair over one shoulder.

"He wasn't ready. So I decided not to wait around." She shrugged, her glance encompassing Rachel. "If someone doesn't know your worth, why stand still, waiting for things to change?"

Rachel stumbled as the bridge met the cycling path. Khattak's hand was swiftly at her elbow. They avoided looking at each other. Alizah's matter-of-fact statement applied to them equally. Khattak had wasted years pushing away a woman he'd finally admitted he loved. And Rachel knew no matter how long she was willing to wait for a man she admired, the outcome wasn't going to be the one she'd foolishly hoped for.

This had always been Alizah's most disconcerting trait—speaking plainly without apology. Willing to face the worst. And now, as then, Rachel wondered how a girl so much younger than she possessed such resolute courage when it came to facing her pain.

The answer lay in the reason she gave them for studying in Saint-Isidore. She had been accepted into a graduate program in journalism, after having taken time off to acquire relevant work experience. Now she was following the trail blazed by her sister Miraj.

They'd reached the top of the hill and looked back at the town spread below, shrouded in darkness except for the lights of police cars that marked off the scene at the mosque.

"You're saying they're connected?" Rachel asked.

Alizah led them around the side of the main admissions building, which struck Rachel as quite similar to the church, with its gray stone pediments and ogival windows. These were paired up at the front and arranged as trios along the eastern façade. The building's fenestration was modest, but its central portal could have graced Trinity College. A police car flagged them down, pulling up on the drive under the building's portico. Rachel held up her ID and asked if there was any news. The driver shook his head and circled back to the exit.

To the west side of the main college was a student center, fashioned in a more modern style with sleekly positioned Greek columns. The windows were crosshatched with sparkling panes, their bright and angular symmetry marred by a set of broken panes at the end of the row.

Alizah unlocked a door at the back and flipped on the lights. They were standing in the middle of a corridor lined with mahogany doors. Each of the doors was papered with flyers. A nameplate beside each door denoted the presence of various student clubs.

The door Alizah had unlocked was marked off with two rows of orange duct tape establishing an amateur cordon. Rachel instantly knew why. The nameplate on the door indicated that the space had been allocated to the university's Muslim Students Association or MSA. The door itself had been defaced by a giant swastika. On either side of the frame, a series of graphics had been taped to the wall, each depicting an explicitly racist, fully bilingual cartoon. The orange tape formed a boundary around these graphics, and the door itself was taped across.

"This break-in happened two days ago." She explained her role as an active member of the MSA, closely connected to other Muslim students and to the Muslim community in town. She knew the congregation at the mosque, and she would personally know many of the families who were impacted by the tragedy. "They trashed our office, stole our electronics, and did this to the door. I taped it off because although we asked campus security to notify local police, no one has been here yet. I wore gloves." She said this a little shyly to Khattak. "I didn't touch anything. I've photographed this with my friend Amadou's camera and with my phone. Two sets stored in different places. I've also kept a record of my correspondence with the administration. And of the calls I made to Inspector Lemaire."

"Wait. You've met Lemaire before? Doesn't he work homicide in Montreal?"

Alizah fished a small, square wallet from the back pocket of the jeans she wore tucked into slim black boots. She removed a card from the wallet and passed it to Rachel. It was Lemaire's business card; Rachel handed it to Khattak.

"He's been trying to do the same kind of work you do. Every time there's an incident, he rotates through and speaks to the community, assuring them that no problem is too small for us to bring to his attention. He said he's made note of what's been happening in Saint-Isidore."

Khattak was studying one of the graphics on the door. It pictured a bearded man in a turban being chased down a street by a long row of marchers wearing hoods that resembled bishops' miters. But something about the way the hoods were drawn could also have represented the Ku Klux Klan. Except that the faces were unmasked. The same hoods appeared on the graphic next to it, this time worn by a group of men kicking a woman in a burqa who was curled up in a ball on the ground. The manner of drawing suggested that both the woman and the turbaned man were the threat. The viewer's sympathy was meant to be engaged by the faces under the hoods.

Saving YOU, both graphics read in French and English.

"These men are here," Khattak said flatly. "Whoever they are, they're real. That's why Saint-Isidore is firmly on Lemaire's radar. That's why he keeps coming back."

Alizah pointed to another one of the graphics, higher up on the door. A single handsome figure dressed in one of the hoods had raised his hands in prayer just above a motto at the bottom of the cartoon. The same motto was inked across a sash the young man wore on his chest.

Alizah nodded grimly. "We've been dealing with this for a while. And not with much success."

Rachel strained to read the tiny printing on the sash. An electric jolt shot up her spine.

The men in the hoods were called the Wolf Allegiance.

10

Khattak and Rachel photographed the flyers. Khattak put a call through to Lemaire, asking for the immediate dispatch of a crime scene unit. There was more than a strong possibility that the vandalism of the student group's office and the shooting at the mosque were connected. There were certain features in common. The slashing of the door and the spray-painted swastika indicated the same kind of rage that had characterized the furious rain of bullets inside the mosque. But the posters—designed in advance and neatly arranged around the door in order to tell a story—spoke of premeditation. The same kind of premeditation that had allowed a killer to escape the scene of a mass shooting without being caught. A premeditation that would explain the presence of two different types of weapons, as well as the calculation behind the executions in the basement of the mosque. Four bodies in the basement, one in the hallway upstairs—cold, precise, purposefully targeted.

When the crime scene unit arrived, Alizah took Khattak and Rachel to a coffee shop near campus that was open late. It was crowded with anxious students busily discussing the shooting. A few of them tried to approach, but Alizah waved them off with a frown. From their quick retreat to cell phones, he knew it wouldn't be long before reporters arrived.

Rachel went to fetch their drinks and Khattak took the opportunity to say a few words to Alizah. She looked older than her years, in her mid-twenties now, a gravity in her face that was new, a hardening of purpose that showed in her eyes but not her face. She was as beautiful as Miraj had been—perhaps more so now with the maturity lent by the passage of time—the kind of beauty reflected in the silent appreciation of young men in the café, men who would welcome the chance to rescue her from anything that caused her grief.

"You're staring," she said at last to break the silence, a flush rising to her cheeks.

"Was I? I'm sorry. I was thinking of the last time I saw you."

"I wrote to you after that."

"Until you stopped."

The families of crime victims often maintained ties with him—meeting before and after the trial phase of proceedings, sometimes needing to share their grief with someone who knew too well everything they had lost. Alizah had also written to Rachel, but it was Khattak whose career she had followed and Khattak whose advice she sought.

He'd treated her the same way he treated his sisters, though perhaps with greater insight into what she needed from him. A space away from her grief . . . from her family's grief . . . though Miraj would always be the thread that bound the two of them together.

"After the case at Algonquin, you stopped writing."

Alizah traced a pattern on the table.

"I didn't want to be another of your burdens. Or one of your lost causes."

Tears sprang to her eyes.

Khattak lowered his voice. "How could you have thought that?"

She bit her lip.

"Because you didn't write me, either. You didn't call my parents like you used to. You just . . . vanished."

Khattak felt a stirring of regret. He could explain that he'd traveled to Iran, then to Europe and Turkey. He could share the toll those cases had taken, and Alizah would understand. But it wouldn't be the truth. The truth was too sensitive to express. He'd become disturbed by Alizah's dependence on him—worried that she wanted something he couldn't give. After her sister's death, he'd become the significant male figure in her life—too significant. She'd been trying to cross a boundary

Esa would never cross. He'd seen distance as the appropriate response. She'd drawn her own conclusions from that.

Rather than hurt her, he said, "You're right. After the case in Algonquin, I spent some time working on a deradicalization project. I'm sorry if that made you think I'd forgotten Miraj or any of you in Waverley."

Tears slipped down her cheeks. A young man jerked to his feet from a neighboring table, his anger barely contained. He wore a navy-blue blazer over a blue and white shirt. His hair was cut short and well-groomed, his eyebrows a pale shade of blond. But in spite of his good looks and preppy appearance, he projected an air of menace.

"You shouldn't be talking to Alizah without a lawyer. Everything about you screams that you're a cop. Both of you." He jerked his chin at Rachel, who had made her way back from the bar, a tray of coffees in hand.

Alizah passed a weary hand over her forehead.

"Like you care, Maxime. Like you're a friend to anyone like me." Her hands clutched the edge of the table until her knuckles shone white. "Why don't you go back to your Wolves?"

"What the hell is that supposed to mean?"

He took another step closer and Khattak pushed back his chair. Alizah rose to her feet and faced the young man down.

"Ask him where he was tonight," she said to Esa.

"Why?" Khattak asked, his neutral tone deflating the tension in the room. "Who are you?" He spoke to the younger man directly. He was met with a look of scorn.

"I'm not talking to you."

Both hands on her hips Alizah glared at him, her air of vulnerability erased as if it had never been.

"Meet Maxime Thibault. He founded the local chapter of the Wolf Allegiance."

11

Catching up quickly, Rachel introduced herself. A nod from Khattak indicated that she should take Maxime aside. She moved to another booth, grabbing her coffee from the tray she passed to Khattak, aware that he was seeking to de-escalate the confrontation between Alizah and the boy. After a moment's indecision, Maxime accepted her invitation to join him, either not wanting to lose face after what he'd said about the police or because he saw Rachel as a challenge. To disarm him, she called the waitress over and ordered him a drink.

As she slid into a seat opposite Maxime Thibault, she made her own lightning-swift assessment of the boy. Despite his posturing, she thought of him as a boy, maybe a couple of years older than her brother, Zach, who was twenty-three. Suave, smooth, and arrogant, Thibault had a chip on his shoulder roughly the size of Québec. Whether it was aimed at male authority, law enforcement, or something else would take her some time to figure out. His English was fluent, far better than Rachel's French, but his accent wasn't Québécois. It sounded distinctly Parisian, and everything about him spoke of unlimited wealth. The watch on his wrist, the loafers on his feet, the blazer with its discreetly monogrammed logo. He'd even tucked a pale pink ascot into the neck of his shirt. But why was a kid with money stuck in Saint-Isidore?

Granted, it was a much prettier locale than where Rachel had grown up in Etobicoke, but if this kid had been educated in expensive foreign schools what would bring him to this town?

"You're a student at the university?"

She sipped at her coffee and waited for him to speak.

"How did you end up working for one of *them*? Sergeant Rachel
Getty. That's an upstanding name." His eyes narrowed. "You're not a
fucking kike, are you?" He shook his head. "No. If you were, you'd be
in charge. Not kowtowing to a raghead."

The vicious insults were shocking in the context of his appearance.
When had prep school blazers and knife-edge creases taken the place
of white hoods? And if these were Maxime's views, why had he tried
to defend Alizah from Khattak? Despite her lighter skin tone, there
was no way Alizah could be mistaken for a white woman. On the
other hand, her unequivocal beauty could make many an individual
set his scruples aside.

Rachel slouched down in her seat, projecting an air of fellowship.

"Don't think he's wearing a rag, is he?"

Thibault's eyes became glassy. He tapped his nose. "On the inside.
They're all wearing it on the inside, but they take it off to blend. Like
Jews who hope they can fool us by anglicizing their names."

He spoke with an air of such reasonableness that Rachel found herself answering him.

"Don't know how you feel about the Irish. My Da just liked the name
Rachel." She took another sip of her coffee and then she said, "Where
were you tonight? It's obvious you've heard about the shooting."

Apart from the strange glassiness of his eyes, he was too relaxed for
Rachel to imagine that he'd taken part in a mass shooting hours before. He was a young man playing at greater menace.

"On campus," he said. "Hanging out with my friends. Why? Am
I a suspect?"

He sounded pleased.

Rachel shrugged, deliberately offhand. "You can see why I might
think that."

"That's just lazy police work. Just because a cleansing needed to happen doesn't mean I'm the one who carried it out."

The waitress brought his coffee to their table and he reached out and
squeezed her hand in thanks. She smiled at him as if she knew him,
accepting a tip and blowing him a kiss.

The contrast between his behavior and his words was chilling.

"Maybe not," Rachel agreed. "But that Wolf Allegiance stuff. Seems like vandalizing the Muslim students' office might have been up your alley. You're a member, right?"

His white, even teeth snapped shut. "Founder. Far above the Wolves. Vandalism is for thugs, not for those gifted with vision."

"Is that what you are? A visionary?"

"Of course."

"So what's your vision, then? Something apocalyptic? Four white horsemen and so on?"

Maxime's smile was slow and charming. Rachel wondered if he thought it would disarm her. She'd already assessed the fit of his clothes for a handgun. He had a laptop bag on the seat beside him; she'd have paid good money to search it.

"You're mixing your metaphors, *Rachel*. My brothers represent deliverance, not death. That's what makes it so simple. There's a natural order of things. And I think we can agree on who should be at the top."

Rachel sighed. "What about the ones underneath, then? Are you saying what happened at the mosque was justified?"

Thibault inched closer, appraising her. She caught the scent of mint and coffee.

"Have you heard of natural selection?" Even his beautiful Parisian accent couldn't make his meaning less ugly. Rachel let him creep closer. From the corner of her eye, she caught Khattak's instant alertness. She made a quick "I'm okay" motion.

"I'd say needing a gun to achieve it is pretty *un*natural, wouldn't you? Would you happen to own one? Is there one in your bag?" She nodded at the laptop bag on the seat.

Thibault shifted back in his seat, but not before Rachel had seen his blink of confusion.

"That's why women shouldn't be in law enforcement. Leave the thinking to men." He patted his bag. "As if a gun that could do that kind of damage could even fit in this bag."

Rachel sat up straight, focused and intent. "What kind of damage are we talking about? And how do you know about it?"

Maxime choked on his coffee, spluttering a little. He used a napkin to wipe his mouth, but all of it was theater. He was buying himself some time.

"I've seen a lot of movies," he said. "I'm assuming it was an assault rifle. The kind of gun you can get just about anywhere in the States."

Rachel belabored the point. "So you're saying there's no assault rifle in your bag."

His hand tightened on the bag. "That's what I'm saying."

"Mind if I look for myself?" He hesitated and Rachel pressed her advantage. "Natural selection suggests a mind like yours would dispose of the weapon as soon as possible."

No details about the shooting had been revealed on the news. The Canadian press were notoriously taciturn; they would wait for the facts to be established. Canadian police officers were even more so. So Maxime wouldn't know the rifle had been found on the scene and that what Rachel was really looking for was the missing handgun.

Falling into the trap, Thibault shoved the bag at her. "Go ahead, you stupid dyke."

Rachel snagged the bag from his hands and checked each of its zippered compartments, taking her time. She found a laptop, a spare ascot, a student handbook, and some papers. When she moved to unzip an inner pocket, Thibault's hands jerked as if to stop her. She looked up at him and he shrugged.

A hush had fallen over the café. Everyone was watching Rachel search the bag. A couple of Maxime's friends came to stand behind him, their arms crossed over their chests. They were dressed in the same preppy uniform, the lieutenants of Maxime's movement.

"Nazis," she muttered as she dug her hand deep inside the pocket. Something solid bumped against her knuckles. She fished it out. It was a mobile phone.

"That's mine," he said sharply. "Put it back."

Puzzled, she slid it back, her hand brushing against a piece of paper. Seeing Maxime tense, she slipped the sheet of paper from the bag and laid it on the table. Though he met her gaze defiantly, he didn't say a word.

It was a copy of one of the flyers she had seen at Alizah's office.

12

Lemaire sent members of his team to pick up Thibault, extending an invitation for Rachel to join the interview. Khattak told her to go, he'd walk back and join her at the trailer where Lemaire had set up camp.

It was nearly midnight and the temperature had dropped. When Alizah told him she intended to return to help the families at the mosque, he walked her back. He didn't want her out alone on the streets after midnight. He offered her his jacket, but she refused.

"Maybe it was for the best that you didn't write," she admitted. "I needed to figure things out on my own. I needed to start again, and now I have."

The dark shadow of a desecrated mosque lay between them and for a moment they observed it in silence.

"Something about you is different," she said. "You seem lighter somehow."

He was surprised by her observation. "After what's happened here?"

In her usual forthright way, she said, "You haven't faced what's happened here yet. It's too soon for it to be real. You seem . . . happier. Have you met someone?"

Alizah smiled a little sadly at the quick response she read in his face. "Does she love you?"

She must, Khattak thought. *She did.* Sehr hadn't stayed in Greece to hurt him. Or to make him pay for his long years of silence. She might not accept that the time they had spent struggling to find their way was warranted—valuable, even—but she wasn't the kind of woman who thought her mystique increased the more she held herself back. Like Alizah, she was forthright about what she wanted.

He smiled sideways at her.

"Not nearly as much as I love her."

He changed the subject. They were close to the mosque and he still had questions to ask.

"Do you think Maxime Thibault is the one behind the attack?"

She took some time to consider, kicking a small stone over the bridge into the creek. A river of mist shrouded the bridge, making it seem cut off from the town spread out below.

He wouldn't think about what waited at the mosque.

He would focus on the assailant.

The mass murderer.

Alizah's breath whooshed from her chest.

"I wonder if he's clever enough. I'm not sure that he is. But I have this feeling—"

He could no longer see her in the fog. Her voice was as cool and shadowy as the moonlight silvering the fog.

"Whoever did this found it easy to disappear. Maybe that's because they're one of us."

"Someone from the mosque?" he said sharply.

"No." Her voice floated back at him. "I meant someone from Saint-Isidore. Someone we know, go to school with, work with—someone who can keep their composure after they've committed an atrocity. I don't know if that fits what I know of Maxime, but there's a chance that it does."

Her face appeared again. She was hugging her bare arms and Khattak insisted she take his jacket. She buttoned it close around her, easing into its warmth.

After a moment, Khattak commented, "He was certainly behind the vandalism of your office. Yet at the same time he was protective of you—do you find that odd?"

She answered with some reluctance. "He wasn't like this when I first met him. We started off as friends." She looked embarrassed. "It took me a while to see that he wanted more than friendship. But before I could figure out a way to let him down, he fell in with this other crowd, and then he became someone else. He became the kind of person who could join the Wolf Allegiance." She shivered. "It flies in the face of everything he now stands for, but he hasn't stopped pursuing me."

Khattak's stomach churned. "Has he threatened you? Or harassed you?"

Or anything worse? he wanted to ask but couldn't bring himself to.

She flashed him a compassionate glance, and he was struck, as always, by Alizah's self-possession. Her friends were likely among the dead at the mosque, yet she tried to reassure *him*.

They were silent until they reached the mosque. There were families gathered in the parking lot, alongside other members of the congregation. Alizah nodded at them, seeing people she knew.

Turning from him, she said, "I'll be all right. I'm going to stay here until they leave; then I'll go home with one of the families. They're going to need support. I won't walk back to campus on my own."

They both remembered that Miraj had been alone by the lake on the night of her murder.

"You didn't answer me about Thibault." He tried to suppress the protectiveness in his voice, the concern that exasperated Ruksh, the older of his two younger sisters.

Alizah heard it anyway and reached out to press his hand.

"He's never touched me," she said. "He won't. He prides himself on some twisted notion of chivalry. I've asked myself if the way he harasses us on campus or down at the mosque is simply his way of getting my attention."

"Then he's not a racist? He's just looking for a way to impress you?"

"Oh, he's a racist," she said matter-of-factly. "A Nazi through and through. And I don't mean that as a casual slur; it's the Wolf Allegiance's stated ideology. But he hasn't been able to let go of me, and surprisingly, that's not completely at odds with the Wolves' ideology. They like the idea of submissive Asian girlfriends who take their orders from them."

For a moment her mask of preternatural calm shifted, and he witnessed the raw and very real pain beneath it. "But I've known men like you, Esa. So why would I look at him?"

He was too humbled by the words to respond. He took out his phone to check for an update from Lemaire, hoping to change the subject. He frowned as he saw a text from an unfamiliar number.

I've been waiting for you. Now that you're here, let's begin.

The text had the unsettling language of a threat.

Seeing his frown, Alizah peered over his shoulder to read the text.

"Does this seem like something Thibault might say?" he asked her. "Or that he would have one of the members of his group send?"

The number flashed up as unknown. She looked dubious. "We call them the Wolves or the Allegiance. How would they have your number? They're not hackers. They're just bored and easily distracted."

But the graphics on the MSA's door had been sophisticated, well-timed, and well-placed. Was it possible that the graphics had gone up first and someone driven by cruder instincts had been inspired to spray-paint the swastika? Did the act of vandalism somehow mirror the dual nature of the attack at the mosque?

Alizah was watching his face.

"Amadou would know," she said. "What's going to happen to him, Esa? Can you protect him? Can you get me in to see him?"

"He said the two of you were friends, and that you'd told him about me. Did you have some reason for thinking I'd come to Saint-Isidore?"

Alizah tilted her head to one side. Though his jacket was oversized on her, she looked anything but defenseless. She was measuring him, weighing what she wanted to say.

"I'm reminded of a five-act play." She pointed down at the mosque that had now become a crime scene. "This is the fifth; the vandalism of our offices counts as the fourth. But there were other things that happened before this. I wanted to call you after the first, but both Amadou and Youssef said that we should wait. He thought we could handle things ourselves."

Suddenly her calm deserted her, and Alizah began to cry. With great gulping sobs she said, "We waited too long. *I* waited too long. This is my fault, Esa. Everything that's happened—each of the acts—is because of something I did."

"No, it isn't."

He offered the words softly, not drawing close, not reaching for her to console her. She needed to stand alone, just as she needed to cry. It wouldn't be the last time.

He didn't know what she was referring to, but he didn't need her to elaborate. He knew exactly what Alizah was trying to tell him.

The massacre at the mosque was a climax.

The case was about beginnings.

13

"TAKE NO PRISONERS" CAMPUS RADIO CALL-IN SHOW
[Translated from the French]

TODAY'S HOST: ALIZAH SIDDIQUI

ALIZAH: Welcome to the program, Alain. I understand that you have some concerns about how the Saint-Isidore mosque shooting is being portrayed in the national media. You think the coverage is making Quebeckers look bad.

ALAIN: I do. All we want is to hold on to our culture and heritage.

ALIZAH: French language and culture, just to clarify?

ALAIN: Yes, what's wrong with that?

ALIZAH: Nothing at all, but why can't others hold on to theirs, Alain?

ALAIN: Because . . . they're not like us. They're against us.

ALIZAH: From the shooting at the mosque, it would seem like it's the other way around.

ALAIN: I'm not talking about the shooting, I'm talking about Québec.

ALIZAH: Fair enough. But don't you think that at some point that's where all this "they're not like us, they're against us" rhetoric leads? One day you're writing a "Québec First" Facebook post. Then to kick it up a notch, you and your friends form a quiet little anti-Muslim group. Two months later, you've got forty thousand members. And the next thing you know you're organizing, getting guns, and somebody goes off-script. Unless that *is* your script.

ALAIN: You're putting words in my mouth. I didn't say anything like that.

ALIZAH: I'm just asking you to think about where this leads. Why even start this up?

ALAIN: I'm talking about Francophone rights. I won't apologize for being Québécois.

ALIZAH: I'm not asking you to. I'm saying maybe don't assume being Québécois gives someone the right to shoot up a mosque.

ALAIN: [angry] You're forgetting we were here first!

ALIZAH: [very quietly] So that means French culture is what matters? You should be able to hold on to it, preserve it, pass laws that make sure it's protected, and get the whole country to agree?

ALAIN: [with pride] Yes! Now you're getting what I'm saying.

ALIZAH: By that logic, what about Québec's First Nations? *They* were here first. *They* deserve to preserve their culture, languages . . . treaty rights. They don't want to be erased by an onslaught of people who don't act or look like them.

ALAIN: You cannot compare the accomplishments of the French civilization with savages who hunt the buffalo.

ALIZAH: [softly] And you *don't* think your sentiments are racist? When what you're saying is that it's not so much that the French were here first—before the immigrants and other riffraff—it's more that French culture is superior, and that's why it should be protected at the expense of everyone else.

ALAIN: Obviously. Would you rather see a woman in a bikini on a beach, or in a shroud you could wrap around a corpse?

ALIZAH: So then what you're really talking about is French supremacy. *White* supremacy, if I'm hearing you correctly. Does that make you a white supremacist?

ALAIN: I didn't agree to come on your show so you could insult me.

ALIZAH: This is a call-in show. I didn't solicit your call in particular. But are you saying it's an insult to be called a white supremacist?

ALAIN: [sullen] You're calling me a Nazi.

ALIZAH: That was your word, not mine. [pause] Are you definitively telling me that you're *not* a Nazi and you *don't* support white supremacist beliefs?

ALAIN: Fuck off and die, Paki bitch.

[Call terminated.]

ALIZAH: And that concludes the latest episode of *Take No Prisoners,* where we discussed white nationalism in Québec. Thanks for tuning in.

14

Maxime Thibault was brought in to be interviewed. The flyer Rachel had found in his notecase linked him to the destruction of the MSA office. They couldn't ignore that link: that unfettered act of vandalism could now be seen as a precursor to the shooting at the mosque. The flyer Rachel had found in Thibault's bag was suggestive of the first possibility. But the interview with Maxime Thibault didn't take place in the incident room. Instead, Thibault was taken to the local police station, the interview conducted personally by Lemaire while Khattak and Rachel watched from the other side of a semi-transparent window.

Within moments, it became clear that like Étienne Roy, Thibault was receiving treatment that had not been meted out to Amadou Duchon. Lemaire had established a relaxed atmosphere; they had the camaraderie of two men who knew each other well. As she listened to the pace of proceedings, Rachel's disquiet deepened.

"What the hell *is* this?" she muttered to Khattak. "It should be obvious that Maxime Thibault's group of neo-Nazis is responsible for defacing that door, and more than likely that they played a role in the attack. Thibault is probably the ringleader."

Khattak shared what Alizah had told him with Rachel. She supposed it was something to consider—that Maxime was like a little boy who pulled a girl's pigtails for her notice—but it certainly wasn't the whole story. His poise and self-confidence, his utter lack of remorse—whatever role his group played in this place so close to the nation's capital, he was thinking of more than Alizah. Something ugly was festering under the surface of this town.

She'd sensed it outside the mosque. She'd felt it at the hospital and in her interactions with local officers. As if they all knew a secret Rachel hadn't figured out. And now someone was bringing Thibault a piping-hot cup of tea.

Rachel's eyebrows shot up. Thibault was a suspect in a terrorist attack. What if he flung the tea in Lemaire's face? But Lemaire didn't seem worried. He was slumped back in his chair, his arms folded over his chest, and he sounded as though he had no more on his mind than a chat with an old and dear friend.

"He's trying to gain his confidence," Khattak murmured.

Rachel shook her head. "No. They know each other, sir. There's already a pattern there. Listen to the way Thibault keeps calling Lemaire '*Patron.*' I've got a bad feeling about this. This guy should be in handcuffs."

One of Lemaire's team members took exception to Rachel's words.

"Don't tell us how to do our jobs. There are no guns registered to Thibault. He has no criminal record. He's never even been charged with something as minor as public disorder."

Rachel shifted to face the other man, whose name she hadn't caught. Photographs from the mosque's multiple crime scenes were scattered over his desk.

"Public disorder doesn't seem so minor now, or haven't you noticed?"

He scowled at her, but when Khattak flicked him a glance he subsided into his seat. All Khattak said mildly was, "There are other ways to get a gun."

They both turned back to the interview. Lemaire asked Thibault about the vandalism on campus. He shrugged it off.

"They're making something out of nothing. It was just a little harmless fun."

"So you're admitting you papered the office with those flyers?"

Thibault smirked. "Can't deny it, can I? That cow of a woman saw it in my bag."

Lemaire adjusted the edge of the table with care. "I'm sorry, who?"

"The Anglo kike. The one who looks like the side of a mountain."

Rachel's ears burned; her body was abruptly doused in sweat. She'd heard worse—on the ice, at home, at work—but never in front of Khattak. Or someone like Christian Lemaire. She froze, not looking at the others in the room.

Khattak faced her head on.

"He's a Nazi, Rachel. The only thing that's ugly here is him."

Thibault was grinning over at the window like he knew, and again Rachel was struck at the rot concealed behind his smooth façade. The days of skinheads were over; the racists had changed their guise.

She gave an offhand shrug. "I'm not bothered. I'm pretty sure I could take him."

His head down, Lemaire's officer grinned into his collar. His whisper was thickened by his Québécois accent, but Rachel heard him anyway.

"Kikes like to talk big."

Khattak leaned forward and rapped on the window. Lemaire looked up with a frown. He eased out of his chair, leaving Thibault to cool his heels.

When he entered the outer room, his gaze lingered on Rachel's flushed face.

"Sir," she said to Khattak. "Don't."

Khattak ignored her. He pointed to Lemaire's man.

"Your officer just insulted my partner—I want him off this case."

Lemaire's eyes widened with surprise. He jerked his head at his subordinate. They exchanged a rapid volley in French, the younger man with a sulky cast to his face.

"He insulted you?" Lemaire verified.

Rachel's face was burning. But she looked Lemaire dead in the eye.

"I've heard worse. So has Inspector Khattak."

He frowned over at Khattak. "I'm concerned that we're a little short of manpower."

Khattak looked over at Thibault behind the glass. And then back at Lemaire's officer.

"*I'm* concerned about the excess of Nazi effluvium, when we're interrogating Nazis."

"Nazis?" he challenged Khattak. "That's a little harsh, isn't it?"

"They've been painting swastikas. That's what I find harsh."

Lemaire barked something at his officer, who quickly escaped the room.

He made a polite half-bow at Rachel. "You won't have to deal with him again." He noticed Khattak's skepticism and said, "What? What fault have you found now?"

But Khattak didn't tell him, and at his urging Lemaire returned to the interview.

Rachel sighed, her hands clenched into fists. She didn't need Khattak to fight her battles. It made her look weak when she needed to appear as invulnerable as any man on the team.

"You've heard a lot worse about yourself, sir."

"It's different for me, Rachel."

Rachel sized Khattak up, his grave demeanor, his steady presence. As usual, it made her furious. "Christ Almighty, sir. Why the hell are you so calm? You *know* what's happened here. And I'm pretty sure you know which way the wind is blowing."

As usual, he was patient with Rachel—dignified in a way she couldn't hope to emulate when she was giving free rein to her anger.

"I actually prefer this, Rachel. I prefer it when the enemy comes out into the open. It's the ones who smile at you while they're plotting in the dark that I've learned to worry about. That's why I called him out."

Her voice a little scratchy, she said, "That wasn't your sense of chivalry kicking into overdrive again?"

He shook his head, his smile a little wry. "What you think of me, Rachel. Perhaps it was a little of that. But mainly, I'm beginning to worry that as gruesome as the shooting is—as wretchedly evil—there's more going on in this town."

Rachel had been thinking the same thing. She nudged Khattak to put it into words.

Glancing at Rachel, he rested a hand on the glass partition.

"Sometimes the monsters we fear aren't on the opposite side."

15

"You can lead this interview, if you like."

They were in the lounge, which had been emptied out so Lemaire could have the room to himself to speak with Père Étienne, now that the interview with Thibault had concluded with his release. They didn't have anything to connect Thibault with the shooting yet, but that didn't mean they wouldn't find something as their inquiries progressed.

The station was overheated, the lounge cramped and stuffy, not a place where big men could find themselves at ease. Various flyers had been posted to a bulletin board, notices of services available to the community tacked up between posters of wanted men. Members of biker gangs, tattooed according to their creed, featured heavily in this mix.

Rachel found a chair that she thought might accommodate her size, leaving the sturdier one across from it for Lemaire. She felt a little uncomfortable at his unexpected benevolence, though it was far less troubling than the fact that this was the place he was planning to interview Étienne Roy.

A junior officer ushered Roy into the room. He was urged to the room's only sofa, and a cup of coffee was placed at the table by his elbow. He was then asked in deferential tones if he needed anything else. As he expressed his thanks in a still-dazed voice, Lemaire signed off on reports brought to him by another officer.

"One hour," he told his team. "We make no public statements before then, and if he doesn't like it, the mayor can kiss my ass."

Rachel's ears perked up at that. Her favorite kind of cops were ones who hated politicians, and if Lemaire fit into that category she was willing to cut him some slack. She switched her attention to Roy. He was younger than she'd expected, perhaps fifty years of age, with a face that revealed that this was his first real encounter with tragedy. He seemed muddled by the events that had just unfolded.

Rachel wondered how such a helpless individual could oversee the needs of a large congregation, let alone summon up the dispatch to carry out a crime like this.

Lemaire sat down heavily across from her, angling his chair between Rachel and the priest. He nodded at her and she began. He might not like her technique, but if he was giving her carte blanche she knew what she wanted to ask.

"Why were you holding the assault rifle, Père Étienne?" She sensed Lemaire's surprise at the precision of her accent and her use of the correct form of address. She ignored it, keeping her eyes on the priest. She followed up her question by repeating it in French and asking if he'd prefer for her to conduct the interview in his own language.

Étienne Roy blinked at her, his eyes large and round behind his owl-shaped glasses, his lashes sandy and sparse. His hands trembled in his lap. He answered her in English.

"I don't know. I don't know what compelled me to pick it up. It was there on the floor, and when I saw the bodies everywhere . . . I thought perhaps I should move the weapon out of the way."

Her voice cool and precise, she said, "You're saying you didn't fire the weapon? It wasn't you who opened fire on the people who'd come to pray at the Al-Salaam mosque?"

Lemaire's sharp eyes shifted to Rachel, but he didn't interrupt.

Roy expelled his breath on a sob. "*Fire* it? No, of course I didn't. Those were my friends inside the mosque—even were they not, I am a man of God. I would never take the life of another of God's creatures."

He appealed to Lemaire, who waved the appeal aside.

"*Désolé*, Père Étienne. Please, just answer our questions. It will help us to resolve this."

So he'd made up his mind, Rachel thought, with a quiet little flicker of protest. She'd been starting to like Lemaire. But he'd released Thibault with a warning, while Amadou was still under guard. Not that Rachel believed anyone at the scene was entitled to the benefit of the doubt—she was trying to fulfill her mandate, the mandate that required her to treat all suspects as equal, with the same presumption of innocence.

"Where did you enter the mosque from?"

"The side entrance."

A small corroboration of Amadou Duchon's story. If he'd entered from the side door, it was conceivable that Amadou wouldn't have seen him. Nor would the priest necessarily have seen Amadou.

"Before or after you heard the attack begin?"

He looked uncertain, confused perhaps by her phrasing.

"I didn't hear the attack. I just—I heard people crying. I thought I heard a young man calling out."

"Did you recognize his voice?"

"Not—not in all that chaos. But later I saw Amadou, outside in the parking lot. He was being arrested."

"Did you hear him *before* you entered the mosque, or after?"

Père Étienne shook his head. "I'm not sure. Things were happening so fast. I'm trying to reconstruct what happened in my mind, when I really should be at my church. I need to set up services for the families who are grieving tonight. My congregation will be eager to help."

"Will they?"

Rachel stared at the priest without blinking, wondering what he would make of the starkness of her question. He rubbed his beard, made an abortive little swipe for the cross he wore at his neck, then looked from Rachel to Lemaire and back.

"Yes," he said. "Of course. Why would you think otherwise?"

Rachel considered her options. She could confront him with the things that were on her mind, the inside information she and Khattak had gleaned from Alizah, or with tidbits from the rancorous anti-Islam debate taking place in the province of Québec. Or she could stay quiet in her seat and wait him out. She chose the latter option, and after a moment of tense silence Père Étienne hurried into speech.

Without being prompted, he took them through the scene from the moment of his arrival to the instant he'd picked up the gun. He'd been running late for a meeting with the imam. He met with the imam regularly to discuss an interfaith initiative they'd undertaken with a local rabbi. Because the imam wasn't in his office, he'd entered the hallway to search for him, realizing he might still be at prayer.

He hadn't noticed the body in the hallway right away, heading straight into the main hall. What he'd seen there had caused him to drop to his knees.

Rachel looked the priest over. He was wearing the same clothes he'd been wearing at the scene; they hadn't been entered into evidence. In silent witness of Père Étienne's words, the knees of his dark brown slacks were discolored. Possibly by blood. His shirt was also stained.

"I think that's when I heard the voice—someone calling out for help. I went into the hallway and saw a man's body at the far end. The gun was beside it on the floor. I couldn't believe what I was seeing. It was such a shock. There was so much blood in the prayer hall. There was more at the end of the hallway. I went to the man—I turned him over to see if I could help." His voice broke over the words, his pupils growing larger, his breathing harsh in his chest. "I couldn't. I was certain he was dead. So I picked up the gun to make sure no one else could use it."

"Did you call the police? Did you check on anyone in the hall?"

Shame crept over his face and the priest bowed his head.

"I should have done something. I should have done more to help. I was stunned, Christian; you must believe me. By the time I gathered myself together, the police had arrived to secure the scene. You were there, *mon fils;* you saw. You were the one who took the gun away."

Lemaire reached over and patted the priest's knee, a gesture that shocked Rachel. Did no one at this station observe protocol? Not even the man in command?

No wonder a member of Lemaire's team had felt confident enough to call her by a racial slur. She cleared her throat with some fanfare.

"Père Étienne, you said you left the imam's office and observed nothing to distress you in the hallway. You went straight into the prayer hall without any idea of what you'd see there, is that correct?"

He nodded. "Yes. That is exactly how it happened. It is my duty to tell you the truth."

"You were in the habit of visiting the mosque, you said. You knew the congregation."

"Yes," he said again. "Of course. We organized many joint activities for our congregations. Along with the Temple Beth synagogue."

"So you'd be familiar with observances inside the mosque."

Bewildered by her line of inquiry, the priest nodded again.

"Hmmm."

Rachel looked down at his footwear, scuffed and bloodied from his presence on the scene. She leaned closer to him, her sharp brown eyes unwavering as they examined his face.

"Perhaps you'll be able to tell me then, if you thought nothing was amiss before you entered the hall, why did you enter the prayer space while you were still wearing your shoes?"

Étienne Roy went still, a boneless stillness that failed to conceal his distress or the slight glimpse of a strange emotion roiling beneath the surface. Lemaire swore to himself in French. Rachel waited both men out.

At last, Roy spoke, with an air of irritability.

"It happened so quickly, I am still in shock. I may have the sequence of events wrong. I might have seen the body in the passageway, and therefore rushed into the hall. To tell you the truth, *mademoiselle*, it's become something of a jumble in my mind. I will need long hours of reflection before I can be certain."

Rachel's smile didn't reach her eyes.

"*Pas de problème*, Père Étienne. Take all the time you need. There's just one other matter I'd like to clear up, if I may."

"I don't think—"

She breezed over the interruption.

"If you saw the body in the passageway first, did you also then notice the gun?"

16

WOLF ALLEGIANCE CHAT ROOM
[Translated from the French]

SUBJECT: PÈRE ÉTIENNE IN CUSTODY
CLOSED GROUP

BROADSWORDBEN: WE NEED TO MAKE A MOVE. WE NEED TO GET HIM OUT.

MAXIMUMDAMAGE: IT'S COOL.

NINEINCHNAILER: HOW IS IT COOL? THEY'VE GOT OUR FUCKING PRIEST.

MAXIMUMDAMAGE: WE HAVE PEOPLE INSIDE. PÈRE ÉTIENNE HAS PEOPLE.

WHITEVICTORY: AND WE SHOULD TRUST YOU WHY?

MAXIMUMDAMAGE: YOU READY TO TAKE ON THE BIG DOG?

[WHITEVICTORY HAS LEFT THIS CHAT.]

MAXIMUMDAMAGE: ANYONE ELSE?

BROADSWORDBEN: JUST GIVE US SOMETHING.

MAXIMUMDAMAGE: THEY'RE NOT DOING ANYTHING TO PÈRE ÉTIENNE. THEY KNOW THE MOSQUE IS A BASE FOR TERRORISTS.

FLAYALLTHEPLAYERS: YEAH, BUT WHAT IS PÈRE ÉTIENNE TELLING THEM?

MAXIMUMDAMAGE: HE'LL SAY WHAT HE HAS TO SAY. THE QUESTION IS WHAT IS HE THINKING. WHAT IS IT HE'S *NOT* SAYING.

NINEINCHNAILER: SOUNDS LIKE YOU KNOW THE ANSWER.

(continued...)

MAXIMUMDAMAGE: DON'T *YOU*? IF YOU'RE ONE OF THEM, YOU FOLLOW THE RELIGION OF WAR AND IF YOU FOLLOW THE RELIGION OF WAR, THE CHRISTIAN GOD SAYS YOU'RE THE ENEMY.

WE'VE BEEN PLAYING BY THE RULES WHILE THEY'VE BEEN CHOPPING OFF HEADS. SO JOIN THE CRUSADE. JOIN US BECAUSE OUR VALUES ARE TRULY FUCKING SUPERIOR.

FLAYALLTHEPLAYERS: IMPRESSIVE. YOU REALLY THINK A PRIEST WOULD TALK LIKE THAT?

MAXIMUMDAMAGE: FUCK IF I KNOW WHAT YOU GUYS WANT FROM ME.

FLAYALLTHEPLAYERS: NO, THAT WAS GOOD. IF THAT'S WHAT PÈRE ÉTIENNE TOLD THEM ALL I CAN SAY IS THAT'S GOOD.

NINEINCHNAILER: YEAH, BUT WHAT ABOUT THE AR-15? HE WAS FOUND WITH THE GUN IN HIS HAND.

BROADSWORDBEN: CHRIST YOU'RE OBSESSED WITH THAT GUN.

NINEINCHNAILER: IF WE'RE FIGHTING A GLOBAL WAR AT SOME POINT WE NEED TO ARM.

MAXIMUMDAMAGE: JUST LAY LOW FOR NOW. KEEP AN EYE ON THAT MUZZIE COP.

BROADSWORDBEN: WHAT ABOUT THE DEVIL'S DUO—A & A? YEAH, THEIR OFFICE WAS TRASHED BUT THEY'RE STILL ON THE RADIO. YOU WANT WE SHOULD MAKE IT PERSONAL?

MAXIMUMDAMAGE: I SAID LAY LOW. I'LL TAKE CARE OF THE REST.

17

Khattak had sustained an uneasy relationship with Diana Shehadeh for years. Sometimes their work overlapped; sometimes they were at odds over a direction Diana argued he should have taken pursuing a particular inquiry. Diana didn't hold back when it came to telling Khattak where she thought he'd erred, lately with greater frequency. He was under no illusions about how the current investigation was likely to play out. If Diana couldn't influence him, she would cast him as an adversary and demand a recalibration of his efforts. And of Community Policing.

It was nearly four in the morning. The scene outside the mosque had been cleared, and they stood together at the far end of the parking lot, away from the glare of the lights set up outside Lemaire's center of operations.

Khattak was hoping that a little conciliation in advance would buy him some flexibility as the investigation rolled on. They waited while the last few bodies were loaded into mortuary vans, and quietly and privately they offered prayers over the scene.

Alizah's insights were as sharp as ever. She was right: he hadn't faced the shooting at the mosque—not what it truly meant. He didn't want to. He wasn't certain what shape this new reality would assume or what it would bleed from him when it had ended.

Diana's phone had been buzzing since he'd come to meet her, and now she turned it off and put it away.

"Can we just talk about this honestly?"

For once, she didn't sound confrontational. Her tone was despairing, at odds with the aura of invincibility she projected during her inter-views. She was young and attractive, her chestnut hair tamed into waves that framed her intelligent face. Her professional dress was like a uniform—her suits either black or navy blue, her blouses buttoned up to the throat. She'd been on her feet since she arrived, either coor-dinating the MCLU's response on her phone, or seeking information from various law enforcement agencies, or lending an ear to those who'd waited outside the mosque through the long hours of uncer-tainty.

"Of course, Diana." He gave her a respectful nod. "I'm happy to speak to you, as long as you aren't confusing honesty with full disclo-sure."

A curious frown settled on her brow. "Why shouldn't I?"

"Some matters must remain within my discretion while the inves-tigation proceeds."

She gave an exasperated sigh, pinching at her collar again.

"Can there be any doubt about what's happened? The priest was found with the gun in his hands. The whole point of being at the scene is to ensure they don't try to make that go away."

"There's always doubt," he warned her. "These are still early stages. We have to ask ourselves why a Catholic priest who served on an in-terfaith committee with Al-Salaam's imam would devise an attack against the mosque. Does that make sense on its face?"

Diana's head swung around to the mosque, then back to the activity at the trailers.

"Just whose side are you on?" she asked moodily.

Esa suppressed a sigh. These were the kinds of comments he loathed. A construction of binaries, where people were either with you or against you, with no common ground in between. He'd hoped that a leader of Diana Shehadeh's caliber would be well past these questions by now.

But any response he made along these lines was bound to sound condescending.

He spoke cautiously, hoping she'd hear his undertone of humor: "I'm on no one's side. I am for justice—no matter who it's for or against."

Diana had been asked the same question about her loyalties during a now-infamous parliamentary debate. Khattak had just quoted back Diana's indignant response.

She wanted to be angry at him, but a smile twitched the corners of her wide-lipped mouth.

"You *would* remember that."

He smiled, too, a little rueful. "Hard to forget the way you made your mark."

She rubbed the back of her neck, releasing the tension there. Then, almost as if grasping his cautiously tendered olive branch, she said, "So what can you tell me, Esa? What are your honest thoughts about what will happen next?"

"There's a search on—if Étienne Roy isn't responsible for the shooting, then someone else is, or he may have had an accomplice. But there are two things you should know up front."

He told her about the vandalism of the student office, and in more detail he walked her through what might happen to Amadou Duchon. He watched the angry color rise to her face, the tightening of her lips, the frown that had become habitual. He would have been wiser not to ask, but sometimes, like Rachel, his emotions colored his perspective.

"Is this becoming too much for you, Diana? You haven't had an easy tenure as head of the MCLU."

He was expecting her to flare up like his sister Ruksh often did when he expressed his concern, but the tentative trust between them held.

"Walk me to my car," she said. "I should get over to the hospital."

Esa took her briefcase from her while she unlocked the door of a small red Volvo. It wasn't a rental car. She must have driven down, as soon as the shooting had made the news. No wonder she was tired.

"It's gotten worse and worse," she admitted. "Did you know we published sixty op-eds this year? You'd think they were meant to be educational—to address specific hate crimes—but God, Esa. Half of them were on *policy*. Official government policy. Of course, it's not just Québec. You must have heard what's been happening in Alberta."

Esa nodded. When he'd been called to Saint-Isidore, he'd been working a case linked to two extremist groups in the province of

Alberta who were seeking to defend so-called Canadian purity against the Islamic threat. One was called Wildrose, the other the Three Percent. They held an ideology in common with the Wolf Allegiance.

"We've been engaged in this work for so long. You, me, so many others—yet a terrorist attack anywhere in the world and we're right back at the beginning."

"Diana—"

"I'm sorry, I meant attacks on the *Western* world." There was a cynical droop to her mouth. "When attacks like these happen in Somalia or Pakistan, they barely register a pulse."

At the look of sympathy in Esa's eyes, she bristled and said, "Every day, it's something new. There's no laying down our arms."

The statement fell into a sudden hush, painful and disquieting.

After a moment, he asked her, "Are we at war, Diana?"

She slid into her car, nothing agreed between them on how to proceed, nothing yet resolved.

She gestured at the mosque, small and strangely ominous in the glow of the outdoor lights. At the mortuary technicians, traveling back and forth through the doors, in the process of cleaning up.

"They're certainly at war with us."

18

Esa spent some time canvasing both the parking lot and the mosque. Though he was careful not to interrupt the officers still working the scene, he tracked the different entrances and exits, moved from the basement back to the main hall of the mosque, trying to estimate for himself the amount of time the shooter was likely to have spent inside the mosque and the possible routes he might have taken. When Esa had finished considering several different scenarios, he pulled out his phone. He had several missed calls—one from the hospital that might have been Amadou trying to reach him, another from Alizah, and two from Rachel. Something must have happened.

Before he could call Rachel back to clarify, his phone buzzed with a text delivered by an encrypted service. He read it quickly.

> I've been wondering who's important to you. It looks like Shehadeh is a player.

Esa scanned the parking lot, suddenly conscious that he was alone in a corner, some distance away from the lights. He picked up his pace, heading to the entrance of the mosque, passing members of Lemaire's team as they came and went, with no sign of Lemaire himself.

Instinct told Esa to act on the message. He needed to get Paul Gaffney out here so he could take Esa's phone apart. Gaff was the tech specialist at Community Policing, and he could play a role in the greater investigation as well.

Esa scanned the parking lot. Whoever had sent the message had witnessed his conversation with Diana. It could have been anyone. One of the technicians, one of Lemaire's team—a stranger in the shadows. The shooter returning to the scene to witness the aftereffects.

Khattak moved to the perimeter of the lot, scanning the streets on the other side of Lemaire's headquarters. He knew the trailers were temporary; Lemaire would commandeer operational quarters soon, but Esa was checking for cameras. Lemaire should have set them up as part of his surveillance of the scene, but Esa couldn't see them. There were no businesses this close to the mosque, no cameras on the streets, either. But he remembered that when he'd walked down the hill with Alizah and Rachel there had been signs that cautioned against speeding. Perhaps somewhere in the area there were red-light cameras. He'd find out. But first he had calls to make, and he wanted an update from Rachel.

The first call he made was to Diana Shehadeh. She needed to be careful, in case the texts were more than a prank from someone in the Wolf Allegiance. Gaffney would be able to tell him how they'd accessed his phone.

Before he could relay his warning, Diana interrupted him, a note of relief in her voice.

"Can you get here right away?"

She had already reached the hospital.

"What's happened?"

"Some good news for a change. The student, Youssef Soufiane, is out of surgery, and he's regained consciousness. He'll be able to tell you what happened inside the mosque."

A hand gripped Khattak's shoulder. He wheeled around to find Christian Lemaire with Rachel at his side.

"Diana, I'll call you back." He looked at the scene beyond them, the signs of increased activity. "What is it? Have you found the second gun?"

"Youssef Soufiane is ready to speak," Lemaire said.

"Yes, Diana Shehadeh just told me."

Lemaire hesitated and Khattak hastened to reassure him. "We've worked together in the past, but obviously I'll say nothing that would compromise the investigation."

The two men looked at each other, a conscious weighing of the priorities of each. Something in Khattak's face seemed to set Lemaire at ease.

"*Bon,*" he said. "Let's go."

He led the way to his car, Khattak sliding into the passenger seat, puzzled by the look on Rachel's face.

As Lemaire pulled out of the lot, he answered Khattak's question. "No luck on the gun yet. We'll have daylight soon; we'll be able to search the creek."

"What about your priest?"

Rachel leaned forward to answer him. "Hard to say what's going on there, sir. There were some inconsistencies in his statement, but he might just be in shock. He's been fingerprinted and his clothes have been taken for testing. Shoes, too."

Khattak nodded. He was glad Rachel had caught that for herself. He held up his phone to show the others the text he'd been sent, but when he searched for it, it had vanished. Just like the first one he'd received.

And then he realized. Whoever had sent him those texts had used an encrypted service so that the texts would self-destruct after he'd clicked them open.

"What is it?"

Khattak turned to Lemaire. "There's someone else we need to consider." He explained about the texts, but Lemaire shrugged them off.

"You don't have them?"

"I'll screenshot the next one."

"You think there will be another?"

"I'm certain of it. You know what messages like this can lead to."

Lemaire's deep voice rasped in his throat. "They're like anonymous letters. They're meant to assert control. Someone is toying with you, Khattak."

Esa didn't want to exaggerate his own sense of worry, but he was concerned by the threat to Diana.

"It might be wise to assign an officer to Diana Shehadeh for as long as she's here."

This time Lemaire parked in the emergency entrance, throwing his keys at a member of his team.

"I don't have enough officers on the ground. Let's wait and see, shall we? This might not be anything other than a college boy's prank."

"Some prank," Rachel muttered.

But Khattak left it for now. If he pressed Lemaire, Lemaire might ask him to turn his phone over for forensic analysis, and he preferred that a member of his own team be the one to run that diagnostic.

Soufiane's room was at the opposite end of the hall from Amadou Duchon's. A pair of Sûreté officers were leaning over the reception desk flirting with the pretty nurse. Diana Shehadeh was outside the door, giving Soufiane's family some privacy.

The trio of girls Khattak had noticed earlier was still there, the girl named Chloé hovering anxiously near the door, yet making no demands. Alizah was nowhere to be seen. The guards were still on Amadou's door.

"Lemaire." Khattak kept his voice down. "You don't have a guard on Soufiane."

Rachel had noticed, too. She'd taken up watch right outside Soufiane's door.

Lemaire nodded at the reception desk. "My men are right there. He's a victim, Khattak; he barely survived the attack. There's no chance he did it himself."

The words gave Esa pause. Had Lemaire really not considered the obvious?

"If he witnessed the attack, he's a threat to the shooter. What if the shooter returns?"

Lemaire jerked his head in the direction of Amadou's room.

"We have the shooter under guard."

"Lemaire—"

Khattak pulled him aside. Diana Shehadeh was only steps away. If she caught wind of Lemaire's words, the whole complexion of the case would change. Instead of a police investigation, they'd be dealing with a national scandal.

"What?" The other man sized Khattak up.

Khattak spoke each word slowly and deliberately.

"Amadou Duchon is not your shooter. Which means Soufiane is still at risk. If you don't believe me, call in a profiler. Unless you already have one on your team."

There'd been no time for a substantive team briefing yet because Lemaire's INSET team was fully occupied: coordinating the search, processing the multiple crime scenes, dealing with the victims' families, reporting to the mayor and the premier, and dealing with the press and the public. But they'd need to present a theory of the crime soon, from which their joint strategy would emerge. They needed a profiler at that meeting. Someone who would tell the members of Lemaire's team, and Lemaire himself if necessary, what Khattak already knew.

The shooter was going to be a young white male, disaffected and full of rage, prey to radicalization. It wasn't Amadou Duchon, who had tried to save his friend's life. It was also unlikely to have been Étienne Roy, whose actions required an explanation but were not necessarily incriminating.

They had released him after his initial interview, but Maxime Thibault fit the profile.

But to have sat there in that café so calmly, just hours after the shooting, he would have had to be a psychopath. Yet there was something about the texts sent to Khattak that strongly suggested Maxime as the culprit.

But he would withhold judgment. It was much too early to guess.

More pressing at this moment was his need to determine exactly what kind of an officer Christian Lemaire was. Superintendent Killiam had left the scene. There was no one on the ground to enforce her directive, and if Lemaire was half as good at assessing character as Khattak considered himself to be, he'd know that Khattak was unlikely to make a personal complaint. He could railroad the investigation in a particular direction if he chose to and take on the MCLU's opposition merely as a matter of course.

The tone of political discourse in the province suggested that such an outcome was possible. Except that Lemaire wasn't a politician. He was a decorated police officer with a stellar record in homicide. There wasn't a hint of corruption attached to Lemaire's name.

Khattak waited for his response. He watched as Lemaire reassessed the officers he'd assigned to the floor. Seven team members in total: five men and two women, all of them white. Four were at Amadou's door, two at the reception desk, and one was keeping an eye on the elevator. Lemaire strode to Amadou's door, snapping orders to his team. The men at the reception desk snapped to attention at Soufiane's door. Two of the women joined him, while a third officer took up a post by the elevator.

Lemaire beckoned to Khattak. He made no apology, gave no explanation for his actions. What he did say with a faint softening of his voice was, "Perhaps you'd like to speak to Youssef Soufiane first."

19

Rachel moved out of the way of the Sûreté officers, glad that whatever Khattak had said had prompted a reconsideration. The ward should be locked down. She was worried that it wasn't. Why were the girls dressed in black still permitted to hang about the elevator? Chloé with her pale face and hair and slight outbreak of acne along one cheek appeared to be the youngest. The others paid more attention to the Sûreté officers than they did to Chloé, who was hovering at the fringes of Youssef Soufiane's room.

The young man's family had left the room shortly after Khattak had entered. A small woman wearing a head scarf and a long, demure gown brushed past Chloé, deliberately pushing her aside. The woman's husband tutted at the girl as he passed, while Soufiane's other relatives swept by the girl as if she weren't there.

Her trembling, "Mr. Soufiane," was swallowed up by the silence. The hand she'd raised to attract their attention fell to her side. Rachel caught a glimpse of a small black tattoo on the inside of the girl's wrist. It was a delicately drawn rendering of the fleur-de-lis on the flag of the province of Québec. The very tip of the lily was edged in red.

The girl's personality was timid, but the tattoo at her wrist hinted at unexplored depths.

Rachel approached her, flashing her ID.

"Your name is Chloé, right?"

The girl glanced up at Rachel like a startled creature in the wild.

"It's Chloé Villeneuve, but how did you know?" she whispered in French.

Rachel switched to the same language.

"Alizah Siddiqui told me. You're friends, right?"

Chloé's slim shoulders relaxed, and when Rachel nodded over at the waiting area she followed her to a seat in the lounge. Chloé sat forward in her seat, a posture that allowed one wing of her hair to cover the acne on her cheek. Rachel felt a pang of sympathy. She'd been just as self-conscious once, never quite sure what to do with her hands or how to arrange her long limbs in a way that no one would notice.

"You're here very late," she said to Chloé. "Do you know Youssef well?"

"He's my friend."

Her blank despair said otherwise.

"Do you know if he's going to be okay?"

Rachel looked back at the door. Khattak was still inside the room, Lemaire was speaking quietly to Diana Shehadeh in the corner. From what Rachel had learned about her, Diana would be negotiating access to Amadou Duchon. She wondered for a moment if Lemaire would give in, studying his reassuringly solid frame.

Sensing her interest, he glanced over at her. Rachel flushed, quickly turning back to Chloé.

"The surgery went well and now it's just a matter of waiting to see how well his body recovers. He's out of immediate danger, but he's not all the way out of the woods."

Chloé's relief was palpable. She'd check with Khattak to see if the young man had asked for her.

"Is he your boyfriend?" Rachel asked directly.

Chloé shook her head, her thin lips trembling. "No. I wish he was, but Youssef said no, his family wouldn't accept it. They immigrated from Morocco. Youssef was born here."

"So what are his thoughts?" Rachel probed. "You're a pretty girl; it must have been hard for him to turn you down."

Hope flashed into Chloé's eyes. "Do you think so?" she asked.

"Didn't Youssef?"

Youssef Soufiane's family had gathered in a corner of the waiting room, taking up the rest of the seats. Chloé flicked a nervous glance at them to see if they were listening. Youssef's mother glared at the girl, frowning under her head scarf. But the young girl sitting beside her offered Chloé a hesitant smile.

He's going to be okay, she mouthed.

Chloé sank back into her seat, the tension easing from her body. She pushed a lock of fair hair behind her ear.

"Youssef was really kind to me—just like Amadou is. He could have taken advantage; he knows that I'm . . . stuck . . . on him. That I like him, I mean. But he told me he wanted to marry a girl from his own background, one who can speak Arabic as well as French, and he didn't want to waste my time by offering me anything less."

Surprised, Rachel said, "You're both young to have spoken of marriage."

Chloé blushed. "I know. But that's how they do it in his family. Either you're with someone for the purpose of getting married, or you're not with anyone at all. He likes me. But maybe not in that way."

She risked a glance at Youssef's mother.

"I think—I think if his mother liked me, it might have made a difference. But Youssef would never want to hurt his mother. That's what makes him so different." She gave Rachel a searching glance. "He's not all about himself like most of the others."

Rachel was touched by the sweetness of the tribute, innocently offered and steadfastly believed. It must have hurt a girl as tenderhearted as Chloé to have faced such a harsh rejection from the Soufiane clan.

"How did you meet Youssef—and Amadou, as well? You mentioned that you know him."

"We're all at school together. Different programs. Amadou takes night classes in the journalism program. Youssef is studying engineering."

"And you?"

"Graphic design." She turned her wrist to show Rachel the tattoo. "I designed this for our group."

"Your group?"

Suddenly abashed, Chloé dropped her chin to her chest. "The girls over by the elevator. They're my friends. We thought we'd get one together—they asked me to design it."

"Does it mean anything?" Rachel asked, pointing to the tattoo.

Chloé offered her a shy smile.

"It's the fleur-de-lis," she said, as if someone outside Québec wouldn't know that. "And we're the Lilies of Anjou." She blushed again. "It's just a silly clubhouse name. It doesn't really mean anything. It gives us an excuse to hang out and talk about things we like."

"Such as?"

Chloe sounded embarrassed. "Oh, you know. The power of the feminine in nature, and so on. We sometimes meet in the woods and try to commune."

Though the words were offered without much confidence, they did suggest a reason for the lily tattoo as a symbol of the same.

"And was that all?" Rachel persisted, trying to get a better sense of who the Lilies were.

Chloe's renewed blush was so vivid that Rachel guessed that the group of young women most likely confided their secrets in one another. Including their romantic inclinations.

Which brought her back to Youssef.

"How did you find out that Youssef had been shot?"

"We were supposed to meet Youssef and Amadou at the mosque after prayers. We usually hang out in the evening."

"You mean with your friends, the Lilies of Anjou?"

Chloé shook her head. "Me and Alizah. She's our friend, too. The others came to the mosque later. After the news had spread."

Rachel stared at her, trying not to betray her intense interest in the statement. Lemaire had said there had been no witnesses at the scene, apart from Amadou and the priest.

"Chloé, am I the first police officer you've spoken to tonight? Has anyone else taken your statement?"

Chloé looked confused. She chewed a strand of hair between her lips. "No. Should they have?"

Keeping her voice even, Rachel asked, "What time did you arrive at the mosque tonight? Before or after the shooting?"

Chloé paused, perhaps alerted by the note of suppressed excitement in Rachel's voice.

"I heard it," she said. "But I wasn't there. I was just making my way down the hill. And I heard these sounds. *Rat-a-tat, rat-a-tat.* I'm sorry I don't know how to describe it. Just that sound—like muffled firecrackers, I think. Very close together, very loud. So I began to run."

At Rachel's questioning look, she added, "I knew it wasn't firecrackers." And then with a deep sigh, she sank all the way down in her seat and added, "We have a problem in this town."

No kidding, Rachel thought. Khattak had already used the terms "hate crime" and "terrorist attack" to describe the shooting at the mosque. Now someone turned up the volume of the television in the waiting room, and as the prime minister appeared on the screen every head in the waiting area swiveled to watch. Rachel had met the prime minister earlier this year at a dinner at Rideau Hall. He was clearly shaken by the news, his statement clear and concise. He called the attack a cowardly act of terror and urged the nation to come together.

Looking around the ward—at the Sûreté officers, at members of the Soufiane family, at Diana Shehadeh and the Lilies of Anjou—Rachel didn't see much faith in the prime minister's assurances. Diana Shehadeh looked angry, the officers skeptical, and Youssef's family simply bewildered.

"What kind of problem?" Rachel asked Chloé.

"Listen," Chloé said, shrinking from another hostile glance from Youssef's mother. "I don't think we should talk about this here. Do you have a card? Can I call you?"

Starting to feel a little bleary-eyed, Rachel handed her card to Chloé.

"I'll tell you what you want to know, but will you let me know if you hear anything about Youssef? Like his visiting hours or anything?" She cast a longing glance at his door as she moved to the elevator. Rachel had the feeling that Chloé was holding something back.

Rachel dropped her voice. "Is it about that group that calls themselves the Wolf Allegiance?"

Chloé hesitated before the open doors. The two girls dressed in black joined her in the elevator, blocking her from Rachel's view. Were they simply being protective, as friends who belonged in a small, closed group? Or did they have something to hide?

She didn't have a chance to hear Chloé Villeneuve's answer.

20

"Youssef," Esa said. "Do you feel up to talking with me? Are you comfortable speaking in English, or should I request a translator?"

The young man in the bed had a face that was pale beneath the even brown tones of his skin. He was younger than Esa had expected, his densely clustered curls giving him the appearance of a boy, an appearance enhanced by his expression of youthful wonder. He studied Esa for several moments, then answered him in Arabic.

Esa demurred in the same language, expressing his disappointment that he didn't speak it. The few phrases he knew were not enough to sustain the conversation they needed to have.

Youssef switched to English, his fluency greater than Esa's in French, the slurring of the words along his tongue suggesting the drowsing effect of medication.

Gently, Esa took him over events at the mosque, easing him into describing the moment of the attack. It had happened so quickly that Youssef wasn't sure what he'd seen, whether he'd been shot first or last. His respiration began to accelerate, his breath rasping in his lungs.

"I was in prayer," he said. "I didn't see. Who shoots someone in the back?" He choked over the words. "When I fell, I heard people screaming. I turned my head to the side to see. I heard footsteps. I thought the shooter was coming closer to make sure I was dead."

Intent now, Esa asked, "Did you see him?"

Youssef hesitated, as if he was making sense of what he'd witnessed. "I saw—someone dressed in black. I saw—Abubekr. He was trying to protect Adam. It happened so fast. The shooter stood over Abubekr.

He shot them both—just like a spray. The bullets scattered everywhere; it was so loud that I felt it . . . here."

He dragged the hand that was attached to the IV up to his chest.

A nurse entered the room. She made a disapproving noise in her throat, taking Youssef's hand and placing it back under the sheet.

"His blood pressure's rising. Whatever you're doing, it's time for you to stop. He shouldn't be disturbed."

Her French was plain enough for Esa to understand. He answered her in English.

"I'm sorry. I need to ask him something else. It won't take me a minute. Could you wait outside?"

She reached over and patted Youssef's curls. Murmuring to the boy in French, she asked, "Do you want me to get rid of him? This is the last thing you need."

Youssef managed a tired smile. "*C'est bon.* I can answer."

The nurse flounced to the door, quivering with primness. At the door she turned and said, "Inspector Lemaire is waiting for you outside."

When she'd gone, Esa turned back to the boy.

"Youssef. This is important. Can you tell me about Amadou? Can you tell me what you remember about Amadou?"

The nurse had lowered Youssef's bed, and now his head sank deeply into the pillow. Tears slipped down his face through lashes as thickly tangled as his curls.

"It felt like I was alone for a long time. But I had a sense that the shooter was still at my side—I'm not sure why. I must have passed out, because I don't remember how long I lay there. But when I became conscious again, Amadou was holding on to me. He was trying to bandage me up. He must have saved my life."

"But he wasn't with you during the shooting?"

"No. He had a meeting with another friend, so he didn't want to wait around. He must have heard the shooting and come back."

Such a narrow window, Khattak thought. *Between Amadou's departure from the mosque, the shooting that had begun in the basement, and the all-out assault in the main prayer space. How quickly the assailant must have moved.*

But at least part of Amadou's statement was borne out by Youssef's recollection. Why would Amadou have come back to save someone he'd just shot? If Amadou was the shooter, why risk being found at the scene?

He needed to ask Youssef the question point-blank.

Leaning closer so Youssef could hear, he said, "Was it Amadou you saw, Youssef? Was Amadou the shooter?"

Youssef coughed, tears watering his eyes.

"No—no—I told you. Amadou came back to save me."

Cursing himself for doing so, Khattak pushed a little harder.

The boy's eyes were closing, he was almost asleep, but Khattak needed to be sure.

"How do you know, Youssef? How can you be sure it wasn't him?"

The boy's hands relaxed on the bedsheet, his breathing evening out. He closed his eyes without speaking. Khattak waited another few moments, hoping for a change. It didn't come until he was at the door.

Youssef struggled against the effects of the medication, pushing himself up on his elbows. Panic shone through his eyes.

"'Ya Allah, ya Allah,'" he recited.

Esa took his hand. "What is it? You mustn't upset yourself, Youssef."

"It wasn't Amadou; it wasn't."

"Did you see the shooter's face?"

Youssef's eyes were wide with horror, the realization new.

"It was a *woman* who shot me. She looked at me when she was done."

"You saw her face?" Khattak gripped his hand.

"I couldn't. No one could see her face. She was wearing a black abaya."

21

"Any news?"

They were in Lemaire's car headed to the team briefing, where a fully functioning incident room was in the process of being organized out of offices loaned to Lemaire's team by the mayor of Saint-Isidore. Khattak had also requested that Paul Gaffney, Community Policing's cybersecurity expert, be added to the team, and Gaffney was en route now, though he wouldn't reach Saint-Isidore in time to make the meeting.

Khattak answered Lemaire's brusque request by giving him the essence of Youssef Soufiane's statement. Lemaire whistled out loud. He shot a glance at Rachel in the back as he turned down the main road.

"What do you think?"

Rachel appreciated the fact that he was seeking her input. Many senior officers didn't.

"One, I think you need to release Amadou Duchon. Soufiane confirms his story, which makes Amadou a hero. There's no reason he should be under guard, except for his own safety." She'd grown a bit more politically savvy since her time at Community Policing. She wasn't oblivious to the racial undercurrents in Québec. "Think about the optics. You release a white man at the scene found with the weapon in his hand. But you put a black paramedic who was trying to save lives under arrest. I don't think you appreciate the shitstorm you're calling down on your head, sir."

"Lemaire." He made another turn, pulling into a parking lot and usurping a spot at the front. "You don't frame it as a matter of justice,

I notice. You think a Québécois cop isn't susceptible to that kind of appeal?"

Rachel caught the smile that Khattak quickly suppressed. She glared at him. He was used to her lack of tact; he was probably happy that it was Lemaire's turn to get a taste of it. He didn't interfere, leaving her to talk herself out of what she'd just said.

"Nothing to do with you or the Sûreté, sir. Happens in every jurisdiction, including ours. I take it as a matter of justice every single time. Not everyone I've worked with does. Not like Inspector Khattak."

Lemaire didn't seem pleased by the endorsement. Neither agreeing nor disagreeing with Rachel's assessment, he said to Khattak, "You're sure about Duchon?"

"I'll accept all responsibility for the decision to release him."

Lemaire slammed out of the car. "Not necessary. My choice, my responsibility."

They stared each other down in the parking lot.

"We only have a few minutes," he warned. "You're worried about Duchon. What about when I announce that the suspect was wearing a burqa? What do you think will happen? They'll connect it to Duchon. Then it explodes and goes national."

"Yes." Khattak's response was dry. "I could write the headlines myself."

"Sirs." Rachel's sharp interruption drew both men's eyes to her. "You're making an assumption. Just because Youssef Soufiane saw a woman dressed in a robe doesn't mean that's who the shooter was."

"No? I'm not following."

Isabelle Clément was waiting at the top of the stairs. She signaled to Lemaire and he nodded. Feeling the pressure of the time, Rachel made it quick.

"It's the easiest disguise in the world. It stirs up the kind of trouble Saint-Isidore has been trying to keep under wraps. It explodes the whole Charter of Values debate. And it targets a community that some in Québec are all too happy to demonize. As Inspector Khattak could tell you, it's not all that different in Ontario. You should have seen what happened when a local politician tried to table an anti-Islamophobia motion."

She wanted Lemaire to believe that she possessed no innate anti-Québécois prejudice. That wasn't who she was or what she stood for. If she believed otherwise, she wouldn't be Esa Khattak's partner.

"I did." Lemaire's hostility eased. "It wasn't pretty. Neither was Saint-Isidore's Code of Conduct." He motioned to Isabelle Clément that she shouldn't wait for them. The press liaison turned on her heel and disappeared inside the building, unflustered by her dismissal.

"What exactly happened with the Code of Conduct here? What inspired the need for it?"

Lemaire stretched out his back and sighed. "They have quite a lot of foreign students at the university. It raised the profile of . . . certain activities." He flicked a glance at Khattak, indicating that he should explain.

It was Khattak's turn to sigh. "Observing the month of fasting, and so on. The ordinary things that make up to day-to-day life."

Lemaire cleared his throat, sounding a little embarrassed. "So at a town meeting here, someone protested these . . . foreign practices. And it was moved that newcomers needed to be warned."

"Not against Ramadan," Khattak corrected. "Nor against the mosque. No, the Code of Conduct was meant to address the fear that Muslims in Saint-Isidore might take it into their heads to start cutting off hands or stoning women. The Code was meant to warn them off."

Rachel knew Khattak's poker face quite well. Despite the seriousness of the subject, she caught the quick twitch of his lips.

"Put like that, it does sound rather ridiculous. They didn't spell it out when they were drafting the Code—they didn't come out and say 'we don't want Muslims here.'" Lemaire sounded fed up by the fact that he was splitting hairs. "But that's, in effect, what it came to. Islam is seen as a danger to the secular values of Québec. And someone took that lesson to heart. My team will be working for weeks to solve this, and nothing they do will be right."

He spared Khattak a brief glance of commiseration.

"You've been through it, eh? You know what I'm talking about."

It was an oblique reference to the parliamentary hearing where Khattak had been compelled to clear his name of suspicion. It told Rachel that in the little time Lemaire had had available since the shooting, he'd found it necessary to do a little digging.

But the place of sympathy he'd arrived at shattered another of Rachel's assumptions.

"Okay," Lemaire said to Rachel. "You've made some good points. We can't leap to conclusions just because the shooter was wearing an abaya. But we do have to consider whether the shooter may have been a disaffected member of the mosque. Someone with a personal grudge. We can't ask the imam. But Père Étienne or Rabbi Avner might have heard something through their interfaith group. We should follow that up."

"We should also ask Alizah," Khattak suggested. "She and Amadou were involved in the mosque. If there's something to what you're saying, Alizah won't have missed it."

"No," Lemaire agreed, with a decided lack of enthusiasm. "Your young friend pays very close attention to everything that happens in this town. She never fails to remind me of things I've overlooked."

"I can follow up with Alizah, if you'd prefer."

A droll note in his voice, Lemaire answered, "Yes. I'm sure you make an entirely different impression on the mademoiselle than I do."

Khattak's eyes narrowed, but he didn't respond. Rachel rushed in to fill the silence.

"Youssef's testimony does give us something, though. It explains a hell of a lot about how no one had time to escape."

"Go on."

With Lemaire's blue eyes fixed on her face, Rachel swallowed.

"The shooter entered through the women's entrance dressed in an abaya. The abaya concealed the guns. So whoever was wearing it was able to take them by surprise."

22

It was five in the morning now. Everyone was edgy and desperately in need of sleep. But their INSET team would be working through the next few days without snatching more than a few hours of rest here and there.

Rachel's ponytail was beginning to hurt. Slinking down into her chair and waiting for Lemaire to begin the briefing, she released it from its rubber band and gently massaged her scalp. Lemaire gave her one of his penetrating looks, making a quick survey of her face and hair before turning to one of his aides. If it had been her former boss doing it, Rachel would have found an excuse to leave the room.

But Lemaire had only looked; he hadn't leered. And then he'd looked away.

She combed her fingers through her straggly hair, pondering this. Was she getting a vibe from Lemaire, or was her lack of sleep affecting her otherwise incisive thought processes? He didn't look her way again, so she rubbed her eyes, wondering how Khattak was faring without rest. He was standing at the front of the room with Lemaire, leaning against a whiteboard, his hands in his pockets, letting his gaze range over the material the team had collected.

Crime scene photographs were still being processed and tacked to whiteboards. There appeared to be some confusion as to what to prioritize. Most of the investigators and technicians had come in from Montréal, along with an experienced team of pathologists. The local police were not equipped to deal with a crime of this scope, yet they didn't appreciate being muscled out. Unlike Khattak, who was scrupulously polite when asked to advise on a case, Lemaire wasted no time smoothing ruffled feathers. In one way, Rachel admired it. In another, she knew that the person who would bear the brunt of the local cops' displeasure wouldn't be Christian Lemaire—it would be Esa Khattak.

Lemaire nodded at someone she couldn't see. Rachel turned to look behind her. At the back of the room the premier's press liaison stood with her briefcase in hand, still as smoothly poised as she'd been hours before. She'd changed her clothes and was wearing more practical footwear—but other than that, everything about her appeared the same.

Khattak's charisma had had no impact on Isabelle Clément. She was entirely focused on her job. She gave off an air of chilly competence and Rachel sympathized. Clément was an attractive woman in a nearly all-male environment. Whether at City Hall or among police officers, she would be guarded against giving anyone she worked with what they perceived as an opening. Perhaps the rhetoric that reached her ears was more sophisticated than what Rachel so frequently dealt with, but it amounted to the same thing in the end. Unwanted, unwelcome attention that hindered a woman's performance of her job.

Not to mention the uncounted cost of prolonged psychological stress.

She glanced at Clément's hand for a wedding ring, even as she knew that a ring on a person's finger made no difference to a would-be harasser or to anyone who thought he was entitled to personal attention.

Maybe she was constructing an artificial sense of solidarity with Clément because she was so often the lone woman in the room, just as Khattak was nearly always the sole senior investigator who was also a person of color.

Here the INSET team was uniformly white, including the officers seconded from the Sûreté. Rachel's mouth quirked as she realized the senior pathologist was a woman of South Asian background, neatly rounding out a stereotype. She looked impatient and frazzled, wearing a lab coat with the kind of pocket protector that had been popular decades ago, rammed with pens and highlighters. She was tapping her foot impatiently, as though counting the minutes until she could return to where she was needed. She didn't look as though she suffered fools gladly. Like Clément, she looked entirely capable of handling Lemaire, Khattak, or anyone else who thought about obstructing her work.

Lemaire invited the pathologist to speak first. He introduced her as Dr. Sunny Agarwal.

"English or French?" she snapped, a question that summed up the language politics of the province.

Lemaire nodded at Khattak, a gesture of respect.

"English. For now."

One of the doctor's assistants handed out a one-page summary of her findings. She didn't go over the number of dead and wounded; it was there for them to read. She did explain that two different guns had been used at the scene—one a 9mm handgun, the other the AR-15. She was also able to give them a sense of how many shots had been fired from the handgun and how many from the assault rifle. Casings were still being recovered from the scene.

"I won't waste your time with the details. We'll have a reconstruction model for you by the morning, so you'll know exactly where the shooter or shooters stood. There wasn't a lot of movement or panic on the shooter's part. No one got close enough to intercept him, though we are still testing for DNA. There is one thing, though, that stands out."

She motioned to her assistant for a whiteboard.

She tacked a sketch onto it. Every officer in the room leaned forward to peer at it. Watching them, Dr. Agarwal made an exasperated noise. She took a black marker and drew a set of three large black dots that even those at the back could see.

"I spoke to the surgeons who worked on Youssef Soufiane. He was shot three times in the back, but not with the assault rifle. He was shot with the handgun. And he was also stabbed." She shook her head at herself. "No, sorry. I don't mean stabbed. He was *marked*." She put a photograph up on the board beside the three black dots, showing a faint tracery on Youssef Soufiane's back.

When no one in the room responded, she clicked her tongue. She took up the marker again, this time tracing a pattern between the dots.

Rachel bit back a gasp.

Because what the shooter had done was quite deliberate.

He'd marked Youssef Soufiane with an emblem of Québec.

In this case, the fleur-de-lis.

When Dr. Agarwal was finished, Lemaire spoke next, then Khattak. A private conference between the two men and Clément yielded the decision to immediately release Amadou, while keeping him under watch. Clément would make it clear in her statement that there were no eyewitnesses to the shooting and that there was no one who could identify the suspect. The information about the black abaya would not be released, though it broadened the scope of their search.

Lemaire addressed the room, this time in French.

"So now we are looking for three things: the handgun, the knife, and the abaya. It is for certain that the shooter will find the possession of these items too hot. They will either be destroyed or discarded. And if it is the latter, we must determine where. Do we have anything on the assault rifle or the handgun?"

The ballistics technician stepped forward. He held a report in his hand that he passed to Lemaire.

"Nothing on the handgun, sir. But we've gathered some information on the AR-15."

"That was quick," Lemaire said.

"That's because we matched it to one in our database. It matches casings collected from another crime scene."

The whole room became alert. Rachel itched to steal the report from Lemaire's hands. Perhaps sensing her intense interest, he set the report down on her desk. Rachel quickly flipped through the pages.

"Continue," he said to the technician.

"Two years ago, there was another murder committed with the AR-15."

"What murder? Where?"

The technician seemed bewildered by Lemaire's sharp questions. Stumbling over the words, he spit out, "Montreal's Rue Sainte-Catherine's shooting. It was used to kill a member of a biker gang. His name was Michel Gagnon."

A whisper ushered through the room as the case took on an entirely new complexion. Québec had a long history of biker gangs who trafficked in guns and drugs and who spewed violence against one another in the streets of Montréal and all over the province. Michel Gagnon was a former drug lord, leader of an infamous motorcycle gang. He'd been killed in a drive-by shooting. There were no witnesses to the shooting, at least none who were willing to speak. No one had claimed responsibility for his death. Not even rival gangs. No one had wanted to strike that spark, but the war between the gangs had raged on for a decade.

Now at last they had a clue that could lead them back to the night Michel Gagnon had been murdered. And the use of the fleur-de-lis symbol carved out on Soufiane's back could easily be attributed to the gang's Québécois *de souche* philosophy, the French-language formulation of "old-stock Québécois"—a code word for white identity. Which meant that the gang members were also French nationalists, with a supremacist twist. Immigrants from North or West Africa, like those who had settled in Saint-Isidore, would never be welcome in their ranks. And as the home of one of the first Codes of Conduct, Saint-Isidore was the ideal battleground.

Lemaire dismissed the technician, addressing himself to Rachel.

"Looks like you were right about the danger of making assumptions. This shooting wasn't carried out by a disaffected member of the Al-Salaam congregation. It looks like Montréal's gang wars have landed in Saint-Isidore." He glanced over at Isabelle Clément, whose main concern was how these developments would play in the media and reflect on the premier of Québec. "We should be asking ourselves how they knew to come here. And taking a very close look at Maxime Thibault's chapter of the Wolf Allegiance."

Rachel raised her hand to ask a question.

"I'm a little confused about the members of this Allegiance. Were they on the local cops' radar before the shooting at the mosque? Do they have broader community support, or do you consider them a fringe element?" She thought about what Alizah had told them and added, "Apart from the break-in at the MSA student group's office, I understand there were previous incidents. Could you speak to that?"

Again, that unfamiliar look appeared in Lemaire's eyes. Something elusive balanced between assessment and appreciation.

"Excellent questions," he said. He scanned the room, pointing to a young man at the back. "You're local, Constable Benoit. Can you advise us on previous incidents?"

A young man in uniform scrambled to his feet, so astonished to find himself the center of attention that he flushed to the tips of a pair of ears that stuck out like the blades of a fan. He asked permission to speak in French, and both Esa and Rachel nodded their assent.

Though he was nervous, the young officer's summary was a model of concision.

The first incident had consisted of a call-in show's quarrelsome host asking for listeners to suggest amendments to the proposed Code of Conduct. That discussion had precipitated a deluge of abuse against Saint-Isidore's small Muslim community that the host had actively encouraged. Each suggested amendment recommended a greater curtailment of the rights and freedoms of this community, until an all-out ban was proposed. Borrowing language from the rest of Canada, a stand was made against barbaric cultural and religious values.

Shortly after the program, some individual or group had broken the windows of the local synagogue and the mosque.

The second incident had taken place under cover of night. On Easter morning, a pig's head, fresh with blood, had been left on the steps of the mosque before the first prayer of the day. No one had claimed responsibility, but a note had been stuffed inside the head: *Pigs deserve pigs. Pigs go home.* A report had been filed with the SQ from the area, but the note inside the pig's head had disappeared before it could be tested.

Then exactly one month before the mosque shooting, the imam's car had been set on fire in the parking lot while he was inside leading prayers. No one was hurt in the incident, and again no one claimed responsibility. The incident was investigated by both local police and the fire department, but no suspects had been named and the case was still considered open. The police had recommended that the mosque consider setting up security cameras. Within a week the cameras had been smashed. When the mosque committee had replaced them, the new cameras had been stolen. No usable footage had emerged from either set.

Philippe Benoit finished his recital and sat down, a hush settling in the room. Lemaire let the silence build. Rachel knew what he was doing. He wanted his team to consider that all along the violence had been escalating—that there had been warnings before the assault on the mosque that the local police either had been too inexperienced to field or had chosen to downplay. She couldn't tell which of these theories Lemaire was inclined to believe, but something about Constable Benoit's recital puzzled her.

"There's still something missing, isn't there? What's the connection to the Wolf Allegiance?"

Lemaire let the constable answer.

Awkwardly poised between sitting and standing, Constable Benoit stumbled over his response. "Ah . . . I'm not certain."

Lemaire gave him a friendly smile.

"Come on," he said. "You've done good work. Think it through. You know this town better than any of us."

Flushing beet-red again, Benoit straightened his shoulders. He was applying himself to the task—his embarrassment was not a cover for dim-wittedness; he was merely overwhelmed to be relied upon by an officer of Lemaire's stature.

"There's no direct connection I can point to, sir. It's just that this group—the Wolf Allegiance—they held some kind of party to celebrate each event. And I did some digging through their online channels: they were most pleased each time an act of vandalism occurred." He switched to English. "They egged each other on."

"How did you keep track of this?" There was genuine approval in Lemaire's voice. Constable Benoit began to gain confidence.

"It was the young lady—Miss Siddiqui. She stopped by the station many times. I thought she was right about the things she was saying," he said simply. "So I began to take an interest."

Rachel looked from Lemaire to the young constable. There was an opening here if Lemaire chose to take it. He could ask Benoit whether he had reported his concerns to his senior officers and what, if anything, they had done about it. But it would put the young constable in an untenable position, because his immediate bosses would be sure to hear what he'd said.

Something was rotten in good old Saint-Isidore, all right. Rachel wondered what Lemaire would do.

"You're an independent thinker," Lemaire said curtly. "You're an asset to this team, Benoit."

Looking like he couldn't believe what he'd just heard, Benoit mumbled his thanks. He would have sat down again if Khattak hadn't intervened.

"You mentioned online channels."

The young man nodded.

"So you have some expertise in this area?"

He nodded again, apparently tongue-tied, perhaps wondering if the axe was about to fall on his neck. Khattak gave him a reassuring nod.

"Good. We have a team member coming in—Paul Gaffney."

A murmur of surprise rippled through the room. Gaffney was a legend in the Royal Canadian Mounted Police, the federal police service. It looked as though his legend had spread to the Sûreté.

"I'd be grateful if you would consent to being paired with him. There's something I need you both to look at."

Khattak didn't elaborate, and overwhelmed at his good fortune, Benoit's mouth went slack until he collected himself enough to indicate his assent. He cast an admiring glance at Khattak, his sheepish gaze lingering for a moment on Khattak's face.

Lemaire rattled off assignments, indicating that Rachel and Khattak should join him in his office, where Isabelle was already waiting.

"You know something I don't?" he asked Khattak, referring to his reassignment of Benoit.

Khattak gave him a friendly smile. "You'll know it, too, once Gaffney gets to work."

23

WOLF ALLEGIANCE CHAT ROOM
[English-language page]

SUBJECT: ANY TIPS ON THE INVESTIGATION?
COMMENTS OPEN

BROADSWORDBEN: YOU HEAR ANYTHING?

FLAYALLTHEPLAYERS: THEY LET DUCHON GO. HE WASN'T CHARGED.

BROADSWORDBEN: EVERYONE KNOWS THAT. I'M TALKING ABOUT INSIDE INFORMATION.

MAXIMUMDAMAGE: THE COPS HAVE SOME HEAT ON THEM FROM THE FEDS. KHATTAK AND THAT WOMAN.

BROADSWORDBEN: GETTY.

MAXIMUMDAMAGE: YEAH, GETTY. SHE'S DOGGING LEMAIRE WAITING FOR HIM TO GO WRONG.

NINEINCHNAILER: WHAT KIND OF HEAT?

MAXIMIUMDAMAGE: THEY MISSED SHIT. THE PIG'S HEAD, THE FIRE, THE CAMERAS.

FLAYALLTHEPLAYERS: THE SYNAGOGUE.

FRENCHKISSER: THE MUZZIES COULD HAVE DONE IT. THEY HATE THE JEWS MORE THAN THEY HATE EACH OTHER.

WHITEVICTORY: THE PIG'S HEAD WAS ME. I ALSO DID THE BACON ON THE DOORKNOBS. NO ONE REPORTED THAT?

NOHA TEHERE: YOU KNOW BACON DOESN'T HURT US, RIGHT? WE DON'T CATCH ON FIRE OR ANYTHING. YEAH, IT'S GREASY AND IT DOESN'T SMELL GREAT, BUT WE HAVE WINDEX FOR THAT.

MAXIMUMDAMAGE: LURKING IN OUR CHAT ROOM AGAIN, ALIZAH? GUESS YOU CAN'T LEAVE ME ALONE. NICE NICKNAME, BY THE WAY—NO HATE HERE.

NOHA TEHERE: YOU PUT THAT TOGETHER? I'M JUST TRYING TO KEEP YOU HONEST.

MAXIMUMDAMAGE: MAYBE WE DON'T WASTE TIME TALKING.

NOHA TEHERE: YOU NEED TO STOP THREATENING VIOLENCE IN A PLACE WHERE WE'VE HAD A MASS SHOOTING. UNLESS YOU ACTUALLY DID IT, AND YOU'RE LOOKING TO ESCALATE. IN WHICH CASE, YOU'D BE STUPID TO ADVERTISE HERE.

BROADSWORDBEN: SOMEONE NEEDS TO BE TAKEN DOWN A PEG.

MAXIMUMDAMAGE: SHUT UP, BEN.

NINEINCHNAILER: NO NAMES.

NOHA TEHERE: OH COME ON. EVERYONE KNOWS WHO YOU ARE. JUST OWN YOUR NAZI IDEOLOGY.

MAXIMUMDAMAGE: SO EVERYONE WHO DISAGREES WITH YOU IS A NAZI?

NOHA TEHERE: IF THEY CALL FOR EXTERMINATION. I'M A LITTLE PICKY LIKE THAT.

MAXIMUMDAMAGE: NO ONE HERE SAID THAT.

NOHA TEHERE: YOU HAVEN'T BEEN PAYING ATTENTION. ONE DAY IT'S GOING TO BE TOO LATE.

WHITEVICTORY: LOOK AT THAT. SHE SOUNDS LIKE SHE CARES ABOUT YOU. TALK ABOUT ARYAN NATIONS! WE GET ALL THE GIRLS. #muzziepussy

MAXIMUMDAMAGE: SHUT THE FUCK UP. ALIZAH, GET OUT OF HERE NOW.

NOHA TEHERE: COME WITH ME, MAX.

FLAYALLTHEPLAYERS: WHAT THE HELL'S UP WITH YOU, BRO? YOU GONNA LET THIS BITCH OWN YOU?

BROADSWORDBEN: YOU WON'T LET US TAKE HER ON. YOU GOING SOFT?

(continued...)

NINEINCHNAILER: I'LL TAKE HER ON. SHE LOOKS LIKE SHE'D SCREAM REAL SWEET.

NOHA TEHERE: I'D SCREAM FOR THE POLICE, YOU MEAN. MAX, COME WITH ME, PLEASE.

MAXIMUMDAMAGE: GET OFF OUR MESSAGE BOARD, BITCH.

24

Rachel shamelessly eavesdropped as Isabelle Clément took Lemaire to task.

"You're lighting a conflagration if you're thinking of pitting *pure laine* Québécois against an immigrant population."

"I am?" Lemaire raised an eyebrow, not the least intimidated. "*I* didn't draft the Charter of Values. And we are well past the point of considering minorities immigrants. They've been here for several generations."

Isabelle Clément made a little moue of distaste. "Not long enough for the *pure laine*."

"I don't give a damn about the *pure laine*. I have a killer to catch, and I don't give a good goddamn who it is—or what community they spring from. Twelve people are dead, Isabelle. And more will probably die in hospital. What would you have me do?"

Isabelle took the question quite seriously, as if Lemaire had offered her an opening.

"I would prefer—as would the premier—if you didn't release Amadou Duchon just yet. The moment he's released, he opens his mouth as to why he was detained. And there are legitimate concerns about his background."

This time Rachel couldn't mask her dislike of Clément, her earlier solidarity evaporating.

"Background?"

Isabelle flashed her an impatient look.

"I don't mean that he's black. I mean all the agitating he's been doing with this other congregant of the mosque." She snapped her fingers, trying to recall the name. "The one who calls you all the time," she said to Lemaire. "This—this Alizah."

"Al*eezah*," Khattak clarified the pronunciation of Alizah's name. "But protesting the actions of a group like the Wolf Allegiance is not a reason to detain him. Amadou's only crime is that he tried to save his friend's life, and was caught in the wrong place."

Isabelle gave Khattak a dismissive look that Rachel knew her boss was unaccustomed to. He was usually met with overwhelming feminine interest.

"Your politics are racial, Inspector."

"What makes you think yours aren't?"

Rachel's eyes widened. It was a direct, unequivocal challenge, which Khattak had never issued before. Offered coolly and politely as if Khattak was unconcerned by Isabelle's contemptuous dismissal. He rubbed a hand along his newly grown beard for emphasis. And Rachel took a minute to think about why Khattak had let his beard grow out and why he'd chosen not to shave it off the instant he'd heard they were heading to Québec.

Isabelle scowled at him. "What do you mean by that?"

Khattak's response was stated so evenly that it took Rachel a moment to realize what he'd said.

"Identity politics aren't just black or brown. Sometimes they're old stock, *pure laine*—with a fleur-de-lis etched in blood for emphasis."

The press liaison fell silent for a full minute. When she spoke, her voice was shaking.

"How dare you speak to me like that? How dare you make that kind of assumption about me?"

"But you're perfectly free, of course, to make any assumption you like about me or my racial politics."

Khattak's smile was cold, echoed by the lift of a sleek black eyebrow.

Isabelle's face flushed, a line of sweat forming on her brow. Rachel almost felt sorry for her. Isabelle deserved Khattak's rebuke—which had been delivered quietly—but confronted with her own hypocrisy, she seemed to be at a loss. Her hands were trembling at her sides.

She took a quick breath, but she didn't look to Rachel or Christian Lemaire for support.

"You're right, Inspector. I deserved that. I owe you an apology. It's not an excuse, but I'm under some pressure from the premier." Embarrassed, she added, "I've never had to be the public face of anything like this."

"Thank you."

Khattak said nothing else to let her off the hook, and Rachel was amazed by the change in his demeanor. He rarely let a colleague suffer discomfort on his account; he was much more likely to be the one to smooth over personal conflict.

She decided they needed a moment alone. This wasn't how they usually proceeded on a case. Khattak focused on the facts; it was Rachel who led with her heart.

Her concern must have been evident, because when she looked away from Khattak it was to find Lemaire studying her, an expression of great interest on his face. Alarmed by it, she said, "So what is our position, then? What happens now?"

Lemaire came to a decision. "Let's get Duchon home." He summoned one of his officers to arrange Duchon's release before continuing. "I've got camera footage in from the main street. The team is studying it now. If we get anything, we'll expand our search beyond the creek. Until then, I suggest you all get a few hours' rest. We'll begin again in the morning."

He conferred with Isabelle, emphasizing what she could state publicly and what it was necessary to omit. She repeated her apology to Khattak before she made her excuses and left.

Lemaire gave them the address of the hotel where he'd checked them in, and Rachel followed Khattak out into the late summer night. They'd come straight from Toronto to the scene of the shooting, their presence too urgently required to delay by dropping off their gear. They were edging toward dawn now, and the subdued activity down the road at the mosque seemed almost unreal.

"Can't believe this happened here, sir. I can't believe some lunatic walked into a mosque and murdered twelve people, then took the time to mark one of his victims with a fleur-de-lis."

She offered to drive the rental car to the hotel and Khattak let her, wearily pressing his palms against his eyes.

"Are you all right, sir?" She hesitated, thinking of how he'd spoken to Isabelle. "This must have hit you hard."

She kept the windows down to reduce the stifling heat in the car but also so Khattak could look away if he chose.

He didn't. He did the same thing Lemaire had done, studying Rachel closely, examining her face for something she couldn't guess at. Signs of support? Loyalty? Judgment?

An unpleasant thought struck her. Surely he didn't imagine that she saw the case any differently than he did—that she and Isabelle were allied in thinking that peace should be purchased at any cost.

"Rachel," he said slowly, his deep, attractive voice sending a sudden shiver down her spine. "I've been thinking about the fate of Community Policing."

She shot him a look of alarm. Had she missed something, something that had been seriously troubling him?

"You're overdue for a promotion. I know Superintendent Killiam thinks so as well."

Rachel spoke through lips that had suddenly gone dry. "Well, that's great, sir, but that doesn't change anything at Community Policing, does it?"

Khattak's hands were clenched, setting off alarm bells in her head. "You'd make an excellent director," he said.

"Sir." She slammed on the brakes at a traffic light she'd missed. "*You're* the director. You're the one who brought me on board. I wouldn't want to stay on without you." She cleared her throat, deeply uneasy. "You're not thinking of leaving, are you?"

There were no other cars on the street, so Rachel put the car in park. She turned in her seat to face him. He gave her a curious look, deep and searching and entirely new to the parameters of their relationship.

When he didn't speak, Rachel plodded on.

"Is this about Sehr? Are you thinking of getting married?"

He hesitated, so Rachel plunged in.

"That doesn't have to change anything, sir. I'd be very happy for you."

Now at last, Khattak smiled. The smile she knew, sweet and teasing, and the ramrod tension in her spine eased.

"It's not about Sehr. I haven't spoken to her about this. I wanted to speak to you first."

Rachel swallowed. She tried not to blink at the turn the conversation had taken.

"You can talk to me, sir." She tendered each word carefully. "You know that, I hope."

"I do." Still he hesitated, choosing his words. "What happened at the mosque . . . what happened at the station, it reinforced something I've been considering. I don't know that I add value to this job anymore."

"Is this because of your run-in with Diana?"

He shook his head. "No. She didn't say anything I haven't already heard. From everyone." He looked defeated. "Except you. And Sehr. We both saw a value in working from the inside. But Sehr's not a prosecutor anymore, and I'm not sure that my future still lies with Community Policing."

Very carefully, Rachel asked, "You're saying you think you haven't been effective?"

His mouth twisted, and at the bitterness of his expression Rachel's heart sank.

"I'm saying that it's hard for me to walk into a mosque where twelve individuals who share my faith have been murdered . . . most likely because they practice it . . . and do nothing other than stand back as a neutral observer."

Rachel felt the tears well up in her eyes. Khattak swore softly.

"Rachel—"

"No, it's all right, sir." She willed the tears not to fall, rubbing a quick hand across her eyes. "I'm fine. But how can you call yourself an observer? There's nothing neutral about you."

"There isn't?" He sounded disturbed.

"No." She forced a laugh. "Working with you—it's like seeing the mirror image of myself. You project neutrality, but you're ferociously committed to the work. Look how you stood up for Amadou. You forced that onto their agenda, you *know* you did that, right?"

"You're giving me too much credit. Lemaire doesn't strike me as a bigot."

She scoffed at the explanation. "You don't give yourself enough. You've got more that you want to say, is that it? You can't take the pressure? The only senior brown cop—the only Muslim? Come off it, sir. What do you think it's like for me? For any woman who tries to slog her way to the top? You remember our first case? You remember Salvatore Costa?"

A reluctant smile edged the corners of his mouth.

Heartened by it, Rachel went on. "He was such a pig. Every single day he made a comment, just not loud enough for you to hear. Then one day I come in and he's got a nudie calendar tacked up on the board and he's watching for my reaction. 'Come on, Rachel,' he says. 'Don't break a guy's heart. Stick your picture up there. You can be Miss January—just you and a hockey stick, that would do it for me.'"

Seeing Rachel's face through the glass door of his office, Khattak had opened his door and taken in the scene. He'd ripped the calendar from the bulletin board in a single concise gesture, turned to Sal, and said, *Get your things and get out; you're no longer a member of this team.* Then he'd looked around the room at the rest of them—Paul Gaffney, Declan Byrne, Rob Sharma, and he'd said in a tone that lowered the temperature in the room, *If any one of you attempts to harass Sergeant Getty or any other female colleague, I will personally see to it that he's out of law enforcement.*

They'd looked at Khattak, guilty and embarrassed. They hadn't been part of it, but they'd allowed it to continue with their silence. A silence Sal had read as tacit endorsement.

Khattak had called only Rachel into his office.

I know it's hard to fight this, Rachel, given what happened at your last post, but I wish you would. You'll have my backing, and you won't have to face it alone.

She'd looked at him in horror, stammering an apology, and after seeing her panic he'd let her escape and put the incident behind her. But the entire team had been required to attend training on the issue of harassment. A confidential reporting system had been established, but after Salvatore had left there'd been nothing further for Rachel to report. At least not on her own team. In the field, there were always outliers, but Rachel's confidence had skyrocketed once she knew she had Khattak at her back.

"You showed up," she said simply. "You didn't just talk the talk. You made everything about being a cop better. You should know what a difference you've made."

They were at a crossroads. To the north of the bridge was the campus. To the south, the creek meandered off into the woods, while parallel to the road ran a set of train tracks, the mournful notes of the horn sounding from a great distance, adding pathos to the early dawn.

Khattak cleared his throat. Rachel was glad he didn't thank her, because she didn't know how much longer she could swallow back her panic at the thought of him leaving her behind.

"I think I'm failing, Rachel."

She wasn't buying that.

"You're just angry. I think you've been angry for a while, but you've trained yourself not to show it."

She started up the car again, aiming a lopsided smile at Khattak.

Startled at her words, he met her gaze. She couldn't help herself. Her whole heart was in her eyes. He swallowed at what he saw there. Her personal faith in him. He reached out for her hand and squeezed it hard.

Her voice rough with emotion, she said, "Maybe it's time for a change."

25

Squeezed in beside Khattak, who'd stretched out his long legs in front of him, Rachel sat back on the small sofa in the campus radio station, enjoying the warm rapport that existed between herself, Alizah, and Khattak and into which Amadou Duchon was now being inducted.

She'd managed a few hours of sleep back at the hotel and now she felt ready for the new day's challenges, though her worries about Khattak were gnawing at a corner of her mind. He didn't look like he'd slept all that well, though there was something about his good looks that was enhanced by the shadows under his eyes. She would have envied it except that she knew he'd probably stayed up praying for the souls of the victims. She hoped he'd have a chance to rest later that afternoon.

The campus studio was cozy—Alizah was seated behind the desk; Amadou wandered in and out of the sound booth, testing sound levels while Alizah fiddled with the microphone. One wall of the room was covered in a collection of vinyl records that made Rachel's mouth water—so many of her favorites were there—Bowie, Joni Mitchell, Blue Rodeo. They were crammed into a corner shelf at eye level, a little at odds with a wider selection of famous Québécois singers and North African rai. Tacked to the back of the door of the sound booth was a signed Céline Dion poster, the singer posing in a shimmering gray minidress, her sincerity blazing from her eyes.

Was it hanging there as some kind of cool-campus-kid mockery?

Amadou met her gaze solemnly. With perfect seriousness, he said, "She is still the queen."

Rachel tried to seem like she agreed, though she unironically preferred The Police.

"You're okay?" she asked Amadou, studying him. "No aftereffects?"

"I'm okay." His demurral was at odds with the weariness in his face. "A black man learns very early what to expect from police." The words were neither bitter nor resigned. They spoke of matter-of-fact acceptance, belied by the gleam of resistance in his eyes. And despite her extensive training in community relations, Rachel couldn't think of a response that wouldn't come off as dismissive of Amadou's experience. She simply nodded, holding his gaze.

She had thought that Alizah and Amadou would be at a vigil outside the mosque or at the hospital trying to get word on whether there were any survivors of the night's attack. She also thought that the shooting might have driven Alizah home to Waverley—considering the memories it must have brought back.

Fists banged on the glass window of the studio. A look of disgust on her face, Alizah pushed the mic away and stood up, smoothing her hands against her jeans. It was Maxime Thibault who'd rapped his fists against the glass—perhaps in a greeting, though the group of young men around him made obscene gestures at Amadou. Maxime's fixed stare didn't waver from Alizah. Slowly, he ran his tongue over his lips.

She scowled in fury, but Khattak didn't let her intervene.

He stepped outside, speaking too quietly for them to hear, but whatever he'd said, the young men moved off. As Khattak stepped back into the studio, Rachel caught the explicit racial slur aimed at his back.

She wasn't surprised—Thibault had used an epithet to her face; why would he spare Khattak?

"You need protection from them." Khattak said this to both Amadou and Alizah.

Her tone scornful, Alizah replied, "From a gang of preppy thugs? I don't think so."

"No." Khattak shook his head decisively. "From Thibault. He's exhibiting classic signs of stalking. And that can escalate quickly."

Amadou nodded wisely. "I've been telling her, sir. She doesn't listen."

Alizah looked over at her friend, a sweet smile breaking on her face.

"I have you, Amadou," she said simply. "You never let me out of your sight."

"Ya Allah." He patted his chest once with his fist. "Now you know why."

"We have to do the program today," Alizah explained. "It's more important than ever."

"Why?" Khattak kept his eyes on her face and she blushed.

"You didn't hear the morning drive time? Pascal Richard is already sharing his crackpot conspiracy theories—riling people up. He's not the least bit apologetic for his role in this."

"Who's Pascal Richard?"

Alizah and Amadou answered together, feeding off each other's words.

"He's a local radio shock jock."

"He's a cretin."

"He's a monster. He's been fanning the flames of racial bias here since the passing of the Code of Conduct."

"His following is enormous—his show has been syndicated and he's drawn all manner of crazies to this town. His shows are an example in incitement."

"Incitement to what?" Rachel broke in. She was thinking uneasily of the sections of Canada's federal Criminal Code that spoke directly to hate crimes. She hoped Alizah and Amadou weren't exaggerating the impact of a lone voice on the radio.

"To hate," Alizah said. "To all the things that have happened here."

"The Wolf Allegiance's anti-Islam rally," Amadou supplied.

"The pig's head at the mosque."

"The attack on the synagogue."

"That time they set fire to the imam's car."

"It's endless—there's a new obscenity every day. I don't mean like the shooting last night. I'm talking about the little things that led up to it. That's why Alizah petitioned for her own radio show on campus. As a rebuttal to Pascal's, so we could take them on."

"I couldn't have done it without you, Amadou. You're the one who rounds up all the guests. You're the one who takes the call-in abuse."

"They abuse you, too," Amadou said gently. "Just in a different way."

"It's much worse for you."

"Is it? Max is not after me."

"Amadou—"

"Alizah," he chided.

Their byplay reminded Rachel of one of her mother's favorite movies, *His Girl Friday,* where Cary Grant and Rosalind Russell had starred as a pair of battling journalists with snappy patter and rat-a-tat dialogue that had always delighted Rachel. In the case of the movie's two leads, the banter had been a means of expressing sparkling romantic interest. In Alizah and Amadou's case, it was the empathy of two friends who knew each other well and who could be counted on to have each other's backs.

A little like Rachel and Khattak.

Which reminded her again of the conversation she'd had with Khattak in the car; she wondered whether she'd convinced him not to give up on their work. Without him, their unit would be left rudderless— and without much difficulty she could imagine it being dissolved.

Khattak's quiet voice cut into her thoughts.

"You said today's show is important. What are you planning for today?"

An apprehensive note crept into Alizah's voice. She fiddled with the microphone, avoiding Khattak's gaze.

"We're having a memorial. By reading out the names of the victims from last night."

Khattak's eyes narrowed.

"That information hasn't been made public because we haven't had time to notify all the victims' families. We're also waiting on news from the hospital. So how could you have a list?"

Braving his gaze, Alizah answered, "Diana Shehadeh gave it to us. She didn't say that we couldn't use it. In fact—"

"In fact?"

"She's the guest on our show today."

Khattak looked over at Rachel, who squared her shoulders.

"That's a terrible idea. We've been keeping a lid on things here, so far. Speaking to Diana Shehadeh will only blow that up. You're not ready for that, Alizah. None of us are."

Alizah was wearing her hair in a long, dark braid. She leaned over the electronics board, and the braid fell forward. She was considering Rachel's words seriously. She'd grown up in the intervening years, a measured young woman who had taken time off from school to work after her sister's death and who had now nearly completed her graduate degree. She seemed to be heavily involved, not only in her program of study but also in a range of extracurricular activities that included the Muslim Students Association and her program on campus radio. What she had to say in response caused the hairs on the back of Rachel's neck to stand up.

"That's what they said when we showed up to council meetings to make our position known on the Code of Conduct. When politicians refused to speak to us, they said we were stirring things up. It's what the police said when we reported Pascal Richard for hate speech— and then later, when we began to document each incident. 'Let's keep a lid on things. Let's not let them blow up.' Well, they just blew up at our mosque."

Amadou moved closer to Alizah. He didn't touch her in any way, yet his solid presence was clearly a source of comfort.

If it were Rachel, she would have hugged him. But through her work at Community Policing, she'd learned that observant Muslims did not engage in casual contact with members of the opposite sex. She'd seen as much with Khattak—until he'd lowered his guard with Sehr, the woman he hoped to marry.

She'd also seen him with Alizah—protective, the way he was with his younger sisters, but mindful of an appropriate distance.

He wasn't as reserved with Rachel. She could tell that their relationship—as partners, as friends—fell into a different category in his mind. A category of one, where you could count on your partner to save your life as often as she spoke her mind.

This was one of those times when Khattak would have to speak.

And she wondered how closely his private thoughts might reflect Alizah's.

But he was a law enforcement officer first.

"No, I'm sorry. Even if Diana gave you the list, she has no way of knowing if it's accurate or up to date. It would be irresponsible to misinform the families. You know that, Alizah. It's not something I need to explain."

The fleeting pain that showed in Alizah's eyes was a quiet confirmation of his words.

Amadou rapped his knuckles against the sound equipment. He was staring beyond Khattak's shoulder at the hallway where students had begun to line up at the glass, some waving at Amadou, others whispering and pointing.

News about Amadou's detention had gotten out.

Amadou ran his thumb over his lips. He didn't wave or smile or even fling up his head in a confrontational gesture. His quiet dignity spoke for itself as he met the gazes of the others head on. One by one they dispersed.

He shifted his attention to Rachel, taking her by surprise.

"What did you think I would do?"

Discomfited, she didn't answer.

"What about the interview?" Alizah asked.

Khattak considered it. "Diana Shehadeh usually finds a way to speak her mind. If you're not prepared for that, your interview might result in the same outcome. Do you think you can handle her?"

Alizah smoothed her palms over her jeans before she answered. "We're mainly going to speak about the vigil." She bit her lip. "There's a rumor that Maxime's followers are planning to stage some kind of rally. We want to make sure our vigil isn't disrupted."

Rachel thought that was a terrible plan.

"Won't drawing attention to their plans on public radio only encourage more of them to show up?"

Alizah was quick to respond. "It's not directed at them. It's an appeal to the rest of the citizens of Saint-Isidore. To show up for the victims of the shooting."

From the way his brows drew together, Rachel could tell that Khattak was thinking the same thing that she was. The vigil would require police protection. If Étienne Roy was not the shooter, the suspect was still at large. And what better opportunity for the shooter to make his mark than by disrupting a peaceful vigil.

"Even if we don't advertise it, people will still show up. This just allows us to do something to honor the memory of our friends."

Khattak's attention was distracted by the press of students on the other side of the glass. A few young men—tall, broad-shouldered, physically fit—were making obscene gestures at Amadou, who ignored them, going about the business of setting up the show. One was staring at Alizah with a fixed, unwavering gaze. Khattak turned back to the others. He spoke to Amadou.

"You'll wait for me to attend the vigil. I'll escort you both personally."

Rachel watched as a silent communication passed between the two men.

"We'll wait," he agreed. He indicated the students on the other side of the glass with a sharp lift of his chin. "But what you're seeing out there is nothing new. It's not something you can protect us from after the two of you leave."

He made the possibility of their departure sound imminent, irreversible. Beneath his calm expression, Rachel sensed a very real despair. Had he been expecting more from them? Something he hadn't articulated because he didn't know how to put it into words?

"You just have to deal with it. It happens every day."

Khattak shook his head, but he wasn't discounting Amadou's words or his experience. He was bringing them back to the matter at hand, the matter that was weighing on their minds.

"Not like this," he said. "A mass murder at a mosque is not something that happens every day. And God forbid it should ever happen again."

He turned on his heel suddenly and banged a fist on the glass, holding up his ID. The students quickly scattered.

"Alizah." His tone was peremptory. "You said you heard a rumor about Thibault's plans for tonight. Where? How did you hear it?"

She didn't speak, fiddling with her braid, suddenly seeming much younger than her age.

"It wasn't a request, Alizah."

Sparks flashed in the young woman's eyes. She wasn't used to this side of Khattak, and Rachel had to admit she hadn't had much experience of it, either. He was cold, concise, focused, sparing little time for her feelings.

Firming her lips, Alizah said, "It's not my secret to tell."

Khattak's gaze switched to Amadou, who shrugged.

"Émilie Péladeau warned me."

"She's a student here?"

A glance passed between Amadou and Alizah. Then with a hint of discomfort, he nodded.

But there was more to it. Rachel had looked over the list of names Christian Lemaire had collected—family members and friends who were anxiously awaiting news at the hospital.

"She was at the hospital last night," she put in. "Is she related to one of the victims?"

But she already had a sense of the answer. "She was with Chloé, right? One of the girls dressed in black?"

They both nodded.

"That seemed like something," Rachel pressed. "The black clothes, Chloé desperate for news about Youssef. Why were they there? Why do they have an ear on the ground for trouble from Thibault?"

Somewhat stiffly, Alizah answered, "The girls you saw last night— they have their own group. They call themselves the Lilies of Anjou. Sometimes they hang out with Maxime."

Rachel's eyebrows shot up. That wasn't quite the vibe she'd picked up from the girls at the hospital. They hadn't seemed anything like arm candy for a group of neo-Nazi thugs.

"But Chloé is crazy about Youssef. Why would she have any sympathy for Thibault?"

Alizah hesitated. "Everyone on campus knows Max. He has a charming side and he's really popular. People get drawn into that before they find out anything else. Once they do, it can be . . . difficult . . . to refuse his friendship. Or to figure out a way to cut loose."

She sounded as though she knew something about the subject, as if it was a reason for her to stand by the young women she'd just described.

"And Émilie Péladeau?" Khattak interjected. "The source of the rumor? What was she doing at the hospital?"

Amadou's gaze fell to his hands. He answered with an air of palpable embarrassment, flicking Alizah a discomfited look.

"We might as well tell the truth. Émilie was there for me."

26

Amadou gave them directions to the office of the dean of the university. Their conversation wasn't finished, but Lemaire had just called with an update.

Rachel waited as Khattak listened to the other man on the phone, then laid out his own plans for the morning. Covering the phone with his hand, he spoke to Rachel: "Étienne Roy has given Lemaire permission to search both the church and his house for the handgun. He's asking if you want to go with him. He'll collect you on the way."

Surprised and a little disarmed, Rachel agreed, approving of the concise manner in which Khattak laid out his concerns. Khattak put his phone on speaker, treating Rachel to Lemaire's litany of curses. The vigil was the last thing they needed, but if they tried to shut it down outside the mosque, mourners would find another place to gather. He concurred with Khattak that they needed to mobilize an immediate response. When pressed on the safety of Amadou and Alizah, Lemaire advised that it was better to speak in person, after the team regrouped.

"I'll meet you at the station in an hour," Khattak said, terminating the call.

Outside the dean's office, he asked Rachel to take out her notebook, rattling off a list of tasks that included setting up a meeting with the dean, another with Diana Shehadeh, and the task of tracking down Émilie Péladeau.

"We need background on this group—the Lilies of Anjou. Also, I want a list of the incidents reported to the dean, and the action the university took in response. When you have that list, get it to Diana Shehadeh and ask her to be at that meeting. Oh, and one more thing, Rachel."

Rachel looked up, her pen flying over her notepad. "Sir?"

"Make sure Gaff's settled in and connect him with Constable Benoit. There's a task I'll need him to do for me, but I don't have the evidence yet."

Perplexed, Rachel stared at him. There was something about his expression that warned her not to inquire further.

"What about you, sir? Where are you headed?" She tried to suppress the anxiety in her voice.

"I'm going to see Pascal Richard."

Dismayed, Rachel said, "You won't be able to shut him down. It's a freedom of speech issue, sir."

She could tell that her boss was choosing his words with care—reminding himself that Rachel wasn't the enemy, that she wasn't responsible for the anger simmering just beneath his impassive exterior.

"It's strange, isn't it, how much latitude hate is granted, the insidious way it creeps in under the protection of the law. People like Thibault are given the benefit of the doubt far more often than we are."

By "we" he didn't mean police officers. It was obvious he meant members of minority communities—communities he identified with. Rachel couldn't fault his conclusions. Freedom of speech as a value was nearly sacrosanct. And under its broad umbrella, groups like the Wolf Allegiance had not only come into being—they were flourishing.

Not a lot of consolation to the families of the dead.

Had it crossed over? she wondered. Speech into action, hate into blood?

Khattak had used a similar phrase once when discussing the Christopher Drayton case—the case of a Bosnian Serb war criminal . . . a fugitive from justice who'd ended up in Canada.

How quickly the violent ideals of ultra-nationalism led to hate, how quickly hate to blood.

She struggled to clear her thoughts. This was Québec, *la belle prov-*

ince, not a distant land torn by a war fueled by nationalist identities. This was a blip, an anomaly—something that had happened once before with the shooting of young women at École Polytechnique— and now there was a new lone wolf, this one possibly radicalized online.

She was convinced that the shooter would turn out to be a white male between the ages of twenty and forty, who was deeply disaffected, without genuine community ties, and who might have a history of domestic violence.

This case was ugly because of the target—the shooter at École Polytechnique had targeted women engineering students, a different kind of ugliness—but it wasn't emblematic of the greater violence she was beginning to believe Khattak feared.

Though she couldn't discount that it had happened in Saint-Isidore, or its infamous Code of Conduct, the code that may have been responsible for lighting the flame.

Khattak was waiting for something more from her, but Rachel didn't know what else to say, so left it at, "Just be careful, sir. I bet this guy has a lot of experience riling people up. Don't let Richard mess with your head, sir. Don't let him get to you."

Khattak's razor-sharp smile was thoroughly unsettling.

"I'm the one who's planning to get to him."

Leaving Rachel to team up with Lemaire, Khattak sorted through the details of the case in his mind, mentally arranging a list of questions to prioritize. The issue of first importance was not only to uncover the location of the missing handgun but also to determine how two such weapons had fallen into the hands of the unknown shooter. Gun control laws in both the province and the nation were strict. The question of access to the weapons used in the shooting suggested a high degree of premeditation and a deliberate attempt by the shooter to cover his tracks.

They were looking for a psychopath, perhaps. The executions in the basement of the mosque represented cold, controlled rage. But what of the upstairs shooting—the spray of bullets and the hate embodied in the message drawn on Youssef Soufiane's back? Still controlled, Khattak thought. Operating under pressure in a high-stakes environment, the shooter had kept his calm and exited from the scene safely.

And if he was able to project himself as undisturbed by the night's events—if he was in some way celebrating them even now—that meant he might have the coolness of nerve required to return to the scene tonight, to keep tabs on the investigation, or to surveil the planned vigil.

Even to attack again, if he was willing to accept the much greater risk of being caught.

Who had the self-possession to carry out such an attack and also have access to a gun linked to organized crime? Khattak ran over a list of names in his mind: Roy and Amadou at the scene. Thibault or the Lilies of Anjou by implication, though he wasn't certain of the role either had played. As important as the timeline on the night of the shootings was the need for a timeline that tracked the incidents mentioned by Alizah and Amadou from the passing of the Code of Conduct to the shooting at the mosque last night. There had to be something there—a trigger they'd overlooked. And there was also the question of the role Pascal Richard had played.

Which reminded him of something he'd forgotten to ask Rachel. But better to go through Gaffney directly. Pulling into the parking lot at the radio station, he called Gaffney and explained what he wanted. It was mind-numbing, time-consuming work, but there was a reasonable possibility that Gaffney's efforts would yield a lead.

He ended the call, following the directions to the third floor, where Richard was busy in a program meeting. The receptionist pointed Khattak to a waiting area where a student intern crossed his path, a young man with a brush cut, dressed like another of Maxime Thibault's acolytes, but with an attitude of pleasant cooperation. Discovering that Khattak wasn't fluent in French, he switched politely to English.

"Do you save the recordings of Monsieur Richard's call-in shows? On tapes or discs, I'm not sure of the technology involved?"

The intern, whose name was André Martin, nodded. "But they only go back as far as six months."

Not long enough, Khattak thought. But it was a beginning.

"I'll need those recordings. I'd appreciate if you'd have them delivered to my car."

André's mouth gaped. He looked perturbed by the request; he'd guessed the connection between Khattak's request and the shooting last night at the mosque.

"I'm not sure . . . I don't think I can decide that. You'd have to ask my boss."

Khattak gave him a quizzical glance.

"Do you think he might have some reason to refuse?"

Now André seemed truly alarmed, stumbling over his words as he searched for an appropriate response.

Surprising Khattak, he answered at last, "If the reason you're asking is because of last night, I think he'd mind very much." He cast a furtive glance behind him at the door. "Pascal is not the type to take the blame for anything on his own shoulders." With a sudden flash of perception, he added, "He's not smart enough to understand the obvious. It's all a game to him."

Khattak watched the young man closely. "It's not a question of conviction, then? Nor of deep-rooted ideology?"

André didn't hesitate. "Not at all." He gestured expansively at the closed door. "Pascal is a clown."

"And yourself?" Khattak canvased the young man's haircut and clothing again. "Would you say you subscribe to a particular set of convictions?"

"What do you mean?"

"You work for Monsieur Richard," Khattak said. "You're sporting a certain form of dress. It's . . . suggestive."

André swallowed, his large Adam's apple bobbing in his throat. He looked as though he were about to cry, a sensitivity at odds with his appearance.

"No matter what Pascal stands for, this is a good internship. A step up the ladder for me. I don't share Pascal's views, whatever his actual views may be. And I can assure you, I'm not one of Thibault's Wolves. I'm a military cadet—a certain professionalism is expected."

The door behind André opened and, very much on his dignity, he excused himself from Khattak's presence.

In other circumstances, Khattak would have been abashed and offered the young man an apology. In this case, he didn't. He was weighing André's denial against his unexpected revelation: as a military cadet, André would have had extensive training in the use of firearms.

Pascal Richard leaned back in his chair, stretching his arms out behind his head, blocking the view from a suite of windows—and what a view it was. Perched above the lake, framed by a blossoming forest of maples and alders, where the cool gray water rolled over a stony ground in an undulating rhythm, the picture window opened on to a terrace that was set with a bistro table and matching chairs. A window nearly as large on a perpendicular wall gave him a view into the next-door studio, where a different broadcast was airing. From a wall of windows, the studio shared the spectacular view of the lake and the wraparound outdoor terrace.

With its framed vanity photographs and awards and impeccably chosen furniture, the interior of Richard's office was immaculate.

Khattak wasn't sure what he'd been expecting—a senior figure who may have served as a mentor to Maxime Thibault, well-groomed and self-possessed, perhaps. Or a loud, brash personality along the colorful lines of Canadian icon Don Cherry. Instead, Pascal Richard more closely resembled Cherry's longtime counterpart on *Hockey Night in Canada*, the likable Ron MacLean.

Richard wore a pinstriped shirt with cuff links. His brown hair had a natural wave and was worn loose and long in the front. His attractive face was permanently creased with laugh lines, and he looked Khattak over with an unconcealed and vivid interest. He was fluently bilingual, and the resonant timbre of his voice was perfectly suited to his work.

He didn't look anything like Khattak's conception of a purveyor of mainstream hate. But appearances didn't mean anything, as Khattak had learned again during his last case investigating two murders on the

Greek islands. He skipped over the preliminaries and asked Richard to provide an account of his actions the previous evening, curious to see the man's response to a direct approach.

"You think *I* carried out the shooting?"

"Did you?"

"Hell, no." He gestured at a trophy on his desk in the shape of an oversized microphone. "That's the only weapon I require."

Khattak found this answer revealing.

"Who do you consider your enemy, Monsieur Richard?" He rested his arms on Richard's desk, a tactic designed to encroach on Richard's territory. "Who are you armed against?"

To his surprise, Richard mimicked the gesture, leaning in close enough for Khattak to smell his aftershave—woodsy and pleasant like Richard. He took his time looking Khattak over, a wicked spark in his eyes.

"Not who you're imagining," he said easily. "Not someone like you."

Khattak was caught off-guard. By both the implied intimacy of the remark and the suggestion that Richard had recognized him. Richard seized his advantage.

"Come on," he said with a grin. "You're famous, Inspector Khattak. You have a legion of female fans. Maybe some men, too. Meeting you in person, I see why."

It was a flirtatious comment, offered by a man with considerable charm of his own. Esa wondered if Richard thought he would be rattled by the other man's interest. He wasn't, though he shifted back in his chair.

"Look," Richard continued. "I'm deeply sorry about what happened at the mosque. But it is in no way connected to my program or to me. I was at a bar last night—having a drink with friends from work."

Khattak remembered André.

"Is your intern old enough to drink?"

"Who, André? Yes, he's old enough. We invited him along."

"Was he with you the entire night?"

"The entire night?" There was a swift spark of interest in Richard's eyes. "I couldn't say for certain—everyone has their own thing, pool, darts, chatting up someone who shows an interest. He came with us. I'm not sure when he left."

He noted down the names of Richard's prospective alibi witnesses. But when Richard went on to specify time and location, it left a window open. Not only for André, but also for Richard himself. And he wondered if the man realized that. In a crowded bar, it would have been easy to slip away and return later. Or simply to have gone on home, as Richard admitted to doing himself. He made a mental note to ask Lemaire to follow up on the activities of both men.

"Now if someone like you had been there, I might have found it worth my while to stick around."

When Khattak ignored this, Richard challenged him directly.

"Are you a homophobe?"

It was Khattak's turn to offer a smile of some charm. "Not at all."

"Well, I'm not an Islamophobe." Richard said this with manifest aggression.

"Your program suggests otherwise."

"Can you specify a particular program?"

Khattak's phone signaled the arrival of a text message. He ignored it for the moment.

"What about this morning's? I understand that you invited your callers to share their theories about who was behind the shooting."

"So?"

"Monsieur Richard." Khattak's voice deepened with a note of warning. "You focused on Amadou Duchon."

Richard rose to his feet in a sudden motion. He ambled over to his vanity wall, stopping before a photograph of a ceremony. In it, he was being handed the key to the city by the mayor of Saint-Isidore.

"Not me," he clarified. "The police did. Your colleagues, I believe. I just ran with it."

Khattak rose, too.

"Are you not at all concerned about inciting violence against a young man who bravely ran to the scene to offer his aid to the wounded? Or were you unaware of that?"

Richard turned from the wall, and Khattak noticed that the collar of his shirt was drawn up unusually high at the back, a slight misstep in an otherwise polished appearance.

"I thought he was in police custody."

"Did you?" Khattak pointedly fell silent, pushing the door to Richard's office ajar. The sound of a radio broadcast filled the hallway— it wasn't Richard's station. It was Amadou's rich voice in the midst of an interview with Diana Shehadeh. "You're paying attention to campus radio. An unlikely rival for a man in your position. Which suggests that you thoroughly understand the dubious achievements of your program. Some *would* call it incitement."

Richard's eyes flicked over Khattak again, making a personal calculation.

"Would *you*?" he asked.

"That depends. I'd like to borrow your recordings so I can make that determination for myself."

For a moment, he thought Richard would refuse. Instead, the other man shrugged.

"You're welcome to them. I've no doubt that Amadou and his feisty counterpart have your ear—but you won't find evidence of incitement on my show. And even if you do, incitement isn't a crime."

Some types of incitement were, Khattak thought. He studied the photograph that had drawn Richard's interest. He recognized several faces in it, including those of Christian Lemaire and Isabelle Clément. His mind drew connections that left him shaken. The three figures in the photograph represented law enforcement, politics, and the press— and they had deemed Pascal Richard's program worthy of honoring with the key to Saint-Isidore.

He was reminded of something Alizah had once written him, something she had adopted as her motto.

The battle is everywhere, all the time.

"You have a platform," he told Richard quietly. "Some would say that it confers a moral responsibility."

Richard shrugged this off. "I'm not the voice of public morality. Ratings. Dollars. Entertainment. That's the business I'm in."

Grimly, Khattak said, "There's a direct connection between your business and what happened at the mosque last night."

Richard took offense at the words.

"That's a pretty big leap. There's a difference between letting people air their grievances on my show and some lunatic setting out to gun down innocent people."

Khattak knew different.

"I'm afraid it's not as great of a leap as you think."

He clarified certain details about the nature of Richard's program. Richard made arrangements for André to deliver the recordings to police headquarters with the air of a man who had nothing to hide and less still to apologize for.

Unconvinced, Khattak thanked him for his time. But at the door Richard detained him by voicing another question, his tone clipped, the words hesitant. Esa looked up from his phone. He hadn't had a chance to read through his messages yet.

"Would you like to get a drink with me tonight? It doesn't have to be alcohol."

Without a trace of discomfort, Esa declined the request. "I'm afraid it would be inappropriate."

Richard moved closer, his eyes on Khattak's face.

"Because of your investigation?"

Khattak nodded. "That. And the fact that I'm hoping to be married soon."

He checked his messages on his way to the car. An update from Rachel on which of the tasks he'd assigned that she'd been able to accomplish. And some cryptic muttering about Lemaire taking her to check out Père Étienne's church, which for the moment he ignored.

There was another message waiting for him through a new delivery service. He clicked it open as he stepped into the sunlight. He looked back at the building to find Richard watching him through the window.

He was struck by a pang of menace. It wasn't because of Richard. It was as a result of the message waiting for him on his phone.

Richard doesn't want you nearly as much as I do.

This time Esa remembered to take a screenshot.

27

PASCAL RICHARD SATELLITE RADIO SHOW
[Translated from the French]

RICHARD: So you guys hear about this group of Goth girls here in Saint-Isidore? First I thought they were Allegiance groupies. Turns out, no. No wolf heads for them, just delicate little pansy lilies on the insides of their wrists. That's how you spot these bad girls. They call themselves Lilies of Anjou. Posers or not, you decide.

One of them is pretty sweet—let's call her Ém. So this Ém chick is all hot and bothered about some biracial newcomer. He doesn't look biracial, mind you. He's blacker than the inside of a coal mine, but she doesn't care, she's after him, day and night. The fact that he's at the scene of the shooting, he's arrested—none of that puts her off. What can I tell you? Some girls like to roll in the mud. Now let me tell you the good part. This dude—this black-as-night hombre from the gateway to hell—he doesn't want her. He's not assimilating, my friends. He doesn't speak French. He speaks some shit-for-brains patois, whatever passes for *la langue française* in that Senegalese backwater he's from. So why is that a problem? I think you know the answer to that.

These people, the ones who won't let a woman show her face, they don't *want* to be Québécois. Because they think they're goddamn superior. *We're* the cockroaches, my friends. Don't let anyone tell you different.

Okay, Marie—who do we have on the line?

MARIE: We have Paul on the line.

PAUL: I've seen the way the Lilies go after those guys. Those guys will
   fuck them, no problem, but then they go home to Maman for a sweet
   little virgin.

RICHARD: [laughs] Sounds like you could use a sweet little virgin yourself.

PAUL: [laughs] *Va chier,* Pascal. Fuck you. [pause] Yeah, probably. But
   they're throwing themselves at these guys. They should be wearing
   burqas.

RICHARD: You'll get no argument from me. You part of the Allegiance?

PAUL: [pause] Better if I don't say.

RICHARD: I wouldn't worry, man. They get some excellent pussy.

PAUL: Fuckin' A.

RICHARD: Wait, man. Help me out here. You said "guys," plural. It's
   not just Ém and the black guy? Who else is getting their panties in a
   wad?

PAUL: [laughs] That little dopey chick. She's pretty in a crack-addict way.

RICHARD: I love me some heroin chic.

PAUL: [laughs] Exactly, dude. But I'm guessing she's out of luck now. One of
   them's out of circulation.

RICHARD: You talking about that kid in the hospital—Youssef Soufiane? That's
   cold, dude.

PAUL: I'm just saying what you're saying. We're the cockroaches, man.

RICHARD: You wanna drive them out, you better be there to put
   pressure on the mayor. You better have rung the phone off the damn
   hook on the Code of Conduct.

PAUL: Don't worry, we've got it covered. [HANGS UP]

RICHARD: Marie, I gotta say that kid was lit. Who's gonna compete
   with that?

MARIE: How about someone who thinks you're shit? We have Réj on
the line.

RÉJ: You know who's a shit-for-brains, Richard? You. You're like primordial
sludge that never crawled out of the sea.

RICHARD: What's the matter, babe? You've got no arguments so you resort
to—what do you libtards call it—ad hominem attacks?

RÉJ: You're a sexist, misogynist, racist piece of shit. You're inciting violence
by demonizing our neighbors. You would have fit right in, in
Nazi Germany.

RICHARD: Ooooh. Fancy college girl with college words. You go to the
Université Marchand? [pause] Hey, I know who you are. You're the ugly Lily.
You're the dyke, Réjeanne Beaudoin. [silence] You still there, bitch? Sorry, I
meant "butch."

RÉJ: Did you just out me on your program, you homophobic fuck?

RICHARD: I thought you libtards were all about owning who you are.
All that gender-fluid, nonconforming crap. [growls in throat] Girrrrrrrl
power. But be honest. Are you a girl, or are you one of those freaks in
between?

RÉJ: You would know. Heard you hit on Khattak. You know who he is, right?
The Muslim cop they sent to clean up your mess.

RICHARD: Is that your fantasy, freak? Or do you have a crush on someone at
Al-Salaam like both of your horny friends?

RÉJ: You're a walking Charter violation. And you're a fucking awful Québécois.

RICHARD: [chuckling] Walking Charter violation, that's a good one. But
freedom of speech, babe, freedom of speech. Or don't they teach you that
at the School of Libtards?

RÉJ: They teach us to recognize Nazis. You're a danger to everything
we stand for.

[Call terminated.]

RICHARD: That was a live one, friends. Sounds like our friend
Réjeanne needs a good old-fashioned screw to loosen up everything that's
tight. I know she's a dyke, but let's hope our brothers in the Allegiance are
willing to take one for the team.

28

With Khattak busy at Richard's studio, Rachel accompanied Lemaire to Père Étienne's church for a preliminary search. The old stone church had been built in the late 1800s. It was too circumspect and discreet to be considered a cathedral, built on a smaller plan without the requisite connecting galleries or stone buttresses. Its rose-gold stone was wrapped in curling tendrils of ivy and warmed by bright swathes of sunlight. The garden was overgrown with tiger lilies that swayed in the breeze under a surfeit of hedges. It was poised at the summit of a modest hill, and something about its character suggested a place of sanctuary. Of homecoming.

Rachel had stopped attending church the third year after her brother, Zach, had run away. Her parish priest had had nothing to offer her by way of hope except the empty promises of a distant saving grace. The priest's bond with Rachel's father had been too strong for him to question why Zach had run away or to ask what there might have been in the home to drive a teenage boy away. His charity didn't extend to Rachel; he'd made her feel as though her concerns were a nuisance and that she would be better off submitting to her father's authority.

But Père Étienne's church was nothing like that cold space that had seemed to condemn Rachel's sorrow, mocking her despair with the lonely silence of judgment. Someone was playing the organ with a light hand, the music evoking the dance of spring . . . budding life . . . intemperate joy. The worn oak benches gleamed gold in the chapel light, the end of each pew dressed charmingly with wildflowers. At the altar someone had potted pink and gold chrysanthemums in a pale blue jug. There were no calla lilies, and none of the flowers were white. The jewel-toned rose window threw arrows of blue and green light over the altar and down across the transept.

The entire scene was resonant with hope.

"It is a beautiful church," Christian Lemaire said, observing Rachel's reactions. "You are Catholic?"

"I think so," Rachel said cautiously.

"You don't know?" There was warmth in the blue eyes that regarded her, but Rachel didn't think Lemaire was mocking her.

She had climbed the three stairs to the chancel, and now she placed both hands on Père Étienne's lectern to give herself time to answer.

"Whether it's a mosque, a church, or a synagogue, I don't see God stepping in to help. Look at last night's shooting."

She was standing in a spot where the rose window cast a shaft of orange-gold light over her hair; the wisps of hair at her neck spiraled out in fiery trails. When she noticed Lemaire staring at her, she quickly stepped out of the light. He turned away, gesturing at the organ loft above the chancel, where the church's pipe organ was fixed in glorious display. They couldn't see the organist from where they stood, but the music continued without a break, swelling up into the grand emptiness of the nave.

"We should cover every inch of this place," he said.

Rachel was dubious. Though the church was modestly built, it suggested any number of places to hide a weapon, and that was excluding the garden. She moved away from the lectern.

"Would you mind beginning with our local musician?" Lemaire asked.

"Any particular reason why?"

Lemaire came closer, looking down at her from his great height. Did he resent being challenged? Or did he just not like explaining himself? She hadn't gotten that vibe from the way he'd singled Benoit out for praise among a group of more experienced colleagues. She faced him squarely, waiting.

"The musician is a young woman. She might relate better to you."

Rachel had no idea what prompted her to challenge Lemaire. She should have asked him how he knew the organist. Instead, she offered, "You don't think you have what it takes?"

Her words were rude and uncalled for, but Rachel was more appalled to hear the note of flirtation in her voice. A scalding blush climbed to the roots of her hair. From the hint of devilment in Lemaire's eyes, he was thoroughly enjoying her embarrassment.

He didn't lean in to crowd her. He just waited an appreciable moment before he said, "You tell me."

The heat blazing through Rachel became an inferno. She could feel herself perspiring under her navy-blue shirt. She struggled to regain her composure, blinking several times rapidly and running a dry tongue over her lips.

"Christ, sir, I'm sorry. That was completely out of line."

Lemaire's pleasant laugh sounded in the nave.

"Rachel." He shook his head, still enjoying her discomfiture, but not in a manner that amplified her humiliation. He was sharing the humor of the moment with her. "You don't need to call me sir. I'm not your boss. I'm your temporary partner. A colleague, maybe a friend. If you can't bring yourself to call me Lemaire, perhaps you might try 'Christian.' You don't mind if I call you Rachel?"

He moved a short distance away, finding a small door that Rachel had missed and turning its iron knob.

Rachel took a few calming breaths. He'd put the control back in her hands, not pressuring, not insisting, just suggesting another way of looking at things . . . at him. He'd said nothing out of line in return, merely teasing her a little, the way that Khattak sometimes did. Except her reaction to Lemaire was nothing like her response to Khattak— whom she'd come to think of as the truest friend she'd ever had. With Lemaire there was something more. A hint of excitement . . . and if she didn't ruthlessly squash it down . . . a growing sense of attraction.

Realizing she'd been silent too long, she nodded.

"Yes. You can call me Rachel."

She slipped under his arm to open the door.

It led to a narrow staircase that would take her up to the organ loft. She was unsettled by the thought that Lemaire might be watch-

ing her climb and wondering why he'd preferred to search the nave
and transept himself. He couldn't be covering for Père Étienne or he
wouldn't have suggested the search to begin with. She should feel flattered that he'd asked her to partner him. Instead, she felt somewhat
cautious—was he keeping an eye on what she and Khattak were up to?
Or was this a means of ensuring that Khattak was out there on his
own? She couldn't say the INSET team was hostile to their presence,
but no one had laid out the welcome mat, either. Except for Christian Lemaire.

Rachel shook her head at herself. Damned if he did, damned if he
didn't. Maybe she should cut him a little slack. At the top of the stairs,
she peered over the railing to watch him search. He'd begun at the
last pew and was thorough in his methods . . . checking every hym-
nal, each footrest, the spaces beneath the loosely cushioned benches,
the collection boxes stacked at the outer end of each row. So he wasn't
faking it—he was really looking for the gun, despite his treatment of
the priest.

She was beginning to think she understood it, connecting it to her
own experience at her parents' Catholic church. Their priest had
wielded influence, even amidst that small congregation. In a place like
Saint-Isidore, where the institutions of power seemed inextricably
linked, the relationship with Père Étienne might be one that it was
necessary to preserve.

"Who are you?"

A sharp, sardonic voice interrupted Rachel's reflections. The flowing music had ceased. The organist who asked the question was not
who Rachel had expected to find playing such evanescent music.

It was one of the three girls who'd been at the hospital, the one
with short black hair that was sleek and glossy, dyed neon blue at the
tips. She had a pointed, unmade-up face and a skin like thick Irish
cream. She was still wearing the black coat, the collar tacked straight
up. Rachel noticed now that a series of baroque antique silver pins
had been substituted for buttons on her coat. A silk scarf at her throat
in a blaze of vermilion completed her ensemble.

The girl was an original. She was also beautiful, but not in a conventional sense. It was something about her expression—the sheer force of life contained in her vivid blue eyes. She watched Rachel with an expression of skepticism, and she must have deduced who Rachel was because she'd spoken in English with a strong Québécois accent. Rachel answered the girl in French and asked her name in turn.

"Réjeanne Beaudoin. I'm a student at the Université Marchand."

"You're local?" Rachel asked, wondering why she was persisting with her French when the girl was answering in English.

Réjeanne nodded. She straddled the bench, resting one hand on the keys. Strong hands, Rachel saw. And the right hand was shadowed, the blue and green tints of a bruise showing at her knuckles.

"For my sins, yes."

"Why do you say that?"

"You have to ask?"

It was an oblique reference to the shooting. To the chaos that was expanding to claim all of Saint-Isidore. Maybe that's why Réjeanne was at the church, losing herself in the transcendent music she had played.

"What hymn was that?" Rachel asked. She was deeply interested in music, the legacy of being the daughter of Lillian Getty, an aspiring concert pianist who had retired upon her marriage to Don Getty. Rachel knew a lot of church music, but she hadn't recognized the piece Réjeanne had played.

"Nothing you know."

Listening to the girl's sharp, uncooperative responses, Rachel had a better sense of why Lemaire had suggested she conduct the interview.

She leaned against the railing. "It wasn't a hymn really. I'd call it 'Concerto of Spring.' It was bursting with hope . . . but it was tender beneath its energy."

Réjeanne looked at Rachel more closely.

"You play," she said.

"I'm learning." Rachel smiled. "My mother was a pianist. She taught me a little about music. But I can't play anywhere near as well as you." She tipped her head back to catch the fragments of light the rose window scattered over the organ. She had a sense of being suspended out of time—in a place of utmost harmony. She wished Réjeanne would take up the music again.

"I'm a music student," Réjeanne said, after a pause. "That was my own composition."

Rachel looked back at her, alert. "It was beautiful." She considered the girl's age. "You must be some kind of prodigy."

Réjeanne didn't smile, but her expression lightened. Her free hand played with her scarf.

"Not really," she said. "I hear the music, of course. But it's been a lifetime of grueling study."

"If you have a keyboard, you should play that at the vigil."

"That's not how Muslims conduct their mourning."

The words took Rachel by surprise. They suggested an intimacy with the Muslim community that Rachel hadn't expected from Réjeanne. Another assumption, despite the fact that she and Khattak had been advised that the members of the Lilies of Anjou knew Youssef and Amadou. She reconsidered, sharpening her focus.

"You were at the hospital last night. Did you know any of the victims of the shooting? Is that why you were there?"

"I was there for my friends. They wanted to be there."

"I talked to your friend Chloé. She was anxious to know about Youssef Soufiane's condition."

"Who wouldn't be?" Réjeanne was fencing with her.

"Were *you*?"

"Of course. I'm a human being. Don't let the getup fool you." She shook her hair out of her eyes, caressing the neon-blue tips with thin white fingers.

"Is that the only reason you were there? To support Chloé?"

Réjeanne's eyes blinked, catlike. "No. There was also Amadou to worry about. Émilie was worried about him."

"But not you. Not personally."

A private smile etched Réjeanne's lips. "Not personally. Men don't interest me." She paused, waiting to see if Rachel had drawn an inference from her words. She ran her hand lightly over the organ's keys. "What interests me is music, nothing else."

"Not quite nothing," Rachel pointed out. "If you were at the hospital, if you know something about Muslim funeral customs, your friends must matter to you."

"Of course they do."

She turned back to the organ, rearranging her posture and her limbs, bringing her hands to the keys. A gentle refrain floated through the alcove, evocative of longing and loss.

Rachel scanned the alcove as Réjeanne played, searching for places where someone might have hidden a gun. Apart from the organ, and the bench Réjeanne was sitting on, there were no repositories in the alcove, no additional places she could search. Unless there was a way of dropping the weapon inside the organ's wind-chest. She put the question to Réjeanne.

"How does the organ sound this morning?"

Réjeanne fingered the keys beneath her hand.

"Fine. Sublime. Like it's only been waiting for the morning to come alive."

A dead end there, then. But Rachel would still check.

Addressing the girl's back, Rachel said, "Where were you last night after nine p.m.?"

She received an answer she wasn't expecting. The girl turned the melody dark, casting a glance at Rachel over her shoulder.

"I was in the woods."

"The woods? Alone at night?"

A stroke of apprehension shivered down Rachel's spine.

"I didn't say I was alone. I was with my friends, deep in the woods. Far away from the mosque. I don't know if it would have been better or worse to have been there."

Rachel refused to be distracted, though the shape the music had taken, dangerous and disturbing, was giving her a feeling of queasiness.

"What were you doing in the woods? Practicing a ritual?"

The girl's hands froze on the keys. "Why would you ask that? Being fond of nature doesn't make me some kind of witch."

It was Rachel's turn to score a point. "No, you're not, are you? You're a Lily of Anjou. I'm just not sure what that is."

She let the silence build. It served a purpose. No matter how poised this gifted musician was, she couldn't be certain her secrets were safe from a detective. Everything Rachel asked her had a point to it. Réjeanne revealed things even when she withheld information. As Rachel waited for a response, she moved to the side of the organ, peering at its pipes.

"What are you doing?" Réjeanne asked sharply, the music coming to a close.

Rachel looked at the girl, her face spattered with droplets of light, soft and expressive with sympathy. Her words were a sharp contrast.

"I'm trying to determine who murdered twelve people last night."

Réjeanne raised a hand to her throat, her wrist twisted outward.

The same tattoo that had stamped Chloé's wrist was delicately etched on her skin.

She hadn't thought of it before, but now Rachel considered the meaning of Youssef Soufiane's knife wounds. And the fact that someone had taken the time in the midst of pandemonium to carve that emblem onto Youssef's skin. The fleur-de-lis again.

What had Réjeanne and her friends been doing in the woods at night?

And what were the rituals of the Lilies of Anjou?

29

Réjeanne denied any further knowledge of events and refused to explain her activities in the woods. She slipped away down the staircase without a backward glance, pausing only to collect a coffee-colored satchel that thumped against her leg. When Rachel examined it more closely, Réjeanne hitched it over her shoulder and fled.

Why? What was in the bag that Rachel couldn't know about?

Frowning, she turned her attention to the bench. It was expensive, padded with oxblood leather, but it didn't open. In fact, the bench was locked. Rachel would need to find the key. Perhaps it was in Père Étienne's office—she'd have to look for it to rule the bench out as a hiding place for the gun.

That left the organ itself. Maybe there were openings at the tops of the pipes. Some of them were large enough that an object could have fit inside. But Rachel couldn't reach the top of the wind-chest from the floor. She moved the bench closer to the organ. It was better, but not ideal. She had to perch on her tiptoes to reach the top. Carefully, she braced herself against the pipes. But she'd leaned over too far. She slipped a little on the bench and her free hand came down on the keys. The discordant sound filled the alcove.

Lemaire called up to her.

"I'm fine." But her breath came out in a gasp that indicated otherwise. She heard movement from below. Perhaps Lemaire was coming up to join her. Better hurry in that case. She was hardly at her most elegant, stretched out over the pipes.

She reached up on her toes again, positioning herself more securely.

She had enough height now to see into the pipes, whose inner reaches gleamed in the light, unmarked by layers of dust. The passageway was clear, but the light didn't reach to the bottom.

If she stood on the organ itself, her view would be unobstructed. But maybe it was worthwhile to see how well her hand could fit inside the largest of the pipes first. It was a stupid place to hide a gun because an organ in such good repair was probably serviced regularly. Still, she needed to cross it off her list.

Teetering now, she reached her hand inside the pipe. The gleaming metal was warm. Experimentally, she flexed her hand, stretching it as far as she could. *Yes,* she thought. A handgun could fit inside the pipe. She changed the angle of her hand to be sure, bracing it inside the tube. Suddenly something pushed against her leg. A door banged and she heard a rush of footsteps. As her foot slipped on the bench, her hand was wrenched from its position with a painful twinge. Her body overbalanced and she flew back toward the railing.

A whimper escaped her lips as she fell, narrowly missing the hard stone rail and the open chasm below.

Christian Lemaire caught her mid-flight, but the weight of her body unbalanced him. She landed on him with a thud, all of it happening so fast that she couldn't sort it out in her mind.

She lay still for a few moments, struggling to catch her breath. She became aware that her elbow was digging into Lemaire's ribs and that he was lying quietly beneath her. She scrambled off his body, mortified by her clumsiness, but Lemaire didn't stir. His eyes were closed, his breathing winded.

Then she noticed the giant bump on his forehead.

It was bleeding. He'd intercepted her fall, but he'd caught his head on the rail.

Horrified, she took out her phone, her fingers trembling over the numbers. And then she realized the only line she'd been given was Lemaire's. She tried Khattak instead. Before she could complete the call, a low groan sounded from Lemaire.

"I'm all right," he said with a vestige of his former teasing tone. "Don't panic. No need to call an ambulance."

Easing away from him, Rachel whispered, "Are you sure you're all right?"

"That was quite a stunt," he teased. "Remind me to put in for combat pay when I'm working with you."

"I'm so sorry! Inspector Khattak is usually the one to suffer the results of my enthusiasm."

Lemaire leveraged himself up from the floor on one elbow. He eyed Rachel with mock suspicion.

"Enthusiasm, eh? That's what they're calling it now?"

Rachel couldn't suppress a smile. "I'm sorry," she apologized again. "I'm like a bull in a china shop. I hope I didn't damage the organ."

But she didn't turn to look, her gaze fixed on the bump at Lemaire's temple. She found a tissue in her pocket and held it against the steady trickle of blood.

"I've seen the way you move. I wouldn't call you clumsy. Anyway, it wasn't your fault. Someone pushed you, Rachel."

Her startled eyes flew to his. "You saw them? Was it Réjeanne?"

He shook his head, then groaned at the effect of the movement.

"That's it," Rachel decided. "I'm calling someone."

Lemaire caught her by the wrist, staying the call. She felt a stunning flash of awareness and saw it reflected in his eyes. His voice a little rough, he said, "Not necessary. Just help me get up."

With a doubtful look at his bulk, Rachel helped shoulder Lemaire to his feet. He took his time, leaning against the railing.

"Were you out for a moment, sir?"

"No." His breathing evened out. "I was just mortally embarrassed by my failure to catch you. I didn't want to face your wrath."

Rachel gave him a crooked grin, disbelieving.

"Isn't that more embarrassing than just admitting you were knocked out cold?"

When Lemaire smiled back at her, she felt her heart seize up in alarm. What was happening to her? She'd never reacted to a man like this—not even to Nathan Clare, a friend of Khattak's. She'd had a brief entanglement with Nate that had come to nothing in the end.

Now the storm of her response to Lemaire broke over her like a wave. She was deeply, viscerally attracted to him.

Trying to push past the stunned realization, she concentrated on what he'd said.

"How did you know someone pushed me?"

"It was a reasonable guess." He gestured at the wall on the far side of the bench. "There's another door there, behind the curtain. I was coming up the stairs to check on you. Whoever pushed you used the other door. I didn't catch them in the act—I saw the curtain rise as the door slammed shut."

He looked doubtfully over the railing. "I could have chased them. But I thought it might not be a good idea to let any harm come to Khattak's cherished partner."

Rachel blushed at that.

Lemaire gave her a lazy smile. "What?" he asked. "It's obvious in the way he talks about you, in the way he defers to your opinion."

Rachel cleared her throat. "That's just good police work, sir. I'm an excellent detective."

Lemaire's smile broadened. His gaze flicked to the bench: it was a comment on Rachel's near disaster.

"What were you doing?" he asked.

"Looking for the gun. There was something a little too dismissive about Réjeanne's answer when I asked her if anything about the organ was off."

"I didn't notice any discrepancy. The music was resplendent."

Rachel gazed at Lemaire without speaking. That was exactly the word she would have chosen to describe Réjeanne's soaring composition. Feeling overwhelmed, she gripped the edge of the rail.

"It was just an instinct," she said quietly.

Lemaire frowned. He leaned over the bench and ran his hand over the keys. The notes came out full and round. Rachel shivered at the sound—at the unintentional closeness between herself and Lemaire.

"I'll send in an expert to take a look. In the meantime, there's still Père Étienne's house."

Concerned, Rachel pointed to his bruise. "Shouldn't you get that looked at first?"

The bleeding at Lemaire's temple had stopped. He motioned for her to precede him down the stairs. She'd thought he wouldn't answer, but his wicked murmur reached her.

"If I stumble on the way down, at least the landing will be soft."

30

At the station, Khattak turned his phone over to Paul Gaffney. The latest encrypted message had self-destructed, but between Gaff and Benoit, they were prepared to tear his phone apart to find out who had sent the threatening texts. There had been three in total now, and each message indicated the sender's proximity to Khattak, with such thorough knowledge of his movements that he was beginning to suspect someone on the INSET team. He looked over to where the team coordinator was keeping track of each officer's assignments and adding them to a timeline.

He didn't intend to share his discoveries with anyone other than Rachel and Lemaire. He couldn't expect Lemaire to keep him abreast of developments if he didn't do so in exchange. Lemaire accepted his request for discretion, hurrying off to a meeting with Isabelle Clément, while Rachel brought Khattak up-to-date.

Neither of them had any solid leads. There were gaps in alibis, there were unaccounted-for movements by parties tangential to the crime, but there was nothing concrete for any of them to go upon—except to keep trying to track the firearms.

Gaffney came over to join them, a new phone in his hand that he handed to Khattak.

"Someone keeps trying to call you; I've forwarded your calls to this number."

Whoever was threatening Khattak hadn't called. They'd only sent text messages. It could have been an escalation, but when he checked the new phone the number that registered was Alizah's. He called her back at once, dismayed to hear the panic in her voice.

"What is it? What's happened?"

He sorted patiently through her words. When he made sense of them, he was shaken by a futile sense of rage. He soothed Alizah into silence, promising to call her back. Lemaire was still busy with Clément. Staring blindly around the room, he noticed Rachel watching his face, waiting her chance to speak.

"Did you have a chance to interview Étienne Roy today? Could you determine what kind of state he's in now?" He heard the grating demand in his voice, but Rachel took no offense.

She shook her head, her ponytail flaying her cheeks.

"We need to see him at once. But first, I need you to tell me about the church."

"Why? What did Alizah say?"

He looked around the room. At every station, officers were hard at work, gathering information, collating facts, busy in subsets of briefings, developing a theory of the shooting. In the office behind a glass door, Lemaire and Isabelle Clément were engaged in what looked like a shouting match, though they were making an effort to keep their voices down.

Everything was happening quickly and with urgency, yet Khattak felt suspended in the moment, apart from it all, watching through a filtered haze.

Rachel tugged at his sleeve. He heard her voice as if from a great distance away.

He'd locked everything down from the moment he'd gotten the call to come to Saint-Isidore. Walking the blood-soaked halls of the mosque, waiting for the vans and ambulances to carry their cargo away—studying the bullet holes in the mihrab from a safe, clinical distance. But it was getting to be beyond him, from what could be expected from a man like himself—a man who'd grown too solitary and closed in by his faith.

With each new case, there were those who looked to him for something he'd never been able to adequately impart. Like the boy Din, at

Algonquin Provincial Park. Or the group of young dissidents in Iran—Taraneh reaching out to him, needing him, asking him to stay. Or Alizah facing him down at her sister's funeral. As solitary a creature as he was, as much a prisoner of grief.

He blinked back sudden shaming tears, grateful for the strength in Rachel's hand as she tugged him out of the room, into the fresh air of the parking lot.

It was time for *maghrib* prayer and he was in a town with a community that observed prayer, but he couldn't attend because the mosque was still cordoned off. He longed to be in the divine presence, yet at the same time he recoiled from it.

"Esa," Rachel insisted, using his name to focus his attention. "Please tell me what's wrong. What did Alizah say?"

He brought his eyes to rest on Rachel's upturned face, on the anxious concern for his well-being that blazed from her kind dark eyes.

He was gripping her hand with a force that appalled him, but she didn't try to pull away.

He forced himself to let go, to monitor and slow the pace of his breathing, counting under his breath, in the same inexorable rhythm that he rehearsed on his tasbih. Rachel waited at his side, not pacing, not pushing . . . just there.

Then he told her simply, "Youssef Soufiane just died."

She didn't say anything at first, her face hollowed out by shock. She gnawed her lower lip; she was giving herself a moment to come to terms with his words.

What could she say? What was there left to say?

He'd needed Youssef to survive the grim and terrible reckoning that had taken place at the mosque; now he too was gone, his life extinguished in a fit of violence and rage. With an added mark of cruelty: the lily on his back. There would be no shielding Youssef's family from this truth. The act of washing the body, the rituals of *ghusl*, would leave no truth untold. They would see the nationalist symbol and have to face the fact that Youssef had been killed because of his beliefs.

The beliefs that had made him a person who wasn't wanted in Saint-Isidore.

And Khattak asked himself the question whether it wasn't just Saint-Isidore and whether there was a place in this world where any member of his community could live unencumbered and at peace.

He could see his own distress reflected in Rachel's face.

"Ah, I'm sorry, sir. Who else knows about this?"

Khattak looked back at the station. "Lemaire and Clément, probably. They'll have to make a statement, because nothing will stop Diana from holding her press conference now."

"Makes sense. I'd like to tell Chloé myself, before she hears it from anyone else."

Khattak made an effort to focus on the case. "You've ruled her out as a suspect?"

"Gaff is pulling up background on the names I gave him, but I can't see Chloé using an assault rifle. If she did, she wouldn't have turned it on Youssef. It's clear to me that Chloé was in love with him."

"Rachel—"

They thought of the same case, a case they had worked in the past, where the love between two people had been weaponized, resulting in terrible injury.

"I mean, it's not absolute. We should dig into these Lilies of Anjou. They're friends with Alizah, they're on the fringes of the Muslim community, but they're not entirely distant from Thibault. Still, my money is on Thibault. He has a bit of a god complex. Arrogance like that could maybe speak to method."

"We need a profiler," Khattak said. "Lemaire shouldn't waste any more time."

"I think if you mention it, he'll probably listen."

The offhand way Rachel offered the advice made Khattak appreciate that she was getting to know how Lemaire operated. And if that was the case, it made more sense for Rachel to request that a profiler be assigned to assist them.

"Sir? What about Roy and the church? What did you want me to do?"

That soaring sense of loss engulfed him again at the words.

How could the summer night brush against his senses with such

ardent warmth, carrying the scent of blossoms and fresh pines? It reminded him of where he'd begun. Of what he'd hoped for when he'd
first begun.

It reminded him of Miraj Siddiqui's blank face on a table at the
morgue.

Gruffly, he said to Rachel, "The mosque will be sealed for some time.
I don't think it's a good idea, but the congregation is looking for another place to pray."

He left Rachel to sort out matters with Lemaire, choosing to walk
through the backstreets to the church. Étienne Roy lived in the small
house beside it, on call for the needs of his parishioners. He welcomed
Esa into a parlor full of books, where a pair of ginger tabbies were
curled up on an overstuffed sofa. More composed than at their last
meeting, and sporting an ecclesiastic collar, Père Étienne shooed the
cats from the sofa and invited Esa to sit down.

His kind eyes probed Esa's face.

"You look troubled," he said.

The genuine concern in his voice shifted the ice encasing Esa's
heart.

"I should be asking about you. What you witnessed was unthink-
able for a civilian. Especially for a man of the cloth."

Père Étienne wheeled an antique wooden tea table to a spot that was
a comfortable distance between their seats. He poured tea from what
Khattak recognized as a vintage tea set patterned with historic Québécois inns.

"It was terrible," Père Étienne said quietly. "You think you know the
devil, then you realize you don't until you see the proof of his work."

This insight interested Esa. "You attribute the shootings at the
mosque to something . . ."—he hunted for the right word and settled
on, ". . . supernatural?"

Père Étienne placed a wide-rimmed teacup in Esa's hands. The eyes
that looked into his were deep and guileless. He was more fragile than
Esa had first guessed; there was a tremor in his hands on his cup that
Khattak attributed to incipient palsy.

"We've both seen it in the course of our work. We know the devils that inhabit the human heart. That's what I have seen in the church."

He gave Khattak a short lesson on the history of Saint-Isidore's church, then turned the subject back to Esa's visit.

"You were involved in interfaith work with the imam. You must have thought highly of him. His congregation will need a safe place to pray. Would you be willing to offer the church? Knowing that it might result in another disturbance? And knowing that I have grave doubts about it myself?"

Père Étienne was nodding before Esa had even finished his request.

"Anything they need shall be theirs." He hesitated. "If the altar and the Savior on the cross will not disturb them?"

There was such a bright warmth in the priest's eyes that Esa found himself giving in to it. Needing it. With no change in his expression to give himself away, he knew he could no longer think of Père Étienne as a suspect.

"Whose heart would not be lightened in the presence of the son of Mary?"

A corresponding warmth brightened Père Étienne's face. For a moment they were not priest and police officer, bound by their respective duties. They were men whose work had left them seeking a place of grace to heal a deadly divide.

"You look tired, my son, and hungry. Let me bring something to give you the strength to face the duties you have yet to carry out."

He retreated into the interior of the little house, where Esa heard noises that indicated an offering of some kind would be brought to him on a plate. He had an unreasonable hope that it might be a slice of homemade cake.

While Père Étienne was busy, he took a look around the little study, crammed full of books and samplers and handwritten notes on a desk, where in graceful and dignified French, Père Étienne had laid out the pattern of his sermons. Reading his preparations for the coming Sunday, Esa felt as though a small opening of light had arrowed through the darkness.

I do not cause you grief to grieve you. What is your grief except a path to Me?

And there are none among you that I will turn away.

One of the tabbies leapt up onto the desk demanding to be petted. As she did so, her bushy tail dislodged a sheaf of papers. Esa bent to collect them as the other tabby slipped between his feet to brush against his ankles.

He'd been marked by the pair of tabbies as a possible source of affection. Smiling, he stroked his hand over one of the cats, snatching a sheet of paper from beneath her feet. He turned it over and set it on the desk and felt an immediate shock.

It was a copy of one of the flyers that had vandalized the student office on campus. The cartoon that featured a group of men kicking a woman in a burqa.

A china plate rattled as it crashed down on the trolley. Père Étienne's face was white. Gasping at Esa, he said, "It's not—my son, it's not . . ."

Esa's expression gentled. He moved to settle Père Étienne in his seat, taking his trembling hands in his own. He scooped up one of the tabbies and placed her in the priest's lap, giving him something to hold on to. The cat glared at Esa balefully but curled up without further protest.

He fetched a glass of water from the kitchen and held it so that Père Étienne could drink.

Eventually, the other man said, "I know what you must think. I was found at the mosque with the gun. But I didn't—the picture you found isn't mine. It depicts a terrible act of cruelty."

Esa kept his voice even. "It depicts a hate crime."

It seemed to him that Père Étienne wanted something from him, was looking at him as if Esa might have the answer to a riddle that haunted his thoughts.

But Esa had a question of his own.

"Père Étienne. Do you take confession at your church?"

31

Rachel took a deep breath and made the call. If she waited any longer, she'd talk herself out of it again, and then she'd be back where she started. Second-guessing herself for no good reason and delaying a conversation that was more necessary by the moment.

"You have to come back," she said without preamble.

"What? Who is this?"

The voice on the other end sounded disoriented, as she might well be. Sehr Ghilzai had given Rachel her number, but the two women didn't often have reason to connect. Sehr had known Esa as a friend for years and was the woman he'd grown to love after the long period of mourning he'd observed over the death of his wife, Samina.

"It's Rachel. And I'm calling you because I think Esa is in trouble."

Rachel knew she was way out of line making this call. She had no right to interfere in Khattak's personal affairs, and he wouldn't thank her for pressuring Sehr to return from her vital work at an NGO in Greece, assisting Syrian refugees. He'd view it as an intrusion and it was. Rachel didn't care. She would argue about it with Khattak later. If he was thinking of leaving Community Policing, there wasn't much worse that he could do. Raise an eyebrow? Offer a stern reprimand? He'd need stronger weapons than that to dent Rachel Getty's courage.

She launched into a recital of everything that had happened since they'd arrived in Saint-Isidore. Then she discussed the effect she thought it was having on Khattak's mental health. Though they'd grown extremely close as partners, she knew that Khattak often felt isolated and alone. Having Sehr in his life was supposed to change that. But it bloody well couldn't when she was thousands of miles away. And then, Khattak did his damnedest to protect Sehr from the knowledge of anything that hurt him, including the emotional impact of his work with CPS. It was a difficult line that Khattak had to walk in his job, and if Sehr wasn't up to supporting him through it, Rachel couldn't see how Sehr was of any use. It was also past time to call Sehr out on the way she was punishing Khattak for taking so long to come to the conclusion that he loved her, insisting on distance at the very moment Khattak needed her close.

But before she could gather a full head of steam, Sehr cut her off.

"It's good to hear from you, Rachel." Her tone was wry. "And, yes, I've heard the news."

"On Lesvos?" Rachel spluttered in disbelief. Then she was drenched in embarrassment. What if Khattak had called Sehr himself?

"No, no. I'm back, Rachel. I flew in last night."

"Does the boss know?" Rachel asked cautiously.

"I wanted to surprise him. I'm not here for long, but I was planning to see him today."

"We're in Saint-Isidore."

"Yes," Sehr said dryly. "So I gathered."

She sounded sleepy, as if she was still adjusting to the difference in time zones.

"Can you get here right away?"

She waited impatiently as Sehr considered her request.

"I don't think that would be wise. It's better if I wait for your return to Toronto."

An impasse. But not for long. Rachel had screwed up her courage to make the call; she might as well see it through.

"Listen, Sehr," she spoke in the same tone she used when she was mapping out a play for her hockey team. *Get behind the blue line.* "He's not doing well. The shooting has hit him hard and he's talking about leaving Community Policing. He wants me to step in and take his place. That is *not* happening. *You* have to make it not happen."

There was a long pause before Sehr said the only thing that mattered to Rachel. The thing she was counting on Sehr to say.

"I'll catch a flight tonight. Where will I find him, Rachel?"

Rachel gave her the address, feeling a momentary relief. Sehr would be able to fit the pieces back together. That was her special gift. At least, Rachel hoped it was.

Clearing her throat, Rachel asked another intrusive question. She might as well. In for a penny, in for a pound.

"You're still together, right? You won't hurt him?"

"I didn't mean to hurt him, Rachel. I just needed a little time."

That was what had hurt him, Rachel thought. Not knowing if he had anything to count on. To hope for.

"He's not himself," she said finally. "Things here are getting to him." She paused. "This case is ugly and it's going to get uglier. It would be good if you were around."

Sehr's reply was grave. "He makes his own decisions. You know that, Rachel."

Growing angry, Rachel pinched the bridge of her nose, adjusting the phone in her grasp.

"*He* didn't decide that you should stay behind on Lesvos."

"I have my own life, my own work, Rachel." Sehr sounded sad, but Rachel didn't care. What the hell did she have to be sad about? Everything she wanted was right within her grasp.

"Do you know what's unique about your relationship with Esa, though?"

Sehr stayed quiet. Maybe because she had some inkling of what Rachel was planning to say. Rachel steamrollered over the silence.

"When he needs help, he doesn't ask for it. He doesn't think he deserves it. That's because of you."

She hung up before Sehr could respond, breathing heavily, angry at Sehr, angry at herself. *Jesus Christ.* The woman had Esa-fucking-Khattak wildly in love with her, and all she could think of was playing these stupid games. Though maybe Rachel was angry because of how things had played out with Nate. Khattak had given Sehr a chance to work things out. Why hadn't Nate done the same? The answer that rang through her head had plagued her thoughts for weeks: because she wasn't worth it, because nobody wanted her. Just like her father had said.

"Why the ferocious scowl? Who were you talking to?"

Lemaire closed the door to his office, where Clément was making a call.

Rachel put a hand up to her ponytail and tugged at it.

"Just a friend."

He didn't trot out the tired joke in response: *with friends like that . . .*

Quickly she asked him, "Did you hear about Soufiane?"

A team member walking by passed Lemaire a clipboard. He read the update with a frown.

"Yes. I'm doing the press conference now, as soon as Isabelle is free. We'll be holding it on the outside steps. You'll attend?"

"I'd like to observe from inside, thanks. What about the vigil?"

A group of uniformed officers was beginning to gather near the door. They were carrying batons and flashlights, adding their names to a list.

Lemaire signed the clipboard and passed it back to the officer who was waiting.

"It's taking place after sunset prayer in the park. We have about an hour and a half. I don't expect any trouble."

A statement that gave Rachel pause. Why didn't he? There'd been so much trouble already. And as Lemaire believed in Père Étienne's innocence, that meant there was a fugitive on the loose. Who might return at any moment.

She considered her next words carefully, conscious of her place as an outsider on a mainly Québécois team.

"And if trouble shows up without waiting for your permission?"

Damn. That wasn't careful or well-considered at all.

"Why do I feel like you're trying to tell me something?"

"Is the Wolf Allegiance rally on your radar? They're going to be at the park tonight."

Another set of uniformed officers passed between them to line up at the doors.

"What do you think?" He didn't sound offended, so Rachel decided she could push him a little further.

"There are things we need to go over. I received a list from the dean's office of incidents on campus and actions taken in response. I think there are leads there that need to be prioritized."

"Fair enough." He took stock of the smoothly running operation. Clément had finished her call. She flicked her fingers at him in an imperious gesture. When Lemaire waggled his eyebrows at Rachel, she had to choke back a grin.

"Looks like it's time for this show pony to perform."

Rachel took stock of his impressively solid frame. "You're hardly that, sir."

"Christian."

"Christian." A little flare of excitement uncurled in Rachel's stomach.

Was she flirting with a senior officer of the Sûreté? She rather thought she was. And it wasn't nearly as awkward as usual.

"Let me finish this. Then if you want to talk, we can grab a drink on the way to the vigil. Sound good?"

"Or something to eat instead. We didn't break for lunch."

Lemaire gave her a wholly appreciative smile.

"Fine," he said. "An athlete needs to eat."

32

Rachel plopped herself down on Gaffney's desk, so she could discuss recent events with him and Benoit. Despite Isabelle Clément's attempt to commandeer the stage, Lemaire spoke first, gravel-voiced and confident, able to convey the things the citizens of Saint-Isidore most needed at this moment—a sense of reassurance, and an overview of safety concerns that required the cooperation of the town. He made a strong statement in support of the targeted community, and he warned against any activity that would cause further grief to those who had lost their loved ones. The camera panned the people who had gathered to hear his statement. Rachel caught sight of the Lilies of Anjou, grouped together in their black coats.

Made uneasy by the sight, she shoved off the desk and hurried outside, pushing through the crowd until she was close enough to be within earshot of the girls.

Chloé was watching Lemaire with earnest, anxious concentration. It didn't take much for Rachel to figure out what was going to happen next. Someone should have warned Chloé—someone like Rachel herself. Lemaire was already speaking. It was too late to take her aside.

"It is with great sadness that we announce that although Youssef Soufiane was taken to the Hopital de l'Enfant-Jésus for treatment for his wounds, he passed away earlier this morning. The entire nation offers its condolences to his family in their time of grief."

The rest of his words were lost on Rachel. Chloé's face had blanched. She collapsed in the arms of her friends.

Rachel raced to her side, taking her weight in stride. There was an ambulance parked outside the station; a stretcher was summoned and Chloé was lifted inside, Rachel following behind.

Chloé revived quickly, a look of blank confusion on her face, but when she saw Rachel she remembered.

"Please say it isn't true." Tears streamed down her pale white cheeks. Rachel took her hand.

"I'm so sorry, Chloé. It would do no good for me to lie."

"But he was doing better," she whispered through dry lips. "He came through the surgery okay."

Rachel hesitated. Did Chloé need information or comfort? She opted for the latter.

"He's in a good place, now. Youssef is at peace."

Chloé chewed her lip, her eyes wide and full of disbelief.

"How do you know that?"

"Because it's what he believed. He was at the mosque, right? So he had faith there'd be something after all of this." She waved vaguely at the scene in the parking lot.

"But what if he did something wrong?"

The wrenching pain in Chloé's eyes was at odds with her little-girl voice. Rachel's attention immediately sharpened. But she spoke calmly, so as not to frighten her.

"Is there something you want to tell me, Chloe?"

Chloé looked torn. She made a few false starts, but by the time she'd decided to speak something threw her off. Her friends were at the door to the ambulance, peering in. Réjeanne and another young woman Rachel hadn't spoken to yet. Whereas before she'd thought of them as young women who refused to conform, staking out an identity for themselves, she now had a sense of menace. Even of danger, at the thought that Rachel might be threatening their friend.

The unknown woman was holding Chloé's other hand in a grip that seemed painful. Chloé didn't protest. She seemed to welcome the strength of that grip.

"Youssef," was all she said.

"We know." The other girl turned to Rachel with a sniff. "Do you mind? We can look after our friend."

Look after her or prevent her from telling the police something they needed to know? Rachel wasn't sure. She studied Réjeanne, who was watching them with a stillness that seemed unnatural, as if everything inside her was clenched. Could Réjeanne have returned to the church and pushed Rachel from the bench? Did that explain her stillness? Réjeanne gave the third girl a warning glance. She nodded back at Réjeanne, following her lead.

"You were at the hospital last night," Rachel said to the girl she didn't know. "What's your name?"

"None of your business."

The third girl said it with a flat superiority, as if Rachel weren't worth bothering with. But Rachel knew perfectly well who she was. She also had a piece of information she could use to make the girl speak—the girl who must be Émilie Péladeau. But she'd be giving Chloé away by doing so, and she needed Chloé on her side. Chloé had things to tell her; it was just a matter of time.

She eased out of the ambulance with a smile at Chloé.

"Wait!" Chloé swallowed thickly. "What about—what about the funeral? Do you know anything? Would I—will I be able to go?"

She looked so young and wounded, a fragile wisp of a creature encircled by Réjeanne and Émilie, whose black-winged coats made them look like predatory birds. Again, Rachel wondered whether the Lilies were protecting Chloé or themselves.

And Youssef's funeral was such a delicate subject that Rachel couldn't do it justice in the circumstances. She told Chloé to call her later, reminding her that she already had her number. When Chloé looked bewildered, Rachel gave her another card.

"I'll look into the funeral arrangements. Give me a call when you can."

She strode away, joining the group near Lemaire. When she looked back at the ambulance, Émilie had grabbed her card from Chloé and was shredding it into pieces.

33

"That went about as well as could be expected."

Lemaire had found a boulangerie off a side street that was still serving lunch. He was watching Rachel with evident amusement as she made short work of a set of sliders. Throughout their quickly snatched meal, he'd taken phone calls; then he brought Rachel up to speed. The mayor, the premier, other influential political figures, and members of the Sûreté were pressuring him for answers he wasn't in a position to give.

They made the right noises, they spoke about the nation as one family, but they seemed to have blinkers on about what had happened in Saint-Isidore. About what was still happening. Added to those pressures, Rachel knew Lemaire couldn't be happy about the fact that she and Khattak had been dumped in his lap. She could tell that he was used to more deference than she employed when going over a case with Khattak. But he didn't seem to mind the way she aired her questions without much regard for his rank.

He asked her what was troubling her about the shooting.

She took a stick of celery from the platter of vegetables he had ordered and which she'd greeted with disbelief and jabbed it in the air to emphasize her point.

"Three things. The firearms seem inexplicable to me. The handgun and the assault rifle. They don't add up. They don't make sense in the context of Saint-Isidore. Two, this Code of Conduct. I mean, why? What was the point of it—why was it necessary? Whose harebrained scheme was it to begin with? Three, I went through that list the dean gave me. Over a period of two years, it totals forty-seven incidents. I checked with Alizah—the log she and Amadou have been keeping actually totals four times that number of incidents. The dean's list included only those they classified as noteworthy through some system of their own." She bit off the end of the celery stalk. "That's not the interesting part. What's interesting is that despite this pattern of harassment, the dean's office saw fit to do nothing in response. Absolutely nothing. So what are your thoughts on that?"

Her brown eyes blazed with enthusiasm, with interest, with conviction—all of which was undercut by Lemaire's response.

"You think we're a bunch of racists in Québec, don't you?"

Her cheeks flushed and the bitten-off celery stalk froze midair.

Thrown off-balance, she tried to figure out what she'd said that had led him to arrive at his conclusion.

"They seem like reasonable questions to me, sir."

The "sir" was back. Because his words had resurrected the need for formalities. This time he didn't correct her.

"Maybe there's some truth to that. There's fringe elements—no—" He held up a hand before she could interrupt. "Don't quote that study back to me."

"What study?" she asked, bemused.

"The one on Bill 62."

Rachel thought back quickly. After the Charter of Values had failed to pass in Québec, similar legislation had been introduced, namely Bill 62, under the heading of "religious neutrality." Though the new legislation had succeeded where the Charter of Values had failed, civil liberties groups had successfully challenged the section of the bill that prohibited covering the face.

Lemaire didn't seem to find that conclusive.

"The Charter may have been killed," he said, "but its underpinnings never went away. That Bill 62 study told us that seventy-six percent of Québécois still favor banning the face veil, just as the bill prescribes. It's sixty-eight percent in the rest of Canada, you know."

Rather than shying away from his conclusion, Rachel took the bit between her teeth.

"But you know that very few Muslim women choose to wear the niqab. There's not even a hundred of them in the entire province. Why did such a nonissue come to define the election in Québec?"

Lemaire sighed. He must have known that no matter where she was headed with this, there was no getting around certain unpalatable truths. The sooner they cleared the air about it, the sooner they could get on with bringing a murderer to justice.

"If you're asking if this was dog-whistle politics, it was. The face veil is so different from what Québécois know—so alienating—that the issue became a lightning rod. Even among more liberal elements, there were those who weren't able to accept it."

"But that suggests that someone who wears a face veil can't be considered Québécois. If you extend that logic further, it might even suggest there's no such thing as a Muslim Québécois."

The bold statement, stripped to its essence, seemed to hit Lemaire like a punch in the gut.

Because it was exactly what the dog whistles were about.

No one in political life had had the nerve to say as much quite as plainly. But in effect, that's what the Code of Conduct—and the succeeding legislation—stood for. It was dressed up in language about religious neutrality and the values of Québec—it resisted encroachment; it spoke of erasure—but at heart it was a repudiation, of what was considered different . . . other . . . barbaric.

Debates about the Muslim veil had created the specter of a foreign invasion—an intolerable usurpation delivered by the hands of a community who sought religious freedom.

The language of Bill 62, of the Charter of Values, and of Saint-Isidore's Code of Conduct suggested it applied to all communities equally. But its neutrality was a veneer. Its practical application was to exclude those in religious dress from joining in public life. In starker, more specific terms, the proposed legislation stripped a Muslim woman of her dignity and her choice.

As Rachel watched Lemaire struggle to respond, her expression softened into sympathy. Maybe he'd never thought about these things before. Maybe he'd never had to.

"What happened to bring about the Code of Conduct? Was there an incident that triggered it?"

The question connected the various strands of the case, getting to root causes. She saw a new respect in his eyes as she asked it.

"It was the university's fault. They introduced a program recruiting students from North Africa—from the Maghreb: Morocco, Tunisia, Algeria. It was targeted to elite families and it brought an influx of money to the school in the guise of a cultural exchange. Citizens of these countries are educated in the French system."

"That doesn't sound so bad. A lot of universities rely on tuition raised from international students."

"The program wasn't the problem. The issue was that the university did nothing to prepare the community for it. No outreach programs. No citizen exchanges—just a rather abrupt shift in demographics."

Rachel frowned at him. "But there's a mosque here. There must have been a Muslim community in this town before the influx of students."

"It's been significantly upgraded, and it's become more visible in the minds of the people here."

"Are you saying that Muslims who live here should try to stay under the radar—that they should try to disguise who they are?"

"I'm saying that that's what the people of Saint-Isidore came to think. You see these incidents in the news—these attacks all over the world—they were afraid a terrorist attack might happen in their town. That these students would bring it here. You look at the owner of a remote little Québécois pâtisserie, and a woman in a black veil comes to his store to place an order, and what do you think he thinks?"

"Saint-Isidore is hardly remote," she objected. "We're an hour and a half from Ottawa."

"It was too near in time to the attack on the Bataclan, to the mass murder in Marseilles. The people here did not have the language to express their concerns. They thought a change was in the wind, and not one for the better."

"Because they'd assigned collective guilt to a community where no one was guilty of a crime. The same way you arrested Amadou but let Père Étienne walk."

He shifted uncomfortably in his seat. "I didn't say they were right. Only that they began to feel afraid."

"Someone made them afraid, you mean."

It was his turn to frown. "I don't follow."

Rachel counted off on the tips of her fingers. "The Wolf Allegiance didn't appear out of nowhere. Now they have chapters all over the province. You get from the Code of Conduct to a hate group to a shooting because someone is invested in making people angry."

Very mildly, he asked, "What makes you think the Wolf Allegiance is a hate group?"

Rachel's shock was plain on her open face.

"What on earth makes you think they stand for anything else?"

34

Rachel had wrong-footed Lemaire twice now. He took another call, this time from Isabelle Clément. In the meantime, Rachel settled the bill, feeling anxious about the vigil. The outdoor vigil was such a bad idea that she wished there were a way to stop it. There was a simmering tension in the town—the shooting hadn't calmed it; it had ratcheted it up a level. If she were Lemaire, responsible for the safety of the residents and under national scrutiny, she would consider a curfew. But she could only imagine the grandstanding that would follow in its wake.

We will not be cowed by a terrorist attack. We will stand up for our values.

Or did those words only apply when the attack was carried out by extremists who proved in the end to be Muslim?

Better not to ask Lemaire. She'd poked the bear and the bear seemed sensitive, maybe not unduly. She wondered if he realized that there might be a parallel between Muslims who were sensitive on the question of whether they fit into the national fabric and Québécois who were fighting to hold on to their heritage. No need for her to point that out. She was still waiting for answers to other more urgent questions.

They followed a path along the creek bordered by green summer woodland, thick, richly scented, and innocent of the spreading scourge of hate. A place of safety, where Rachel felt like she could breathe.

Lemaire told her his news.

"Isabelle has been summoned to Montréal, though I told her to stay on call. She'll be needed back here sooner than she thinks."

"What does she do, exactly? Besides answering questions on the premier's behalf?"

"She's good under pressure. She used to be a defense attorney. That makes her an expert at spinning implausible explanations."

They shared the grins of two cops who were not particularly partial to those who represented criminal offenders.

"Were criminals her only client base?"

"No. She also had a knack for getting politicians out of a mess."

"What kind of mess?"

"A member of parliament's drunk-driving incident—a cyclist was killed, but thanks to Isabelle the MP wasn't convicted. Then there was a group of councilmen who were caught making use of an escort service. Some minor things, some not so minor. But they all had one thing in common."

"What was that?"

"They required crisis management. Isabelle is an expert at that."

They talked a little more about tracing the firearms. Lemaire had already connected with his colleagues in Vice. If guns had been delivered to Saint-Isidore, that meant there could be a delivery network that was operating beyond their knowledge. They needed to track it down if they had any hope of discovering who had bought the firearms. Even then it was a long shot.

They crossed the bridge over the meandering creek, listening to the soft rush of water over the stones as the warm summer air stroked over the empty park.

The units of uniformed officers that had lined up inside the station were spread out at the perimeters. The streetlamps were few and far between. Rachel couldn't make them out, which seemed like a dangerous omission.

"They have head lamps," Lemaire reassured her. "They'll put them on once the vigil begins."

"Will you be making a statement?"

"No. This is an event organized by the public. It would be an intrusion."

"You don't consider the presence of the Wolf Allegiance an intrusion?"

"I don't know what it is you think we have to fear. We've run checks on each one of their members. They're not registered firearm owners. They would be crazy to make an attempt upon the vigil. It's only a minor protest. Neither they nor we should turn it into something bigger."

Frustrated by his refusal to recognize the problem, Rachel called him on it.

"You know what they're protesting, right? It's not the prayer in the park. It's the people themselves. That seems like something pretty big to me."

When he looked down at her, speechless, she thought he might be starting to understand.

35

When Khattak returned to the hotel to change, the concierge told him a woman was waiting for him in the lobby. He only had a few minutes. He was supposed to meet Alizah and Amadou at their campus office. He hoped they hadn't walked to the vigil on their own, though the campus office wasn't necessarily any safer. He'd had a moment to check the list of incidents that had been reported to the dean of the school. Beneath his calm demeanor, a quiet anger was simmering.

He strode into the lobby, ready to make his excuses, when a woman rose from her seat. She was wearing a long-sleeved dress that flared out at her waist. A hand went up to shift her hair over her shoulder, she turned and smiled at him, and he recognized Sehr. Sehr, home at last.

His heart thudding in his chest, he moved to embrace her.

She took a step back, giving him only her hand.

He held on to it, feeling his pulse race, a question in his eyes.

"When did you get back?"

She made a wry grimace, not shying away from the hunger in his gaze. "Last night. I have terrible timing, apparently. I was hoping to surprise you."

His voice husky, he said, "You have. How did you know—"

"It was on the news. I should have waited for you to come home—" She shrugged her slim shoulders. "But I couldn't."

He felt a pang of fear. It was what he'd wanted, longed for, missed— but he didn't think he was misinterpreting the distance in Sehr's eyes. He told himself she was here, she had come to him, and that was more than he'd hoped for.

"I'm glad you've come," he said. "Does this mean—?"

"Esa, no." She bit her soft lower lip. He wanted to draw her into his arms and tell her he would meet any demands she had if she would end their separation. But he also knew he was asking for an answer that Sehr wasn't ready to give. "I'm sorry, I didn't mean to give you the wrong impression. Rachel called me. She was worried about you."

"Worried about me?" His tone grew cool. "Is that why you came? Because you thought I needed minding?"

He'd made her angry, he could see. She dropped her hand, drew back, a quick frown sketched on her brow.

The apology he should have made formed a cold little knot that he couldn't get past. He felt an unreasoning anger. Why had she come if she couldn't admit what they both believed to be true? Too much time had been wasted. He loved her. He wanted to move forward. He'd made both of those subjects clear to her before he'd left the islands. She'd told him she needed time to think—to reconsider. Especially as she had work that she didn't intend to abandon. She'd resented the way he'd pressured her, and hadn't spoken to him in weeks. It was two months since he'd last seen her, and in the empty space between, self-doubt and disgust had crept in.

Why would she want him after what he'd done? After everything he'd said to hurt her?

"Will you give me a moment?" he asked politely. "I need to change before I head back."

He didn't wait for an answer. He was having to concentrate to keep himself in check. He had to be at the vigil in less than twenty minutes. Then after a full day on the case tomorrow, he was meeting with the families of the victims.

If he couldn't govern himself, what comfort could he hope to give?

He showered quickly and changed his clothes. He hadn't eaten in hours; he hadn't slept the previous night. Perhaps he could persuade Sehr to share a late dinner with him. But instead of returning to the lobby and putting the request to her, he rolled out his red and gold prayer rug and oriented it toward Mecca.

He knelt down on the rug and put his forehead to the floor between his palms. A great desolation rolled over him, a tangle of emotions tightening his throat.

In the posture of *sajdah*, he wasn't conscious of his plea.

He was seeing the bloodstained floors of the mosque . . . the hallway, the mihrab, the bodies . . . he couldn't shut it out. He couldn't shut out who he was. Or how much the murders mattered to him beyond the parameters of his work.

How long he stayed in *sajdah*, his forehead pressed hard against the floor, he didn't know. He didn't find any relief. The tension in his body didn't ease. In that long, dark void that passed between him and the faith he reached for, time had ceased to have meaning. Then at last, he heard a knock on the door.

When he summoned his nerve and opened it, Sehr was waiting outside.

Her eyes roved over his face, seeing the weariness there. They stopped on the red splotch at the center of his forehead.

"Oh, Esa," she said softly. She stretched up on her toes and kissed him on the lips. "I'm so sorry, I wasn't any help at all. You *have* to know I love you. Whatever you're facing, I'm here. I *want* to be here at your side."

A violent streak of hope shuddered through him.

"Sehr—"

"No." She hushed him with a finger to his mouth. "You don't have to make me any promises. The only thing I need is you."

36

Alizah saw Esa long before he reached the campus gates. He was walking hand in hand with a woman she didn't recognize. Though they weren't speaking, he kept her close by his side, sheltered under his arm—the kind of chivalrous gesture Alizah had come to expect from him. As they drew closer and she was able to read the expression on his face, a little flame of jealousy licked at her thoughts. She had no right to feel it. Their only bond was through Miraj, and though she'd tried to convince him that she'd never hoped otherwise, he was, after all, a detective. Her denials hadn't persuaded him—he'd imposed the necessary distance, and ashamed, she had let him go.

She thought maybe it wasn't Esa she wanted, it was what he represented—safety, solace, the promise that things would come right, though she knew they never would now that her sister was gone. Even Esa's kindness couldn't assuage the loneliness of life without Miraj. Which didn't explain Alizah's possessiveness or her sense of resentment of the woman close by his side. Amadou put a hand on her shoulder and squeezed, in a gesture of commiseration.

It required too much effort to tell Amadou what was wrong when she couldn't explain it to herself. She thought of Esa as hers. She'd flourished and matured under his attention; she didn't want anything to change. Even if he saw her as just another wounded bird.

"Alizah." He smiled at her, an unfamiliar light in his eyes. At the note of tenderness in his voice, the attractive woman at his side flashed him a startled glance—a little concerned, a little disturbed. Alizah hated herself for the joy she took in seeing it.

Whoever you are, she thought, *you'll never be bound to him as I am.*

He made the introductions and asked if they were ready to walk over to the vigil. Amadou asked for a moment to speak to him first, leaving the two women alone.

Sehr spoke first, her question friendly and direct. "How do you know Esa?"

Driven by a perverse impulse, Alizah said, "Miraj Siddiqui was my sister."

A pause. And then an expression of such warmth and sympathy flooded Sehr Ghilzai's face that Alizah had to look away, pretending to be occupied by the sight of students gathering at the gates. Her eyes stinging, she cursed herself for making use of the sister she had loved so fiercely that it still felt like her heart was cracked down to its core.

Sehr seemed to know that she couldn't have borne her sympathy, so she asked, "How is your friend Amadou coping?"

Determined to misread her, Alizah said, "With what? Being black in Saint-Isidore?" She shrugged. "As well as can be expected."

Sehr's eyebrows arched. "That's not what I meant." The warmth in her face fading, she said, "I'm no threat to your relationship with Esa."

Coolly, Alizah answered, "I didn't think you were."

Some primal feminine instinct told her that Sehr wasn't as concerned with Alizah's connection to Esa as she was with her own. Sehr didn't know about their correspondence, their attachment, the secrets they shared—that much was clear to her at once.

Alizah's respect for Esa increased. It wasn't his own privacy he had chosen to protect; it was hers. She could only be grateful for that.

Her heart was beating heavily against her chest when Sehr said quietly, almost like a warning, "Esa and I are getting married."

Alizah's fists clenched inside her pockets. She made her face blank under Sehr's probing gaze, wrenched because she knew it was true. She'd seen the quiet joy in Esa's face. He'd found himself again because of this woman with her russet-dark hair and wide, compassionate eyes.

She didn't want Sehr to hate her. Because then she would lose Esa altogether.

Her breath catching in her throat, she made herself say, "Good. He deserves to be happy."

Sehr relaxed at the words. Alizah forced herself to continue, to answer the question she'd batted back at Sehr like a weapon.

"Amadou is managing. He's devastated about Youssef. But I don't think the greater scope of this has struck him yet." She waved a hand at the crowd. "He did everything he could to save Youssef, so this doesn't seem real to him." Speaking more to herself, she added, "None of it seems real. I don't know how we came to this."

Turning her head away, she saw a procession advancing down the hill to the gate, carrying bamboo torches. They were dressed alike in white polo shirts and dark slacks, the torchlight flickering across their clean-cut faces. Their shirts bore identical logos—a reworking of the Québec flag; instead of a fleur-de-lis quartered over a white field, the field was blue. At its center was a white crescent, but in lieu of a star was a tilted fleur-de-lis—a black slash running through both. The crescent and star were symbols of Islam—it was a visual depiction of the Wolf Allegiance slogan: Stop the Islamization of Québec. The same symbol had appeared on a flyer taped to the door of the MSA office.

The Wolf Allegiance's protest had begun, Maxime Thibault at their head. The circle of police officers contracted, and then reshaped itself into a line, creating distance between the torch-bearing group and the community gathered to pray.

Young Muslim men linked their arms, forming a cordon around the prayer. They barricaded three sides of a square. The fourth side was left open so that no one blocked the direction of prayer. The police advanced to fill this space.

The atmosphere grew tense and ugly; the tempo of the prayer sped up. Residents of Saint-Isidore had come out in support, carrying bouquets wrapped in cellophane, or tokens they laid at a makeshift memorial on the ground. Groups of university students carried signs that said: TOUS HUMAINS, LE QUÉBEC EST PAS LA FRANCE and CE N'EST PAS LE QUÉBEC. Instead of torches, the residents carried flashlights. They drifted toward the prayer, a little distance apart.

Someone had arranged a makeshift podium near the gate on the higher ground.

Scanning the crowd, Alizah saw the Lilies of Anjou at the edges of the Wolves' procession, at the edges of the prayer. Observing. Not participating. Perhaps, she thought with dawning insight, that was a safer choice for them to make. A short distance south, just climbing the embankment, Rachel was with Christian Lemaire. When Alizah saw him, her relief was edged with a sense of vindication. Now maybe Lemaire would believe her when she spoke about wolves in their midst.

He'd never taken her complaints seriously, but he couldn't deny them now. He was seeing the proof for himself. But something else was happening. The prayer had finished. The torchbearers were pushing ahead against the police, just as the group of Muslim men rearranged themselves to meet them. Reporters were also pushing their way to the front.

Before Lemaire could reach his officers to issue instructions, the police line re-formed as a barricade, facing the congregation down. Puzzled, the congregants fell back. Reporters stepped into the breach.

A disembodied voice floated over the gathering. Alizah's head swung in its direction.

Diana Shehadeh stood there, a microphone in her hand. There was a glittering look of triumph in her eyes.

In sharp, staccato French, she said, "Doesn't that tell us everything? Even after we are murdered en masse, we cannot rely on the Sûreté to act to defend our rights."

A cheer went up from the Wolf Allegiance. They began a chant. The congregation responded with the rousing cry of "Allahu Akbar."

Someone grasped Alizah's elbow.

"Wait here—all three of you, I mean it. You need to keep Amadou out of this."

Esa pushed past her to the podium. Lemaire and Rachel had broken into a run.

Amadou didn't listen. He disappeared into the crowd.

Alizah glanced over at Sehr. Sehr made a helpless gesture, eloquent in its distress. She didn't stir from her place at the gate, her gaze tracking Esa's progress.

Alizah was already moving. "I have to stop this. I'm the only one he'll listen to. Tell Esa I had no choice."

37

The confrontation had spun out of control. Alizah heard a roar of movement, felt herself swept up in the crowd, pressed between bodies. She caught a fleeting glimpse of Amadou, shoving his way to the front of the group, even as screams and cries sounded from all sides.

She nearly lost her footing twice. If she fell, she had no doubt she would be trampled. She couldn't tell what was happening. Were the police pushing the congregation back, or was Maxime's gang of thugs bearing down against them? Flushed and sweating, she searched the crowd for Maxime.

She'd expected to find him at the center of the confrontation, shoving against the police to get to the small group of Muslims who'd dared to hold their prayer in the park. She heard Amadou's voice ring out. Then feedback from the microphone, where Diana Shehadeh had fallen silent. Then a huge whoosh of air, followed by a battle cry. The Wolf Allegiance had broken through the police line and now they were swarming down the hill.

Some of the crowd stood their ground—including Amadou. Most scattered, pushing past Alizah. Her coat was ripped from her shoulders. A heavy hand landed between her shoulder blades, shoving her down to her knees. Then someone else grabbed her, and she was dragged away by her shoulders. Her heart was thudding too violently for her to summon a scream.

She began to fight back, twisting her body to make herself more difficult to drag. A growl of frustration left her throat.

"Shut up."

She was dragged a little farther to the shelter of an oak and thrust aside. She was left panting on her hands and knees, her hair falling in tangles around her face. Just a breath, then another, then she'd scramble to her feet and run. The knees of her jeans were torn. She could feel the stickiness of blood where both her knees had been skinned.

Someone reached down to grab her under the arms and set her upon her feet.

"I told you not to come tonight."

Maxime spit the words at her.

Alizah combed her hair away from her face with her fingers, staring up at him, white-faced and angry.

He was breathing heavily, his torch discarded, his hair disheveled, his polo shirt covered in grass stains, a thin line of blood trailing from the corner of his mouth. His blue eyes were blazing with emotion; his hands clutched Alizah's by the wrists.

Behind them, the police had begun to impose some order on the scene, Lemaire barking out instructions. She couldn't see Amadou anywhere, her breath catching on a sob.

"Stop it," Maxime snapped. "You're fine. You're safe. Everyone's going home."

"Why did you come tonight?" she snapped back. "What kind of monster are you? We haven't even buried our dead, and this is what you thought you'd do?"

"I don't owe you an explanation, bitch. This is still a free country."

She shook off his grip, twisting around for a better vantage point from which to view the park. The police had arrested several of the stragglers, but in the dark she couldn't make out who they were. Sehr was no longer at the gate. She'd reached Khattak and Rachel, neither of whom seemed happy to see her, yet Khattak held out his hand and pulled her close.

"Who the fuck are you in love with?" Maxime's crude words broke through her reverie. "Amadou or that fucking cop?"

She turned to face him, squaring her shoulders, a belligerent tilt to her chin. Compared to the emptiness she'd felt before, she welcomed the fury brought on by his words.

"Neither. But a frat boy like you wouldn't understand that my world doesn't revolve around a man."

"I saw the way you looked at him over by the gate."

Her eyes narrowed. "You were watching me? You're such a creep, Maxime."

"That's the thanks I get for dragging you out of that mess?"

"The mess *you* made," she pointed out.

"Whatever."

He wasn't able to conceal his hunger as he looked her over. She brushed the dirt and grass from her palms, both her knees still stinging. Before she'd learned about his connection to the Wolves, they had been friends. But once she'd understood his views, once Alizah had made it clear that even friendship wasn't possible as long as Max was allied with the Wolves, something inside Max had curdled into this hate-tinged lust. He couldn't stand himself for wanting her. But he also couldn't stand to let her go.

"Why do you want me, Max? I'm no different from the people you came here to harass. The people you're probably happy were killed at the mosque last night."

"Where do you get off making assumptions like that?"

Though his eyes and voice had darkened, she wasn't afraid of him.

She pointed to the logo on his chest. "Your actions speak for themselves."

She didn't know why she was engaging in this pointless conversation. She should be with the others, searching for Amadou. Esa had moved away, scanning the perimeter. She knew he was looking for her.

She put up a hand and waved to let him know she was fine. The sight of Maxime Thibault at her side seemed to give him pause. He started in her direction. A sudden warm glow flared up in her chest.

Maxime jabbed a finger in her face.

"I never took you for a whore."

She slapped him without a second thought.

"Don't ever call me that." Disgusted, she added, "It's all the same with your kind. You hate minorities; you hate women; you hate anyone who won't bow to your toxic creed."

He stood there silently, his hand pressed to his face. She must have caught him off-guard. He didn't move, didn't try to touch her or hit her back. Not that she would have let him. Her hands were curled into fists, and she was poised on the balls of her feet. She knew how to take care of herself.

"It's not about hate," he told her coldly. "We have the right to defend ourselves, and the Québec we want. Before our culture and history are swept away by the tide."

His hand was still pressed to his cheek, lightly patting the place she'd slapped him.

And though Alizah despised Maxime, she felt a pang of pity as she understood why. She hadn't really hurt him—she couldn't.

The slap was the first time she'd touched him.

Then Esa was there, interposing himself between Alizah and Max, ice in his voice, as he asked Maxime what he'd done.

"Did you assault her?"

Maxime shrugged. "She'll probably tell you I did."

Alizah shot him a furious glare. "I'm not a liar, Max. He didn't hurt me," she told Esa. "He dragged me out of the way."

His voice clipped with anger, Esa warned, "Please find Amadou and go back to your residence. This is no place for you." Then with a little less control, he said, "I told you to stay at the gate, Alizah. Don't make it hard for me to do my job."

She battled an unexpected response to his concern. She read it as proprietary. From Maxime's expression, he did as well.

"I was trying to get to Max," she said. "I thought he might listen to me."

Behind her, Max snorted. He kicked at the grass, dislodging a little clump. He scowled at Khattak.

"Look how she twists us around. You. Me. Amadou. God knows which one of us she wants."

Her cheeks flushed under Esa's steady regard. She glanced at Max, reading the sullen longing in his eyes. She couldn't keep herself from feeling sorry for him, but she couldn't do anything about it. His unsolicited feelings were not her problem. His hate-fueled politics were.

If she owed him Max anything at all, she would have told him the truth.

She'd lost the man she wanted. She would never get him back.

38

There was no amount of damage control Lemaire could do that would be enough now. The vigil had gone just about as badly as Rachel had anticipated, and the fallout would dominate the next news cycle. The premier, the INSET team, and the Wolf Allegiance were under fire to varying degrees. It was rumored that the prime minister would be visiting Saint-Isidore to pay his respects at the mosque, creating additional security problems for Lemaire's team to manage. No progress had been made on the firearms or on the investigation. As a result, Rachel was surprised that Lemaire hadn't been summarily removed from his post, but judging from his discussions on the phone, he wasn't going down without a fight.

There were a handful of police officers left in the park, keeping an eye out for signs of disturbance. While Lemaire was on the phone, Khattak was in the unenviable position of defending his actions to two angry women at once: Diana Shehadeh and Isabelle Clément. Rachel waited for him, her arms crossed under her chest, ready to step in if he needed backup. She was expecting a moment of reckoning from him, not knowing what Sehr might have said. She couldn't ask her, either, because Sehr had returned to the hotel, finding herself in Esa's way in the midst of the ongoing debriefing. Rachel hadn't had a chance to talk to her yet and was still puzzling over whether Sehr's arrival had made any difference to Khattak. He wasn't on the defensive speaking to the two women; rather, he sounded like he was on the attack.

"There should have been stronger measures against the Allegiance from the start. That was my recommendation to the premier."

Diana Shehadeh waved at the mess left behind in the park. "Don't try and cover your inadequacies. If this is your idea of serving the community, no wonder you've been a disappointment."

"I'll speak to you in a moment, Diana. Isabelle, the only appropriate response is to shut down the Allegiance at once."

Isabelle's response was as dispassionate as Rachel had grown to expect. She let her eyes trail over the now-destroyed memorial for the victims, the wholesome signs trodden by angry feet, flowers and stuffed toys scattered over the grounds.

"Inspector Lemaire gave clear instructions to members of his team. That should have been enough to handle the situation."

"They were protecting these murderers," Diana interjected. "They weren't here for the people who came here to pray."

"The prayer was a provocation."

Diana's laugh was bitter. "It seems to me in *la belle province* it's our existence that's the provocation."

Esa turned on Diana again. "This isn't helping. Can you wait for me by your car?"

"Why? So you can cover this up? I don't think so, Esa. I'm here to watch exactly how effective you are."

He shrugged one shoulder, a rudely dismissive gesture.

Sweet holy Christ. What the hell was Khattak doing?

Rachel cleared her throat, intending a reminder that he needed to play fair. He shot her a glance—bleak and resonant with anger. She swallowed a hasty response.

His jaw set, he said to Isabelle, "The mayor's office issued the permit for the congregational prayer. Surely you knew that?"

Isabelle's gaze flicked to Diana Shehadeh.

"It was my understanding that the permit was granted under considerable pressure."

Khattak's response slashed the sudden silence. "Inspector Lemaire did not instruct his team to shrink the perimeter around the prayer. Someone else is responsible for that."

His green eyes were shrewd and insistent.

There was a protracted pause.

Finally, Clément admitted, "Thibault threatened to release a statement to the press declaring our decision to squash his protest as unconstitutional." She moistened dry lips. "He didn't just argue for freedom of assembly. He insisted it was an issue of freedom of expression—he said that Québécois values were being dragged back into the Dark Ages."

Khattak's expression became set. He ignored the group of girls who had come up behind them to clear the litter from the ground. Isabelle's gaze flicked over them and back to Khattak.

"And you gave in to them? Just like that?"

Her response was pure vitriol.

"Are you saying I shouldn't have offered *reasonable accommodation*? Isn't that what you always demand?"

Diana sputtered with rage. "How *dare* you say that? How dare you wield civil rights protections on behalf of out-and-out Nazis?"

Khattak held up a hand and was ignored by both women.

Isabelle's reply was icy. "*My* concern is to represent all the citizens of Québec, not just a group of special interests. I'm sorry if that offends you." Her expression made it clear she wasn't sorry in the least. "Sometimes the truth is hard to hear. But there are no 'safe spaces' in politics." Her tone became sneering, the words directed at Khattak. "Nor in police work, either, I'm afraid."

She stalked away from them to issue instructions to the girls who were trying to repair the memorial. The Lilies of Anjou had come to the vigil, Rachel realized with a start. She had last seen them at the press briefing on Youssef Soufiane's death. She was surprised that only a few hours later Chloé had found the strength to make her way to the memorial. Chloé and the other Lilies were joined by Amadou Duchon, whom Isabelle Clément skirted as if he posed a danger to her. She moved closer to Chloé, and to Rachel's surprise, she gave the younger woman a hug.

Perplexed, Rachel noticed that Amadou was whispering earnestly and at length with Émilie Péladeau. From his body language, he was trying to persuade her of something.

Lemaire rejoined their group. He didn't seem fazed by the dressing down he'd just received from the premier's office. Maybe such things were as commonplace in the Sûreté as they were in Community Policing.

Khattak's new phone made the sound that heralded a text.

Instead of reading it, he beckoned them close and held up the phone. They gathered in a circle as Khattak pulled up the text for them to read.

> Soufiane is dead. One of you will be next.

He took a screenshot of the message, then handed his phone to Lemaire.

"What the hell is happening here?" Diana Shehadeh's horrified gaze moved from face to face. But none of the police officers could offer a cogent answer in the face of so many unknowns.

Khattak's phone sounded again. This time Lemaire held up the message.

> Richard is about to blow the roof off your world.
> Vive la France. Vive le Québec libre!

Speaking through gritted teeth, Diana demanded, "Inspector Lemaire. Can we expect that you'll take some action to defuse another incident like tonight's?"

Lemaire nodded. His evident sympathy seemed to infuriate her further.

"I came to tell you that the mosque has been cleared for use. There won't be a repeat of tonight. The mosque is easier to defend."

The terse, pragmatic words sent a shiver down Rachel's spine.

How could they be speaking of a place of worship like this?

Khattak jerked his head at Lemaire. "I'll head there, now." He addressed Diana. "Come with me and we can talk."

Lemaire nodded. "I'll pass your phone on to your man Gaffney. I've also had a call about security footage. We may have just gotten a lead." He turned to Rachel. "It's late and you need a break. I can catch you up in the morning."

It was true—Rachel was exhausted. But there was too much adrenaline pumping through her veins. With a subtle gesture of her chin, she urged Khattak to take note of Amadou and Émilie. They'd moved away from Isabelle Clément, who was frowning at them over Chloé's shoulder.

Khattak nodded once.

"Amadou!" he called. "We're headed to the mosque. Would you like to join us?"

With a grimace of relief, Amadou removed Émilie's hand from his arm. He detached himself from the group without another word.

Rachel moved away with Lemaire back to the station.

Something about the entire tableau had disturbed her.

And it wasn't the naked threat that had surfaced on Khattak's phone.

39

Diana Shehadeh drove, Khattak in the passenger seat, Amadou in the back of the car, his head resting on the arm he'd braced against the window.

"You didn't do enough," Diana told Khattak. "They're running roughshod over you, over what you're supposed to achieve. When they called you in to head up Community Policing, I thought at last we'd have a voice." She shot him an angry glance as she made a right turn. "But having you here is no different from *not* having you here."

He fought himself for a brief moment. He'd stayed silent too often in the past, and now the rage that simmered beneath his composure was threatening to overcome him. He held it back until she added, "The one thing I've never been able to tell about you is where your loyalties lie. What good are you to us when you're always performing for them?"

She spoke as though there weren't a third person in the car—a witness to the crime, an individual who was implicated in events, though Khattak didn't know to what extent.

His temper snapped.

"I'm sick to God of answering that question. It's *not* a performance."

Diana snorted. "Oh yes, it is. *You* perform for *us*. But time after time, you end up disappointing the audience."

This was so manifestly unjust that Khattak needed a moment to respond. How had he ever imagined that he and Diana were partners—that they'd ever been on the same side?

He shook his head, angry, rattled. "It doesn't work, Diana. These categories you try to box us into. 'Us—them.' It doesn't work. Chloé Villeneuve—she's devastated by Youssef's death. She loved him." He indicated Amadou, listening intently in the back seat. "Amadou and Émilie—there's something there as well. And even someone like Max is able to see Alizah as a person. We're not on opposite sides because of who we are. That kind of thinking is reductive." He clasped his hands together because he wanted to strike something hard. "It's completely dishonest."

He shifted in his seat to look at Amadou.

"Isn't that right, Amadou?"

The young man's expression was curiously defenseless.

"You want to know about Émilie."

"She seemed angry at you in the park."

They had reached the mosque. He motioned to Diana that she should go ahead without them, passing her the keys to the door. He lingered with Amadou near the car, not yet ready to read the secrets of the mosque.

"No, not angry." Amadou tipped back his beautifully shaped head, his eyes as large and inky as the night. "Émilie is a very nice girl. She's always been so supportive. She knows what it's like to be an outsider— she told me she could see it in my face."

"See what?" Khattak kept his voice soft and low, his anger at Diana fading at the rhythmic cadences of Amadou's voice.

"What it's like not to belong. To keep trying and failing because the barriers that surround you are too strong. Too insurmountable." He reached over to pat Esa's shoulder. "You must know what that's like. So does Diana. That's why she's so angry."

Khattak sighed. The brotherhood Amadou was offering wasn't one he had any right to claim. The systemic barriers faced by Amadou as a black man, the ever-present aggressions that battered each corner of his identity, were daily injuries he and Diana didn't share.

Searching for the right words, he said, "Not like you. Nothing like you, Amadou."

"Well. . . ." There was nothing Amadou could add. They both knew it was true.

"What did Émilie want from you, then?"

The young man's muscles tightened.

"She wants something she cannot have. She wants my love. She believes she can save me from the ugliness here by giving me the gift of her love. I have become her project."

There was no contempt in his voice, just a soft, regretful sadness for a girl who'd misunderstood and whose unacknowledged advantages had caused her to lose her way.

"You're not interested?"

Khattak wondered if Amadou realized he was being led through an interrogation. He wondered if he should remind him that it was his job to hunt down the person who had carried out the killing spree at the mosque.

Amadou switched to French, his words caressing the night.

"I want to marry a girl from Senegal. A girl with rich, dark skin and eyes as deep as the ocean. A girl I can take to the mosque who will stand by my side in prayer. She will speak my language, and know my history—I won't have to build a wall; I won't have to tear one down. I want a woman who shares the journey I make to my Sustainer." A sweet smile graced his lips. Ruefully, he said, "I am engaged to be married to a woman like that. Émilie is very kind, very sweet. I value her as a friend without wishing for anything more. Youssef was willing to take that risk, but I want a woman who knows what it is to live in two worlds at once."

The poetic words made an impression on Khattak; they mirrored the relationship he'd had with his wife, Samina, who even after her death held a closely guarded place in his heart. The heart he had only recently opened to Sehr.

"Does Émilie know that?"

Amadou sighed. "She knows, but she hasn't accepted it. She keeps trying to change my mind. I don't mean to be unkind, but she is using the shooting as a means of insinuating herself into my life. I don't want it. I don't think she realizes how dangerous it is for us both."

His attention flagged, Khattak asked, "What do you mean? What danger does Émilie represent?"

Amadou's reply was succinct. "The danger of a white woman involved with a black man—a Muslim—in a town like Saint-Isidore. Plus, she's on the radar of Thibault and his thugs. They used to be friends with the Lilies, so they'll never be able to accept Émilie's attraction to me. They might call me names. The names they call her are worse."

Amadou didn't want to enter the mosque with Esa. It was too soon for him to face the reality that he hadn't saved Youssef after all. Esa let him walk away, thinking over his words. Something Amadou had told him was nagging at him—some casual statement that was more important than it had seemed at the time. It needed attention, yet it wasn't coming into focus. But Diana was waiting inside. He wasn't sure she deserved it, but he knew he had to apologize. To defuse a situation that was adding unwarranted pressure to his investigation.

The shooter hadn't come to the vigil.

But someone had been close by.

Diana hadn't disappeared into the women's prayer space. Esa found her in the main hall, arranging a copious scarf over her hair and shoulders.

She was quiet, her anger calmed, her head bowed as she waited near the mihrab. When she glanced his way, he was startled to observe that tears had streaked her face, tears she made no effort to wipe away.

"How are we going to solve this?" she asked Esa.

Feeling strangely vulnerable, he answered, "We'll make progress, Diana. There's bound to be a break in the investigation. We'll find him."

She shook her head. "I don't mean the investigation." She stepped forward, her hands tracing over the bullet holes in the mihrab. "I mean *this*. How are we going to solve *this*?"

The grief he'd been suppressing rose up in a wave. An electric silence fell between them—and in it everything changed. She wasn't his enemy, trying her best to bring him down. She wasn't sitting in judgment, waiting for him to fail. She was someone who'd worked

tirelessly for a decade, pushing back against forces that were shrinking the perimeters of her world—the gray zone between forces so bleak
and powerful that the simplest act could undo the safety of the bonds
that held them: shared values, a shared humanity, citizenship. No one
on the outside could appreciate the way that each corner of that safety
was threatened.

He pressed a fist to the center of his chest, fighting back the emotion that threatened to betray him. Diana watched him, her shadowed
eyes vulnerable, her shoulders stooped under the weight of this calam-
ity. She wasn't as redoubtable as he'd always known her to be. She
looked small and bereft, mourning what had been and everything that
was yet to be lost.

She knew this was just the beginning. Just as Esa did.

He reached out and took her hand, leading her to a spot in the prayer
hall. New carpets had been laid over where old ones had been stripped
away.

He didn't stand in front of her. He left a gap and took a place at her
side.

He gave the call to prayer, low and rich in his throat, faltering over
the words.

She rearranged her scarf so that it fell in soft folds from her shoulders to her wrists.

When he finished, he turned to Diana, raising his hands to his ears.

"Stand with me," he said.

"In prayer?" she asked, copying the gesture that opened the rites of
prayer.

"No," he answered with a searching look. "Stand with me against
this."

40

Two days later they were no further forward and night was falling again.

"What are we going to do about these threats?" Rachel asked.

Lemaire rubbed the back of his head in response. He looked like he knew she wasn't going to like his answer.

"You should understand we get things like this all the time. Racist abuse, threats, online and on campus, they're quite common. They're pranks, Rachel. They're meant to distract us from our work."

"This feels different," she pointed out. "It's someone who's been shadowing Inspector Khattak." Her glance took in the INSET team. It lingered on a couple of Sûreté officers near the photocopier, who'd taken a break and were now observing their boss. The hum of activity around them continued, a buzz that was comforting and familiar.

Again, she had the feeling that something about Lemaire's words didn't quite fit in with her picture of events—or with the urgency of the shooting. They were in the office he was using as his own, a few framed photographs on the wall. It was nothing like Richard's vanity wall, though she saw a photograph similar to the one Khattak had described—Lemaire, Clément, and the mayor of Saint-Isidore offering Richard the key to the city.

A little shock of alarm ran through her veins. She knew what it was that had tingled at the edge of her consciousness. She pinned Lemaire with a rock-steady gaze.

"You're a senior homicide cop?" she confirmed.

He nodded, watching her.

"Regularly seconded to INSET?"

Lemaire shrugged his massive shoulders. "I have a certain expertise. What's your point?"

She didn't look away.

"Then why are you in Saint-Isidore so often?" She nodded at the photograph on the wall. "Why were you and Isabelle invited to participate in a ceremony glorifying Pascal Richard, of all people? Doesn't seem to fit within the ambit of homicide. Or of national security."

Lemaire turned to look at the photograph behind his head. When he turned back, there was something new in his expression. Weighing. Watchful. A thrill of fear whispered down her spine. The desk was between them, but suddenly she felt his towering presence like a threat.

He cracked his knuckles on the desk, the sound filling the silence.

In a soft voice he asked, "What are you accusing me of, Rachel? Be specific."

Rachel edged closer to the door. Lemaire stepped around the desk, cutting off her access to the door.

Rachel refused to retreat. Her hand thumbed the phone in her pocket. Discreetly, she tapped Khattak's number.

Lemaire was too quick for her, his eyes darting to the hand she'd stuffed in her pocket. He fished her phone from her pocket and tossed it onto the desk.

His laser-blue gaze unwavering, he said, "Go on. You have nothing to fear from me."

Rachel threw up her head.

"Why? Because I'm 'old stock'? I'm what you'd call *pure laine*? Québécois *de souche*?"

"Don't be ridiculous," he batted back. "You may speak French, but you certainly can't claim to be a Québécois."

Rachel didn't want to. But she had to think of something. Her gaze slipped to the gun he had holstered at his hip. He'd have to get her out of the station to his car. She had a very brief window in which to attempt an escape.

"Rachel." His exasperated tone put an end to her plotting, suggesting she'd overreacted. "Why do you *think* I was at the ceremony? Why do you think that photograph is on the wall?"

"It's not just the ceremony," she said rapidly. She jammed her free hand into the pocket of her slacks, withdrawing a crumpled sheet of paper. She held it up as if she were warding Lemaire off with a talisman. "You've made it clear that you're familiar with what's been happening here. You've visited Saint-Isidore several times. Yet you've taken zero action on things that should have been dealt with a long time ago." She brandished the list she'd gotten from the university.

He took it from her hand, reading it over with a frown.

Rachel barreled ahead. "I can't think of a single reason why a senior homicide officer would be on call here. And then having come, why he'd do nothing to halt the activities of a group like the Wolf Allegiance. You didn't detain Père Étienne. And though you should have detained members of the Allegiance, you haven't even bothered to question them."

Lemaire smoothed out the list, resuming his watchful manner. She hadn't yet said what he seemed to expect her to say. Since she couldn't break past him to the common area, there was no point in holding back.

"A lot of people in law enforcement don't seem to have noticed. But Superintendent Killiam did. She told me to watch for it."

Lemaire's eyes didn't shift from her face. "For what?"

"For proof that all levels of law enforcement have been infiltrated by the far right. The alt-right, white nationalists, dress it up however you want. You're just neo-Nazis in the end."

To say she was stunned when Lemaire began to laugh was putting it mildly. He shifted away from the door with a flourish of his hand, seating himself at his leisure, his shoulders rumbling with laughter.

"What?"

Still smiling, he said, "The way you glare at me, *mon amie*. You have quite a way with your superiors."

"You're saying I'm wrong?" Her heart was thundering in her chest.

She flung the door wide but didn't leave. "You're not the head of the Allegiance? You *didn't* orchestrate Saint-Isidore's Code of Conduct with the mayor and Clément?"

Lemaire shook his head, his shaggy hair falling around his collar. "I thank you for that sterling assessment of my character, but no. Take a seat and I'll tell you, since you seem to have guessed quite a bit."

Rachel hesitated, looking at the door.

"It's up to you, Rachel. You're perfectly safe working at my side."

Mumbling under her breath, Rachel took the seat across from Lemaire. He rested his elbows on the desk, studying the suspicion in her face.

"You are quite correct in assessing the problem in Saint-Isidore. There *has* been infiltration. Some elements of the police force here are suspect. We do have reason to suspect the mayor of giving carte blanche to certain disruptive elements in town."

"The Wolf Allegiance," Rachel supplied.

"The Allegiance," he agreed. "But also others. I was assigned to the Gatineau area to root those elements out. To get a sense of the scope of the problem."

"Why should I believe you?"

"You can check with Superintendent Killiam. She's the one who sent me." As a tide of color swept up Rachel's cheeks, Lemaire sought to put her at ease. "Isabelle's excuse is more innocent. She has family in Saint-Isidore."

A low groan escaped Rachel's throat. Lemaire wouldn't have mentioned the superintendent unless he had the bedrock certainty that she would back him up. She'd made a dreadful mistake, and it was one she couldn't back away from. She felt sick with mortification, itchy and uncomfortable in her light summer clothes, under a layer of sweat.

At a loss for words, she whispered, "But why haven't you done anything?" She made a floundering gesture with her hand. "Why did you let it go so far?"

Lemaire's shoulders slumped. For the first time, his bright blue gaze dropped from hers. But he didn't attempt to shield himself.

"Our inactivity was meant to draw them out—to see who might be fueling the fire behind the Allegiance, and what their ultimate goal might be. Someone is making use of these kids, radicalizing a new generation—indoctrinating them into extremist ideology."

"So that's why you appeared to give your sanction to Richard. That's why the photograph is here. You were trying to suggest that you're not someone they need to worry about."

"You seem familiar with the photograph."

"Inspector Khattak described it to me. He said he saw a copy of it in Richard's office."

"Ah." He came to a decision, his voice freshening as he addressed her. "Obviously, we failed at our task. We were unprepared for action. I had to limit my visits here so as not to raise suspicions. That's how I missed the signs."

Rachel nodded to herself. Lemaire's explanation was plausible. But she would still be confirming it with the superintendent.

"You mean the break-in at the MSA's office."

"That. But there was a more obvious clue."

Puzzled, Rachel stared at him. She still had only the blurriest impression of what had happened in Saint-Isidore before the shooting.

"The broken light outside the women's entrance to the mosque," Lemaire explained. "Someone did a trial run. To see how easy it would be to gain entrance without fear of discovery. That's why they vandalized the light."

"And you didn't think to put up your own cameras after that?" Rachel's tone was accusing.

"We were being careful. We didn't want to tip them off."

Rachel frowned to herself. Had it simply been the wrong call? Because its consequences had spun rapidly out of control. And she could see that that truth had just come home to hit Lemaire.

Rachel put in a quick call to Superintendent Killiam to confirm Lemaire's information. When she aired her suspicions, Killiam once again took the time to reassure her about Lemaire's skills and reputation. Rachel hung up, still uncertain. A hand rapped on the door. It was Constable Benoit, an anxious expression on his face, as if it had taken all his courage to interrupt. Though Rachel was glad of the reprieve, she felt sorry for him—she knew what it was like to be that young and green.

"We have something, sir. Would you like—that is, are you available to see the footage?"

The glimmer of a smile in his eyes, Lemaire turned to Rachel. "Are we?"

She swallowed a sarcastic retort, following him to Benoit's station, where a group of officers were gathered. Her colleague Paul Gaffney was among them, and she smiled a welcome at him. It was good to have someone else from Community Policing with them, someone she knew she could trust. Gaff nodded at her.

"Benoit is the one who spotted it. I just cleaned it up."

The attention of everyone gathered at the desk was fixed on Benoit's monitor. At a nod from Lemaire, Benoit hit the play button.

The footage was from a small shop two streets west of the mosque. Its shady, tree-lined lane was dark save for a single streetlamp. For fifteen seconds, the street was deserted on both sides. Then a figure passed directly under the streetlamp, pausing for the briefest moment. The figure pivoted, casting a glance over its shoulder, facing the camera head on.

Ice-cold dread froze in Rachel's veins.

The figure was a woman wearing a niqab and an abaya.

When she turned toward the camera and raised her arm, something else became clear.

The woman was carrying a gun.

Rachel held her breath, her heart kicking painfully at the walls of her chest. Her panicked eyes sought Lemaire's. What the hell did this mean?

Lemaire rattled off a volley of remarks in French, directing his subordinates to keep a tight lid on the evidence and Benoit to turn over the footage without making a copy. They established a chain of custody, Benoit passing the footage over to Lemaire in a signed and dated

envelope. Both Benoit and Gaffney co-signed the seal of the envelope.

"It is essential that this doesn't leak to the media."

One of Lemaire's subordinates spoke up. "Where do we direct our
efforts now? It seems we've been wasting our time looking beyond the
mosque."

"Finish the intake on those who were at the vigil tonight."

"But sir—"

"Do it," Lemaire snapped. "I'll take care of this."

Lemaire's team scattered back to work.

Rachel hung back with Gaffney while Lemaire stormed into his
office and slammed the door. Through the glass panels, she could
see he'd taken out his phone and was shouting at someone on the
other end.

His personality was volatile and intriguing. She much preferred
Khattak's enlightened calm, but she couldn't deny that Lemaire's presence was exciting.

"You planning to stick around?" Gaff asked. "I'm knocking off for
the night."

Rachel sank down lower and whispered, "Is that really the only copy
of the footage?"

Gaff grinned at her, gathering his things and shoving his laptop back
into its bag.

"Are you kidding me? The boss told me to run my inquiries sepa-
rately from INSET's. Just in case. He's not as enamored of Lemaire
as you are."

"Enamored?" Rachel's protest sounded like a squawk.

Gaff walked her out to the parking lot. "Never seen you so hot and
bothered. Not even over that 'gentleman' who couldn't make up his
mind."

Rachel shrugged, pretending that she didn't know he was describing Nate. But Gaff knew her well enough to tease her. She'd left her
phone on Lemaire's desk and thought about going back to get it. But
at Gaff's knowing grin, she changed her mind. She needed a few hours

of sleep. Gaff could give her a ride, and then he could bring Khattak up to speed.

"You don't have to leave because I am. I'm guessing Old Blue-Eyes is quite the antidote to your need for regular sleep."

A reluctant smile cracked her face.

"Shut up and drive," she said.

41

Esa was beginning to feel like he had sandpaper under his eyelids. He'd been working the case around the clock, barely speaking to Sehr. Lemaire had returned his phone, and now a message came through from Rachel. He rubbed at his eyes, the thick lashes tangling, reading over her request. He was aching with fatigue and he wanted to get back to the hotel to see Sehr, the one bright spot in this darkness. But she would have gone to bed by now, so he might as well see what Rachel wanted.

> You need to see this footage. Somewhere away from the eyes of Lemaire and his team. Meet me at this address in 15.

He checked the address with the GPS on his phone. Rachel had chosen a spot on the north side of the lake, a few miles beyond the Université Marchand. There were probably several cafés open late near the university.

He drove through the streets slowly, conscious that he was not as alert as he needed to be to drive. The drive around the lake was circuitous; it was also exceptionally scenic, the antique streetlamps hung with flowering baskets that spilled waves of pink and crimson against a backdrop of trees. The lake itself lay black and silver under the moon, its soft waves dipping to a rhythm that soothed the turmoil of his senses as he rolled down his window to take in the breeze. As it stirred the hair across his forehead, some of his tension eased. He thought he glimpsed a little white boathouse across on the opposite bank, and instantly he was transported back to the town of Waverley and the shores of White Pine Lake.

To a pier in the dead of night where he'd stood over the resting place of a fiercely determined young woman. He was saddened by the memory of her loss.

But that there was too much death in his life wasn't the issue. He'd known that would be the case when he'd committed himself to the police.

What troubled him more deeply than he was able to express was that there was so little justice. He took a turn away from the lake and back into the heart of the town, to quiet streets away from the residential neighborhoods, down a road that led to a series of abandoned lots, derelict and overgrown in the sumptuous summer heat, tiger lilies sprawling in wild, corrosive bunches, tangled with the lacy heads of weeds.

There were no cafés on this road, nor any indication that Rachel was somewhere nearby. They could have met in the hotel lobby—that she'd chosen such a faraway spot suggested that she'd stumbled onto something too provocative to share with Lemaire.

Khattak parked on the street, gazing around for some sign of Rachel's car. The address she'd given him was for a small brown building whose windows were boarded up. The street number was stamped on a listing sign that would soon crash down from the lintel it was loosely attached to. A strong gust of wind would free it—its serrated edge looked dangerous.

Khattak ducked under it, frowning. There was no sign of Rachel having passed this way.

Which seemed a little strange in itself.

He let his hand drop from the door to seek out his phone. He put a call through to Rachel. His frown deepened when he heard the muffled sound of her ringtone from somewhere inside the building. She didn't answer. He tried again and the phone rang in the silence. His sense of danger sharpened. He reached for his gun only to remember that he'd locked it in the glove box of his car. He'd had a presentiment that if he'd gone to the vigil armed he would be laying the groundwork for a tragic confrontation.

He had started back to his car when he heard a shuffling sound on the other side of the door followed by a low moan.

He tried the doorknob and the door parted from its frame with a groan.

"Rachel? Are you in there?"

It was utterly dark inside, a blankness that disoriented. He smelled something—sharp, unpleasant—was it blood?

His hand felt for the flashlight in his pocket, his steps advancing bit by bit. He found the edge of a wall and followed it deeper into the building.

"Rachel?" he called again.

Something was wrong.

He flicked on the flashlight. His wavering steps had led him to a small, dark windowless room. His light flickered into its deepest corners and he was met by a sight that froze him where he stood, motionless and fully alert to danger, and to the recklessness that had made him come this far alone.

He didn't have time to reconsider. As his flashlight made another sweep of the room, he was struck on the back of his head.

When he woke again, there was a musty thickness in his mouth—a roll of cloth had been stuffed inside it. Not far enough to cause him to choke. Just enough to keep him quiet.

Blearily, his eyes opened.

His flashlight had rolled onto the floor, a short distance away. A small circumference of light spooled out near his feet. After a moment's blurry reflection, he realized he was sitting in a metal chair, his feet bound to its legs, his hands bound with a plastic tie behind his back. He could feel a stickiness at the back of his neck where blood had dripped into his collar.

He couldn't see anyone or hear anything beyond the frenzied beating of his heart.

Questions filled his mind.

Where was he? Who had done this? Was Rachel somewhere safe?

He was bound too tightly to shift his position, but he did his best to turn his head.

Behind him, someone had made an effort to disperse the gloom by lighting a single candle. He blinked, trying to clear his vision.

Memory came back in a flash.

He'd seen this when he'd entered the room.

A man in a white robe, wearing a wolf head whose giant fangs were dripping blood.

Black letters were slashed across his chest.

THE WOLF ALLEGIANCE.

He'd stumbled onto the headquarters of Saint-Isidore's neo-Nazi group.

No, that wasn't quite right.

His head aching, he forced himself to think, to remember. He hadn't stumbled onto it. He'd been lured here by a text sent from Rachel's phone, and *then* he'd been attacked.

By whom? Maxime Thibault? Or someone associated with him?

Someone who knew that Rachel had returned to the station for an update on security footage from the area around the mosque.

Pain pounded through his skull. What if Rachel was somewhere nearby? He'd heard her phone ring from inside the building because he'd called it. Twice.

His breathing became panicked; he began to suffocate under the cloth in his mouth.

There was a sudden sharp movement from one corner. The candle flame was snuffed out. He heard the snick of a flashlight as the room was plunged into darkness again.

A presence moved closer to him, taking him by the jaw and jerking up his head. The roll of cloth was yanked from his mouth. The hand at his jaw dropped and the presence withdrew.

He could hear someone breathing, quick and easy breaths.

"Who's there? Who are you?"

There was no answer. He tugged wildly at the ties that bound his wrists, cutting them, the spill of blood slickening the friction. There was another sharp movement. A hard blow landed just below his shoulder.

"Thibault? Is that you?"

A thick and black silence settled in his mouth. He could taste it. He felt his adrenaline spike as fear coursed through his body.

Again, no one spoke.

A hand gripped his throat with a fierce and terrible power, squeezing so hard that Esa couldn't speak, couldn't cry out. The pressure kept on and on until he passed out again.

42

When he came to, slivers of early light leaked beyond the boarded windows to cast a pale opal glow in the room. Light pulsed behind his eyelids. His body ached from its unnatural posture. He was lying on his side, one of his arms pinned beneath his weight.

He scrambled into a sitting position, a wave of nausea surging in his chest.

He fought it, spitting out the bile in his mouth.

Pain shot fiery trails up his arm as it was freed from his weight. He flexed his wrists. He was no longer bound, no longer sitting in a chair, his wrists and ankles freed. But blood was caked at his wrists and thickly matted in his hair. He took stock of his injuries—a throbbing pain in his head and a soreness beneath his left shoulder. Other than that, he hadn't been hurt. He staggered to his feet, feeling his head spin, colors bursting behind his eyes. It took several long minutes to steady himself, his breath rasping in his chest.

His mind sorted through the various strands of the case, trying to weave them together, trying to remember. He'd come here . . . why? What had happened to him?

He became aware of a buzzing noise. His hand slipped into his pocket to bring out his phone. There were a dozen messages on it—nearly all of them from Rachel. One from Diana, another from Sehr. His vision blurred in and out. He couldn't read them.

He stumbled over to a wall and rested his aching head against it, stabbing out numbers on the phone. Rachel answered at once, her words washing over him in a flurry of concern.

He didn't know what he was doing in this room or what had happened to him, so he couldn't tell her. He didn't know where he was, so he couldn't give her the address.

She told him to leave his phone on and she would track it, trying to make sense of his recital.

"Just wait there," she said. "Wait there and don't move a muscle. An ambulance will be there soon."

An ambulance? Why would he need an ambulance? Words slurred on his tongue, but Rachel had already hung up.

He lurched from the room into an entranceway. He was in some kind of deserted office building, emptied of furniture, in the middle of renovations that had been discontinued abruptly, drywall half-erected, timber and rebar shifted off to one side. By gripping the wall, he was able to make his way to the door, an inexplicable sensation of dread mounting in his chest.

Something was wrong. Even Rachel's voice had sounded strangely unfamiliar.

But outside, it was an ordinary summer day, the breeze moving through the overhanging branches of trees that lined the empty street. He squinted against the light of a pale dawn sky, shivering in the fresh air. He spotted his car in the street and made his way over to it, step by painful step, wondering if he had the keys. His pockets felt strangely light. Something told him he should get inside his car as quickly as he could manage and lock the doors. He should get . . . he should get . . .

He should get his gun.

But he didn't know why.

The car was unlocked. Inside the car, he breathed in great gulps of air; he locked the doors and fumbled for the glove box. It was locked and he couldn't find the keys. Maybe he'd left them inside. But something told him he shouldn't go back inside.

His eyes were dry and gritty, his mouth tasted of something unpleasant, and his wrists were sore and itching under their coating of blood.

He looked back at the building, trying to remember.

There had been a sign with a number on it. He'd thought at first of an apartment. There should be a message on his phone from Rachel specifying the address.

But when he checked back through the log, trying to clear his vision, the message was gone.

She'd wanted to meet him there.

He looked at the lintel of the building again.

There had been footsteps in the dust and a sign above his head.

Abruptly, Khattak remembered.

He made his way back into the building. He was listening intently, but he knew that the air in the building was different now. It was deserted. He was the only one inside. Nonetheless, he picked up a piece of rebar, holding it up like a weapon.

He advanced cautiously to the room he'd been in.

Someone had lured him to this building, knocked him out, and trussed him. A candle had been lit to show him a mural on the wall. The man wearing a wolf's head, and beneath it the name of Maxime Thibault's hate group—the Wolf Allegiance.

He entered the room with the rebar in his hand, ready to strike out.

But now the room was empty.

Everything that had been in the room was gone. The chair, the candle, the mural on the wall, even his flashlight. Whoever had struck him had vanished. But how could the mural have vanished? Where was the wolf's head with its threatening fangs? He moved closer to the wall and touched it. It was an old cement wall with a layer of dust that hadn't been painted over. There was no trace of stickiness and no chemical scent of paint. Had he imagined it? But how could he have dreamt an image he'd never seen before?

He thought back to the polo shirts worn by the Wolf Allegiance at the march. The official symbol of the Allegiance was a man wearing a wolf head, but the marchers had worn a restyled flag of Québec, emblazoned with the slogan STOP THE ISLAMIZATION OF QUÉBEC.

It occurred to him now that the slogan had been written in English and not in French. He drew the obvious conclusion. The intended audience hadn't been Québec. The Wolf Allegiance had hoped to broadcast its views to the rest of the country.

He tried to refocus. So it hadn't been some kind of elided dream. He'd seen the mural in the light thrown up by the candle. He examined the floor near the wall for traces of fallen wax, but the floor was clean, layers of dust indicating that no one had traveled over this patch.

He realized suddenly that his reentry into the room was contaminating any evidence the forensic team might find. He beat a retreat, his body refusing to move as quickly as his mind commanded. More light was reaching into the room, spreading out from the corners. It was hurting his head, which still throbbed painfully. He needed a wash and a change of clothes, and something to eat to combat his sense of weakness.

He needed to return Sehr's call. He was swept by dizziness again. Dropping the steel bar, he grasped blindly for the wall, his hand landing on the boarded window. He braced himself for long minutes, breathing in deep gulps of air. Close by, he heard a rustle. When the spots in his vision cleared, he realized that something was caught between the boards. A thick brown envelope—handcrafted, he realized, assembled from pieces of marbled paper. His first name was typed on the outside of the envelope in a sloping Italianate font.

He left it where it was though an urgent need to take hold of it possessed him.

He could hear the sounds of the ambulance, so he made his way back outside to wait.

Rachel jumped out, ahead of the paramedic. Her face paled at the sight of him—he must look worse than he felt. A van pulled up, dislodging members of the crime scene unit he recognized from the mosque.

He gave them a series of muddled instructions as the paramedic urged him onto a stretcher. He chafed at the interval while his vitals were taken and a painkiller was administered. The cuts at his wrists were bandaged as Rachel photographed his wrists.

Khattak frowned at the sight of her phone.

"Is that yours?" he asked, remembering now what had drawn him inside the building. He told her quickly, and she listened, appalled.

"I'd left my phone at the station. I picked it up earlier this morning."

"Same phone?"

She checked it over, going through her camera roll to make certain.

"Yes, it's my phone, sir. Why?"

Khattak struggled to answer, feeling a strange lethargy steal over his limbs. He was finding it hard to focus. He looked at the paramedic and asked him in labored French, "What did you give me?"

"A sedative. You need it."

Alarm widening his eyes, he struggled to make Rachel understand. About her phone. About the mural. About the envelope pinned to the window.

She tried to hush him, to urge him to lie down, but there was something he needed to tell her. He could only manage one word. "Sehr."

He didn't know if he'd made himself understood before he was claimed by sleep.

When he woke, he wasn't at the hospital. He was back in his hotel room lying under the covers on his bed. The curtains on his window were open—it was late in the day; a sleepy twilight had settled over the lake, the clouds tumbling in low dark clusters reflected in the water.

A beautiful, heartbreaking view. He couldn't remember how he'd gotten here. When he tried to sit up, the pain at the back of his head made itself known—a sharp-edged block that weighed him down.

"Esa, please don't move."

It was Sehr's voice, the desperate concern in it a balm for his troubled thoughts. She was still in Saint-Isidore. He'd been afraid that she'd left—frightened off by the Wolf Allegiance or angry at him for having given her so little of his time.

She knelt beside him on the bed, helping to raise him up. She held a glass of water to his lips and urged him gently to drink. Her soft russet hair fell against his face and he took a startled breath, inhaling the subtle scent of her, feeling pleasure break over him in waves.

Her voice shaky, she said, "Your mother is terribly worried."

His eyes sought hers, a question in them.

"I didn't tell her. Someone leaked it to the press, so I called to reassure her. Ruksh flew in to make sure their doctors knew what they were doing."

Trying to inject a note of humor into the situation, he asked, "And did they?"

"You'll be fine," Sehr told him. "But this is your second concussion, so you'll need to take things easy for a while. It's time to let Rachel take the lead."

She was still sitting very close to him, her scent all around him, her skin soft and cool where she was holding his hand. He set the glass aside and kissed her, measuring her ardent response.

She drew back after a moment. "None of that, either. I told you, you're supposed to rest."

When she made to move off the bed, he caught her wrist. He didn't want to waste another moment, no matter what the circumstances were. If he stayed at Community Policing, his work would always be between them. Sehr had been holding back, giving him time to make certain that this was what he wanted. He hadn't known how to convince her of his desire to move forward, given their time apart. Now he knew he needed to be bolder. His willingness to be patient had only deepened her doubts.

He kissed her again lightly. "Marry me, Sehr," he urged her now. "Don't leave me again."

She freed herself from his hold, going to stand at the window and looking out.

"Ruksh is here. And Rachel. They're waiting in the lobby."

"They're not you, Sehr. Don't you know the difference?"

She smiled at him over her shoulder, and the sweetness of the smile made the tension in his head subside. She wasn't going to leave. She'd come to Saint-Isidore to stay.

"Do you have an answer for me?" A hopeful note entered his voice.

She swung around to face him.

"Do you have a ring for me?" she teased.

Elation lit his eyes, transforming the bleakness of his expression. His self-restraint vanished.

"Come here, Sehr."

She acquiesced, letting him take her in his arms, reaching up to hold him close, her fingertips delicately exploring the contours of his skull. But when she heard the rasp of his breath, she slid through his arms like silk, pulling a chair up to the bed.

"I'm not an invalid," he warned.

"I can see that." That teasing note was still in her voice, sending tremors of delight through his veins.

"Then come back to me."

"I shouldn't be with you in your room."

It was the only thing she could have said to reawaken his sense of propriety—of boundaries they both observed. She laughed a little when he groaned, and an answering smile lit his eyes.

"Then you'd better marry me quickly, hadn't you?"

She took his hand in hers, tracing the outline of his stitches. His pulse pounded beneath the careful touch.

"God, Sehr, this is torture."

"No," she said huskily. "Torture is when you vanish without a word. It's watching Rachel call you and you not answering your phone. It's finding out she's called an ambulance because something terrible has happened." She blinked the tears from her lashes. "I'm used to waiting for you, Esa. That doesn't mean I hate it any less."

Fear stabbed through his thoughts. Sehr had often protested the dangerous nature of his work. It was one of the reasons he was reconsidering his job.

"Do you want me to stop what I'm doing? Do you want me to leave this job?" His grave eyes were steady on hers.

Sehr drew a shaky breath, the sound tearing at his defenses. She reached forward to take his face in her hands—hands that were slender and strong.

"You've been asleep most of the day," she said. "So you don't know what's happened. You don't know about the leak of the footage or the way that everything's changed—the way they're looking at us now." She brushed his lips with hers, whispering the words into his mouth. "So no, Esa. I don't want you to stop. I want you to save us all."

43

Late in the day, Rachel, Gaffney, and Benoit sat at the desk in Lemaire's office. He'd given up his office to them so they'd have complete privacy to examine the material from the envelope Khattak had found. Lemaire himself had a more imperative concern. Despite his warnings to the contrary, someone on the inside had leaked the footage of the woman in the abaya to Pascal Richard. Richard had not only made the footage available through his blog; he'd made it the only subject on his program. As a predictable result, the tenor of the national response to the shooting had altered, yielding to a firestorm of hate. Lemaire was stuck in meetings addressing this latest crisis.

A set of photographs were spread across the desk. They were copies. The originals, along with the envelope they'd been in, were at the lab. Rachel had insisted on receiving copies of the photographs, disturbed by Lemaire's admission about the infiltration of the Sûreté by elements of the far right.

The investigation was plagued with additional leaks that made their job much harder. Who was to say that the envelope wouldn't be made to mysteriously disappear? She'd logged it into evidence herself, making sure both Gaffney and Benoit were in attendance.

Now they studied the photographs together. Benoit's eager desire to please was palpable, whereas Gaffney was merely thoughtful, making observations about the type of lens used and the framing of each photograph, laying out the context clues.

His ability to be so calm secretly infuriated Rachel, whose stomach was a twisted mass of worry and suspicion. She'd been popping anti-acid pills to keep a lid on her emotions. She and Khattak had had some bad moments in the past—she expected them as part of her job. But the photographs presented a new and unknown form of menace. She'd waited for Lemaire to act, to respond to Khattak's suggestion regarding the profiler, and when he hadn't she'd made the decision herself, putting a call through to Superintendent Killiam to get the help she needed. And reiterating to Killiam her theories on Lemaire's reluctance to act.

They'd never had an investigation dissolve into shambles like this. They needed immediate course correction, so Rachel had plunged ahead.

"Two years," Gaffney said upon a thorough examination of the photographs.

Rachel frowned at him, a signal to elaborate.

"As best as I can tell, the photographs go back two years. Khattak will have to confirm it, of course, but I'd say that's pretty close."

Rachel swallowed. Hard.

Each photograph on the table depicted a moment in Khattak's life—taken without his awareness. They weren't photographs of his public life, the press conferences he'd given, the accounts of the resolution of various CPS cases—nor even of the Drayton inquiry that had been reported so widely in the press. The photographs were personal, deeply intimate, prying into the corners of Khattak's private life, a grossly personal intrusion.

Many were moments Rachel recognized, moments she had been a part of.

She ran them down one by one, explaining them to the others.

A photograph of Khattak at a bus station. He was standing on the steps of the bus looking down at a young woman wearing a loose black head scarf, sadness and regret in his eyes. The photograph had been taken in Esfahān, a city in Iran.

A photograph of Khattak exiting a mosque in Izmir with a young Syrian man at his side, his face calm and reassuring, his hand gripping the young man's shoulder.

A photograph of Khattak and Sehr on a terrace behind a small Greek hotel, clasped in an intimate embrace.

A photograph of Khattak at his father's clinic in Toronto, taken with a long lens through a window. In the photograph, Khattak was holding a bundle of letters in his hand.

There were other photographs, too. Khattak poised on the edge of the Scarborough Bluffs, rain streaking his face, as he made an impassioned plea. There were also deeply disturbing close-ups taken of the people who mattered most to Khattak. His mother, Angeza Khattak. His sisters, Ruksh and Misbah. His oldest friend, Nathan Clare, and Nathan's younger sister, Audrey.

But there were three photographs on the table that disturbed Rachel more than all the rest.

One was of herself. She was lying on the ice at Algonquin Park as Khattak tried to resuscitate her, anguish distorting his features. The second photograph showed Rachel recovered from her near drowning, Khattak's arms wrapped around her, a poignant relief on his face. She swallowed at the sight of it, at this proof of how much he valued her—of what he was prepared to risk for her, just as she'd been so frantic to rescue him last night. Blinking back furious tears, she pushed the photograph away.

It was the third and final photograph of the group that sent a chill down Rachel's spine.

It was a photograph of Sehr taken when Sehr was alone. But not at her office in Toronto or near the duplex she owned just north of the downtown core.

The photograph had been taken on Lesvos, Greece. Sehr was at the Mytilene airport waiting for a flight to come home. Four days ago she'd been in Greece.

And someone had been following her there.

When Lemaire finally walked into the room, Rachel was brooding over two of the photographs with an expression of deep abstraction. They were the ones of Rachel held fiercely in Khattak's embrace.

Lemaire's eyebrows shot up, but he didn't share his thoughts. Instead, he told her about his appointment at Pascal Richard's station.

"We need to take immediate action. We have to find out who leaked the footage to Richard."

"I'm coming with you to the studio."

She gathered up the photographs, rattling off her theories about the attack on Khattak all the way to the car.

"There are two very clear-cut possibilities here. One, it could be that the Allegiance has had its sights on Khattak for some time. They lured him to that building to work him over, maybe as a warning. Maybe the shooting at the mosque was meant to draw him to Québec."

Though Lemaire didn't agree, he waited for the rest.

"Two. The incidents are unconnected. What happened in Saint-Isidore is connected to the angle you've been working. The infiltration of politics and law enforcement by white supremacist organizations. The photographs left for Inspector Khattak—the assault on his person—they represent something else. Something twisted and frankly terrifying. The Wolf Allegiance logo was just a smoke screen to throw us off the scent."

Lemaire glanced over at her. Though her summary encompassed two equally drastic scenarios, she couldn't hide her enthusiasm and interest. She loved police work, no matter how dark its parameters.

She caught him looking and was genuinely puzzled.

"What?"

He looked at her a little longer, then cleared his throat before he answered.

"Where do you allot the text messages? To the first scenario, or the second?"

Gaffney and Benoit had thus far been unable to dig up anything on the origin of the messages. They'd stripped Khattak's loaner phone of its delivery applications, trying to force his correspondent into another means of contact.

Rachel tipped her head to one side, her ponytail swinging across her cheek. Lemaire reached over and brushed her hair from her face.

A stilted silence fell between them. Rachel inhaled sharply, speaking with a catch in her breath.

"I'm convinced the text messages belong to the second scenario. The photographs go back too far—they suggest a long and disturbing fascination with my boss. It feels like the shooting here was incidental to those pictures—just one more thing they recorded about his life."

"Why lure him to the warehouse then? Why harm him but leave him alive? We've pulled no forensic evidence from the scene. The wall he told us about—the window where the envelope was found. They have only his fingerprints. He talked about a sign near the door. There's no sign there. No chair in the room, no mural on the wall."

She paused, thinking it through for herself. Another ten minutes passed before they reached Pascal Richard's studio, where Lemaire had made an appointment. Rachel wondered if Richard had summoned a lawyer to attend. Whatever she and Lemaire put to Richard now would be broadcast on tomorrow morning's program, making the interview trickier than most.

She charged a little ahead in her eagerness, reaching the entrance to the studio first. Lemaire caught her up, detaining her with a hand on her elbow.

"You didn't answer my question."

Turning back to look at him, she tackled his question head on.

"Doesn't the fact that the scene didn't match Inspector Khattak's description of it make things seem more ominous? To me it seems like someone was playing with him—making him think it was about the Allegiance when in fact it wasn't? And you have to admit that this seems far beyond the capabilities of Maxime's gang of thugs. So maybe whoever took these pictures knew where their home base was, and was devious enough to make use of it." She shifted the packet of photographs, checking to make sure they were secure in her pocket. He knew she'd requested a second set because she didn't trust his team.

"There's a possibility you haven't considered yet, Rachel. Maybe there was no mural. No chair in the room, no flashlight on the floor, no footsteps in the dust. We didn't find evidence of any of these things."

Rachel's thick eyebrows shot up. "You're saying he was hallucinating?"

"I'm saying your partner may have his own reasons for painting this scenario. It's no secret that he's been a vocal critic of the failures of policing when it comes to minority communities."

Rachel took a step back. She opened and closed her mouth without speaking. Gold flints of rage set fire to her eyes.

In a furious voice, she gritted, "You think my boss made this up? That he manufactured his injuries and sold you a pack of lies to get himself some publicity? Did you *see* him?"

"It isn't impossible for the injuries he sustained to have been self-inflicted. In fact, it's rather easy."

Rachel's fury at Lemaire reached such a peak that he let go of her arm.

"You don't see anything but race, do you? If you're not *pure laine,* you're inferior."

He made a quick gesture of surrender, holding up his hands.

"No, no, Rachel. That's not why. You're misinterpreting my motives."

"I'd say they're pretty clear. I doubt you'd accuse a member of the Sûreté of such a reprehensible offense."

Lemaire's response derailed her.

"Inspector Khattak said he hadn't touched the envelope that was stuck between the boards. He waited for the crime scene unit to take possession—isn't that correct?"

Rachel gave him a wary nod. "So?"

Lemaire sighed heavily. "The only fingerprints found on the envelope *and* on the photographs are his."

"*What?*"

"It's true."

Rachel chewed her lip, her mind working furiously.

"He was unconscious for some time," she pointed out. "No reason whoever attacked him couldn't have pressed his fingers to the contents of the envelope without him being aware of it."

"Why would they?" he asked simply.

"To create this doubt in your mind." She fingered the tight knot of her ponytail. "To distract you from the matter at hand. It's pretty consistent, actually." She nodded to herself, convinced of her conclusion. "Just like the footage from the camera. The woman fleeing the scene in an abaya. It's intended as a distraction, to keep us from tracking these crimes to their source. It hides what's really been happening here in Saint-Isidore."

"And what is that, Rachel?"

She watched him flinch from the judgment in her eyes.

"You know the answer to that. Because you're part of the problem."

44

Lemaire knocked on Richard's door. The radio host was alone, unencumbered by a legal representative who would have hamstrung the interview before it could begin. He waved them both to a chair and took his own seat, rocking back in it, flushed and genial with triumph. His program on the footage had been a coup. He'd called it "Twisted Sister" after the woman in the abaya, and supporters of the Allegiance had jammed his lines.

Rachel couldn't begin to imagine how dispirited the families of the dead were feeling now—how shocked they must be by the news that a woman wearing an abaya had fled the crime scene with a gun.

Lemaire glared across the desk at Richard, not bothering with small talk.

"Who was the leak, Richard?"

Richard grinned at Rachel. "Maybe it was the pretty lady at your side."

Lemaire didn't take the bait, waiting Richard out.

Rachel did the same. She'd swallowed her anger at Lemaire's allegations against Khattak and now she radiated patience—a dullness that was designed to set Pascal Richard at ease.

"I'm afraid I can't tell you, Christian," Richard said easily. "As a journalist, I must protect my sources."

"A journalist is supposed to present the facts. That's not how I would characterize the elements of your show."

Richard leaned forward, addressing himself to Rachel.

"My duty is to the citizens of this province. They have a right to be informed of jihadists in their midst—a right to defend themselves, if necessary."

Rachel palmed her notebook and unhurriedly rifled through its pages, until she found the spot where she'd summarized Khattak's comments on his interview with Richard.

"Oh, I completely agree, sir." Her tone was warm and confidential. "But I'm seeing here that when Inspector Khattak spoke to you about the shooting and suggested that the Wolf Allegiance might be behind the shooting at the mosque, you called them 'disenfranchised young men who've been bearing the burden of reverse racism for too long.' Were those your words?"

His chest swelling, Richard affirmed, "I stand by them."

Now Rachel pinned him with her gaze. "So if a white man shot up the mosque, he'd be a disenfranchised youth, whereas if a Muslim woman did it, she'd be a jihadist? Is that right?"

Richard's eyes narrowed. He spluttered a little. "That's not what I said, Sergeant."

Rachel stared at her notebook, pretending confusion.

"You just said that you did. I'm a little curious. Do the people of Québec have the right to be informed of neo-Nazis in their midst?"

Pascal's jaw snapped shut. "You're using the wrong term. The young men of the Wolf Allegiance are not Nazis—they should be called the alt-right. Or white nationalists, if you will."

Quite amiably, Rachel responded, "I won't. I think when you're advocating the removal of a group of people by violent means and when you throw around the term 'white genocide' it's pretty safe to assume we're talking about white supremacists and to call them neo-Nazis." She lowered her voice, mock confiding. "Some of them are actual Nazis. They even have swastika tattoos."

Lemaire followed this up. "You had callers cheering on the shooting today, Richard. The families haven't even had the chance to bury their dead. You have a responsibility as a public broadcaster."

Richard was unfazed. He lit a cigarette without asking them if they minded that he smoked. Rachel got up and opened the window that opened on to the lake. She stood there for several minutes, breathing in the fresh air. She was tempted to walk out onto the terrace.

It wasn't the cigarette smoke she found polluting. It was Richard himself.

"The CRTC hasn't revoked my license. And they would be in the best position to know. Federalists, aren't they?" he said, with a knowing little smile. He'd referred to the Canadian Radio-television and Telecommunications Commission and the standards that broadcasters were required to adhere to.

"I've been monitoring the comments section on your blog. I've no doubt you'll be getting a call from the commission quite soon."

But Richard was undaunted by the warning, his complacency at odds with the precariousness of his position. He blew smoke in Lemaire's face, a gleam of smugness in his eyes.

"Your assault on freedom of expression is most pernicious. You're playing fast and loose with Québec's most sacred values. I can assure you that no amount of religious accommodation will permit you to silence voices of dissent. The people of this province will not stand for it. And after all, there is no relevant law you can hold up as a shield."

"There's the Criminal Code, which has specific provisions against inciting hate," Lemaire rebutted. "As federal legislation, it's more than enough."

Richard's oily grin settled on his lips again.

"No one is inciting genocide here. All we are asking for is a little peace and a little space to live our lives as Québécois. I assure you that no one of consequence will stand in the way of these goals."

Rachel watched Lemaire's brows draw together. He would be wondering who had given Pascal Richard such assurances. The radio bosses for whom he made money? Members of the CRTC? Or the same well-connected politicians who had handed Richard the key to the city? It had the whiff of corruption about it.

Richard stubbed his cigarette out in an expensive crystal ashtray, piled with smoldering butts. He eyed Lemaire with cool insolence. The interview had taken place in English, but now he spoke in French, using well-worn familiar phrases that argued that he and Richard belonged to the same club, the same exclusive group of Québécois *de souche*, where anyone else was a latecomer whose presence simply encroached. And clearly, Rachel was one of those outsiders, because Richard didn't know she spoke French.

The whole thing sickened her. There was a pervasive rot emanating from the corridors of influence and power in this town. If Lemaire was the new broom in town, he needed to sweep it clean. She listened as he took Richard exhaustively through his alibi, finding the holes in it, opening up the possibility that Richard had had enough time to get to the mosque and back without anyone noticing his disappearance.

Angrily, Richard brought his hand down on his desk, just missing the crystal ashtray where the embers of his cigarette still smoldered.

"It's a goddamned Muslim woman. An ISIS bride in niqab. You tried to keep that under wraps, but now everyone in the country knows. Including your precious mosque-goers. You can't put the lid back on the box."

"There's another box, I'm afraid," Lemaire countered. "And I'm quite confident that you would fit within it given the holes in your alibi."

"Aren't you listening, you moron? It. Was. A. Woman. It was one of *them*. It might even have been that little filly Alizah. The one who has Maxime all twisted up in knots."

Lemaire rose to his feet, summoning Rachel with a glance.

"Shall you tell him or shall I?"

Rachel grinned. "You have the floor. I'd hate to interrupt."

Lemaire brought his face within inches of Richard, ignoring his stale, narcotic breath.

"We've done an analysis of the footage. Height, weight, size, length of stride. It's just as probable that the fugitive fleeing the scene was a man."

Richard began to sputter. Christian Lemaire cut him short.

"And don't you realize, Pascal? Anyone can disguise themselves by wearing a niqab. It's no different from a mask. That was the same argument you made when you pushed for the Code of Conduct."

But no matter how hard they pressed him, Richard refused to confirm how he'd gotten the footage.

———

In the parking lot, Rachel gave Lemaire a spontaneous high five anyway.

"It's not every day you catch a Nazi flat-footed."

His mouth had curved into a smile, but at Rachel's words the smile froze on his lips.

"Richard is a serious shit disturber, but I wouldn't call him a Nazi."

A strange expression flitted across Rachel's face. A kind of pity tempered with softness.

"You know when I got up to open the window?"

He nodded, holding himself still.

"It wasn't for the fresh air. I noticed the way he kept scratching the back of his head, and then wincing each time he did it."

"So?" Lemaire leaned against the car, boxing Rachel in with his body. She didn't back off from the proximity.

"I had a look at the back of his head when he scratched at it again." She pulled out the little notebook and flipped it open to show him.

"He'd pulled his collar loose. He had a tattoo on the back of his neck—still a bit red and puffy. Have a good look at it, sir."

"Lemaire," he reminded her absently, squinting at the drawing of the tattoo.

It was of the man with the wolf head. On his chest, a swastika in black.

Lemaire's phone rang. He put it on speaker so Rachel could hear Philippe Benoit's report. Benoit had been assigned to monitoring online chatter about Richard's program, including the comments section on his blog.

"*Patron,* we have another problem," he said now.

"What is it?"

"The Muslims are refusing to pray at the mosque. They say they don't feel safe."

Lemaire shrugged. "Okay. So they stay at home. We're stretched too thin as it is, so why is that a problem?"

"Because Père Étienne has offered them the church. They're hold-ing a ceremony there."

Lemaire swore quietly to himself. Rachel's bright eyes focused on his face.

"Is that public knowledge?"

"I'm afraid so. The Muslim group on campus put the word out. Now members of Thibault's chat room are talking about 'taking back the church.'"

"*Merde.* Put me through to the mayor. And get Clément to meet me at the church."

But Benoit informed him that Clément was in Montreal and he swore out loud again at the news.

Rachel signaled him silently. He covered the phone with his hand. "What?"

"If he's well enough to come, Inspector Khattak should be there."

Lemaire shook his head in dismissal, but Rachel wasn't done.

"Trust me. In a volatile situation like this, you need his presence."

He conveyed the message to Benoit. Then he asked, "Where is Diana Shehadeh? What is her role in all of this?"

He and Rachel waited while Benoit conferred with another mem-ber of the team.

"She's gone back to Ottawa. To brief the prime minister on the Mus-lim community's concerns."

It was Rachel's turn to swear. Their murder investigation was turn-ing into a circus, and Lemaire was clearly losing track of its various threads. With Khattak out of commission, he needed to arrange for personnel at the church.

"*Patron,*" Benoit stopped Lemaire from hanging up. "There's one more thing."

Lemaire shifted a little to draw Rachel closer to the phone. She didn't protest, leaning into him slightly.

"Spit it out, Benoit. I need to get to the church."

"Uh . . . did you request that a profiler join our team at head-quarters?"

"A profiler?"

Rachel started to fidget as Lemaire's hot blue gaze settled on her face.

Benoit sounded as nervous as she felt.

"Her name is Marlyse Sandston. She's waiting for you in your office."

Lemaire ended the call just as Rachel opened her mouth to speak. She needed to explain that the incident with Khattak had sent her instincts into overdrive. But Lemaire dismissed her apology with a shrug.

"I'll drop you off at the station. If this profiler is any good, fill me in on what she says."

Given his easy acceptance, Rachel gave in without a fight.

45

Saint-Isidore-du-Lac Events Page
[Translated from the French]

Statement of the Town Council of Saint-Isidore-du-Lac:

We are grieving and in shock today. We condemn this terrorist attack on a peaceful community targeted in their place of worship. Diversity is a strength of our society and religious tolerance is a cornerstone of that strength. An act of senseless violence such as this has no place in our cities, our communities, or our nation. No one should have to lose their life because of who they are or where they may have come from. This holds true with regard to race, color, sexual orientation, and religious beliefs. Our prayers are with the families who grieve and with all the people of Saint-Isidore. Let us work together to ensure that we never face a day like this again.

COMMENTS

Anon1: Targeted by THEIR OWN.

Anon2: ISIS Barbie! How will you spin this now?

CMorin: THIS WAS A MUSLIM!!! Stop blaming innocent Québécois, stop making statements before you know your facts!!!

ABM: Nothing is the same in Québec. What we were, what we held dear, all of that is gone. One of us had to fight back.

MarioM: ISIS attacks again and yet our PM fails to recognize that Islam is a major threat to our democracy . . . you want more muslim migration, you get more violence.

LiseM: Hypocrite Trudeau . . . did not cry for our murdered soldiers.

ABM: Does not cry for our sons. Will not look after our daughters.

Anon3: Religion of peace attacked by its peaceful congregation might need help to follow the ins and outs of this story.

AlizahS: The police have not confirmed who the shooter or shooters are. This is horrifying speculation causing more pain to the wounded.

JoJoR: Cry me a river JihadiBarbie.

SherylG: Liberal agenda won't work on me. GET RID OF ISLAM IN CANADA.

MareilleA: A woman in an abaya was the shooter? You don't say! What about this Town Council statement now! Take it down at once!

Anon4: Probably Shiite vs Sunni will be my guess can't live with each other over there now trying to do the same thing here.

MarcW: This was friendly fire!

Anon4: Muslims are the problem everywhere in the world. We need to stop being PC.

MarcW: Welcome to the New World Order. They're making sectarian violence commonplace in the West.

Anon5: Never thought to see the day. KEEP THEM OUT!!!

Anon1: Oh don't worry, they'll say it was a white man under that niqab, and the true believers will be on board faster than you can say "Allah Akbar."

RobbieM: They're keeping the statement up when they know it was one of their own, the story will be buried overnight, but if it was a white Christian Québécois the coverage would be wall-to-wall.

MimiL: Good old Canada—wow, we took in a bunch of migrants from countries that sponsor terrorism—who'd ever have guessed things would turn out like this?

Anon4: LMAO.

DDarveau: This is a beautiful town with very kind people who live here, many of whom are praying for the dead and for the families of the dead. But reading these comments I'm ashamed of this town and of all of you.

MFish: No apology from me. This is a wake-up call to our sleeping government. For Chrissake, open your eyes!

ABM: No one's ever cared about our humanity before. If we don't stand up for who we are as Québécois, if we don't think about the future of our daughters, we'll vanish from the pages of history.

AlizahS: Does murdering innocent people in a mosque count as standing up for Québécois identity? Should that be recorded in our history?

ABM: Who said they were innocent?

AlizahS: Your comments are appalling. What crime were they guilty of?

ABM: The same one you are with Max. I shouldn't have to say it.

RGrenier: I'm sorry our government let the Muslim Brotherhood into this country, along with every other terrorist group. Trudeau is a traitor for defending this fascist hate and for bringing those who hate Canadians into our country. Ban them and get him out.

MonaS: Ignorance and intolerance will keep us at war with each other. None of us should go down that path.

EdieQ: Muslims execute Christians everywhere—have you forgotten

(continued...)

ISIS? And now you want us to cry over a handful of people in a mosque? Let them cry over me first.

MarcW: It's called getting ready.

BobbieS: It's called getting even.

AlizahS: Requesting the moderator to shut down the comments section before it comes to the attention of the families of those who were murdered.

MarcW: And now the Nazis are coming after our free speech.

AlizahS: Out of all the comments here, mine is the one that makes you think of Nazis? I hope you recover the spark of your humanity. We're still burying our dead.

46

Esa escorted Sehr into the church, where she quickly became engaged with a group of volunteers who were reorganizing the space to allow for the mosque's congregation to pray. He'd wanted her to wait at the hotel, but like his sister Ruksh, she wouldn't allow her independence to be compromised by his fears. His sister had hugged him close after clearing him to return to duty with the warning that he needed to take more care.

"I can't be the responsible one who keeps tabs on Misbah and looks after Mum. You're not allowed to do anything that takes you out of the running as the caretaker of our family."

She said it with a hint of her old acerbity, but he paid closer attention to the way she was holding on to him, seeking familiar reassurance. He thanked her for coming out to see him and promised not to venture into danger without Rachel at his back.

"When Rachel told you what had happened, you gave her a tongue-lashing, didn't you?" he said to Ruksh.

Smiling, she admitted she'd tried. "But she headed me off. She'd blamed herself a thousand different ways before I got here."

To those who made assumptions about gender roles in his community, he wished they could see the women in his life, his fiercest guardians.

Smiling a little, he sought out Père Étienne in the church's elegant sacristy.

The priest's eyes widened in alarm as he caught sight of Esa's injuries.

"My son, what happened to you?"

Esa strove to set him at ease. His voice had grown hoarse in the short time he'd spent speaking with his sister, and now his throat had begun to ache.

"It was an eventful night, but I'm fine." He hesitated, conscious of the crowd gathering in the church and of the curious glances aimed in their direction. "I need to speak with you, Père Étienne. Is there a place where we could have a little privacy?"

Doubtfully, Père Étienne indicated the confessional. Esa readily agreed, though he hoped that the seal of confession would not remind the priest of his reasons for keeping silent.

A sense of comfort washed over him as Père Étienne joined him in the confessional. He found himself bowing his head, leaning against the little screen, feeling the warmth and safety of the tiny booth enclose him. He felt a lifetime removed from the violence that had been visited on the mosque, and he offered his own quick prayer in the dark.

"How can I help you, my son?"

"Père Étienne, I know being at the mosque after the shooting was traumatic for you; I've tried to give you some time. But you must see from recent events that an ugliness has been set loose."

The priest's disembodied voice floated through the screen, trembling and full of self-doubt.

"That is the ugliness inside the human heart, my son. It exists everywhere, not just in Saint-Isidore-du-Lac."

Khattak couldn't argue with that. But he wouldn't let himself be distracted.

"You went to the mosque that night for a reason, didn't you, Père Étienne? You entered the prayer hall with your shoes still on because you felt the urgent need to give a warning. But you were a little too late. Why did you give that warning?" His voice rasped in his throat, its timbre deep and attractive. "What do you know, Père Étienne?"

There was a long silence from the other side of the screen.

Needing to push him, Esa said, "What happened at the mosque could happen again today—at the church. You have a duty to speak, Father."

"You're asking me to break the seal of the confessional. I have a greater obligation than the one I owe to you. I must stand by my calling."

"Must you?" Esa probed softly. "Will you answer for the dead at the mosque? Will you answer if others are harmed at prayer today?"

A sob sounded through the screen.

Hearing it, Esa relented. He'd have to find another way.

"Père Étienne, will you let me speak? I'll tell you what I think happened, and if I'm right, all you have to do is hold your peace. Your vows remain intact, while you enable me to fulfill my duty to protect the public."

"Very well."

Esa inhaled the scent of cedar in the booth, quickly gathering his thoughts.

"The flyer I found in your office—groups like the Allegiance often identify with their Christian heritage. The Nazis did, as well." He heard the sharp intake of breath from the other side of the screen. He hurried on before Père Étienne could change his mind. "In Québec, of course, religious identity is more complicated because of Québec's history with the church. Would you say it's safe to say that there are generations who have been disillusioned by the church's abuse of privilege?"

Reluctantly, Père Étienne answered, "Though we are working to win back the people's trust, I cannot disagree."

Sensing a little homily to the church was about to ensue, Esa cut him off.

"Groups like the Wolf Allegiance, though, define themselves in opposition to anyone who can't be categorized as Québécois *de souche*."

"I don't understand you, my son."

Khattak clarified his point with care. "I'm saying they're drawn back to the church as a means of establishing their superiority to others—they would see Christians as inherently superior to others such as Muslims and Jews. One of the first things Inspector Lemaire told me when I arrived here was that the synagogue was vandalized first."

Mon Dieu.

Very gently, Khattak finished, "So when members of the Allegiance came to you to confess, you may have thought they were returning to the Catholic faith as a means of showing their repentance. When in fact, the church is a foundational aspect of their supremacy. Père Étienne, I'm so sorry. But they've used you, they've used the church, as a means of harming others."

He heard the rustle of Père Étienne's garments, heard him take in a shattered breath.

"I think you knew this, Père Étienne. That's why the flyer was in your office. You may have asked someone in the group—Maxime Thibault, possibly—for an explanation. You may have counseled members of the group to desist. Because you knew, didn't you? You knew they were committing hate crimes. The pig's head at the door of the mosque, the shattered windows of the synagogue. The swastikas spray-painted in the parking lots. That's why you founded your interfaith group. That's why you began to make your presence felt at the mosque. Because you know that in time hate expands to affect us all."

Khattak paused. His chest was hurting; his throat was numb—he wondered if he should continue. But he thought of Youssef Soufiane; he thought of Amadou and Alizah and everything she'd faced when her sister had been murdered—he thought of the children he and Sehr might raise in a fractured nation one day.

And he made himself go on.

"When you reprimanded them—perhaps in the same confessional where I'm speaking to you now—one of them let it slip. One of them told you they were planning an attack on the mosque. Perhaps you thought you'd dissuaded them, perhaps you only put the pieces together later that same night—and that's why you were at the mosque. You went there to warn the imam. But you also went there to stop someone—perhaps you thought your presence there would force them to reconsider. But it didn't, did it, Père Étienne? And they haven't come back to confess."

A comprehensive silence fell in the little booth. Khattak felt weightless in the dark for a moment, disoriented by the absence of stimuli. His head was throbbing, but he knew he was almost there. He had to

get to the end. He had to induce Père Étienne to speak. Now, and
again later on the stand.

He pressed his face against the screen, stretching the bruised ten-
dons of his neck.

"Who was it, Père Étienne? Who made that confession to you? Was
it Maxime Thibault?"

The silence persisted. Then the priest's hand came up and slid the
screen closed. A long, slow creak indicated that he had exited from
the confessional. When Khattak opened his own door, he was blinded
for a moment by the vibrant warmth in the church. His eyes dazzled
by it, he stumbled forward a step.

A strong arm was there to catch him and set him right.

Amadou whispered his concern. Esa patted his shoulder. His vision
cleared and Alizah was standing on his other side, pain and dread in
her eyes.

"What happened to you, Esa? You look like you've been attacked."

He meant to reassure her, to reassure them both, to promise them
a safety he knew was out of reach. But he couldn't stop himself from
saying, "The same thing that happened here. The thing that will keep
happening now that lines have been drawn. We won't be on the inside again . . . perhaps we never truly were."

Tears filled Amadou's eyes. They glistened like diamonds on his
skin.

"No, brother, don't say that. You of all people—don't say that."

He held up his index finger and pointed it at the sky. He placed his
other hand over his heart.

"Don't tell us that this marks us. Don't take away our hope."

A hot rush of shame swept through Esa's body. Ignoring the ache
in his shoulder, he reached over to pull Amadou into his arms.

"Forgive me, Amadou. Both of you, forgive me."

Alizah's eyes made a desperate appeal—wanting something from
him . . . the same things Amadou wanted . . . comfort, encouragement, belief in a future of safety and belonging. Then she seemed to
change her mind, tilting up her head.

"Amadou," she chided. "Look at what he's been through. Give him a little time." Her eyes swept over the church, lingering on those who'd come to offer their support by joining the Muslim prayer. "We're meant to bear each other up through times like these." With a note of humility, she added, "We did our best with our program today. But we weren't looking to take them on. We were trying to speak to our own."

And he remembered his last day in Waverley, when he hadn't known if he'd failed or succeeded in solving Miraj's murder and Alizah had turned to Rachel and said, *This one will take everything to heart. Hold him so he doesn't shatter.*

She was looking at him now with that same compassion in her eyes. She could be strong for him when he couldn't be. She didn't judge his weakness. Even when things in Waverley had turned out as they had, she'd made him believe the work he was doing mattered. Her faith in him had carried him through things he'd thought he couldn't bear. A man dead at his hands. The loss of those he loved. The dishonoring of his name upon a national stage. And still she'd continued to write him, offering him her belief. He could see it now in her eyes, and he made himself acknowledge the truth.

He loved her.

In some way, he had always loved her. For the faith she had shown in him and the connection she had done her best to keep alive. And then for accepting without protest when the time had come to let go.

She blinked in surprise at the look on his face, jewel-bright tears in her eyes. She pressed her fingers to her lips, a gesture that struck him as a loss.

He knew now why he'd never forgotten her, why he'd given up writing to her with a sorrow he'd never expressed. The loss she'd suffered had changed her, yet her inner belief was undimmed.

And he couldn't fathom how the man she'd loved had thought to look past her to another.

But then love was never made to order—one could spend a lifetime unraveling its mysteries. He was still finding it hard to believe that Sehr had forgiven him his blindness.

The sound of the organ swelled through the nave, the grace notes

of the "Song of Farewell" offered as a counterpoint to Amadou's recitation of the call to prayer.

No accompaniment to the music could have been as profound.

Esa's gaze traveled round the church. He caught sight of Sehr, whose
entrance he had missed. He smiled at her, but when Alizah followed
his gaze and gave Sehr a little wave, Sehr didn't smile back, her eyes
dark as she turned her face away.

Startled, Esa made his excuses. He'd caused Sehr too much misery
to leave her in any doubt about Alizah.

Sehr was his future. He had closed the door on the past.

47

ÉLISE DOUCET'S BLOG
[Translated from the French]

ÉLISE DOUCET
Montréal, Québec

ÉLISE DOUCET: I have no words for how appalled I am that our priest gave up our church to these infidels. Look what they did with it.

ROY GRENIER: More proof they didn't come to fit in. They came to take over our sacred institutions.

EDITH SAUCIER: That black boy. The murderer. He gave their voodoo call INSIDE THE CHURCH!!!

ROY GRENIER: They get everything their way.

ÉLISE DOUCET: Not for long. Not if we speak in one voice, like we did for the Code of Conduct.

ROY GRENIER: We got nowhere with the Charter of Values.

ÉLISE DOUCET: That was just a battle . . . this is the real fight.

PLOUFFEPLOUFFE: Goddamn right. We need to come out and say it; we need the Charter of Values, we need the Code of Conduct, and we need Bill 62. We need laws that represent our values. I'm not going to apologize for having superior values. The Rest Of Canada knows it.

ÉLISE DOUCET: It's *not* that Québec is racist; it's that Québec is right.

PLOUFFEPLOUFFE: Funny how the world follows white culture while refusing to accept that we have the right to protect it.

EDITH SAUCIER: Ha-ha, ROC. White is right. White is might.

ÉLISE DOUCET: There's plenty in the Rest Of Canada who think so, too. They're just hog-tied by the liberals.

EDITH SAUCIER: Père Étienne giving in to Sharia law. What a nightmare.

ROY GRENIER: It's not our land anymore. It's Sharia for all of Canada. Watch for No-Go Zones.

ÉLISE DOUCET: Then do something to fight back.

RONNYP: What would you suggest we do?

ÉLISE DOUCET: Organize. Join one of our groups.

PLOUFFEPLOUFFE: Like?

ÉLISE DOUCET: That should be obvious to you.

PLOUFFEPLOUFFE: I like the young Wolves in the Allegiance. They're the future of Québec.

ÉLISE DOUCET: We *all* need to be Wolves. Unless we're willing to give away more than just our church.

EDITH SAUCIER: I heard the black boy was after our girls.

ABEAUTIFULMERCY: It's not just him. It's all of them. We should be taking action.

ROY GRENIER: I don't care if that makes me sound racist, that's not something we need. There's such a thing as too much assimilation.

(continued...)

CANDLELIGHTVIGIL: I don't care what religion someone chooses to believe in. No one should have to die while they're peacefully praying.

ÉLISE DOUCET: All the more reason why they should have stayed out of our church. And out of Saint-Isidore.

ABEAUTIFULMERCY: They'll figure it out too late.

48

Rachel met Dr. Marlyse Sandston in Christian Lemaire's office. A soberly dressed black woman in her forties, she was seated at the desk and invited Rachel to join her. Slightly intimidated by the doctor's professionalism, Rachel sank down into a chair.

"Thank you for coming on board," she said. "We've been needing your help. We should have asked for a profiler the minute the case came to us."

Rachel passed over the stack of photographs from the envelope. She waited with her arms braced against the desk.

Dr. Sandston studied them for some time. Then she raised her head. "Are any of the photographs more intimate than these?"

Rachel frowned. "Uh—not that I've seen."

"That may rule out a sexual fixation, but it's possible that there will be others that *are* more personal in nature. Whoever took these photographs may be hoarding others. And there may come a time when photographs we haven't seen yet are delivered to Inspector Khattak, at a moment designed to cause maximum harm—personally *and* professionally."

Rachel mumbled her response. "He's not exactly a player, Dr. Sandston. He had his wife. Now he has Sehr Ghilzai."

Marlyse's analytical glance seemed to dissect Rachel's unspoken thoughts. "Every man has his secrets. His amours . . . his private vices."

Awkwardly, Rachel said, "Inspector Khattak is a practicing Muslim."

Marlyse Sandston looked at her pityingly.

"Religion isn't a shield against our needs. I don't want to disillusion you about your boss, but you need to be open to the idea that he may have reasons to keep his own counsel." She pointed to one of the photographs. "This one, for example. What does it say to you?"

Rachel followed the other woman's gaze. Panic swooped through her stomach.

The photograph was new.

It hadn't been among the others.

And it wasn't a copy, like the ones she'd kept in her possession. This one was an original. Someone had been close enough to Rachel to add the photograph to her collection.

The question wasn't when or how. The question was who could have done it?

She shot a panicked glance around the common area—to Gaff and Benoit chatting in one corner. But Benoit had never had access to the photographs. The only part he'd played had been to act as a witness to the transmission of the chain of evidence.

Then who? Who else had access to Christian Lemaire's office?

Marlyse Sandston was still waiting for Rachel's reaction to the photograph. Trying to recover her poise, Rachel took a closer look at it.

It was a photograph of Khattak and Alizah. Though it was a close-up, there were noticeable details in the background. The photograph had been taken at night. There was a blur of movement behind their stationary figures—light glinting off trampled cellophane, the dark shape of an oak tree, and people scattering to the four winds in a panic. And behind Alizah off to one side, the back of a polo shirt marked with the words STOP THE ISLAMIZATION OF QUÉBEC.

Rachel absorbed the details without speaking.

"This was taken the night of the vigil." She struggled to explain, trying to ignore the sense that she owed the other woman an apology. "Events spiraled out of control when members of the Allegiance showed up."

"Yet not so out of control whoever was following Inspector Khattak didn't have time to take this photograph without getting caught."

"Meaning it's someone who blends in?" Rachel asked.

Dr. Sandston tapped the photograph impatiently.

"Look at it, Rachel," she said. "Tell me what you see."

This time Rachel focused on Khattak and Alizah. They were so closely attuned to each other's presence that Rachel was worried.

"Yes." Dr. Sandston was nodding. "You see it, too. Inspector Khattak's pursuer—for want of a better word—isn't taking random photographs. They understand the relationships in his life. They know who's important to him. They might even understand those relationships better than he does himself." Her razor-sharp gaze pinned Rachel. "Is this Sehr Ghilzai?"

Deeply reluctant to admit it, Rachel shook her head.

"Look at the way he's looking at her. And the way she's looking back at him."

"It's not sexual," Rachel flared.

Dr. Sandston cut her off.

"No? But then it doesn't have to be. It's extremely intimate. You can see that she means a great deal to him. But if you look at his body language—" One beautifully manicured fingernail tapped a section of the photograph. Khattak's fists were clenched at his sides, the lines of his face taut with tension. He was poised between a step back and a half-step forward. Moving closer to Alizah. And yet if he'd moved to touch her, the photograph didn't bear witness to the act.

"Who is she?" the profiler asked.

Uncomfortably, Rachel offered, "Her name is Alizah Siddiqui. She's a student at the college here. But we know her from one of our cases. She's become a friend to us both."

Dr. Sandston's beautiful eyes were not inquisitive. She was making a sober assessment. "Was she a witness in your case?"

God, Rachel thought. Dr. Sandston's questions were so penetrating that she would have come in handy during their interview of Pascal Richard.

"She's the sister of a murder victim. We solved her sister's murder."

Something in Dr. Sandston's expression shifted. Her shoulders relaxed and her voice became pensive.

"Then that could explain the intimacy," she said.

Suddenly she smiled, and her smile was so brilliant that she became more than just a colleague who was weighing Rachel's every word.

"You're saying you misread things?"

Dr. Sandston seemed to sense her relief.

"I'm offering you possible interpretations of this photograph based on information you've shared. Nothing more, nothing less."

Rachel stayed quiet.

Sighing, Dr. Sandston continued, "Your faith in your partner is encouraging. It gives me something to work with. If he's the man you believe him to be, he may not have those kinds of secrets to expose." She studied the picture of Khattak and Alizah. "There *are* other kinds of love."

Rachel struggled to make sense of Dr. Sandston's assessment.

"I'm not sure what you mean."

Dr. Sandston rearranged the photographs on the desk, singling out two from the rest.

"That's you with Inspector Khattak, isn't it?"

Rachel wiped the sweat from her forehead, feeling like an insect on a pin.

"Th-they're from another case," she stammered. "He saved me from drowning that night."

"Have you looked at his expression?"

Rachel had no need to. The image of herself in Khattak's arms and the devastation on his face were seared behind her eyes.

"I can see why you defend him; it's obvious that you share a deeper connection than most partners."

Rachel set her chin. "It's not out of line. And it's definitely not personal. We just make an excellent team."

But if Khattak wanted to leave that team, what did that mean for her?

"I wasn't suggesting it was." Dr. Sandston's reply was mild. "I was simply trying to draw your attention to two important points."

Rachel settled back in her chair and crossed her arms. It was a mimicking of her father's unassailable posture. She hoped it made her look strong.

"What points?"

Dr. Sandston arranged the photographs in a particular order. She'd left out the photographs of individuals and included only those that indicated a personal relationship.

"The person who took these photographs has been studying Inspector Khattak for months, if not years. He or she understands him very well. They understand that personal connection is the thing he values most."

Rachel eyed the photographs again. It was a disturbing conclusion. How could someone on the outside—or on the periphery of Khattak's life—understand him so well when Rachel was still in the process of figuring out the things he chose to keep to himself?

"So you're saying it's *not* a stranger. It's someone who's close to him."

Dr. Sandston inclined her head. "That's the likeliest possibility."

"There's another?"

"It could be an extremely astute individual displaying elements of psychopathy."

"Oh, that's definitely better."

Rachel wasn't sure if she was joking. She felt a little bit like the good doctor had just cut her open to examine her insides without offering an anesthetic first.

She backtracked over their conversation, trying to pin something down.

"You said there were two points about these photographs—what's the second one?"

Dr. Sandston's response was inescapably gentle.

"You've said your partnership isn't personal. Perhaps because there's something about developing close relationships that scares you."

Rachel had a sudden sinking feeling that Dr. Sandston knew everything there was to know about her father, Superintendent Don Getty. He'd cast a long shadow in her life until she had carved out her own career. And there were times she still measured herself against him—against the approval that had always been impossible to attain.

But Dr. Sandston showed Rachel the photograph of herself in Khattak's arms again.

"Out of all these photographs, Rachel, this one is the rawest. This one suggests that there is no one else like you in the inspector's life. Your partnership *is* personal. You matter to each other." She smiled at Rachel. "That's *why* you make an excellent team."

Rachel sat there dumbfounded. She couldn't think of anything to say.

Though the photographs represented one of the worst nights of her life, she had wanted to keep them for herself.

Now at last, she knew why.

Marlyse Sandston continued to study the photographs, this time focusing on individuals other than Khattak. She singled one out and slid it across to Rachel.

"Who's this?"

Her expression was enigmatic.

Rachel hadn't noticed it before. It was a photograph of Tom Paley, the war crimes historian who had recruited Esa and Rachel to the Christopher Drayton case, the first case of national significance that she had worked with Khattak. The Drayton investigation had led to a parliamentary inquiry that had for a time compromised their unit's reputation. Paley had been a professional associate of Khattak's rather than a friend—his photograph was strangely out of place among the others.

Frowning, Rachel explained in some detail about the Christopher Drayton case. All the while, Dr. Sandston was nodding softly to herself.

"So Tom Paley has passed away," she said. "Yet when it comes to the dead, there aren't any photos of Inspector Khattak's father or his wife."

Rachel frowned. "What are you getting at, Dr. Sandston?"

"My job is to look for patterns. But there's no pattern here. This photograph is an anomaly. It doesn't belong with the rest. It was included deliberately to point us to something important."

"Tom Paley *was* important to the case," Rachel said doubtfully.

"But not quite as personally to Inspector Khattak."

Though Rachel was puzzled by this observation, she experienced a pinprick of awareness. Like a cat laying back its ears, intuition prickled along her spine. It raged into life when Dr. Sandston asked, "How did Tom Paley die?"

"From a heart attack."

The two women looked at each other in silence.

Marlyse Sandston picked up the photograph and held it up to the light. She considered the other photographs again.

Finally, she said, "No. I don't think he did. Whoever is following Inspector Khattak has been doing more than taking these pictures."

49

This time the cordon the police formed was for the protection of the people inside the church. Members of the Allegiance had shown up but didn't speak. They held up a phalanx of signs, each more ominous than the next. Maxime Thibault was at the head of the group, but like the others he was quiet, casting his mordant glare over anyone who exited the church.

The members of the group were dressed in black. The front row was made up of university students who looked like recruits setting off for boot camp. Behind them was a group of the town's residents—mothers, fathers, grandparents, teenagers, and children. Families from all walks of life. The only commonality was that all the residents were white.

The professional placards they carried must have been printed in the last few hours. Instead of the Allegiance's traditional slogans, they bore the words TAKE BACK OUR CHURCH.

Khattak, Lemaire, and Rachel were standing on the steps, watching the demonstration. Khattak frowned to himself. A reporter who was setting up an interview was framing Thibault as an anti-Muslim activist. This was a new phrase in the common parlance, and to Khattak it was a cause for urgent apprehension. He considered the size of the crowd. Thibault must have warned the members of his group to take no action that would precipitate removal. This time the Allegiance relied on silent intimidation.

Rage burned through Esa's thoughts. He pushed it down, seeing Pascal in the crowd. He was watching him, waiting for him to break.

He held on. But Amadou came up behind him and spoke despairingly to the crowd.

"You know our prayers can't hurt you."

A corrosive little smile settled on Maxime's lips. It was the opening he'd hoped for.

"ISIS might disagree!" He shouted the words, playing to his audience. "Don't they pray for our destruction?"

Khattak put a hand on Amadou's arm. He bent to the young man's ear.

"Get out of here. Don't provoke them. Don't start anything that could hurt the people who came to pray."

He'd given the same instructions to the churchgoers who'd come out to pray with the members of the mosque.

I know you mean well, he'd said to them. *But you won't pay the price of trouble.*

The words had a sobering effect. When the prayer ended, the group dispersed without delay. A few stragglers lingered on the steps, filming the members of the Wolf Allegiance on their phones.

Khattak scanned the crowd again. His gaze stopped on a presence wearing a long black jacket with a hood. Was it one of the Lilies of Anjou? Something about the figure's movement looked familiar.

Rachel sidled up to him, whispering in his ear.

"Are you okay, sir?"

He looked at her, surprised. She sounded more than a little afraid. But he was safe now, unharmed, and if someone in the Allegiance had been behind his assault they'd find that out soon enough. He nodded at her, but he didn't feel up to offering verbal reassurance.

When he turned back to the crowd, the figure in the jacket was gone. He scanned the streets, the parked cars, and the path through the woods to the lake.

Whoever had been standing there had vanished.

Three young women were at the periphery of the crowd, their arms linked in solidarity.

But with whom? The angry young men of the Allegiance, or the worshipers who pushed their children past the protest, sheltered under their arms. The girl in the middle—Réjeanne Beaudoin—was staring right at him.

"This was a mistake," Lemaire said under his breath.

Khattak agreed. "You should have shut down the protest."

Lemaire let out a curse. "I meant the prayer in the church. It's a lightning rod, wait and see. It could burn this whole town down."

"The shooting already did that."

Lemaire shook his head, unable to accept his point of view. Khattak understood. It was Lemaire's responsibility to ensure safe and peaceful assembly, not Khattak's. But Lemaire's concept of safety was conflated with stability. The stability that arose from having given in to the demands of the Allegiance. Freedom of expression balanced against freedom of religion, in the starkest display of privilege Khattak had ever seen.

And he knew that at a fundamental level the police's reluctance to act was emboldening the Allegiance, while those who had just seen their loved ones murdered were running in fear from the church.

"We're not fighting the Crusades, Khattak," Lemaire muttered.

"If the church is the battleground you say it is, I think some of these protesters might be. Ask yourself what it is that they're protesting."

"The use of the church . . ." Lemaire's voice trailed off as Khattak shook his head.

"Not the church, Lemaire. It's never about the church."

He couldn't pin Lemaire down—he didn't know why the other man had come so often to Saint-Isidore without taking decisive action. Rachel had relayed her conversation about a sting operation inside the Sûreté, but Khattak still had his suspicions.

If Lemaire was part of the infiltration of civic and law enforcement institutions by white supremacist elements, that was exactly the story he would have fed to Rachel, who seemed more than willing to be convinced.

"Sir." Rachel gave a discreet nod. Khattak looked over at the Lilies of Anjou.

Réjeanne Beaudoin was trying to attract their notice with a subtle motion of her hand.

Khattak nodded at her. The reporter was fully engaged with Maxime Thibault now. Khattak descended the steps, despite the hand that Lemaire placed on his shoulder to restrain him.

Ignoring Thibault, Khattak said something softly to the reporter.

The reporter shook his head, refusing to listen.

Khattak tried again.

"The shooting is the *only* story here."

The reporter flashed a saucy smile. There was something ugly in it, something complicit. He was clearly taken with Thibault.

"I know my audience, Inspector." He grinned widely at Thibault. "Believe me, the story is here."

50

A scuffle broke out in the crowd. An older woman in an abaya had been blocked from descending the steps by a knot of protesters.

"It's the Twisted Sister!" they shouted.

A stream of other insults followed.

"ISIS killer!"

"Stone the shooter!"

"Send the ISIS bitch back where she came from."

A group of young men from the mosque broke through the knot to form a circle around the frightened woman. A high-pitched whistle pierced the noise. Police officers moved in between the two groups of young men. Reporters rushed to higher vantage points on the stairs, their cameras clicking furiously. A broken bottle flew through the air. It struck the woman on the head. Blood streamed down the left side of her face. A roar of anger shook the crowd. The woman was thrown to the ground, her body covered by two of the young men.

Esa and Lemaire began to fight their way through the crowd, trying to get to the woman.

The entire situation descended into chaos as others joined in the fight.

Bodies pressed up against Esa's, taking punches where they could. He used his arms to protect his face and pushed ahead. There was noise everywhere, shouts, cries, the wail of sirens, police whistles blowing, the press of suffocating bodies fueled by a rush of adrenaline.

All he could think was that the woman in the abaya was about to be trampled.

There was going to be another death to add to the toll of the shooting.

He shoved harder, dodging flying fists, but his movements felt as hopeless as a small boat battered by the pitch of monstrous waves.

He heard the crackle of static.

Then a woman's voice speaking into a megaphone.

It wasn't Rachel, it was Alizah, and her voice was frantic.

"Max!" she called into the crowd. "Max, you have to stop this."

He felt a sudden shift in the press of bodies around him, his nostrils assailed by the acrid tang of perspiration and fear. The bodies fell back a little. When he lifted his head, he could see that more members of the mosque were sheltering the woman on the ground.

He searched for Alizah on the steps. She was holding the megaphone in one hand. Her other arm was stretched out to someone in the crowd. Someone at the center of the disturbance—Maxime Thibault. He stared up at Alizah on the steps, arrested by her appeal.

Khattak watched his face: Max's expression gathered a tightly coiled intensity as he focused on Alizah. The activity around him abated, supporters waiting for his word, though skirmishes persisted on the periphery.

The way Maxime was looking at Alizah raised the hairs on the back of Esa's neck. He wanted to tell her to stand down, to step away, to find another battle to fight, because this one placed her too close to the heart of danger and loss. He shoved his way through the crowd, determined to reach her before Max did.

She spoke into the megaphone again, her soft voice thick with tears. She gestured at the woman on the ground.

"Please, Max, I'm begging you. You're the only one who can make this stop."

Maxime nodded curtly. He gave an abrupt signal with his arm. A hush fell over the crowd. Members of the Allegiance began to run, this time away from the police. Their straggling supporters were taken into custody. A few members of the mosque who'd gotten caught up in scuffles were also led to police vans. A little at a time, the crowd began to disperse, the noise and pressure easing in their wake. The woman in the abaya was helped to an ambulance. Police blocked the attempts of reporters to intercept her.

The shrewd reporter who'd spoken to Thibault earlier hurried back up the steps.

"Who is she?" he asked Max breathlessly.

Thibault and Alizah were still looking at each other—their faces distorted mirrors of each other, reflections of hope and despair.

"Fuck off," was Thibault's response.

Khattak reached Alizah first. He wrested the megaphone from her hand and pushed her behind him, watching Thibault's approach with narrowed eyes. Thibault's eyes moved from Alizah to Khattak and back. He scowled, but Alizah ducked under Khattak's arm, refusing his protection. She reached out and took hold of Thibault's hand.

"Thank you," she said simply. "I know that wasn't easy—not in front of them."

Thibault's breath drew in harshly. He looked down at Alizah's hand as if he couldn't believe she had touched him. For a moment, he did nothing, said nothing. Then tentatively, his fingers fastened around her wrist. He held it as if his lightest touch would break it.

He looked up at Alizah, his eyes burning.

"I did it for you."

He looked back over a desolated ground. Discarded placards, broken bottles, bits of debris wielded like weapons. At Lemaire watching him grimly from the bottom of the stairs. He let go of her hand, his face unreadable and cold. He must have remembered the men who were watching him, the ones who looked to him as their leader.

"It doesn't change anything. I'm not some knight in shining armor."

Alizah moved closer to Thibault and took his face between her hands. He stood there, shocked into silence, letting her hold him in place.

She looked at him searchingly. He couldn't meet the clarity of her gaze, his eyelashes shielding his eyes.

"Just because you're not with me doesn't mean you can't be someone I respect. You were once my friend, Max. You don't have to do this. You don't have to *be* this." She indicated the scene behind him.

"Without you, they're nothing. It will dissipate and end. You could be the one to change things. The one who makes everything better."

Her low voice thrummed with passion, trying to infuse him with belief.

Khattak was unbearably moved. He knew he'd underestimated Alizah—the compassion she was capable of. He made a sound of encouragement.

Thibault's eyes flicked to Khattak. His intrusion had broken the spell between Max and Alizah. Max took a step back, freeing himself from Alizah.

He donned his former attitude like a shield, answering her with scorn. He jerked his chin at Khattak, as if accusing her of something.

"You're a whore," he told her. "So you'll forgive me for thinking, 'Why can't it be me?'"

Alizah shuddered. She'd been holding herself so tightly in Max's presence; then it felt like all the life was leaking from her body. She wanted to crumple up, far away from his hateful words. She thought she'd seen his humanity in his eyes, the warmth she'd known from him in the early days, when she'd thought of him as a friend. He'd shut the protest down because of what he'd once felt for her. But it didn't change the person he'd become. She'd been naïve to think that it would. Love, compassion, kindness—there were some kinds of evil that wouldn't bow to their power. She hated herself for having to learn that lesson again.

"That was brave of you," Esa said close to her ear.

It wasn't. People thought of her as a rebel, as someone who couldn't be hurt, when half the time it was only a front she put up against her fear. It was Miraj who had been the brave one, and it was her memory of Miraj that refused to allow Alizah to give up the fight. But Miraj's restless courage had put her in a grave.

Now this man Alizah had welcomed into the circle of her friendship when she'd first known him had called her a whore to her face. She had to act like it didn't matter, because she had been shouldering the burden of shielding the men in her life—Amadou, Youssef, even

Esa. The desperate need of others to protect her, to claim her, to own her in some small way, was fired any time she gave in to her emotions. And she didn't want to be protected. No one could protect them from what had just happened, any more than they could prevent what was still to come.

A course had been set in motion and it was ugly and dangerous and there was no turning back. There was only getting on with things. Choosing the battles she could fight on her own.

She made herself seem calm, watching as Lemaire led Maxime over to one of the vans.

"I wish I knew why Inspector Lemaire didn't shut the protest down. Why does he keep letting things spiral out of control?"

She studied the few remaining protesters. A reporter tried to approach her, but Esa turned him aside. She wished Diana were here. She wished she had a woman to talk to, someone who would help her make sense of her conflicting emotions. She and Rachel had been close once, but now she wasn't sure if Rachel would understand.

Réjeanne waved to her again from across the road. Alizah frowned. She didn't see Amadou anywhere. Had he been caught up in a scuffle? Or did the police have him? Esa hadn't answered her, and she turned to find him watching the play of emotions on her face. She didn't want to blush, but she couldn't help it.

Her voice a little brusque, she said, "Did you keep track of Amadou?"

He was still watching her, and with a flutter of embarrassment she realized that he was assessing her actions as a police officer searching for telltale clues.

She was saved from whatever he might have said by someone calling her name. Amadou—hailing her from across the road. He'd joined Réjeanne and Chloé and Émilie, and she could see that he needed her as a buffer against the others. Speaking to Esa over her shoulder, she said, "Réjeanne wants to talk to you. Let me see what she wants."

He didn't stop her. When she looked back, he was heading to the ambulance, and she knew his first concern was the woman who'd been attacked. She should have been Alizah's first concern also—but Alizah had a fine-tuned sense that events were moving too rapidly for her to wait, they were escalating . . . and her attempt to reach Maxime might have consequences she hadn't foreseen . . . consequences uglier than what they'd faced so far.

Something told her that whatever the motive behind the shooting at the mosque was, there was a small group of actors at the heart of it. Maxime. Amadou. Youssef. The Lilies of Anjou and herself.

51

When the church had emptied and the remaining officers had dispersed, Khattak had a quick conversation with Lemaire and Rachel. The young men who had been taken into custody had been quickly processed and released. Khattak questioned the wisdom of this, but Lemaire put it down to optics.

"There's no way in hell I can hold the Muslim kids, and if I don't hold them, I can't hold the Allegiance. Not with the circus in town." He gestured at the reporters.

Khattak made his voice sharp. "Are those Isabelle's instructions? Shouldn't she be dealing with this?"

"She has her hands full with the premier. But you can talk to her yourself if you like."

"I will."

He left Lemaire to his work. He'd had a few words with those members of the congregation who remained with Père Étienne. From the agonized expression on Père Étienne's face, he could see the priest had taken his words to heart. Words trembled on his lips that he couldn't bring himself to speak. And then Esa's attention was claimed by two members of the mosque who asked him to visit one of their homes and speak to their community privately. He sorted the details out and walked back outside to find Rachel.

She had been joined by Sehr, and his thoughts brightened at the sight of her. He reached out and took her hand, wondering if she would object to this public demonstration of his interest. Inwardly, he shook his head at himself. The word "interest" was too civilized to convey the depth of his emotion. Taking her hand was like claiming her, as he'd wanted to do for so long. If she pushed him away now, he didn't know what he would do.

She linked her hands with his instead, peering at his face with worried eyes. For his ears alone, she whispered, "I don't think this is what the doctor meant when she told you to rest."

His smile at her was warm, intimate, as he bent his head to hers. "As long as you don't tell Ruksh."

Sehr didn't smile back. "I mean it, Esa. I'm worried."

Instantly contrite, he tugged her closer. "I'm sorry. I did try to prevent this. In the end, I couldn't." The rest slipped out before he could think better of saying it. "Thank God Alizah was able to calm things down."

Sehr didn't say anything, but there was a curious twist to her lips.

A few steps away, Rachel cleared her throat. She had shaded her eyes with her hand and she was looking up at the sky with a frown.

"This is bloody July," she muttered. "Why are there no days without rain?" She hesitated at the sight of Khattak and Sehr, with their hands entwined and the aura of two people exclusive to each other. She was happy to see that things were back on track.

Khattak seemed to read Rachel's mood. He said something to Sehr. She frowned and drew her hand free of his, urging him to go ahead without her.

"I'd like to speak to Rachel for a moment, though."

Khattak nodded, striding across the road to join Alizah and Amadou's group.

Rachel braced herself. Growing up in Don Getty's house meant she'd spent her life learning to anticipate when emotional disturbance might erupt. Sehr was nothing like Rachel's father, yet Rachel could see she was brimming with unresolved tension.

"What is it?" she asked.

She was surprised when Sehr took her aside, under the shelter of a beech tree, drawing her arm through Rachel's. This companionable gesture was so stunning to Rachel that for a moment she lost track of her thoughts.

Sehr sounded embarrassed as she asked, "What can you tell me about Alizah?"

They both looked over at Khattak. Rachel wondered if he knew the warmth he sometimes conveyed—to both Amadou and Alizah. She did her best to explain it.

"We stay connected to the families we meet through our cases— that's part of our remit. But sometimes the families depend on us a little more than they should." She shook her head. "I can't say I blame them. We're often their only source of comfort."

The sky was darkening around them, and as she listened to Rachel, Sehr hugged her arms to her body. There was no chill in the air—just the kind of electrical pulse that gave a forewarning of lightning. She was watching Esa's dark head bent close to Alizah and Amadou, his attention fully focused on the girl.

Sehr's clear and direct gaze met Rachel's.

"So you're saying what he gives her is comfort."

Choosing her words with care, Rachel answered, "I'd call it security. I think he makes her feel safe."

Sehr nodded, as if she was considering this. Whatever Alizah was saying to Khattak, it looked like it had developed into an argument. Her face was tense and angry. Her eyes flashed and her hands were balled into fists.

"And is security all she wants?"

Rachel hesitated. Sehr trusted her. She wanted to be worthy of that trust.

"I don't know," she admitted at last. "What I do know is that Esa hasn't thought of anyone but you."

52

Rachel went over the case with Sehr. She needed a favor. And she knew Sehr's skills as a prosecutor were too valuable for her to sit around cooling her heels while Khattak wrapped up his work. She didn't want Sehr to leave. So she told her about the parts of the investigation where they had come up short and asked Sehr to do a little digging.

"I've already asked Gaff to make room for you. Just try to stay under the radar, in case Lemaire objects. You might also want to check in with the profiler—Dr. Sandston—and get her to tell us what we're looking for. We're missing something here."

She described her conversation with Marlyse Sandston but left out the bit about the photographs. That was for Khattak to share. She'd kept the photographs on her person. She hadn't had a chance to show them to Khattak, though she'd summarized her findings for him.

Now she made her way over to the Lilies of Anjou. Alizah and Amadou had split apart from the others and were speaking to each other in low voices. Rachel had an uneasy feeling that they were talking about their radio show. She made a note to keep tabs on Alizah, who had always been unpredictable when it came to taking risks.

Réjeanne was in deep discussion with Khattak, something cool and sardonic in her face as she looked Khattak over from head to toe. Rachel wondered what she was thinking, but she was distracted by Chloé tugging softly at her sleeve.

Her heart smote her at the sight of Chloé's drowning eyes, her nose and cheeks tinged red, a ball of tissues wadded in her hand.

"Do you . . . do you know anything about the funeral?"

In the press of events, Rachel had forgotten her promise about Youssef Soufiane. She apologized, promising to catch Chloé up as soon as she could. She took in the group dynamics with interest—Réjeanne confiding in Khattak, Alizah and Amadou in conference, Émilie Péladeau shifting her attention between Chloé's conversation and Alizah's. As soon as Émilie's back was turned, Rachel drew Chloé aside.

"There was something you wanted to tell me before. In the ambulance. Can you tell me what it was now?" She lowered her voice. "You said Youssef wasn't always good."

They still hadn't publicly released the information about the markings on Youssef's back. She stole another glance at Chloé's tattoo. The drawings were disturbingly alike.

Chloé cast an uncertain glance at Émilie, but Émilie was now wholly preoccupied by the sight of Amadou's proximity to Alizah.

"What I said to you earlier—well, I didn't tell you the whole truth." The rest of her face flushed as red as the tip of her nose. "Youssef and I wanted to be together. But he said he didn't want to disrespect me. He had to get his family's approval, and his family hated me. That's why we were stuck, because he refused to go against his mother, but he also didn't want to let me go."

She looked so young and helpless as she made the confession that Rachel couldn't believe she'd had the strength and conviction to face down a large, disapproving family.

"What was his mother's actual objection?"

Chloé made a self-deprecating gesture, dismissing herself with one hand. "Well . . ." Her childlike voice faltered. "There's the obvious. I'm not like Alizah or any of the other girls at the mosque. I have this tattoo." Her hands began to tear at the ball of tissue, scattering tiny fragments like snowflakes over a grave. "I wish I didn't, but it's too late to change it now. His mother said it was disgusting. She said I'd defiled myself. But the main reason is because I'm not Moroccan or Muslim. I come from a Catholic background, so I'm not what she wants for her son." A little viciously, she added, "I bet his mother is wishing she'd let him be happy now."

But as soon as she said it, Chloé's face crumpled. "That was an awful thing to say. She's right; I *am* a terrible person."

No, Rachel thought. Chloé was a young girl who'd lost someone she loved in brutal circumstances. She could be forgiven for wanting someone to blame, someone who'd made it clear that Chloé didn't measure up.

"I know she doesn't want me at the funeral, but she doesn't have the right to stop me." Now Chloé sounded tremulous and brave.

"Why not?"

Chloé's fist rubbed against her heart as though the loss of Youssef was a physical ache. The tattoo flexed on her wrist.

"Because. She's not even his real mother."

There was a park bench a few meters away. Despite the pressing threat of rain or the possibility of being interrupted by Émilie, who was keeping an eye on them, Rachel pulled Chloé over to the bench and signaled Khattak. She brought him up to speed, her heart thudding, and let him take over the questioning. Whether Chloé's information was relevant or not, it was a lead they had to explore. Even if Chloé's frankness created problems for her with her friends.

"Can you tell us what you mean, Chloé? Who is Mrs. Soufiane if she's not Youssef Soufiane's mother?"

Bowled over by Khattak's attention, Chloé stuttered her answer. "St-stepmother. She's his stepmother. Youssef's father divorced his mother and later married again. I think Mrs. Soufiane hated me because Youssef's mother gave me her blessing. But when Youssef told his family, th-that's when things got ugly."

"Where is Youssef's mother? Does she live here in Saint-Isidore?"

Chloé's eyes filmed over. Teardrops spattered her cheeks just as the rain came down. She shivered violently and Khattak suggested they retreat to the church.

But Rachel had been watching Émilie's approach. She forged ahead, despite the rain.

"Tell us, Chloé. It could be important."

Chloé drew a shaky breath, trying to compose herself. "She does. I mean, she did."

"Did she move recently?"

Chloé's mouth gaped open like a helpless, floundering child. She stared at them wide-eyed, oblivious to the rain.

"Shouldn't you already know?"

Her breath was the merest whisper.

"Youssef's mother was murdered in the basement of the mosque."

53

"Why didn't you tell us about Youssef Soufiane's mother?"

There was a note of accusation in Rachel's voice. She didn't care if Lemaire didn't like it. He should have listened to Alizah from the beginning. Their phone lines were jammed with messages of hate, siphoning off resources they could ill afford to spare. He should have rooted the hate out at its source; instead, it had flourished to the point where it had emboldened mass murder. His negligence had slowed them down; otherwise they might have uncovered the necessary connections sooner.

"Benoit can pull the victim IDs for you. You can go through them yourself. But what difference does it make? It stands to reason that there were families at the mosque. If Soufiane and his mother were there together, I wouldn't call that a red flag." Sounding aggrieved, he continued, "A father and son were killed together in the main prayer hall—how is that any different? The line you're pursuing—this family discord about Chloé Villeneuve—wouldn't it make more sense if, God forbid, Chloé had been the target?"

Rachel was forced to back down. Lemaire had drawn conclusions that were so obvious that she should have thought of them first. She was itching to correct him, but she didn't have any ammunition.

In a surly tone, she said, "It just seems odd to me. Like it's something we should pay attention to."

Lemaire gave a heavy sigh in response. She knew he didn't have time to debate with her. He'd been hung out to dry by the press for doing too little or for doing all the wrong things. The politicians were marginally happier because now they had someone else to blame.

Distracted by the sight of Khattak cornering Isabelle Clément, he gave Rachel what she wanted.

"Focus on the Lilies. That may be the connection you're looking for. Why did someone mark Soufiane with the Lilies of Anjou tattoo?"

Rachel snorted, mouthing the words *Hate crime* at him. She knew he couldn't disagree when his phone lines were jammed with supporters of the Wolf Allegiance. She watched him rub a hand through his unruly hair. But when he spoke, she could see, he wasn't entirely convinced.

"You shouldn't rule out the possibility that the shooter came from within the Muslim community. You and your boss need to prepare yourselves for what that might mean. For the impact that would have."

Rachel stood her ground. "It makes no sense that the shooter would be a member of the mosque. You're missing the pattern, sir. You're missing the question you *should* be asking."

"Which is?"

"What if these young men who consider themselves *pure laine* murdered twenty people in the name of the *fleur-de-lis*? What will *that* mean for Quebec?"

The corners of his eyes pinched tight.

Because he didn't want to face the answer.

54

In Lemaire's office, Isabelle Clément showed Esa a series of headlines. The prayer inside the church had already gained traction as an item of national news, fanned by the hyperbole that had bloomed from a single image.

The reporter who'd been at the church with Thibault had sold his photograph to all the major outlets. He'd captured the confrontation between Max and Alizah at the church. In it, Alizah was holding Max's face in her hands—they were linked by a visceral emotion.

BEAUTY AND THE BEAST screamed one headline.

BEAUTY FELLS THE BEAST was a slightly more creative take.

The one he found most disturbing stated: NEO-NAZI KNEELS FOR LOVE.

Thibault would be shamed by it in front of the other members of the Wolf Allegiance. He'd have to take some form of action to save face. His weakness made Alizah a target.

He wondered if the French-language press had attempted more circumspection.

Isabelle spared him a weary glance. "The respectable outlets have been careful. The rest are like a toss-up between Breitbart and Info-Wars. The story for them is the desecration of the church by the Muslim prayer." She must have felt the weight of Khattak's silence, because she clarified, "Their choice of words, not mine."

She tapped the monitor with a manicured fingernail, pointing to Alizah's face.

"They've found something to hinge their coverage on. Beautiful girls are news. Regardless of what they stand for. You'd better warn her about this."

He'd tried. And that was before he'd seen the coverage. But Alizah was as stubborn about her participation in this investigation as she'd been in Waverley. He'd told her she needed to fade into the background, to stay away from public gatherings. She'd coolly informed him that she'd promised to attend a vigil organized by the Lilies of Anjou. And that she'd be reporting on the vigil on her program the following morning.

The Lilies' vigil would be held at midnight in the woods, at a pre-arranged location known only to the young women. Outside of the Lilies, only Alizah and Amadou had been asked to attend.

A detail she'd given him as a reassurance. When he'd asked her why she kept up her friendship with the Lilies given their links to Thibault, her response was considered. Like Alizah, the Lilies had been drawn in before they'd known any better. She refused to cast them aside on that basis, particularly given the sincerity of their feelings for Youssef and Amadou.

When he'd told her angrily that she wasn't making his job easier, she'd studied him and said in a careful voice, *I'm a journalist, Esa. It's not my job to give you cover.*

He'd felt the weight of her censure as plainly as if she'd screamed it. But she'd only looked at him quietly, something dark and nameless in her eyes.

That she'd refused his advice was nothing new. He'd never been able to bend her to his will. Alizah's commitment to her own course was something he admired—yet despaired of in equal measure.

Realizing that Isabelle Clément was waiting for him to speak, he used Alizah's turn of phrase. "You'll need to provide some cover for our work. There are too many elements we're unable to control. The Wolf Allegiance. Pascal Richard. Alizah and Amadou's radio program."

He sensed the curiosity behind Isabelle's scrutiny.

"Surely a call to the dean of Université Marchand is all it would take to shut down a student-run program?" She gave a light shrug of her shoulders. "I wouldn't think that many people listen to it anyway."

Khattak felt the same frustration that Lemaire had expressed earlier. "We can't shut down a program that responds to the concerns of the Muslim community while allowing Richard free rein to go on stoking conspiracies." He rubbed his hand along his beard. "We need to stop whoever is leaking inside information to the press—and to Richard, specifically."

He crossed to the other side of the desk and sank into a chair. Isabelle had personalized her office. Beside her monitor was a framed photograph of a group of young people he thought might be her nephews and nieces. She kept her desk and office as neat and orderly as she kept her person—damping down her good looks with a minimum of makeup, her hair pulled back in a knot. Her charcoal blouse served to emphasize her pallor. When she caught him studying her, he quickly looked away.

They sat for a few moments in companionable silence, each preoccupied by the next task, the next thing to be done to tighten the sphere of the investigation, so that it wasn't derailed by the national reaction to the tragedy at the mosque. Or by those who were playing politics.

He decided on his next move, then asked her, "Isn't there any way you can convince the premier to shut these protests down?"

She sighed deeply, folding her hands on the desk. The nails were painted an unobtrusive rose. The tiny lines of worry at the corner of her eyes reflected the same set of tensions that had been weighing on Khattak.

She answered him with a question of her own.

"Do you think you could convince the Muslim community to hold off on public prayer? Could you stop Alizah Siddiqui from airing her program tomorrow?"

Her questions were not accusations. They reflected the weariness of someone who had to serve as the public face of tragedy without having the authority to determine a more compassionate response.

Answering his thoughts, she said, "I can make suggestions, of course, as events unfold. But though I may have the premier's ear, so do many others." Her gaze flicked over Esa with a warning. "Others whose words carry more weight than mine." Unburdening herself, she added, "They need a telegenic face for the cameras. They're not all that interested in the rest."

It wasn't offered as a complaint, yet Esa recognized the note of resignation. He'd heard it from many of his female colleagues, frustrated by unnecessary obstacles or by the difficulty they'd faced being treated with respect by the men who stood in their way. Where they should have had responsible, fair-minded partners, they'd had to learn total self-reliance.

"Do you regret giving up your career as a defense attorney?"

It was a question he'd still not had the nerve to put to Sehr, knowing he was the cause of Sehr's change in career.

Her face relaxed at the question, at the sympathy behind it.

"It was challenging in a different way, but I certainly had a great deal more freedom."

He studied the now-infamous photograph on the wall—Isabelle and Christian Lemaire in company with the mayor, awarding the key to the city to Richard.

"You're thinking it was a mistake," she said. "Probably you think this is where it began."

"I'm more curious as to what you think."

She gave him a long, level look.

"Maybe there is a deeper game than you've been made aware of."

Despite his fatigue, and the persistent headache caused by his concussion, Esa was suddenly alert. "You're saying it's all deliberate? You've been casting a lure, waiting to see who it attracts?"

She didn't answer, simply watching him. Whatever calculations she was making, she was too skilled to betray them. She must have been formidable in the courtroom.

"A dangerous game," he went on. "As it led to all of this. And now there's no action we can take because our hands are tied." He said it with an edge to his voice, stifled by their lack of progress.

He told her quickly about the midnight vigil in the woods and the potential for another confrontation. There was still a killer on the loose—and Amadou and Alizah had only raised their profiles as targets.

"If you need officers at the vigil, that is within Inspector Lemaire's purview."

Esa wasn't put off.

"It's within mine. So there *will* be a quiet police presence and the officers at the vigil will be under my direct command."

Her shoulders tensed at the words. "The vigil is just a small gathering—though I'll wait until it's over before I head back to Montreal." In a completely human gesture, she rested her head in her hands. "Just in case anything goes wrong—I'd like to help those who are suffering this loss. The premier will have to wait."

He must have shown his surprise at this admission of concern, because she frowned and sat back in her chair, shutting off her laptop in the process.

"You don't think me capable of empathy for what these families have suffered?"

"It isn't that. I know you have a job to do. I also know it can't be easy to do it." He wondered if he should try to say something more personal. "None of us have had a chance to reflect upon this tragedy, have we?"

The stern lines of her face softened.

"Any emotion *I* choose to express is seized on as a sign of weakness, whereas the prime minister is celebrated for his tears."

"I'm sorry, Isabelle."

"Why? You, at least, have spoken to me with respect." Her expression lightened. "A little angry sometimes, *non*? But then, I have also been angry at you."

He was astonished when she reached across the desk to briefly clasp his hand.

"*We* didn't make this mess. But we are the ones who will have to clean it up. I'm willing to act on your suggestions."

Khattak didn't think twice. He told her about his private meeting with the families, and he asked her to invite Diana Shehadeh to speak at the press conference she had scheduled for the morning, as a gesture of goodwill and a means of restoring trust.

They discussed the fact that the woman in the abaya who had been injured during the confrontation at the church had scarcely merited a mention next to the drama played out between Alizah and Maxime.

"Ah, God. What a world. You have my word that tomorrow's conference will not echo the disaster of the others." She made a small moue of distaste, unaware that it pursed her lips in a smoothly seductive gesture. "We can no longer afford to speak without betraying our humanity."

Esa smiled at her, encouraged.

"No," he agreed. "Perhaps that's the one thing we *can't* be faulted for."

When Lemaire popped his head in the door to check on how they were getting along, he was greeted by an atmosphere of collegial respect.

Muttering under his breath, he said, "The only good thing to have come out of this." He waved at them to continue and disappeared. Khattak ran over a few more points with Isabelle before excusing himself.

55

On his way out the door, the phone in the inside pocket of his jacket rang. It was a new phone Gaffney had given him. He palmed it, checking the incoming message with only half his attention. He was looking for Rachel. Réjeanne Beaudoin had invited them both to the vigil, waiting for his reaction with mocking self-assurance. When he'd demurred, citing the pressures of the investigation, a spark of amusement had warmed her eyes.

I thought you wanted to solve this, she'd said. *You might find something at the vigil that you've been chasing your tail to find.*

He'd given his usual stiff warning. *Mademoiselle Beaudoin, if you know something of relevance to this investigation, you have a duty to speak.*

She'd smiled more widely, displaying a piercing on her tongue. Brushing off his warning, she'd said something that reminded him of his conversation with Isabelle.

Isn't it time you gentlemen listened to a woman for once?

And as he had with Père Étienne, he wondered what Réjeanne might know.

A shock thrilled through him as he made sense of the message that had just appeared on his phone.

Going to the vigil, Inspector? With all those officers present, you won't see the forest for the trees.

He looked back at the door he'd just closed. The place where he'd reviewed his plans for the officers in attendance at the vigil. The first time he'd done so out loud. The door to Lemaire's office, occupied by Isabelle Clément—the two most senior individuals associated with INSET. Which meant it was more than a leak. To have overheard that conversation in Christian Lemaire's office *as it had occurred* meant that someone had set up surveillance on Lemaire.

He called Gaffney over, and Constable Benoit trailed behind him like an eager and hopeful puppy. Gaffney sent Benoit out to gather the equipment that would allow him to carry out a sweep. Privately, once Isabelle had left. When they were alone, he told Khattak, "You might as well hang on to the phone. It won't make any difference how many times you switch it out as long as you hold on to the same number. Unless you'd rather change it?"

Esa shook his head. There was a value to receiving the texts—no matter how careful the sender of the messages was, each new message betrayed their familiarity with some aspect of the operation. In time, they were bound to make a mistake.

He'd speak to the profiler next. The messages might assist her in creating the profile. He knew she'd been given one of the offices, but they hadn't yet crossed paths.

He was working out a plan in his mind. He'd share it with Lemaire alone. They finally had something they could use to flush out whoever was leaking inside information. Gaffney had already conducted three spot checks on team computers and cell phones; none had turned up anything incriminating.

They weren't dealing with an amateur. Whoever the leak was, he or she was a trained and capable team member who up until now had been several steps ahead.

Gaff reclaimed his attention with a short summary of his conclusions. "The leak and any possible surveillance may not be connected to the messages you've been sent. Even if they are, it's unlikely they have anything to do with the shooting. Right now, we still don't know what we're dealing with. Or who."

"What about the Wolf Allegiance? Has anything broken online?"

Gaff coughed loudly as another officer approached. At the hard look in Gaff's blue eyes, the officer sidestepped and doubled back.

"Plenty," he told Khattak. "All in response to that photograph in the news. They've been piling on Thibault, telling him to step aside. It sounds like an insurrection. He's responded by doubling down with some commentary about the girl. Do you want to see a sample?"

"Give me the gist of it."

"Rape threats, death threats, run-of-the-mill stuff for these guys."

Esa exhaled sharply. He should have assigned Rachel to the sole duty of Alizah's protection. He was impelled by a new sense of urgency—of something transpiring just beyond his grasp—connected to his brief kidnapping and assault? He couldn't be sure. But he could read Gaffney's apprehension.

"That's not why you brought this up."

"Some new stuff, too. Threats of an acid attack. And someone who very specifically promised to finish the work of the shooter."

Benoit approached with an eager smile and a large black bag in his hand. Gaffney waved him off, ignoring his crestfallen response.

"His online name is broadswordben. He says the shooter missed the target the first time around."

"Alizah?" Khattak asked with a sharp spike of concern.

Gaffney nodded. "Not just Alizah," he warned.

"Then who?"

"If broadswordben is to be believed, the target was Amadou Duchon."

Khattak's eyes sought out Rachel, who was at another desk with Lemaire. He made a quick decision as she took the call.

"Send a transcript of that chat log to Rachel's phone. If the Wolf Allegiance *was* behind the attack on the mosque, we need to put this on alert. We need to reach Amadou and Alizah before the Allegiance makes good on its threats."

He read the telltale hesitation in Gaffney's eyes.

"What else?"

The INSET team was on rotation. As new officers crowded into the station, Gaffney ducked into one of the unused offices with Khattak. He brought up the chat log on his phone.

"Something else you should see. Two things, really."

He showed Khattak the photograph that hadn't made the front pages of the main news outlets but was being bandied about between members of the Allegiance with derisive references to the woman whose face was covered in blood from the attack.

It was an utterly callous response to human suffering and pain.

Khattak focused his thoughts until his response was coldly analytical.

"Track them down," he told Gaffney. "There's enough for an incitement charge here." Gaffney nodded, scrolling farther through the chat.

"There may be more to this than we thought. I've been looking at more than the Allegiance, trying to get the mood of the town from various blogs and online sites. You need to look at threats against Duchon specifically."

Khattak was impatient. Amadou had told him this himself already. Amadou's rejection of Émilie had stoked the fires of racial hatred, a scenario in which Amadou couldn't win. He would be targeted as much for rejecting Émilie as he would have been for becoming involved.

But that wasn't what Gaffney showed him.

His hands slick with sweat, Khattak passed the phone back to Gaff.

"They're saying the mosque attack was an operational failure?"

Gaffney nodded.

"What background do you have on Amadou Duchon? Did they target him for reasons beyond the obvious?"

Gaff jerked his head at Rachel, busy at her own desk, scowling as she sorted through a stack of papers.

"Rachel's going through it now."

56

WOLF ALLEGIANCE CHAT ROOM
[Translated from the French]

SUBJECT: BLACK DOG
CLOSED GROUP

BROADSWORDBEN: TIMING WAS OFF.

FLAYALLTHEPLAYERS: MISSED THE TARGET.

BROADSWORDBEN: TARGET BLACK DOG.

DEATHMETALSTRIKE: EVERYTHING ELSE GRAVY.

FLAYALLTHEPLAYERS: MISSED MAX'S BITCH.

BROADSWORDBEN: STILL TIME. GAGNON'S LIEUTENANTS IN PLAY.

FLAYALLTHEPLAYERS: SHOULDN'T HAVE DOUBLE-CROSSED THEM.

MAXIMUMDAMAGE: WTF YOU TALKING ABOUT?

BROADSWORDBEN: DUCHON DICKFACE CROSSED GAGNON. SCRAMBLED UP HERE TO LAY LOW . . . WE LET GAGNON KNOW.

MAXIMUMDAMAGE: GAGNON'S FUCKING DEAD.

BROADSWORDBEN: GANG NEVER FORGETS. NEXT THEY HIT YOUR GIRL.

MAXIMUMDAMAGE: THEY NEED TO FUCKING KEEP AWAY.

BROADSWORDBEN: CAN'T PROTECT ALIZAH ON YOUR KNEES.

YOU NEED TO GET THE FUCK OUT.

(continued...)

MAXIMUMDAMAGE: WHO HAS THE HIT OUT ON DUCHON?

BROADSWORDBEN: I'M NOT TELLING YOU SHIT.

MAXIMUMDAMAGE: IS THERE A HIT ON ALIZAH?

BROADSWORDBEN: FUCK OFF.

FLAYALLTHEPLAYERS: FUCK OFF.

DEATHMETALSTRIKE: FUCK OFF AND DIE.

57

Rachel was still busy with Lemaire, so Esa switched course, making an effort to find the profiler—Dr. Sandston. One of Lemaire's officers directed him to the office at the back. As he moved through the cubicles and subgroups, he noticed conversations trailing off as he passed.

He ignored them, tapping on Dr. Sandston's door. She called to him to come in, but he stopped short when he saw Sehr seated at another desk in the room making notes on a legal pad, her laptop open before her. When she looked up at him, a smile of such sweetness broke over her face that for a moment he couldn't remember why he'd come.

He introduced himself to Dr. Sandston before saying to Sehr, "I wasn't expecting to find you here."

She answered his unasked question by showing him what she was working on.

"I'll have something for you on Amadou's background soon. Did you want privacy for your conversation?"

Troubled, Khattak wasn't certain how to answer. Someone senior must have authorized Sehr's access. If he pushed her out of the investigation, as he very much wanted to, he might alienate her with what she would view as condescension. If he didn't, their personal relationship might compromise it in some way. He was aware of Dr. Sandston's appraisal of their interaction and wondered what judgments she might be forming. Though he hadn't seen them yet, Rachel had told him about the photographs.

Hesitating, he deferred to Dr. Sandston. She invited them both to join her at her desk. She was making a clinical evaluation of his fitness for work, he thought, giving nothing away herself. Rachel had spoken highly of her insights. It reminded him that both he and Rachel had urged that a profiler join the team at the first opportunity, whereas Christian Lemaire had held back, setting back the progress of their time-sensitive investigation, a hindering that almost seemed deliberate.

Khattak realized that he was taking Lemaire at his word—if his ranks had been infiltrated by white supremacists, Lemaire was limiting the number of people who had access to inside knowledge.

He gave her his own summary of events and asked Sandston to share her conclusions.

With that same appraising look, she said, "We're not talking about a single profile here, Inspector Khattak."

"Please call me Esa."

She didn't make a similar offer in exchange; perhaps, like Rachel and Isabelle, she'd learned the necessity of asserting her credentials. Then again, he had no intention of calling this cool, incisive woman anything other than Dr. Sandston.

"There's more than one profile?"

"I think there are three." She listed them in those same dispassionate tones. "The attack on the women's area came first. It was conducted execution-style, at close range, with deadly and determined precision. The shooting in the main hall upstairs with a different weapon suggests something else again. Unchecked rage—a commitment to annihilation. The shooting up of the mihrab certainly suggests a personal, anti-Islam animus."

Esa noted her choice of words. *Anti-Islam,* not *anti-Muslim.* Was the distinction significant?

"And the third?"

"Your kidnapping. The messages you've received, the photographs left for you, the act of causing you physical and emotional duress. That's something else altogether."

A number of questions ran through Esa's mind, but Sehr spoke up first.

"If there were white supremacist markers at the location Esa was lured to, isn't that indicative of the same motivation behind the mosque attack? And then isn't it likely that the same individual was responsible for each of these scenarios? Esa is quite well known. Is it possible the shooting at the mosque was *designed* to bring him to a place where he would be more vulnerable?"

Though she tried to mask it, Esa heard the tremor in Sehr's voice.

"It's possible," Dr. Sandston conceded. "But it doesn't align with certain other elements of the shooting."

"The broken lights," Esa said. "The lily carved on Youssef Soufiane's back."

"Correct."

"What is your theory, then?"

Marlyse Sandston reached behind her to collect several sheets of paper from the office printer. She slid these across the desk to Khattak.

"Controlled, premeditated rage in the basement. Frenzied rage in the main hall. But then the act of marking Youssef Soufiane—controlled again." She showed them a photograph of the carving on her monitor. They both flinched from it, and her cool professionalism eased. "I'm sorry," she said. "I should have warned you. The point is, look at how the lily is carved. There are no hesitation marks, and the pattern itself is perfect—almost artistic."

Esa's stomach clenched.

"You're saying whoever carved it *practiced*."

"Yes. They were deeply familiar with the pattern. But also note that Youssef Soufiane was marked like this in the midst of chaos, while the shooter risked being discovered at any moment. Think about the discipline that would require."

Sehr shook her head, bewildered. "I know shooters like this prepare, but that's not what you're saying, is it?"

Dr. Sandston leaned forward, pointing to one of the pages on the desk. She had created a diagram of the shooting, putting events in chronological order and ending with the moment that had been captured on the security footage—the woman in the abaya looking at the camera.

"What I'm saying is that every moment of this attack was premeditated. The shooter had to consider a number of different things. Who he would kill first and by what method. How he would gain entrance. Whether he would be able to disguise himself and escape. How best he could avoid a confrontation with police." She paused, thinking over her own words. "On the whole, shootings like these are carried out by radicalized white men between the ages of twenty and forty. Shooters who fit that profile are certainly capable of planning." Her fingers traced the route on the diagram. "What they are not capable of is total self-possession in the aftermath of the event. The words 'going out in a blaze of glory' come to mind. But this shooter was able to cover his tracks completely, so much so that we don't know where to look. He also managed to implicate the targeted community."

Sandston raised her eyes to Khattak's face.

"The shooting was personal. It wasn't a random act of violence, which means—"

Khattak interrupted. He'd finally understood what she'd been trying to explain. "Which means we have to identify who the target was. Do you think it was Youssef Soufiane and his mother?"

"It may have been." She showed him the position of bodies in the main hall. "But it may have been the imam. It may also have been this father with his small son."

"Could it have been Amadou Duchon? Or Alizah Siddiqui?" He explained about the threats that had been made against them online.

A certain alertness entered her expression at his mention of Alizah. He felt Sehr straighten in her seat beside him and made an effort to keep his voice neutral.

"Of course, I can't rule it out, but if Alizah and Amadou were the targets, someone who had planned so meticulously would not have left their absence to chance."

"So what do the online threats signify, then?"

"I would say they're incidental. Not to Amadou and Alizah's well-being—to the profile of the shooter."

A little of his worry eased. "What about the link we found to biker gangs? There's now a suggestion that Amadou was on their radar, though I don't know why."

Sehr turned to look at him. "I may have found something relevant in the files."

"Tell me, Sehr."

He knew his voice was different—softer, the tone more intimate— when he spoke to Sehr, but he couldn't help that. It was why he tried to separate her from his work, a distance she was steadily erasing.

"Inspector Lemaire ran a number of successful operations against the gangs. He himself testified against key members of Gagnon's club. Just as Isabelle Clément once represented Gagnon during the course of her work as a defense attorney."

"Does that speak to the profile?" He referred the question to Dr. Sandston, who shook her head.

"A personal attack on either Lemaire or Clément would not have been staged at a mosque."

"There was something more on Amadou," Sehr said. "It's actually very sad, Esa—I thought he might have told you. Amadou's brother was a casualty of the wars between the gangs. He was killed crossing the street—a case of being in the wrong place at the wrong moment. Amadou hounded Gagnon trying to get justice for his brother. Just before Gagnon's trial, Amadou was badly beaten by one of Gagnon's goons. He escaped to Saint-Isidore-du-Lac."

Khattak went over the chat room transcript in his mind. This new information explained the references to Amadou.

If a biker gang thought Amadou Duchon had escaped their delivery of justice, the motive would have been personal indeed. And the window between Amadou's leaving the mosque and reentering it to speak with Youssef was nearly negligible. Even the most prepared shooter might have missed the target. The chat log seemed to confirm this.

Yet he couldn't simply assume that Amadou had been the target. He needed to consider other possibilities as well. If Amadou *wasn't* involved, why had the mosque been targeted? Could it have more to do with the politics involved?

Isabelle Clément and Christian Lemaire were two high-profile individuals associated with the investigation. Could the mosque have
been chosen as a target to draw either Isabelle or Lemaire—perhaps
both—back to Saint-Isidore to expose them in some manner? Suppose the shooter had known about Lemaire's efforts to root out elements of the far right in the Sûreté. Or suppose they'd thought if the
shooting could be blamed on a Muslim woman wearing a veil it would
widen support for the ban on the face veil, ensuring that the premier
would not be subject to the pressure to reconsider his position. And
Isabelle Clément was the premier's public face.

Esa knew there were holes in his logic, but his head had begun to
ache and he couldn't condense his thoughts into appropriate action.
It was time for him to reconnect with Rachel to try to find answers—
it was how they worked best.

"Could you say if the shooter was a man or a woman?" he asked at
last.

Dr. Sandston spread out her hands, but it was not an admission of
failure.

"As the shooting was orchestrated, it could easily be either. If we
found the missing handgun, that might give us a little more to work
with."

Yet despite extensive searches, the handgun had still not been found.
Which led Esa back to the question of infiltration. If the investigation had been compromised in some way—

Dr. Sandston cleared her throat. "I think we should talk about what
happened to you now, Inspector Khattak."

Khattak's response was sharp. "Because you don't believe the incidents are connected."

"Precisely." She gave Sehr a warm smile. "This is something the inspector and I should discuss on our own."

Sehr didn't take offense. She shut down her laptop and gathered up
her purse. Her hand brushed Esa's wrist and his whole body warmed
at the contact.

"I'll find us some refreshments. I have a sense this isn't done."

58

Rachel was still chatting with Lemaire when Sandston called her on her phone, asking her to bring the photographs back to her office. A little awkwardly, Rachel excused herself. A moment later, she was at Sandston's door, Philippe Benoit at her shoulder.

Bashfully, he said to Khattak, "I've got something you should look at here."

"Will you give me a moment?"

Benoit nodded eagerly. "I'll just brief Inspector Lemaire."

Rachel hustled him out of the way, closing the door behind her.

"I reckon you have another admirer there, sir. Try not to break his heart."

Khattak grinned, amused as she'd hoped by her irreverence.

Dr. Sandston pointed to a chair. When Rachel had taken her seat, she was asked to lay out the photographs on the desk.

"All of them?" A tangible note of alarm raised the register of her voice.

Marlyse Sandston gave her a chiding glance. She knew why Rachel didn't want to be around while Khattak went over the photographs. But she had to concede when Sandston said, "How can Inspector Khattak protect himself against things he doesn't know?"

Dr. Sandston arranged the photographs in a pattern. Khattak studied them with a frown. Like Rachel, his attention was fixed on the photo of Sehr in Greece. Then his lean and elegant hands touched the photographs taken in Iran and Turkey.

"He's been following me for some time."

Dr. Sandston let the assumption on gender stand.

"Yes."

"To be in Iran and Turkey at the same time as I was would have required detailed knowledge of my movements. Advance knowledge, as it's difficult to arrange the visa to Iran."

"Yes," Sandston said again.

"Yet he had me at his mercy and took no further action."

"He's taken further action." Sandston's reply confirmed Rachel's own thoughts. "The text messages—the taunts. He's trying to rattle you, to push you into making a careless mistake."

Rachel's chin jutted out. "Because he wants Inspector Khattak off the case. He knows it's just a matter of time before we figure out the shooting."

But even as she said it, she knew it was wrong, a fact confirmed for her by Dr. Sandston's swift shake of her head.

Rachel pretended not to notice when Khattak slid the pictures from Algonquin toward him. He fell quiet and neither woman interrupted his perusal of that evening at the lake.

"A terrible night."

He didn't elaborate. But then with a snap of anger in his voice, he added, "For someone else to have been there, yet refuse to offer their help . . . Rachel nearly died that night."

Dr. Sandston stayed silent as he turned to look at Rachel. She made an effort to meet his gaze, her face uncomfortably flushed.

"I appreciate that you saved me, sir."

She watched him swallow, unused to seeing him so defenseless.

"You saved *me*, Rachel. I thought you knew that by now."

She let that sink in, a ball of warmth settling somewhere deep in her chest.

Her blush deepened as she met Dr. Sandston's probing gaze. She remembered the other woman's words.

There are many kinds of love, Rachel.

Khattak broke the ensuing silence.

"Are these photographs threats? To my family—to Sehr and Rachel?" His fingertips lingered on the photograph of himself with Alizah.

Marlyse Sandston nodded. "Quite clearly. To anyone you care about."

"You're concerned about escalation." Frowning, he pulled the photograph of Tom Paley aside from the others.

"If this was a case of stalking, escalation *would* be at the forefront of my mind."

She reached across the desk for the photograph of Paley and held it up to the light.

"It's not?" Khattak sounded puzzled.

"I'm afraid not."

Rachel knew where this was headed. She bit back a sound of protest.

From Khattak's impatience, she could see that he thought Dr. Sandston was deliberately holding back. Whereas Rachel knew the doctor was simply gathering herself to tell him.

"It can't be a case of escalation, if it begins with murder."

Khattak looked at her, shocked.

She touched the photograph of Paley.

"Sergeant Getty told me that your former colleague Tom Paley died of natural causes—of a heart attack. But we need to consider *why* Paley's photograph was left for you with the others. And whether the person who took these photos has been acting to harm you from the start."

59

Esa found Philippe Benoit in conference with Lemaire.

"Join us," Lemaire said, shoving a chair at Esa with his boot.

"Anything?" Esa rubbed the back of his head. The ache was growing sharper and more persistent. "Constable Benoit wanted to show me something."

Abashed at being the focus of their interest, Benoit's freckled skin acquired a tinge of pink. His Adam's apple bobbed up and down. But despite his nervousness, he gave a concise summary of his report. He'd been tasked with the long, hard slog of going through Richard's radio broadcasts over a period spanning two years. What he'd found was an interview Richard had conducted after Saint-Isidore's Code of Conduct had passed. Richard had invited a man named Stéphane Marchand onto his show.

Khattak didn't know the name. He didn't remember it from his review of key members of the Allegiance.

"He wasn't a member of the Wolf Allegiance," Benoit clarified. "Marchand and another man by the name of Jean Roussel were two of Michel Gagnon's chief lieutenants. They were both brought up on a manslaughter charge for the killing of Bilal Duchon—Amadou Duchon's brother. But Bilal Duchon's killing was accidental—he wasn't the target; he was caught in the cross fire. Roussel was convicted of the crime, but Stéphane Marchand had an alibi."

Khattak's eyes widened. So they were back to Amadou's brother. Could Amadou have been the reason Marchand had accepted Richard's invitation to come to Saint-Isidore? He followed this up with Lemaire.

"Why would Richard have hosted Marchand on his radio show? Surely not to speak about the killing of Bilal Duchon. I'm guessing Marchand would want that safely buried in the past."

Benoit placed his large hands on his knees and squeezed.

"No, Inspector Khattak, you're quite right. Marchand was invited onto Richard's show to speak about the Code of Conduct. His appearance here had nothing to do with Duchon."

"Why would a lieutenant of Gagnon's be invited to Saint-Isidore to speak?"

Benoit was red eared in his eagerness to get his story out.

"There was a fundraising campaign aimed at raising the profile of the Code of Conduct. Stéphane Marchand was the driving force behind that campaign. And as you know, Richard himself was the one who called for the Code from the start."

Khattak thought this over. It was clear that Benoit was suggesting Pascal Richard was their man. He glanced at Lemaire, who'd crossed his arms over his chest, his head tipped back and his eyes half-closed, mulling his own private thoughts.

Esa couldn't stop himself from saying it.

"What price the key to the city now?"

To his surprise, Lemaire grinned. "So you're not always as polite. You know how to throw a punch." He nodded at Benoit. "Continue, please."

"The reason the charge against Marchand didn't stick in the Bilal Duchon case was not only because of his alibi. Marchand is known to move guns and drugs for Gagnon. But there's not a single firearm registered in his own name."

"He keeps his hands clean," Khattak noted.

"More than that," Lemaire concluded. "He's a natural conduit for an unregistered gun."

Which meant that Richard could have obtained access to the weapon used in the shooting.

Khattak drove himself to his next meeting, overriding Rachel's protests. He'd convinced her not to leave Sehr's side until he returned.

He was due at the home of Youssef Soufiane's family, where he expected to meet Alizah and Amadou. Once the vigil was over, he'd insist they both be brought under police protection. Until then, he didn't intend to allow either out of his sight. And when he could, he'd find a moment to ask Amadou about the killing of his brother.

The Soufiane family owned a home on the upper slope of the town at the north end of the lake. Their back garden was populated with oak trees that feathered down to the lake. An outdoor gathering had been organized. The order of events would be evening prayer, Khattak's address, and then a large communal dinner, with the food provided by members of the community.

He parked his car and slid his tasbih onto his wrist. Next he slipped a clean white kufi from his inside pocket and settled it over his hair. His beard was growing in thick and dark, though he'd trimmed it close to his jaw. He'd made the conscious decision not to shave it the moment he'd heard about the shooting. His beard could be taken as a signifier of faith; he hadn't wanted the Muslim community to harbor any doubt.

As he was greeted by the Soufiane family and invited to join the prayer in the yard, he felt as though he'd exchanged one identity for another. Here among this group of Québécois Muslims whose origins could be traced to every corner of the globe, his sense of being on guard subsided. The community was ready for him—prepared to receive him as their own, though they spoke many different languages that Esa didn't speak and his French was only adequate at best.

He was invited to lead the prayer. Instead, he chose to give the call to prayer, cupping a hand to his ear. He did this for a reason. It was an assertion of who he was, both publicly and privately. The families would hear him call out the *adhan* with the grace of a thousand past recitations and they would know who he was. But in shaping the Arabic words into their centuries-old rhythm, Esa would also be speaking to himself.

Accepting himself, the mask set aside for now.

The *adhan* wasn't quite a song, nor was it a chant. Its recitation was something measured in between, an offering of grace to the heart.

When he'd finished, he turned to take his place among the rows of the faithful, where several of the women were crying. There was a young woman at the back wearing a royal-blue veil. She raised her face to the sky; he recognized Alizah.

She wasn't crying. She looked more lost and alone than he'd ever seen her, something in her posture reminding him of that night in Waverley, the extreme pallor of her shock as she'd come face to face with the knowledge of the violence done to Miraj.

Alizah was too young to have seen the dead, yet he knew she had the fortitude to face it. He found himself standing in a prayer row between Youssef Soufiane's father and Amadou Duchon. Their shoulders brushed against each other as they prayed. By the time they'd arrived at the supplication, Soufiane was helplessly sobbing.

Esa was moved to comfort him, but Soufiane's wife came to take him away to the house. A young man Esa recognized from the prayer at the church invited Khattak to come forward and speak. His eyes ranged over the small group of men and women of all ages and backgrounds, though the majority were of North African descent. The university students were gathered to one side, sprawled upon the grass as they watched him. And he witnessed how deeply entwined Amadou and Alizah were in this community, staying close to the others.

He reported on the progress of the investigation, trying not to sound officious. When he'd finished, he offered the words he found most difficult to relate. He'd rehearsed them in his head and he'd asked Diana Shehadeh for her advice, but in the end they'd both agreed. Though they wanted to calm the fears of the community, reassurance would have been dishonest.

"We believe the shooter is still at large, and may be armed. I advise you to stay away from the mosque, and to avoid any other public gatherings for now. Though I appreciate the need for community at the moment, it places your children in danger."

As he'd expected, there was an angry murmur from the students. One of the young men challenged him. He identified himself as Rami, Youssef Soufiane's brother.

"They have claimed our families and our mosque; now you're asking us to hide from their hatred? We won't do it. We're not afraid."

"You should be," Esa said grimly. "I know I am." Ignoring Rami for the moment, he turned to the women in attendance, all of whom were veiled for prayer. "Sisters. Those of you who cover outside your homes, I urge you to travel in larger groups, preferably with a male member of your family."

"So this new French secularism—this Code of Conduct secularism— is one that imprisons our sisters at home? Is this what they call liberation?"

Esa stifled a sigh at Rami's words, but before he could determine what to say Alizah stood up, allowing her veil to flutter to her shoulders. A warm recognition passed over the faces of the students in the group.

"The shooting was an act of terror, Rami. And the terrorist is still at large." With a painful twist in her voice, she added, "Your parents can't afford to lose another son."

And she stood there and recited the names of the dead, until a pool of silence blossomed over the night.

60

Diana Shehadeh found Esa a little later, sitting at a small, round table in the garden, waiting for Amadou and Alizah to join him. He'd moved through the crowd, speaking to each member of the small community, listening carefully to anything they needed to share about their grief. Consoling the families of the dead was not a new experience for him, yet rarely had he known a community struck so deeply and so hard. They exchanged phrases in Arabic, and even when Esa couldn't understand what was said, it was the language itself that brought comfort—its lulling, rhythmic cadences, its history as a sacred tongue that could connect him instantly to any Arabic speaker at any time or place across the globe.

"I think that helped," Diana said. She'd brought over a plate of appetizers and companionably they shared the meal as she told him what the MCLU had set in motion when she'd gone to Ottawa. They'd issued a constitutional challenge to the Code of Conduct and to Bill 62, citing violations of the Canadian Charter of Rights and Freedoms, the supreme law of the land.

"Beyond constitutional issues, we need this case to be prosecuted as an act of terrorism, with hate crimes added to the indictment."

Moodily, Khattak said, "We haven't caught the killer yet. We can't say with certainty that hate was the motive here."

Instead of getting angry, as he expected, Diana looked at him with pity.

"Oh, Esa. Haven't you faced it yourself?"

He surprised himself by giving her an honest response. "I don't think I want to. There are times when I need to look away."

Her voice was still soft when she said, "You can't. None of us can anymore." She waved at someone on the other side of the garden. He looked up and saw Amadou, whose great dark eyes reflected his own sense of melancholy.

The dusk prayer would always break Esa's heart.

The difference was that the weight of it was deeper.

He took a long sip of his drink.

"What will you say in the morning? At Isabelle Clément's press conference?"

A smile touched Diana's lips. "Thank you for getting me invited to that, by the way. I think I might take her a little by surprise."

Esa's own smile turned wry. "She promised me that this is one conference that won't go off the rails."

With a touch of asperity, Diana said, "I won't say anything beyond the things this country needs to hear." But when she put her hand on his, he recognized it as a gesture of fellowship. They were both on the same side now. They would have to be, until they could fight their way through. "Do you remember when you were offered the job? Director of Community Policing. You called me and we talked into the night."

A slight smile curved his lips.

"You had so many doubts, so many concerns about all the different ways you might be used. I asked you what you wanted to achieve."

"I remember."

Though in truth he'd forgotten how generous Diana had been, becoming more and more closed off, so that each of them had gone on to fight their battles alone.

"You said you wanted to achieve whatever measure of justice you could for communities just like ours. And I said you should take the job. Do you remember why?"

Years had passed since that conversation had taken place, but now he recalled her words with a shiver of premonition. She had predicted the fallout from the rise of groups like the Allegiance. Conditioning, she'd call it. But what she'd said had cracked open the truth, like a thin and jagged spike.

You have to do this, she'd said. *What we're facing is just the beginning.*

61

Alizah couldn't eat with the others at the gathering. She was too tense and her stomach was still roiling from her confrontation with Max, and now from the sense that she'd forfeited Esa's trust. Perhaps because she'd insisted on heading to the vigil in the woods. Or maybe because she'd accused him of using her to give him cover. There was also a chance that he might have drawn back because Sehr Ghilzai didn't like her.

She pushed a heavy wing of hair from her face, finding a corner of the Soufianes' garden where she could speak to Amadou privately.

"You have to tell Esa the truth. Leaving him in the dark like this isn't fair. It might put him in greater danger, and you know he's already been hurt."

"He's going to think I'm involved."

"He's the one who insisted on your release. He wouldn't have done it if he thought you were involved."

Amadou shrugged his powerful shoulders, the movement so effortlessly graceful that Alizah wished she were like her sister Nazneen, the artist, who would have captured the gesture on canvas. But she was more like her sister Miraj. Doggedly after the truth.

Something was going to happen at the vigil tonight. That's why she needed to be there.

"What happened at the mosque has nothing to do with Michel Gagnon or his flunkeys."

"Or your brother?" she asked Amadou softly.

Amadou blinked to hide the moisture that sheened his eyes. "Bilal is gone. It's time to let him rest in peace."

Alizah's white teeth bit at her lower lip. There was something she needed to say to Amadou—he and Youssef had been her steadfast partners in the battle against the insidious poison seeping through the veins of Saint-Isidore. But she was afraid that putting it into words might make Amadou think she blamed him, when she didn't. No matter how carefully she said it, she could still see it going wrong.

"Spit it out, Alizah. Tell me. You can tell me anything. Even about Maxime." He shrugged again. "If you want him, we'll find a way to get him on our side."

Startled, her eyes flew to his.

"I don't want him; why would you say such a thing?"

When Amadou wisely didn't speak, she knew he was thinking of the photograph she hated. The one where she'd taken Maxime's face in her hands. Anyone looking at it would draw the wrong conclusions. Including Esa. But Esa had seen their interaction firsthand. Surely he wouldn't think she'd set aside everything she believed in for someone like Max?

Or maybe, she thought wryly, she was protesting too much.

Amadou's voice boomed in her ear.

"If it's not about Max, then what? Whatever you want to say, say it to me, Alizah."

Their eyes met and held, eloquent with fear. At last, Alizah exhaled on a sigh, her arms clasped to her middle, as if still in the posture of prayer.

"I just wanted you to know that you didn't bring this . . . madness . . . to Saint-Isidore. You didn't kill Youssef, and you aren't responsible for what happened at the mosque."

Amadou's shoulders sagged.

"So you *do* think it was a hit."

They'd kept a close watch on Wolf Allegiance's online chatter. And on other online platforms. The comments after the prayer at the church had terrified them both.

"I don't know what I think it was. Gagnon's men. Max's followers—or maybe Maxime himself. I don't know. I just keep thinking . . ." Her voice trailed off.

"What? Tell me," he said again.

"I keep thinking about that woman in the abaya. The one caught on camera. Who was she? Why did she have a gun?"

She glanced around the garden, her gaze moving from face to face.

"It couldn't have been one of us. It doesn't make any sense. Then why was she wearing an abaya?"

"If you dive into the abyss, go all the way to the bottom."

Her heart skipped a beat. She was afraid to ask Amadou the meaning of his words, and unconsciously she cast a yearning glance at Esa. His clear green gaze was focused on her, solicitous and intent. She wanted to speak to him—to go to him—but she was afraid of what he might say.

Amadou tugged at her arm. "By wearing the abaya and getting caught on camera, the shooter succeeded at the most important thing."

She looked back at him. In a whisper, she asked him what he meant. But she should have known the answer.

"He put the blame for our tragedy on us."

Esa was quiet at Alizah's side as they followed Amadou across the stone bridge to a path that led deep into the woods. At the bridge, there were views of the mosque, the church, and the university on the hill. Some forty minutes later as they headed west of the town, they were surrounded by trees in the thickly forested wood, their path shadowed by the murmur of water. The officers whose presence Esa had requested were waiting at the edge of the clearing they approached.

"Where's Rachel?" Alizah asked, feeling her absence.

Esa looked at her briefly, and she felt herself floundering, though she kept her face composed.

"With Sehr."

So he'd sent Rachel to Sehr but was here with her himself.

She hugged his concern to herself, refusing to admit what it meant to her.

The rain had cleared away the humidity, and the night air was crisper than it had been in the Soufianes' garden. She'd worn a long-sleeved sweater knowing the night would grow cool. She'd been to the Lilies' meeting place before, both as a matter of personal curiosity and in the process of coming to understand them. The meeting place was a thickly forested spot deep in the heart of the woods, where a secret pond much smaller than the lake was set in a circle of trees. An hour's walk east would see them back in the center of town, but at the moment it seemed as though they'd stepped through a portal to a quiet, unfamiliar world.

Émilie and Réjeanne had often discussed the sacred nature of circles, and Alizah had sometimes tagged along. She knew there was more to it, though. The Lilies were rebels, outsiders who'd been scorned for their ties to the Muslim community. The woods made them feel safe . . . special . . . a place where no one intruded, where they were free to be themselves. To explore what they called the feminine in nature.

But Alizah had also accompanied them so she could keep an eye on Chloé, who was younger and more passive than her friends. Her views were often swept aside by the other girls' stronger personalities. So watching out for Chloé was Alizah's gift to her friend Youssef, the one person who'd been able to reach the fragile girl inside. Chloé had blossomed under his attention, and Alizah was uncomfortably reminded of the letters she herself had written to Esa.

In the center of the small lake, some twenty feet from the shore, a miniature dock was anchored to the bottom by a set of posts, one of which supported a bird feeder with a slate-gray roof. Alizah drew in a breath, savoring the bite of the pines and the smell of rain-washed earth. The path was littered with small stones, and little pebbles found their way into her shoes.

She'd wound her shawl around her torso to keep warm, and whimsically she imagined herself as a bluebird guiding others into the woods.

When they were all assembled at a little clearing by the lake, Réjeanne intoned a strange set of words in French—rustic, arcane, empty of meaning. As she spoke, she sketched an incantation in the air. Alizah stole a glance at Khattak, wondering what he made of Réjeanne's actions. His expression was impassive, even faintly bored.

Réjeanne had dropped her knapsack on the ground and now she opened it, taking out her phone and setting it on a rock. She hit a button and an intricate little melody drifted over their heads. Next she produced a miniature, leather-wrapped bundle and lit a match to a fragrant pouch of herbs.

Émilie took Chloé by the hand and pushed her into the center of the clearing. Réjeanne circled Chloé, holding a bundle of sage aloft in her hands. Its smoky-sweet scent made Alizah cough.

As Réjeanne continued to circle Chloé, she recited a kind of eulogy. She spoke of Youssef Soufiane and of other victims of the mosque shooting the Lilies of Anjou had known. While she spoke, Émilie knelt on the ground beside her knapsack, taking out a set of lanterns, painted a faded gold. She lit the lanterns with matches from a little matchbook. The matchbook was from the café near campus where Alizah had taken Esa and Rachel.

A rustling sounded from somewhere behind them and Alizah turned to look. Esa nodded to the officers on the perimeter, who swept their flashlights back over the path they'd traveled to the lake. Nothing moved in the dark. There were only the sounds of the forest. The wind brushing lightly over the maples, small creatures scurrying swiftly over ground. The slow, warm benevolence of the lulling motion of the waves.

Esa switched his flashlight off, observing the trio of Lilies perform their dance to the music from Réjeanne's phone. Their flowing skirts trailed behind them as they danced.

Though they performed the dance with quiet concentration, Alizah sensed that something was off. The scent of sage turned acrid as it burned. Without having moved, she found herself between Amadou and Esa, shielded from unknown danger. Émilie's concentration was broken. She scowled over at Amadou, whose body sheltered Alizah.

As the music wound down, Réjeanne intoned, "Let the lanterns of death carry your grief away. It's time, Chloé. Time to mourn Youssef and let him go." She wheeled suddenly, her arm falling in a graceful arc, and whispered straight at Khattak, "Let your husband go."

The other girls went still. Somewhere over the lake, the cry of a loon punctured the darkness. Émilie began to push the floating lanterns out toward the mooring post in the water. She'd lit the candles inside, and now in the immutable darkness of the woods the candles glimmered like fireflies bobbing above the waves.

Chloé tugged the long sleeves of her dress all the way over her hands. Then she put up her hands to her face and began to cry, not daintily as she'd done before, the tips of her ears and her nose red, but with harsh, convulsive sobs that shook her fragile frame.

Réjeanne abandoned her act and snatched Chloé up in her arms.

"Shhh, shhh, it's all right. You can tell them about Youssef, Chloé. It's time to tell them the truth."

62

Esa's gaze tangled with Alizah's. He looked over her head back at the way they'd come, thinking of how Lemaire had refused to assign an officer to Sehr for protection. He needed Rachel here. This was the kind of thing she excelled at; she had already established a bond with Chloé.

As the girl began to calm in Réjeanne's arms, Esa asked Réjeanne, "They were married?"

Chloé's sobs had turned into hiccoughs. Réjeanne rubbed her back in a circular motion.

"Right here in this clearing," she said. "We served as witnesses. Youssef's mother was here, too."

Esa's eyes squinted against the darkness, trying to see Chloé's face without the use of the flashlight.

"Who officiated the ceremony?"

"I'm surprised you don't know. It was Père Étienne."

Réjeanne's statement carried the weight of a confession, but Alizah couldn't make out its import. She looked at Esa again, observing the tension in his face. The confession meant something to Esa that she hadn't grasped.

After a pause, he asked, "A Catholic ceremony?"

Réjeanne nodded.

Esa gestured at the clearing. "With a similar set of rituals—the dance and so on?"

Réjeanne smirked. "Not in front of Père Étienne. He would have accused us of witchcraft."

"I'm surprised he was willing to venture outside of the church. He couldn't have thought it proper." Now he addressed Chloé, his voice grave and deep. "Did Youssef become a Catholic?"

Chloé raised her ravaged face to his, her body propped up by Réjeanne.

"His mother said he could, so he did."

But something in her face gave her away.

"It wasn't real," Esa guessed. "It was a means to an end, the end being that he wanted to be able to claim you as his own."

"Yes." Her voice came out in a whisper. "We belonged to each other."

From the corner of his eye, he saw Amadou move away to the edge of the water where Émilie was still setting the lanterns adrift.

"You didn't tell us that before." He gentled his voice, speaking to her the way he would to calm a frightened child. "Chloé, can you tell me anything about the lily that was carved on Youssef's back? Did that have something to do with you? Or with the Lilies of Anjou?"

She shook her head, the frantic motion sending her long, pale hair flying about her face.

"No, no, never—I would never have done that to Youssef. And especially because—"

Suddenly bored, Réjeanne released her hold on Chloé and stalked away to join Amadou. There was a small smile playing about her lips that reminded Esa that she'd said he would find what he'd been searching for in the woods.

"Because?" Esa prompted.

Chloé held up her arm and pulled back her long sleeve. She turned her wrist outward to show him the delicate tattoo.

"Youssef didn't like my tattoo. He asked me to get it removed. But my family said that I shouldn't."

Khattak's gaze flicked to Alizah, who he knew would understand. Many Muslims believed that the body should be returned to God without altering His creation. A permanent mark such as a tattoo was at odds with that belief.

But why did any of it matter?

"Did Réjeanne and Émilie know? Did anyone object to you having the tattoo removed? Were you planning to get rid of it?"

Chloé's hiccoughs had subsided and now she was able to speak clearly.

"I would have done anything for Youssef. But we weren't even married a week. I didn't have time to do as he'd asked me. I told Réjeanne. But she was the only one."

Another dead end. He thanked Chloé for telling him. After a moment's consideration, he asked Réjeanne to join him at the edge of the lake, where he pressed her for the rest.

She didn't answer his question about the tattoo, though there was a stillness about her, as though she was expecting something else from him. The clever little smirk was still on her lips

"Réjeanne." His voice darkened with caution. "If you know something, a murder investigation is a dangerous place to keep secrets."

She stretched, letting her sleeves fall back along her strong, white arms.

"I'm not keeping secrets. I brought you here to reveal them."

Her gaze drifted over the lake. She pointed to something in the distance. He switched on his flashlight again: it lanced across the water, tracking the path of the lanterns. Two of the lanterns had bumped up against the dock and stopped there.

He swept his flashlight across the lake twice before he saw it. Then he called in the officers who'd stood back observing the scene.

Someone had drawn an arrow pointing up to the bird feeder on the post that faced the shore. Something dark was wedged into the opening of the feeder. He trained the flashlight on the bird feeder's mouth. It took his mind a moment to sort out what he was seeing.

Amadou saw it first.

He looked back at Chloé and Alizah and said, "There's a gun out there on the lake."

63

Though she was tall, Rachel had to jog to keep up with Lemaire's brisk pace. He was calling team members in from each of the inner offices. She'd left Sehr with Dr. Sandston and a sternly worded warning not to wander off on her own, offering Sehr the tried and true: *If anything happens to you, the boss will never forgive me.*

In the center of the large room, team members gathered, ready to report on progress. Dr. Agarwal was back with another update on the series of autopsies her team had performed. She had no further forensic evidence to share, but she gave the go-ahead for funerals to proceed. Lemaire nodded. His blue eyes swept the room—a blue that reminded Rachel of the pieces of Caithness glass she'd used to decorate her condo.

She noticed something else, too. Roughly a third of the team members were missing. Lemaire barked out orders at the others. They hustled to the small armory at the back to don protective gear. Everyone seemed to be in on a secret that Rachel didn't know.

Except for Gaffney and Benoit, both crouched in front of their computers, stabbing away at something Rachel couldn't see.

Gaff nodded at Lemaire. "We're good to go."

"You'll need a vest," Lemaire told her.

"We're going out on a raid?"

She followed him to the armory, her mind full of questions. Lemaire had told her about infiltration. He hadn't told her that he was prepared to act. But all those sidebars, those team meetings, when she'd thought he'd been instructing his team on the investigation into the shooting, this was what he'd been doing. Setting up the takedown to pull in members of law enforcement suspected of working with the Allegiance by catching them in the act. Proof of which must have been established while she'd been busy with the shooting.

She shouldered into her vest, watching as he did the same.

"I'm surprised they found one to fit you."

His dancing blue eyes found hers. "They could have asked you," he told her. "You've been tracking me pretty good."

Rachel's thoughts shorted out, a hot red stain climbing her face. Before she could stammer a reply, he went on, "Just like I've been tracking you."

Rachel blinked several times, but Lemaire didn't drop his gaze; it was rock steady holding hers. Finally, she said, "You're an excellent cop."

"Yeah?" It came out like a lazy drawl. He tossed her a helmet with a black visor and took another for himself. "So are you. Is that all it is?"

Her fingers clutched the helmet helplessly. Lemaire's unequivocal expression of his interest floored her. He came closer, helping her fasten her vest. Rachel's breath hitched in her chest. He was so close— so big that he surrounded her, like the men she sometimes played hockey with. He smelled like summer wind and fresh pine, tall and strong as an oak. He used the vest to tug her a little closer, his teasing softening at her obvious bewilderment.

"I'm your senior officer. As long as we're working together, nothing can happen here." He fastened the vest and let go. "But you should know I want it to, after this is over."

Rachel needed a moment to collect her thoughts. For whatever inexplicable reason, this roughly attractive man was expressing his interest in her. But there was none of the queasiness or helpless rage she'd felt with her former boss. He'd stepped away, giving her space if she wanted it. But space wasn't what she needed. She was imagining Lemaire pulling her close with that same lazy smile and tugging her into his arms. She wanted to get close. She wanted to *be* close.

"Ready, sir."

Another officer interrupted them. Rachel watched Lemaire reel off a list of instructions. She could have slipped out of the armory and left them to it. She could have turned tail and run. Instead, she waited for Lemaire to finish. He was nearly ready to head out. He cocked his head at her and waited. She stepped into his space, reaching around him to fasten his vest, letting her hands linger on his chest.

"You're not anything like him. And I want it to happen, too."

Now the blue eyes blazed at her and the cocky grin disappeared. He gave her a short, brisk nod.

"Good," he said gruffly. "Then let's get this done."

Gaff caught her on the way down the steps.

"What is it?" She lifted the visor to look at him. And then remembered to ask him to keep a close watch on Sehr.

"Where's Khattak?" she added.

"Still at the vigil, why?"

"Benoit and I tracked down each member of this team—nearly all seconded from the Sûreté du Québec—with white supremacist ties." Lemaire looked up at them from the bottom of the steps and he hesitated. "There are some anomalies. I'd prefer it if Khattak had your back."

"What kind of anomalies?"

"Rachel!" Lemaire called her to come. It wasn't a request.

"I haven't figured it out," Gaff muttered. "But something's off around here. Even about this sting." He drew her aside so Lemaire couldn't overhear. "I've seen the way Lemaire looks at you. But maybe he's trying to distract you from something else."

Rachel's face was white under her helmet. She climbed into the van. The driver shifted smoothly onto the main road, and Rachel tried to get her bearings as they drove past the station and around the bend of the creek. For a moment she could glimpse some of the town's landmarks from the center: the university, the town hall, and the church. Lemaire had insisted that she take the seat across from him. Swallowing hard, she'd listened. She couldn't be wrong about him, she told herself. It couldn't be an act—what would be the point?

But a cold, analytical part of her brain provided the answer at once.

To draw you away from the Wolf Allegiance. To disguise the extent of their infiltration into the Sûreté and our INSET team.

And what better way to distract her than to pretend an interest? He was the one who'd repeatedly asked her to partner with him, leaving Khattak on his own, an act that served a twofold purpose. Neither one of them had backup. And neither one had the chance to get inside Lemaire's operation. And the worst part was that it was entirely consistent with Lemaire's actions from the outset of the operation.

The arrest of Amadou Duchon. The free hand Lemaire had given Thibault and his thugs. His lack of response to Alizah's list of hate crimes. The way he'd failed to dig out Pascal Richard's ties to neo-Nazis . . . right down to not noticing the swastika at the back of Richard's head. His failure to offer protection to Alizah and Amadou or to put a watch on the mosque. He'd taken no action on a profiler or on following up on who might have been responsible for the assault on Khattak.

In fact, he'd dared to suggest that Khattak had contrived the entire incident to focus the investigation where he wanted it: squarely on the Allegiance and their ilk.

Something niggled at her memory. Some small, insignificant detail.

There was something Lemaire had dismissed.

It slipped through her mind, elusive and dark.

She listened to Lemaire go over the raid with the tactical team commander, in his strong, dark tones, and forced herself to think. It had happened almost at the beginning; it was almost the first thing Khattak had singled out.

What was it?

The van hurtled around the corner past the empty parking lot of the mosque. Someone had made an attempt to wash out the spray-painted swastika, covering it with patterns in green. Abruptly, Rachel remembered.

The synagogue was vandalized first.

And Lemaire had done nothing in response.

Not even when Khattak had warned him to make the synagogue a priority.

Her hands shook in her lap, her fingertips ice-cold.

These were things he would have done, not to entrap others, but because he himself was behind them. The photograph on the wall in his office lurched up in her memory.

He'd given a neo-Nazi the key to Saint-Isidore.

Wasn't that proof of his corruption? What greater proof did she need?

She'd been disarmed from the first by Superintendent Killiam's recommendation of Lemaire. And then by the personal interest he'd used every opportunity to express. If he'd been conducting a sting, he would have wanted to lock things down and keep them quiet.

Instead, he'd invited her in. And he'd given Khattak and Gaffney a free hand.

She sucked in her lips in a bitter grimace, tears forming in her eyes behind the visor.

They were tears of humiliation.

Because of course she'd fallen for it—for him. She'd stupidly imagined that a man like Lemaire might actually be interested in her.

And then she was struck by a far more terrible thought. Sick to her stomach, Rachel began to sweat.

She had only Lemaire's word for it that he'd seen someone push her from the bench in the church. She'd heard only one set of footsteps approach.

What if Lemaire himself had pushed her from the bench?

He'd struck his head because he hadn't been able to move out of the way in time. And then he'd used her ensuing concern to his benefit, seeing at once the ways in which she could be manipulated.

He must have known about her father. As a police officer, he'd be familiar with the profile, with her vulnerabilities. She'd always have the need to prove herself to a man in a position of authority. He'd used that—used her.

A furious rage replaced her self-pity.

Lemaire had wanted her here in this van. She didn't need to be here. She should have been with Khattak.

He looked up at her and smiled.

She sketched a stiff smile in return, a painful movement of air between her lips.

Like a death rattle, she thought.

He must have seen it, too, because he asked, "Are you all right?"

She took too long to answer. He leaned across the open space, whispering, "Don't be afraid, Rachel. I'm going to take care of you."

64

It had taken some time to retrieve the gun. A call out to Gaffney to mobilize resources while keeping things quiet enough to prevent a leak had resulted in Benoit showing up to fetch it with the appropriate gear. Now Khattak entered the gun into evidence, frowning at the empty station. He'd insisted that Alizah and Amadou accompany him; he left them waiting in the lounge.

Gaffney found him a few minutes later and brought him up-to-date.

Grimly, Khattak said, "Our communication with Lemaire seems to be a one-way street."

When Gaffney told him the rest, his response was so fierce that it brought Sehr out of Dr. Sandston's office.

"What's happened?"

"Nothing," he said, trying to soften his voice, aggrieved at the sight of her in the center of a perilous storm. He had to get her out of the station so he could focus. But the warning Dr. Sandston had given him was too serious to ignore. She had suggested that his stalker had targeted others connected to him in the past. If Tom Paley hadn't died of an innocuous heart attack, if his death had been part of some twisted campaign against Khattak, that meant he wasn't dealing with a stalker. Khattak was dealing with a killer.

"Something," Sehr persisted. "Tell me, so I can help."

He throttled the angry words that rose to his lips. He tugged her out into the lobby, his hand on her wrist possessive, thrilled by the answering flame in her eyes. Until he realized that it was anger—anger in place of passion.

He'd worked too hard to arrive at this place with Sehr. If he went on as he had in the past—as he had with his sisters, ruthlessly overprotective—he might end up losing what he'd worked for, as he had with Ruksh. He expelled a harsh breath. If he was going to do this, he wouldn't hold anything back.

"Rachel is out on a raid with Lemaire. He hasn't kept me informed and I'm concerned that there's a reason for that—that he's put her in danger on purpose. And with the photographs, and the messages, and the attack—" His expression was so fierce that she grimaced. "God help me, Sehr, having you here—defenseless and at risk—is preventing me from doing my job. I can't focus when you're in the way. But I don't want you anywhere else."

She studied his face in silence, drawing it out so he had time to get himself under control and think back over what he'd said.

A flash of alarm passed through his eyes. "Sehr—"

In the clear, precise tones of a prosecutor, she said, "What makes you think I'm defenseless? Do you think I just wandered into the midst of a refugee crisis without taking any steps to prepare myself—to *protect* myself?"

She was using the same tone she used when she conducted a cross-examination.

Angrily, he said, "*I* was taken by surprise, and I'm a police officer. Forgive me for thinking that you might be more vulnerable than I am."

Her reply was measured. "It's *because* I'm a woman that I take sensible precautions. For example, Inspector Khattak, I would not have attempted a rendezvous with my partner at an unknown location without calling to check with her first. I would not have entered an abandoned building on my own in the middle of the night. I would have called for backup and waited. So you tell me, Esa Khattak. Which one of us is more reckless when it comes to taking risks?"

He stood in front of her speechless, and she smiled. She reached up to stroke his forehead where the bruise had grown more noticeable. Gently, she said, "You're allowed to worry, but I'm not? Do you think it's been easy for me so far away from you in Greece?"

"Sehr—"

Her arms circled his neck. "Now is when you kiss me."

He didn't need to be told twice. When at last she broke away, her mouth was full and throbbing. His lips strayed over her temples, pressing kisses into her hair.

"It's stopping that's the hard part," he said. "Once you let me start."

She pressed herself closer, and he relished the weight of her in his arms, soft and supple and strong. This time she kissed him, her hand reaching up to stroke his jaw.

"Keep the beard," she teased. "It has definite possibilities."

When she saw the surprise on his face, she asked, "Was that too much?"

He recovered himself at once. "It's never too much, Sehr. If anything, it's not enough." With a deepening of his voice, he said, "Does this change things? Do you want a traditional wedding?"

Full of fanfare, laughter, music, and food—the kind of wedding he'd had with Samina years ago. Sehr was watching his face. The rueful smile that touched her lips turned his heart over.

"Three-to-six functions, taking us months to arrange?" The teasing look was back in her eyes. "You haven't asked me properly yet."

And he damned well wasn't going to in the middle of a police station.

"Oh, I'll ask you. I was just hoping for a concession."

Her expression became serious. To stop her from saying something he knew would hurt, he kissed her again, pushing past the boundaries he knew she was trying to observe.

But he'd mistaken her. Her hands tangled in his hair; she gave in to the kiss wholeheartedly.

"I don't want any of that," she muttered against his mouth. "I don't need it; I don't even need the ring. I just want you, Esa. I've waited a long time. I don't want to wait any longer." She was breathing harshly against his lips, driven as much by anguish as by love.

Gaffney stepped into the lobby. "I've got Superintendent Killiam on the line."

Khattak squeezed Sehr's hand and let her go. His conversation with Killiam was brief and to the point. The only progress he could report was that they thought they had found the gun. Benoit was processing the details.

But when he shared his suspicions about Christian Lemaire, Killiam asked him bluntly, "Has he treated you badly?"

Esa frowned. His experience with Lemaire had no bearing on the suspicions he'd just raised. If he was honest with himself, stopping himself making things personal was also the only way he was able to focus on his job.

"He's kept me out of the loop."

Killiam disagreed. "He's kept you informed through Rachel, and left you to do the work you were sent to Saint-Isidore to do. Have some faith in your partner. She's an excellent judge of character."

Killiam ended the call. Khattak strode to the armory, calling Gaffney to join him.

"Just a moment, sir."

Benoit waved him over to his desk. "The gun you brought in. The ballistics were a match to the handgun used in the executions. It was a legally registered firearm—it wasn't connected to Gagnon, or any of the biker gangs."

Khattak doubled back.

"But it doesn't make any sense."

Reading the name over his shoulder, Khattak felt as though he'd stepped into quicksand.

Because the gun involved in the shooting was registered to Youssef Soufiane.

65

The raid on the Wolf Allegiance's headquarters went down exactly as Lemaire claimed to have planned, designed to entrap police officers who'd been working with the Allegiance to stir up trouble in Saint-Isidore and to subvert the investigation into the shooting at the mosque. He'd divided the targets into three groups, assigning his handpicked team into the mix alongside officers seconded to INSET. Now the tactical team reported in from the other two locations. They had the arrests in hand—they'd taken their targets by surprise.

Lemaire's team acted last. His presence in the center of the operation gave them a tactical advantage. He leapt out from the back of the van, summoning Rachel to follow. She made herself count her breaths, trying to hold on to her nerve. When she stepped out of the van, she recognized the location.

It was the same building where she'd picked up Khattak, after the attack. She saw the sign he'd mentioned before listing in the wind. The target location was the same place where Khattak had been assaulted and nearly choked to death.

She tipped her visor up slightly for a better look at Lemaire's face.

What kind of game was he playing?

What was waiting for her inside?

Lemaire snapped his fingers and the team divided in two. Now in the warm silence of the summer night, Rachel followed his lead. There were six other officers with them. Four went ahead, circling around the back. Lemaire kept her behind him and signaled the other two.

In a minute, the door was breached.

"Go!" Lemaire shouted. He drew his weapon.

Rachel followed at his heels, her hand feeling for the reassuring weight of her gun.

Inside, the scene was chaotic. Men crashed through the back entrance. Everyone ran. Tall, broad-shouldered men with brush cuts threw down chairs. Rachel stumbled over a chair, her leg getting trapped inside it. Someone aimed a fist at her head and she ducked, flattening her shoulders so the man went sailing past her. There were candles lit against one wall. As she fell, she saw the image of a wolf's head on the wall.

Someone kicked at her, a heavy boot against her ribs. She swiftly rolled to one side, scrambling back to her feet. A shot was fired from the outer room and she whirled to face the sound. Whatever Lemaire had planned, he'd underestimated the number of men he needed. At least one of the men inside had escaped, and two other officers were down. Someone had lit a smoke bomb. Coughing, Rachel pulled the visor closer to her head. She scrabbled over to check on a man on the floor. He was bleeding from a blow to the head.

One of the members of the Wolf Allegiance dived in her direction. Her heart thudding in her chest, she waited. When his arm came down on her throat, she slammed her fist into his ribs. He was tackled by an INSET team member and forced down onto his knees. Rachel grabbed the injured cop on the floor and dragged him off to one side. A foot kicked out and connected with her visor. Stunned by the blow, she fell back. When nothing else followed, she ripped the helmet from her head. Her visor had been smashed and now she couldn't see through it, though it would have been safer to keep it on. Staying low to the floor, she searched for an opening—for an opponent she could take down.

There was a gunshot, followed by another.

Most of the men in the room had been subdued, members of the Allegiance, but also a few officers Rachel recognized from the first team briefing. But Lemaire wasn't in the room. She wiped the sweat from her eyes, pushing back sticky strands of hair. She dried her palms on her slacks, then reached down for her gun. Her hand closed on empty space. She'd lost the gun in the fight. She took hold of her baton instead, hearing the sounds of a struggle somewhere deeper inside the building.

She pushed through the smoke, blindly following the sound. She called out a warning in her strongest voice. No one responded, so she stole along a corridor to a passageway at the end. The smoke thinned out as she moved, too late to stop her from tripping on a piece of re-bar and crashing through the room beyond. She fell awkwardly on her wrist. Her baton rolled out of her reach. Blinking through the dust, she saw that it had come to rest against a man's black shoes.

Awkwardly, she stumbled to her feet.

She was alone in the room with Lemaire.

And his gun was pointed at her head.

The blood rushed from her head. She held up her hands in surrender.

His burning eyes locked on hers.

"Don't move another step."

A whimper escaped her lips. She took a trembling step back.

"I said don't move."

"Please." Her aching whisper hurt her throat. "I'm asking you not to shoot."

His gaze flicked over her shoulder and back to her sweating face. Terror colored her vision, the scent of it acrid and hopeless. She was out of moves—she couldn't stop him. And she knew from the lethal purpose in his eyes that he wasn't going to change his mind.

Then a tiny corner of her mind registered the sound of movement, the harsh breath of another person at her ear—someone close enough to save her.

She made a life-or-death decision and feinted back.

Lemaire aimed his gun and fired.

Rachel was on the floor, gasping. She felt a heavy weight collapse over her chest; blood began to ooze from her neck. She thought she'd screamed, but the sound came out as a croak. Her whole body was on fire, her chest convulsed in reaction, her ears ringing from the gunshot. She was breathing in dust and debris, choking on the smoke in her mouth. The weight on her chest grew heavier, the blood sliding down her neck under her clothing, pooling between her breasts. Her hands scrabbled to touch the wound, but they were weighted down as well.

She couldn't breathe. She was suffocating in her own blood.

Then the weight on her chest shifted. What had felt like a drowning embrace was lifted from the floor and shoved aside. Lemaire straddled her body and pushed her down. He'd taken off his helmet and gloves. His hands made a thorough search. They came away red with blood.

"Christ, woman. I told you not to move."

He shouted something into the other room, stripping the vest from her body with hands that shook. She was drowning in sweat and blood, but still she tried to call for help.

Lemaire shifted aside and pulled her up in his arms. He braced her against one knee, pressing his glove to the wound at her neck. His free hand brushed the hair from her face, and then there were others in the room—paramedics who laid her down again and switched her over to a stretcher. The room was suddenly filled with blinding light. She felt the sting of anesthetic at her neck, dizziness darkening her thoughts.

She heard someone say, "Missed the artery. Did you get him?"

And saw Lemaire nod once.

Through a haze of smoke and dust, she struggled to make sense of the chaos in the room. Her chest was no longer aching. Lemaire had stripped off her shirt as well as her vest, and when she looked down at her torso she couldn't see a bullet wound. Her fingers traced over her ribs and sternum. There was a biting sting at her neck, but she seemed otherwise unharmed.

Her gaze followed the movement of the paramedics. They were lifting another body onto a second stretcher. He was dressed like a member of the Allegiance. A paramedic stopped to kick away the gun still clenched in his hand. It was taken into evidence by another officer.

"Still smoking," the officer said.

"I don't know how he missed," Lemaire answered. "She stumbled right into his path."

Rachel raised her eyes to his face and saw that he'd lost his normal healthy color.

"Why didn't you listen? I told you I had it covered."

She was shivering violently, trying to make sense of the sequence of events. The heavy weight that had trapped her body, that sense that she'd been on fire . . . Lemaire snapped at someone behind her. Her half-naked body was wrapped in a cotton blanket.

"It doesn't need stitches," the paramedic told her. He'd cleaned the wound from the bullet that had grazed her, and set a thick bandage in place. "Doesn't mean it won't hurt like hell."

Rachel nodded absently, her gaze still fixed on Lemaire.

"Christ, woman," he repeated. "You just took years off my life. Is this what you do to Khattak? No wonder the man's on edge."

The words sounded fuzzy in her ears. She jerked her chin at the dead man on the stretcher. "He's the one who shot me?"

Lemaire's head came up with a jerk. His hot blue gaze found hers.

"What the *hell* did you say?"

The minute he said it, Rachel knew.

She had no answer for his outrage.

He spoke to her slowly, measuring out each word.

"You thought I was aiming at you."

"Please." Rachel choked back a sob. "Christian, I'm sorry. I lost my bearings in the smoke."

He knew it was more than that. Hostility darkened his face. He leaned down, putting his face close to hers, his blue eyes bleak with regret.

"I was wrong about you, Sergeant Getty. You were never a member of my team."

66

Three days passed before Rachel was able to insist on being discharged. Esa was at her bedside, where she was grumpily listening to the doctor, who'd seen too many of the dead to give in to Rachel's demands.

"I'll certify you unfit for duty if you keep putting up a fuss."

"That's blackmail," Rachel grumbled.

"Well." The doctor hooked a clipboard over her arm. "Blackmail would be the least offensive thing to have happened in Saint-Isidore for months."

"She'll stay," Khattak told the doctor firmly. "Until you say she can go."

The doctor's eyes ran over the bruises on his face and neck.

"You're not looking too good, either."

"Ha!" Rachel said. "That's gotta be the first time someone's said that to you."

The doctor hid a smile at Khattak's embarrassment. "I'll work up your papers," she promised Rachel.

Rachel studied the bruise on Khattak's forehead. "We're quite a pair, aren't we?"

He tried not to grin and failed. "Decorated officers."

"What made Gaff suspicious of Lemaire? I screwed up there. He's not going to want to work with me again." She didn't need to state aloud that she'd repaid Lemaire's trust with unstinting disloyalty.

"Oh, I think he will," Khattak told her, nodding at the door.

Rachel's temperature shot up. With everything that was going on at the station, Lemaire couldn't be at her door. All hands were needed on deck.

"He's asked the nurse about you at least a dozen times over the last few days. He's waiting for me to leave."

"You probably shouldn't," Rachel said. "He might throttle me in my bed."

He'd avoided answering her question about Lemaire, so doggedly she asked it again.

"Gaffney's leads point to a senior figure as the leak. That's why the raid went south. The officers recruited to the Allegiance had a few minutes' warning of the raid. Gaff thought the leak might be Lemaire because Lemaire didn't take anyone into his confidence. But we know now he was right to keep what he knew to himself."

"Where is Gaff now?"

"With Sehr."

He didn't have to tell her that he didn't trust any of Lemaire's officers with Sehr's safety. There might be others associated with the Allegiance who had escaped the raid.

"And the kids?"

"Outside waiting for me. Alizah wants to see you. And we need to talk to Chloé." He looked a little discomfited as he asked, "Now that you're back on your feet, could you be the one to speak to her?"

"Why me, especially? You usually have more luck with women."

He told her what they'd learned about Youssef's gun, that it was the weapon that had been used to murder the women in the basement of the mosque. And Chloé had to know something about the gun.

"You made a connection with her—you'll be able to draw her out." He hesitated as if he would say more, and Rachel suddenly had an inkling of what might be in his mind—her brother, Zach, and her work with troubled youth—she quickly straightened up.

"Let's get me discharged. Lemaire's operation may have been a success in terms of rooting out white supremacists in law enforcement, but we still haven't caught the shooter at the mosque."

Feeling like a new woman after a brisk shower in the washroom attached to her hospital room, Rachel mumbled a question at Alizah as she pulled a fresh shirt over her head.

"Youssef was a good friend of yours. Do you know why he had a gun?"

With a curious note of detachment in her voice, Alizah asked, "Rachel, weren't you paying attention to the list of incidents I gave you? We reported them to the dean. We also reported the break-in, but the administration took no action. We also informed the police about the vandalism of the mosque and synagogue, but again no one took any action."

Drawing her jacket back on, Rachel holstered her gun at her waist. Lemaire had found it for her and placed it in her hands with that still-banked fury in his eyes. She'd have to work up the nerve to deal with him, once they'd run the killer to ground. They were close to untangling this whole mess. She gave Alizah a summary of Lemaire's operation, watching the girl tilt up her head. Alizah shivered in relief.

"I wish Inspector Lemaire had told me what he was doing," she said. "All this time, I didn't think anyone cared." She handed Rachel her jacket and helped her shrug it on. "When no one was willing to re-spond to our complaints, we felt endangered and *that's* why Youssef got the gun. The threats against Youssef and Amadou were becom-ing serious because of their involvement with Chloé and Émilie."

Alizah abruptly went still. She turned to look at Rachel, the words falling slowly, sounding like they'd come from a great distance away.

"Why are you asking me about Youssef's gun?"

From the wary look in her eyes, Alizah had already begun to sus-pect.

"The gun we recovered from the lake was registered to Youssef. You didn't recognize it?"

Alizah shook her head, her eyes deeply shadowed. "I'd never seen it. I didn't even know what kind of gun it was." Rachel could see that she was trying to put the pieces of the puzzle together but finding it impossible to do so.

"This can't leave the room, Alizah. The gun used in the basement executions turned out to be Youssef's gun."

Alizah took a faltering step back. She came up against Rachel's hospital bed and sank down in the chair across from it. She bent over her knees and put her head in her hands, speaking to herself.

"Didn't *anyone* read that list?"

Rachel squatted down on her knees in front of Alizah, wincing as the movement pulled at the bandage at her neck. "What do you know that I don't?"

Alizah's head came up, her green eyes filled with fury. "I *gave* you the list, Rachel. I put it in your hands myself. You took it to the dean."

Instantly Rachel understood. "The campus break-in? The gun was taken from your office along with the electronics you had reported stolen."

"That's where Youssef kept it."

But Rachel's memory was excellent. While the break-in at the office had been reported, the stolen gun was absent from Alizah's complaint.

Alizah rubbed at her eyes. "I reported everything except the gun because I didn't want to get Youssef in trouble."

"But all this time you knew the gun was out there? You blamed the Wolf Allegiance for the break-in, but you never thought to tell us they might have Youssef's gun?"

But Alizah didn't need her rebuke. She was already blaming herself.

"The news only reported that Père Étienne had been found with an assault rifle. They didn't mention another gun. Neither did you."

"But surely to God, if you thought there was a gun in their possession, you should have reported it to us."

"I know," she whispered. "There was so much going on, I didn't have time to tell you."

Rachel was watching Alizah closely. Something didn't add up. She'd never known Alizah to be anything other than forthright, but something in her face had shut down.

"Maybe you didn't think a member of the Allegiance took it. Maybe you had a reason to think someone you knew might have needed that gun. Maybe it was the Lilies of Anjou, as part of their rituals in the forest. Maybe that's how they knew where the gun was." She caught the subtle shift of Alizah's glance. "No? Who, then?"

But she only had to think of the person Alizah had been insepa-
rable from since Rachel and Esa had arrived in Saint-Isidore.

Alizah was trying to protect Amadou Duchon.

Alizah pushed herself out of the chair and sidestepped Rachel.

"I swear to you, Amadou wasn't the shooter at the mosque."

"He was there that night."

"To pray. Youssef was like a brother to him; he tried to save his life."

"Amadou *had* a brother," Rachel said.

Alizah's face was pale, her skin clammy. But she didn't say anything
more.

A heavy hand knocked on the door. Lemaire stepped into the small
room, instantly making it smaller. His gaze slid from Rachel to Alizah.

"What's happened?"

"Nothing!" Alizah's voice broke. She whirled on her heel and left
the room, leaving Lemaire with Rachel.

He looked her over, his gaze lingering on the bandage at her neck.
Frowning a little, he said, "Should you be up and about?"

"I'm headed back to work."

The silence between them built until Rachel finally cleared her
throat and spoke. "Listen, Christian, I'm sorry. Things happened so fast
that I didn't have a chance to think them through."

He put up a hand, cutting short her apology. "I may have been a bit
hard on you. Gaffney told me he was the one who misdirected you." He
shook his head. "What you must have been thinking in the van."

She dropped her gaze, both embarrassed and contrite. "I *am* sorry.
It just . . . made a lot of sense. There's a leak at the top somewhere. No
one else came to mind."

He scratched the back of his head, his blue eyes fixed on her face.
"You were thinking like a cop. That's what you're supposed to do. I'm
not saying it didn't sting—but I'm guessing it hurt you more."

Rachel's insides tightened. Suddenly it became imperative that
she not stick around to hear the rest. She searched anxiously for her
purse. Lemaire's gaze followed hers. He got to it first and dangled it
by the strap. Rachel stayed where she was, an ache making itself felt
inside her chest.

Grimly, she raised her chin and looked him dead in the eye.

"Don't beat around the bush, Lemaire. Say what's on your mind."

A slow smile of appreciation broke across his face.

"You've got guts; I'll give you that."

His amusement faded and he took a step closer to her, looking down into her face.

"You thought this wasn't real. You thought I was using it to keep you from finding out the truth." His expression softened. "You've known some shitty men, haven't you, Rachel?"

She shrugged, pretending indifference, though her heart was beating loudly enough to make her think he could hear it.

Lemaire closed the distance between them and kissed her, cupping her head in his giant hand. When he let her go and took a step back, Rachel's eyes were closed. The pounding was now in her ears.

"So what do you think?" he said easily, waiting on her answer.

She opened her eyes. Her breath puffed out on a gasp.

It would be so easy to take the coward's way out. She'd done it with Nate in Greece. She'd known Lemaire for just over a week. It should be easier this time.

Except it wasn't.

She'd believed the worst about him and he was standing right here, that teasing smile in his eyes. Giving her another chance, if she was brave enough to take it.

"You Francophones talk about your feelings a lot. I prefer actions to words."

His grin widened. "Yeah?"

"Yeah."

"Then show me."

Rachel took him at his word.

67

Esa caught Alizah by the arm as she stumbled from Rachel's room.

"What is it? Why are you crying?"

She rubbed the back of her hand across her face. "I'm not."

She tried to shake off his hand; he tightened his grip. He'd insisted that she and Amadou accompany him to the hospital. Lemaire had assigned Philippe Benoit to watch over them. He'd just come on shift and was waiting for Alizah nearby.

"What did Rachel say to upset you?"

She angled her body away from his, signaling Amadou, who was waiting at the end of the hallway. "I have to go."

Esa caught hold of her other arm and pulled her around to face him. The messenger bag she was wearing slid across her back.

"Not until you tell me what's happened."

She struggled to free herself, but she didn't call Amadou for help.

"Let go of me, Esa, please."

He didn't.

"Alizah—"

Angry tears formed in her eyes. She stopped fighting him, letting him hold her by the arms, shaken by the way his grip had changed to something gentle and protective.

A silence held. Finally, she said, "Why are you doing this to me? Why are you touching me when you know—" She couldn't make herself finish.

He let go of her arms at once, and a pained smile came to her lips.

"That's what I mean," she said softly. "You're not in this, you have Sehr—but you can't seem to leave me alone."

She saw his regret, his immediate understanding, and it struck her like another kind of pain. To bury her confession, she said, "Rachel told me about the gun."

Now he was watching her differently. Trying to assess her reaction.

"Youssef had it for protection. He kept it on campus at our office. That's where the break-in was. I didn't think it was relevant because I didn't know you were looking for a gun."

His green eyes narrowed to slits. He didn't believe her. Or at least he didn't believe she'd given him the whole truth. And she wondered how he'd learned to so easily read her secrets.

Very softly, he said, "You had to know that *any* missing firearm would be relevant to us."

She shrugged, rubbing her arms where he'd held her.

He followed her action, frowning. "Did I hurt you?"

A blush stained her cheeks, heightening her discomfort.

"No." She tugged her sleeves down over her wrists. "It's nothing."

Because she couldn't tell him the truth.

I wanted to touch the place you touched me.

The only way to get herself out of this was to answer his question. Or . . . at least part of it.

"I was upset because Rachel thought I knew who'd taken the gun. I didn't." Her mind working quickly, she added, "If I had something on Max, I wouldn't keep it to myself."

But he was too clever for her, and she saw him glance past her to Amadou, waiting at the end of the hall. He must have guessed the reason she hadn't asked Amadou to join them.

"Did you think *Amadou* had taken the gun? Just as a precaution?"

She couldn't answer this—how could she? She wanted Esa's trust but not if it came at Amadou's expense. She veiled her eyes.

"May I go now?"

He ignored that. "We've flagged your name in several online discussions about the shooting. Including Wolf Allegiance threads about

Amadou's brother, Bilal. You may have been worried about Amadou's safety. If he was the one who stole Youssef's gun, that might have seemed reasonable to you."

Conflicted, she stared up at him. Hoping he would give her a little more. When he didn't, she whispered, "Amadou wouldn't have vandalized our offices. Not even as a smoke screen."

Esa's eyes stayed on hers.

"Who discovered the break-in?"

She didn't know if it was a trap, but she answered honestly. "Amadou did. Then he called me."

"He might have taken the gun *after* he discovered the damage."

She tugged at her sleeves again, a nervous, betraying gesture.

Struggling to find the right words, she came up with, "You've seen what's happened here—you know what happened to you." Her eyes traced the bruise on his forehead. "I'm not saying he did, but wouldn't it make sense that if Amadou took the gun, he took it for his own protection?"

The look on Esa's face was one she recognized. He'd looked at her that way once—in Waverley. On the day she'd finally learned who had killed Miraj.

It was the limitless sympathy one would extend to a child.

Quietly, he said, "A gun has other uses, Alizah. Youssef's was used at the mosque."

Her heart shriveled up at the words.

"Amadou didn't do it. You're supposed to protect us from this—how could you think he's guilty of killing one of our closest friends?"

She waved to Amadou, shifting away from Esa. But Esa swung her back around. This time he made no apology for his touch.

"Where are you going?" His tone warned her not to put him off.

"To the radio station. We still have a show to do."

"I thought your program airs in the morning. You shouldn't be out this late."

Alizah swallowed at the look in his eyes. He thought she was lying again.

"Pascal is doing a special broadcast. The dean managed to get us equal time. Maybe to make up for not taking action on my earlier reports."

"How long is the broadcast?"

"We'll be done by midnight."

"You're already a target. Why do you want to provoke whoever has you in their sights?"

She glared at him, furious. The messenger bag on her shoulder flipped forward. He read the slogan she had printed out and taped across its flap.

#JournalismIsNotACrime

Quietly intense, she muttered, "It's not a provocation, either. I'm standing up for us. I thought you'd want me to."

"Dammit, Alizah, I'm telling you *not* to do this."

His grip was so tight now that it was hurting her, but Alizah didn't care. She welcomed the harshness of the contact. She relished the power she had to get under his skin like this. Her sense of triumph reached him and he flushed, a dark color rising in his face.

Her instincts at war, she said, "Well, I don't answer to you. Unless you're hoping to change that."

His brief laugh mocked them both. "Even if I did, you wouldn't listen to me, so don't hold it up as incentive."

Alizah blinked at this. "*Would* it be incentive?"

"Don't twist what I'm saying. I want you to go straight home."

A sudden bleak acceptance descended on her thoughts. He was right. She had been willing to twist it. She'd seen what she wanted to see, when all she had really shared with him was her love for Miraj. Not once had he indicated otherwise. Not once had he crossed that line. That look on his face in the church—it didn't mean Esa was hers or that he wanted to be. All she had to do was look at him with Sehr to know the truth. A staggering pain swamped her senses. But she would never let him see it.

She forced herself to speak. "I'll go home *after* we've done the broadcast."

He put up a hand to the bruise at his temple and rubbed the area around it. He glanced at Constable Benoit, who was wisely pretending not to listen.

"Keep a close eye on her. On both of them." He gestured at Amadou. "Make sure you see them safely home." Benoit nodded. Esa turned back to Alizah. "Don't say anything to rile up Thibault. We didn't track him down in the raid, which is why you need to be careful."

She couldn't bring herself to reassure him. She was angry in a way she knew he didn't deserve. None of this was his fault. But she needed a reason to blame him.

He didn't let go when she tried to tug herself free. He waited for her to face him.

When she did, he said calmly, "I know you're angry at me. But I also hope you know I'm trying to keep you alive."

For a moment, her eyes were locked on his. But she couldn't—*wouldn't*—speak.

Resigned to her stubbornness, he let go of her hands with an angrily muttered curse.

Alizah wished he hadn't. She wished he were holding her, still.

Until he said with conviction, "I wish to God I'd never met you."

68

Rachel and Khattak met up in the hallway.

"Got a call from Gaff," she told him. "He says he's come across something in the online chatter we should take a look at."

Khattak looked tired to his bones, so she added, "I can take care of it, if you want to get some rest. Sehr's already at the hotel, probably a good idea for you to check on her."

"You're sure you don't mind?" He rubbed a hand across his eyes, making her glad she'd made the offer.

"Lemaire's heading to the station." She glanced around. "What happened to the kids?"

"They went back to campus to do a live broadcast. Constable Benoit is with them."

She whistled under her breath. "Not a great idea, sir."

He met her gaze with perfect understanding. "Alizah doesn't listen to me."

His anger sounded personal. Bitter. To cheer him up, she said, "Benoit is pretty diligent. Plus, he wants to impress you. I'm sure they'll be okay. But I'll check in from the station."

"I'd be grateful if you did. I won't be away long."

"Take until the morning, sir. You look beat."

He gave her that smile that never failed to disarm her. Appreciative and a bit amazed.

"You're the one who was shot. *You* should be taking a break."

Rachel's shrug was unforced. Trying not to make too much of things, she said, "That was more of a bee sting. Besides, I like working with Lemaire."

Lemaire was waiting for her at the exit, pointing impatiently at his watch.

Grinning now, Khattak said, "I'm fairly certain Lemaire enjoys it more. Let him go ahead. I can drop you at the station and we can catch up on the way."

She nodded, striding off to let Lemaire know.

By the time Khattak had brought the car around, she'd organized her thoughts about the case. She slid into the car, checking her purse for snacks. She found a Coffee Crisp and a fig bar. Khattak accepted the latter, which left Rachel with the chocolate fix she'd craved.

"Knock yourself out," Khattak said as the crumbs from her chocolate bar flew everywhere. "For once, I don't care about the car."

Mumbling through a mouthful of chocolate, she teased, "That's only because this isn't your BMW." Making quick work of her snack, she summarized the case for him.

"I'm thinking what's most relevant here is what we learned from Dr. Sandston. We're looking at at least two profiles and, from what I've seen, two separate cases. Your kidnapping and assault are one. The attack on the mosque is the other."

"And there are the leaks. I find them confusing. They're tied to the investigation, but the messages are specific to me. Either someone's following me or they've bugged our offices."

Rachel dabbed at her lips with a tissue. Wafer crumbs fell into her lap.

"Probably both, sir. But like we talked about earlier, the text messages to you fit a different profile—the profile of a stalker. The leaks to the press and to the Wolf Allegiance are coming from a separate source. Someone higher up like Lemaire."

Khattak glanced at her briefly. "Not Superintendent Killiam?"

Rachel considered the possibility. "Maybe. But there's a gap between events and when I'm able to update her, though I've made a few calls. Our leak is moving in real time."

They pulled up in front of the station. She stayed in the car; there was plenty more to say.

"We need to consider a personal motive that's not related to you. Like Dr. Sandston said—maybe the shooting had a target. It could have been gang related, and therefore about Amadou. It could have been directed at the father with his little son—Abubekr, I think his name was. Or at Youssef Soufiane and his mother. Or this could be a case of neo-Nazis run amok. The Wolf Allegiance has popped up everywhere *except* at the scene of the shooting."

Khattak opened the windows and shut off the engine. Warm air filled the car, wrapping around them both.

"They're not mutually exclusive, are they? A Wolf Allegiance member like Max has a personal animus against Amadou as well."

Rachel turned to face him. "Oh yeah? What's that?"

"He's jealous of Amadou's closeness with Alizah."

Rachel nodded. "I'm worried about the way she ends up at the center of things."

Khattak surprised her by saying bitterly, "Maybe she *makes* herself the center."

At his unexpected burst of anger, Rachel felt like apologizing for Alizah.

"They think they're indestructible at that age."

Khattak's hands gripped the wheel. Rachel could nearly hear him thinking.

"She isn't," he offered at last.

"It might not be about her, either," Rachel said doubtfully. "I know she's been a catalyst here—with her radio program and the way she challenges Thibault." She shuddered. "God, what a little creep. But this could be about the Lilies of Anjou; they seem to be everywhere, too. And it was their involvement with Youssef and Amadou that seemed to rile everyone up. Again, it could tie in to the Allegiance— they'd hate that more than anything else."

Fatigued, Khattak rested his head on the wheel.

"Except Muslims," he said quietly.

Rachel wondered if she should pat his back. Her hand hovered

awkwardly before it dropped to her side. She looked up at the doors
to the station and thought of Lemaire's press conference on the stairs.

"We've been thinking the leak has to be highly placed, but maybe
that's not the case."

Khattak raised his head and looked at her. "Who else would have
that kind of information? When and where a raid's going down?"

Rachel mulled the answer aloud. "It could be someone with an ear
to the ground. The same someone who bugged Lemaire's office. Someone we think of as invisible."

At the flash of unease on Khattak's face, Rachel knew he'd come to
the same conclusion.

"Christ," she said. "He *does* have the necessary tech skills. And we
invited him in."

"I sent him off with Alizah."

Khattak turned on the car. "See what Gaffney wants. Then get
Lemaire and meet me at the campus. Let's pray Alizah and Amadou
made it to their show."

69

Despite the lateness of the hour, the station was crowded with cops. Moving quickly, Rachel grabbed a can of pop from one of the vending machines before she found Gaff at the cubicle he shared with Philippe Benoit.

"You figure out who the leak was yet? Because I have a theory I don't think you're going to like."

Gaff frowned at her. Team members were everywhere. He pulled her into the closest office, his laptop tucked under his arm. Rachel flicked on the light. She perched at the edge of the desk, which turned out to be Clément's. Luckily, Her Royal Uptightness had clocked out for the night.

"Is Dr. Sandston still here?"

Gaff shook his head. "She left a while ago. Lemaire dismissed all personnel who weren't involved with the raids. I think cleaning house is his priority."

Rachel nodded. "I'm worried about the boss going off on his own. Does your evidence point to Benoit?"

Gaffney opened his laptop to show her a single white page.

"This is what I've collected from a number of different online sources. There's a name that seems to recur. I noticed it because on one of these platforms there was direct engagement with Alizah Siddiqui."

Her heart racing, Rachel scanned the page. The first two references were from the blog of a woman based in Montreal by the name of Élise Doucet.

FLAGGED:

[Translated from the French]

EDITH SAUCIER: They are decent French boys who have been shamefully maligned.

ABEAUTIFULMERCY: Decent French girls, too.

ÉLISE DOUCET: In the new Québec, everyone's a racist.

CANDLELIGHTVIGIL: We need to change that. We need to change the way they talk about us.

ABEAUTIFULMERCY: The change has already come.

FLAGGED:

[Translated from the French]

EDITH SAUCIER: I heard the black boy was after our girls.

ABEAUTIFULMERCY: It's not just him. It's all of them. We should be taking action.

ROY GRENIER: I don't care if that makes me sound racist, that's not something we need. There's such a thing as too much assimilation.

CANDLELIGHTVIGIL: I don't care what religion someone chooses to believe in. No one should have to die while they're peacefully praying.

ÉLISE DOUCET: All the more reason why they should have stayed out of our church. And out of Saint-Isidore.

ABEAUTIFULMERCY: They'll figure it out too late.

Rachel read the first two entries and looked at Gaff.

"Okay. They're talking about Amadou. But it doesn't seem all that different from the rest of the commentary. I don't see Alizah's name."

She also didn't see Benoit, and she breathed a little easier, though she was itching to be on her way.

"Keep reading. I've cut and pasted another section from the replies to the Town Council's statement on the shooting. I think ABM and ABeautifulMercy are probably the same person, given their preoccupation."

Rachel scrolled down the page, squinting closely at the screen.

FLAGGED:

[Translated from the French]

ABM: Nothing is the same in Québec. What we were, what we held dear, all of that is gone. One of us had to fight back.

ABM: Does not cry for our sons. Will not look after our daughters.

ABM: No one's ever cared about our humanity before. If we don't stand up for who we are as Québécois, if we don't think about the future of our daughters, we'll vanish from the pages of history.

AlizahS: Does murdering innocent people in a mosque count as standing up for Québécois identity? Should that be recorded in our history?

ABM: Who said they were innocent?

AlizahS: Your comments are appalling. What crime were they guilty of?

ABM: The same one you are with Max. I shouldn't have to say it.

Rachel didn't get it. She looked at Gaffney, perplexed.

"I don't see a theme."

He snorted. "I thought you were some kind of prodigy. ABM is obsessed with the daughters of Québec. She keeps talking about protecting them."

Rachel paused, fitting the facts together.

"You think this is about the women who were killed in the basement?"

Exasperated, he said, "That's not who she means. Given the online chatter about Amadou, I think she means Amadou and that girl—Émilie Péladeau. You mentioned her when you told me about the Lilies of Anjou. Have you spoken to her about the shooting?"

No, Rachel realized. A huge oversight on her part. She'd talked to Chloé and Réjeanne, but she'd dismissed Émilie because Amadou had dismissed her.

The lanterns on the lake that had led them to the gun.

She swallowed noisily.

"You think this is some kind of revenge on her part? And that's why she engaged with Alizah? Because she was jealous of her?"

"I don't know. I just thought it was interesting. Also, I don't think Benoit is your leak. I tracked the calls that were made to the press and they didn't come from the station or from any of the phones registered to Lemaire's team."

"You can't rule them out. They may have used a burner phone."

"They didn't. They came from an actual number I was able to trace."

"Wow," Rachel commented. "I wasn't expecting that."

Gaff's weathered face broke into a grin. "No one ever said these guys were smart."

"Max?" she guessed. "Maxime Thibault was the one?"

Which, if true, would raise additional questions. Max had no insight into their investigation. Or into Lemaire's raids. They were still missing a connection. She took a sip from her drink and tried to think.

"Wrong again. The number is from the switchboard at Pascal Richard's studio."

"What?"

In her excitement, Rachel spilled her drink on Clément's aggressively tidy desk. Grinning broadly, Gaff fished out a pack of tissues and handed it over. She mopped up the mess with great care, drying off the bottom of a framed photograph of a group of young people, curtailing the spill before it could reach Clément's keyboard.

"He did have a swastika tattoo."

But would Richard have been so negligent as to leak information from his own phone line? She studied the photograph of Lemaire handing Pascal the key to the city with a sense of unease.

"So?" Gaff asked her. "Does that help?"

Rachel gnawed at her lower lip.

"I think so. At least I should let Khattak know, so he can check out for the night. He went after Benoit."

Gaffney nodded and signaled for her to call.

She got Khattak on the first ring.

"It's not Benoit," she told him. "Alizah and Amadou are safe."

Khattak wasn't in his car. He sounded like he was walking through a large and empty building, his footsteps echoing on stone.

"Where are you?" she asked.

"Still on the campus. Alizah and Amadou weren't at the radio station. I'm checking the MSA office now."

Rachel remembered the long empty hallway lined with mahogany doors. This late at night, the building would be deserted. But if Alizah and Amadou weren't doing their broadcast from the campus—

She made the connection quickly, her heart plummeting to her feet. She snapped her fingers at Gaffney.

"Can you get Richard's broadcast on your laptop?"

Gaff didn't ask why. He reached over to scoop his laptop from the desk.

"Rachel, what's going on?" Khattak's voice sounded in her ear, terse and afraid.

Rachel quickly filled him in.

The sound of Richard's program filled the room. Rachel put her phone on speaker.

But it wasn't Richard she heard debating the outcome of the raids. The voice she heard was Alizah's.

Khattak swore and checked his footsteps. He'd stopped moving, but Rachel heard an echo down the hall.

"Sir. I don't think you're alone there."

There was a long pause before Khattak spoke, lowering his voice.

"Get over to Richard. I'll meet you there."

"I'm heading over to you."

The footsteps sounded louder.

"It's just Père Étienne, Rachel. It's nothing to worry about."

Before she could object, Khattak cut off the call.

She stared at Gaffney, wordless. "Call him back," she said. "And get Lemaire and anyone else you trust. Meet me in the parking lot."

He left at once, forgetting his laptop on the desk.

Frowning, Rachel reached over to grab it. When she spun it around, the page he'd saved leapt up at her from the screen. She read the transcript again. Khattak's bitter words whispered into her mind.

She makes herself the center of things."

But *was* Alizah at the center of this crime?

Almost idly, she read the words she'd failed to notice before.

[Translated from the French]

But if the transcript had been translated into English . . .

She read it again, puzzled. Something niggled at the corner of her mind. She took a deep breath and closed her eyes, shifting pieces of the case around.

She'd gone to the hospital with Khattak to interview Amadou Duchon.

The lounge had been crowded with people she didn't know waiting for news on the fate of their loved ones, among them the Lilies of Anjou. But in that chaos, there had also been many officers of the Sûreté—men and women whom Khattak had called to account for failing to stand at their posts. Or to control the scene.

And others, *including* Alizah.

The names on the page danced up in her mind.

And then not a name but a word. A carefully chosen word.

Rachel's eyes snapped open. She glanced around the office almost blindly. She focused on the word and then she knew.

She knew it all. She knew who the target at the mosque had been and why.

She knew who had carried out the shooting.

It made a dreadful kind of sense.

Swallowing a cry of fear, she grabbed Gaffney's laptop and ran.

70

"What are you doing here, Père Étienne?"

The priest was wearing his collar under a long black jacket. A bulging notecase was gripped tightly under his arm. He gestured at the row of offices, his eyes deep set and dark.

"I have a chaplaincy office here. I sometimes come here to work. I caught sight of you."

Khattak studied the other man's face. The past few days had not worn well on him. He seemed smaller, shrunken, gravely uncertain, harrowed by the experience at the church and by the murders themselves.

Khattak hesitated. He couldn't afford to wait, but he wanted to hear what the priest had to say.

"Are you prepared to help me, Father?"

Père Étienne glanced back at the MSA office door. It was still sealed off, this time by professional police tape. Though without a guard at the door, anyone could slip under it to tamper with the scene. The faint scruff of Père Étienne's tonsure was disheveled, his beard roughly overgrown, his eyes red rimmed. The secrets of the confessional had taken a toll.

He couldn't seem to look away from the swastika on the MSA door.

"Père Étienne?" Esa prompted.

The priest's eyes slid to his. Measuring. Judging. Praying for absolution.

Esa gave up. "I can't wait, I'm sorry. Alizah and Amadou are in danger."

He started down the long corridor, filled with regret. Anything Père Étienne could have told him would have helped. But as with Alizah, the gruesome realities of the shooting had sheared off a layer of his restraint.

"Wait!"

He heard a sudden thump. Père Étienne's notecase had slipped from his hands, spilling his papers on the floor. Esa strode back to him, a pulse flickering at the corner of his mouth.

Père Étienne bent to gather up the contents of the notecase. "My son—"

Esa handed back the pages of a hastily written sermon. "Père Étienne, what *is* it?"

"You asked me about confession—"

The silence stretched out in the hall. Père Étienne gave him a name.

And the name he spoke made Esa turn and run.

The building in which Richard's studio was housed was dark. Esa raced up the steps to the door. He tested the handles. Locked. He'd called for backup. Still minutes away. Rachel was en route, accompanied by Lemaire. His phone rang just as a text buzzed through.

He took the call and ignored the text. As Rachel's terrified voice sounded in his ear, he noticed several shards of tempered glass scattered across the pavement. He looked up above the door. The outdoor lights had been shattered. As recently as this evening.

He looked back the way he'd come. The parking lot was empty except for a handful of cars. One was his; the other was Benoit's patrol car. From its license plate, he was able to identify the third as Richard's. And that was it. If Richard was airing his broadcast, he was doing it with a skeleton staff.

Rachel's panic was bleeding into him.

He hoped he'd been right to place his faith in Benoit. They had nothing on Richard, who wore his sympathies openly. More important, from the breakdown of the image of the figure fleeing the mosque Richard's height wasn't a match. Richard was simply too tall.

Esa tried the door again, rattling the glass, Rachel's voice still chattering in his ear.

"Slow down, Rachel. I can't understand your French."

Rachel said it again. Her words froze him in place.

Carefully, he raised his head and looked around the lot. With his free hand, he reached for his gun. But the lot was still deserted. There was no figure clad in a long dark jacket as there had been outside the prayer at the church.

He used the butt of his gun to break the glass and opened the door. He tried the elevators first. Locked for the night. He ran to the stairwell that led to the third floor.

"Get here," he said to Rachel.

He heard her say, "Two minutes," before he shut off his phone.

On the third floor, Amadou's voice filled his ears. He passed the abandoned reception desk, the hallways dark, the soft light pooled on the floor coming from the studio itself. His hand reached for a light switch. The hallway lights stayed dark.

Listeners were calling in to the show. Amadou and Alizah took turns fielding the calls. At the sound of Alizah's voice, relief swamped him like a wave. And then he listened more closely, edging toward the studio in the dark. He didn't hear Richard. And he didn't think Richard would have given his broadcast into Amadou's hands. Or into Alizah's—even with her experience.

His hands were slick with sweat. He adjusted his grip on his gun, wishing he'd brought a flashlight. Nothing stirred in the hallway. He could make out the shapes of desks and chairs and on one side a bank of cabinets. He checked quickly, but no one was hiding on the far side. He moved forward a step and tripped over something he hadn't noticed. He looked down at his feet. A faceless mass was huddled there. He turned it over with his foot, bringing out his cell phone and using its light to see.

The silent mass was Philippe Benoit. He was bleeding from a wound on his head, his gun missing from its holster. Khattak knelt down beside him, testing for his pulse, his own heart kicking up speed.

He hit Rachel's number with his thumb just as a shape loomed out of the darkness and threw itself at him. He dropped his phone and rolled aside. His assailant leapt at him again.

Khattak stuck out his leg and tripped him. He landed a foot away, cold black metal sliding across the floor. Khattak holstered his own gun swiftly, wrestling with the strong, dark shape. They thrashed across the floor. Khattak gained a little traction and threw his attacker aside. Whoever it was, he landed next to Benoit, knocking himself out when his head thumped hard against the floor. Khattak pinned his body to the floor, wresting his arms behind his back.

He heard the clink of metal; then a weak voice spoke in his ear. "Would these help?"

Benoit had managed to raise his head. He was holding his handcuffs in his hand.

Khattak used them to lock down the suspect.

He turned the suspect over as Benoit whispered, "I'm sorry. He jumped me when I went to check the lights."

Khattak put a finger to his lips. "Can you get up?"

Benoit shook his head, then groaned. "I don't think so."

Khattak looked down at the suspect he'd just handcuffed.

He recognized Pascal Richard's intern, André Martin—the young man who served as a military cadet. The one he'd accused of looking like one of Maxime's disciples. André Martin was the name Père Étienne had given him.

"He's the one who jumped you and took your gun?"

Benoit nodded. "Yes."

Khattak searched for Benoit's gun. He couldn't find it. He'd lost it along with his phone.

"Phone," he whispered to Benoit.

Benoit passed his over, and Khattak switched on its light. He swept the floor, the hallway, the corners of the reception area. The gun was ten feet away. He eased over to it and picked it up. He checked it. It was loaded. He gave it back to Benoit.

Something glinted in the light from Benoit's phone. Khattak turned to look. The light had silvered across the buckle on André's belt. Khattak read its engraving to himself.

FLAYALLTHEPLAYERS

He recognized the name from a Wolf Allegiance transcript, but it didn't make sense in light of Rachel's warning. From Benoit's expression, he recognized the name as well.

"Backup will be here any minute," Esa promised. "Don't take your eyes off him."

Benoit nodded at him wearily. Esa squeezed his shoulder and moved on.

He'd cleared the area behind him. He was in the passageway between Richard's office and the door to the studio. The ON AIR sign that should have warned him not to interrupt the broadcast wasn't on. He put his hand on the handle and considered.

Was the broadcast actually airing? Or had it been a ruse to draw Alizah and Amadou to the studio? He couldn't hear Richard's voice, but the calls coming in were real enough.

Carefully, he opened the door. When he pushed it wide, he caught sight of Richard in the control booth at the back of the right side of the spacious room. With his headphones on, Richard was carefully screening calls at a soundboard, in lieu of his regular technician. He still had access to a microphone that was presently switched off. Khattak guessed that Richard had wanted to control every aspect of this particular program and would weigh in when he wanted to shift the discussion in a particular direction. The booth was protected by a glass partition, but Richard was clearly visible behind it.

On the left side of the studio several feet away from the floor-to-ceiling windows, Amadou's back was to Khattak at the large and durable host's desk, which had been set up with two microphones. He was answering a call that Richard had directed to him—a disturbingly venomous outpouring, if what Esa could hear was anything to judge by. Alizah was facing Khattak from the opposite desk at a second microphone, a digital clock to the side counting down the time in red.

Alizah looked up at Esa. Her eyes went wide at the sight of the gun poised in his hand. Esa put a finger to his lips. He motioned to Alizah to drop down behind the desk. The minute she did, he scanned the studio.

There was no one else in the room. Behind the glass partition, Richard caught sight of him. Shocked, he made a move to pull off his headphones, but Esa stayed him, motioning him down. Richard's hand moved suddenly, cutting off all sound. The studio was filled with dead air. Uncertain now, Esa moved so that he was between Richard and Amadou, who still hadn't turned around.

Amadou remained oddly still.

The lights in the studio were dim. But Amadou was staring straight ahead, his gaze fixed at a point on the picture window.

A single shot shattered the glass. Alizah stifled a scream.

And then there was another presence in the room.

71

"Too little," she said. "Too little, far too late."

"Isabelle."

Esa kept his gun trained on her, just as the lethal black weapon in her hand was pointed straight at his heart.

He recognized the gun. It was a Glock 19, a gun commonly used by law enforcement.

If she'd fired one round to shatter the window before she'd climbed inside from the terrace, she still had more than enough ammunition. He moved closer to her cautiously. He wanted to shove Amadou behind him, but he still wasn't sure about Richard.

"Amadou, get under the desk," he urged.

"He moves and he dies," she warned. "I came here for him, after all."

"You can't get away with this, Isabelle. Lemaire is already here." He could hear the sirens at a distance. He knew it would soon be true.

Her tone became lightly mocking. "Not in time to save you, I'm afraid."

"Isabelle!" Richard squawked a protest. Esa kept his eye on Alizah, who was far too close to Isabelle's side of the desk to give him any peace.

Isabelle glanced behind him at Richard.

"Pascal."

"What the hell are you doing?"

She shifted the gun so that it pointed at Richard, for whom the glass partition would provide little protection. Esa inched closer to Amadou.

"I gave you the key to the city for a reason. But to you, it was only sport. Still, you served your purpose in the end." She nodded to herself, her blond hair spilling out in waves from under her cap. She yanked it off. She was dressed entirely in black, and she moved with the same controlled litheness as the figure he'd seen on the tape.

Esa took another step closer to Amadou, who still hadn't shifted to the side. His hands were clenched on the desk. He wouldn't be easy to move out of the way if the opportunity came.

"What purpose?" Khattak asked. His gun was still trained on Isabelle, his arm locked firmly in place.

"Stirring up the people of this town. Riling up all of Québec. Especially those like André Martin and Maxime Thibault. It was so easy in the end. But you—" The gun now shifted back to Khattak. Her pale eyes glinted with triumph. "You were slow to catch on."

From the corner of his eye, he saw that Alizah had moved farther under the desk, easing closer to Amadou.

His tone conversational, Esa responded, "How could I? The texts you sent me were from an encrypted source, and you didn't say a word when you had me at your mercy."

She frowned at him. "What texts? This is the first time I've had you at my mercy."

He played along. "Then how was I supposed to guess?"

But Rachel had guessed. Rachel's sharp mind had put it all together.

"Who else could have been the leak? Who else do you know who had access to the footage of the woman in the abaya at the scene of the shooting? I didn't leak it myself—I put in André's hands. Just as I had Pascal hire him, as a personal favor to me."

Wheezing a little, Pascal drew his attention to her, his voice clearly audible from behind the glass. "You're the head of the Allegiance? You're the one who hit the mosque?"

Khattak's free hand moved to Amadou's shoulder. He pressed hard, letting him know what he wanted.

"No!" Isabelle said sharply. "He's the one I want. You won't be able to save him."

"Why, Isabelle? What has Amadou ever done?"

With a sudden move, she switched her gun to her other hand.

"Because he nearly saved him," she said coolly. "That's why he has to pay."

Esa shook his head, miming confusion. His arm had begun to stiffen, but he could hear the sound of police cars speeding into the lot.

"Saved who, Isabelle? I don't know who you mean."

"Youssef. All my hard work, all my careful planning. He nearly saved Youssef's life."

"Why would that matter?"

A droplet of sweat formed on his forehead and slid into his eye. He blinked rapidly, trying not to lose sight of where her gun was aimed.

But he'd pushed her too far. She took three steps forward, pressed her gun to Amadou's head, and spit the words in his face.

"Because Chloé Villeneuve is my niece. And Soufiane polluted her. He and his mother both—the one who told him to marry her."

Amadou gasped at the feel of the gun against his temple. Alizah's involuntary movement struck a jarring note in the silence.

"There's time enough for Alizah."

Esa struggled to quash his sense of panic.

"There isn't," he tried to say calmly. "You can't escape, even if you make it out. Listen to me, Isabelle. You don't need Alizah or Amadou. You need a high-profile hostage. Keep me and let the others go."

She tipped her head to one side, her blond hair obscuring her face.

"No," she said quite coolly. "Although you *are* a high-value target." She moved her gun from Amadou's head and pressed it against Esa's chest. She used it to draw two lines against his chest, and he realized she'd marked him with a cross. "If I killed you because of who you are, it would show the rest of you that none of you are safe. And after you? Diana Shehadeh, perhaps."

"Fine," he said carefully. "I accept your terms. Make your point with me. The others are insignificant. They'll be forgotten as quickly as the people you killed at the mosque."

"Esa, no!"

Alizah scrambled out from under the desk. Isabelle swung around to point the gun at her, in the process jolting Esa's arm. His gun was knocked from his hand. Quicker to react than he, Isabelle scooped it up. She held herself out of his reach. With one hand, she cradled her gun to her chest. With the other, she aimed at Alizah.

His face went white and she laughed.

"How perfect it would be if I killed her with your gun. How poetic. Just as I killed Youssef with the gun he bought for protection. What a mercy I spared him the AR-15. A *beautiful mercy*, in fact."

"No." Esa couldn't breathe. He knew this moment. He'd seen it in his nightmares. He knew when a suspect was poised on the brink of a desperate act. "Isabelle, this *isn't* the way."

He heard the pounding of footsteps up the stairs, the shouts as Benoit and Martin were discovered. But the sound was hollow in his ears—a lifetime away, a distance he couldn't bridge. And the last thing he'd said to Alizah was something he'd never be able to retract.

"It's the *only* way."

Amadou shouted hoarsely to distract her, but all Esa heard was the shot.

The sound shattered the night.

Esa shivered with terror, frozen in place, but absurdly the sound he heard in his mind was the melody in the woods.

Tinny, haunting, cold.

As cold as Alizah would be.

72

"Sir—are you all right?"

He felt himself shaken roughly, Rachel's voice in his ears.

"Esa!" She shook him again until he focused. He noticed the bits of broken glass on her shirt. Her arm was bleeding from a scratch. She'd hurt herself, somehow.

He couldn't look past her—wouldn't.

She reached up and murmured in his ear.

"It was a clean shot; she'll be okay. Until she ends up in prison."

And then he dared to look over at the window, where Alizah was leaning weakly against the wall, Amadou beside her.

Isabelle Clément had fallen at his feet. Lemaire's team took over, and he and Rachel were ushered from the room, along with Pascal Richard.

Lemaire stood in the center of the chaos, pulling it all into order—the role that was usually Khattak's. Esa grabbed Rachel's hand.

"You shot her?"

With a cocky grin that didn't fool him, she answered, "From the window. A nice clean shot to the shoulder before she could make up her mind."

"How did you know she was here?"

She jerked her head at Richard. "When our friendly neighborhood Nazi turned off the sound in the studio, he switched on the speakers outside. Lemaire came up the stairs; I made my entrance from the back." She gave him a crooked smile. "Saved your bacon is what I did. Course that might matter more if bacon was actually your thing."

A hoarse laugh sounded from his throat.

"Believe me, Rachel, it matters."

"We're even now, right?" she said warily. "Me on the ice, you here?"

Esa shook his head with the ghost of a smile. The inroads Rachel had made into his heart still had the power to surprise him.

"No," he said firmly. "You still have the upper hand."

Alizah was perched on a desk in the hallway. A female officer took her statement while Amadou hovered close by. Esa stopped to speak to him, console him, but in the end it was Amadou who had wisdom to share. Perhaps wisdom he'd gained through the process of losing his brother.

"He watches over you," he said. "He watches over me. And even if I had found myself with Youssef, I would only be closer to Him."

Amadou was taken aside by the officer waiting to debrief him.

When Esa reached Alizah, she had finished giving her statement. She looked up at him, shivering, a question in her eyes.

He gathered her up from the desk and hugged her as fiercely as he could.

"What I said to you was unforgivable. It would have been the last thing you remembered."

She pulled back a little and smiled at him through her tears.

"No," she contradicted him. "What I would have remembered is the way you begged Isabelle to take your life instead of mine."

He swallowed. Knowing what she would say.

"Alizah—"

"I love you, Esa. I have for a long time now."

He couldn't think of an answer, but after a moment he said, "You know I'm marrying Sehr. All I have to give you is this."

He knew she'd understand even if he didn't have the words.

With a faint smile of surprise she whispered, "Anything you give me is enough."

73

They had gathered to brief Superintendent Killiam on the arrest of Isabelle Clément.

Khattak had appropriately given Rachel the credit for the break in the case, and following his lead, Lemaire had ceded the floor.

The nature of Rachel and Khattak's partnership became clear. Rachel spoke freely, occasionally checking with Khattak, who either nodded or added a few words of his own. He didn't interrupt unless Rachel asked for his thoughts.

"It was Sergeant Gaffney who spotted it," Rachel was saying modestly. "He brought me the transcript, and when I translated it back into French I realized that ABeautifulMercy was an unimaginative restyling of Isabelle Clément's name. Clément: 'merciful,' Belle: 'beautiful.' And if ABM and ABeautifulMercy were the same anonymous commenter, they were both preoccupied with the daughters of Québec. Each of them pushed for action. I mean, plenty of others did as well, but when Gaff ran his check Isabelle was in Montréal on the days she posted her comments on the Montréal blog."

"She's a white supremacist?" Killiam clarified.

"The worst kind of Québec nationalist." Rachel glanced over at Lemaire, blushing at the reminder of her mistake.

"And her name was how you made the connection?"

"Well, that, and I knocked my can of pop over on Clément's desk. There was a photograph on her desk, I cleaned up the frame but didn't really notice it at first. But after I made the connection, I looked again. That's when I noticed that Chloé Villeneuve was in it."

"And Chloé Villeneuve is her niece."

Almost apologetically, Rachel said, "Inspector Lemaire did tell us almost right from the beginning that the reason Isabelle came to Saint-Isidore so often was because she had family here. As for the rest—" Rachel nodded politely at Dr. Sandston. She reached behind her and snagged the remote for the blinds, using it to let a little light into the room.

"Dr. Sandston is better equipped than I am to fill you in on the rest."

Marlyse Sandston edged forward in her seat, the light gilding the warm, dark tones of her skin and glossing over her cheekbones.

"There were two shooters at the mosque; that much was clear to me when I crafted the profile. Just as it was clear that one mind directed the shooting—and most likely directed the activities of the Wolf Allegiance. The motive was simply rage: rage that Soufiane's family had rejected her niece Chloé—a *pure laine* Québécois girl." Her deeply black eyes were knowing when she added, "It's funny, isn't it, when the shoe is on the other foot? When the despised group disapproves of members of the comfortable majority." She drew a steady breath. "Then, Youssef Soufiane's biological mother *did* approve of Youssef and Chloé's match. Along with Père Étienne, she took part in their marriage ceremony. This was a bridge too far for someone of Isabelle's convictions. She wanted to punish Youssef for daring to cross that divide. No doubt she had his gun stolen from campus by a member of the Allegiance. Chloé may have told her that he'd bought a gun for protection. And Isabelle might have thought it was poetic to kill Youssef with his own gun—a cold, clear execution."

"Yes," Khattak put in. "That's more or less what she said at the studio."

"But the frenzied shooting in the prayer hall doesn't fit your profile, Dr. Sandston," Killiam observed.

"She would have given the AR-15 to one of her disciples."

"In this case, André Martin, who worked for Pascal Richard. He's admitted to pushing Rachel at the church," Lemaire added. "As for Isabelle, we knew she was a defense attorney before she came on board as the premier's press liaison. We knew her firm was involved in Michel

Gagnon's defense—her criminal clientele included members of his gang. I should never have overlooked her. Otherwise, I would have considered what she might have gained in exchange for representing Gagnon. She would have had access to her choice of weapons."

He gestured for Dr. Sandston to continue. She gave him a gracious nod.

"Isabelle carried out the executions. André Martin was just another angry young man who found his voice with a gun—a profile we're all familiar with. We shouldn't have missed this, but given that the INSET team was infiltrated by members of the Allegiance, it's likely that his background check was altered—sanitized for our benefit by someone on the inside. And note how this ties into the fact that other than Inspector Lemaire—who was relentlessly thorough in tracking supremacist infiltration of law enforcement in his province—we haven't been paying enough attention to the radicalization of white men from relatively privileged groups. They're being co-opted into identitarian groups, and this is a phenomenon we should be keeping track of."

Killiam nodded to herself. "That leaves the lily on Youssef Soufiane's back."

Dr. Sandston took a moment to think this over. Finally, she said, "Isabelle, again. I'm sure the knife will be recovered during a search of either her home or her temporary accommodation in Saint-Isidore. It would be dear to her," she explained. "As the means by which she left her calling card. As Inspector Khattak advised me, Youssef had asked Chloé to have the tattoo of the fleur-de-lis on her wrist removed. The symbolism is remarkable."

Killiam's gray eyes were sharp and intent.

Sandston continued, "A Québécois Muslim man of Moroccan ancestry asking a Québécois Catholic woman to literally erase a symbol of her identity to accord with his own religious preference. When Isabelle carved the lily on Youssef's back, she was taking that on."

Killiam sighed. She adjusted her glasses, rubbing the tip of her nose. "Terrible. What about the gun at the lake?"

Lemaire answered this. "Martin has confessed that Isabelle asked him to plant it at the lake because that was where Chloé's marriage ceremony took place. It was her way of rejecting the marriage—and of pointing the finger in another direction. Réjeanne says she saw it there the night after the shooting. She waited too long to tell us. She couldn't tell who was aligned with the Allegiance, because there was no official response to complaints about the acts of vandalism she must have attributed to the Wolves. It says something that in the end Inspector Khattak was the one she decided to trust."

A fair enough summary, but Rachel was following her own train of thought. She looked over at Lemaire with a challenge in her eyes, but when she spoke she chose her words with care.

"I'm wondering if Isabelle did anything to give herself away in your meetings."

Lemaire must have spent some time retracing their private conversations.

"Nothing at all. She elicited my sympathy in fact, by letting me know she was a mouthpiece for the premier, and didn't have any real power in her hands. She was used to being overlooked. Disrespected, even, as a woman."

Khattak nodded his agreement. "That's also what she did with me. So I wanted to be sure that nothing I said or did gave her the same impression."

Martine Killiam grimaced. "Clever. Given how gender politics have been shaking up the force, she disarmed you both at the start." A small smile edged her lips as she considered Rachel. "And you she probably didn't like."

Rachel grinned. "I tend to have that effect."

As Khattak started to demur, Rachel laughed outright, easing the tension in the room.

Full of restless energy, Lemaire stood up and paced the room. "I confided in her more than I would have done otherwise. To show her that respect. That's how she was able to leak so much about the case."

Taking over from Dr. Sandston, he summarized his operation as concisely as Rachel had, and when he'd finished, Killiam concluded,

"Inspector Khattak isn't the only one to have a target on his back. Your actions will not be popular, I'm afraid."

Lemaire shrugged without any attempt at bravado. "This is better for the SQ, better for Québec. Let's see what happens next."

"At least the premier has seen fit to give you a commendation."

Lemaire ducked his head, a little embarrassed. "At first, I thought he may have been another plant. Maybe handpicked by Isabelle."

"I'm surprised that Richard wasn't, given all his on-air opinions."

"He's mainly an opportunist. He doesn't much care how he makes his money."

"The swastika on his neck would seem to suggest otherwise," Killiam cautioned.

"He used it as an entrée into a select group. But we'll be going through every utterance on his program. If there's a way to charge him, we'll find it."

"And this Amadou?" Killiam asked. "And Alizah Siddiqui, whom we ignored for so long? *Is* there a hit on them?"

"No. Nothing official. Gagnon's gang is not involved. This was all Isabelle. But there's no way of predicting what radicalized young men will do. I should have paid more attention to those incidents she reported. She tried so hard to get them on my radar, but I refused to expand my focus from my operation; I thought I had room to maneuver."

A failure shared by them all.

"What about Maxime Thibault?" Killiam asked. "How will you make sure now that he stays away from Amadou and Alizah?"

Lemaire spread his hands. "If he's convicted of inciting hate as the founder of his chapter of the Allegiance, that will keep him away. But if those charges don't stick, unless he directly threatens them with violence, there's not much more we can do."

"We'll make them stick," Killiam said grimly. "But until this dies down, Alizah and Amadou should be keeping a lower profile. As a matter of their own safety."

Khattak shook his head, the purple bruise on his forehead standing out in sharp relief against his paler skin. "Alizah won't be quiet. You should expect more trouble from her in the days to come."

Disturbed by this, Killiam said, "Of the kind you suffered? How did Isabelle Clément pull off the attack on you?"

Khattak looked quickly at Dr. Sandston.

"She denied it. She also denied sending me the texts."

Lemaire leaned against the conference room table. Rachel watched him closely, holding her breath.

"By the time you were assaulted that night, Isabelle Clément had returned to Montréal."

"André Martin, then," Killiam offered.

Lemaire shook his head. "He had checked in with Pascal. He was at the studio all night."

Killiam frowned. "Then we've missed someone else they roped in to do their work. And there will be others who infiltrated the investigation, the ones we still haven't caught. Keep at it until you find them."

"Ma'am," Rachel said to Killiam. "Mind if I have a private word with Inspector Khattak? Can you finish up here?"

The superintendent nodded. Rachel turned to wink at Lemaire before she left. He smiled back at her and went on with his report.

Rachel led Khattak down to the cafeteria, where in short order she found herself in possession of an inventive take on what should have been an appetizing serving of poutine. It was garnished with cilantro and lime, and gamely Rachel dug in. Khattak asked for tea, but when it came he grimaced at its flavor and pushed his paper cup aside.

In the windowless room in the basement cafeteria, he studied Rachel's face, reading the concern she no longer bothered to hide.

"I'm all right," he told her. And then teasing her, he added, "And you're more than all right, it would seem."

Rachel admonished him between oversized bites of her meal.

"How does you being stalked add up to feeling all right?"

She shoved the bowl of poutine at him. He refused it with a show of horror.

"I get it." She waved a hand at his face. "You don't want to mess with the pretty."

She felt like she'd scored when he laughed.

"Your compliments, Rachel." He was grinning as he shook his head, which made her all the more reluctant to bring up what was on her mind. She took a breath—and a healthy bite of poutine—and plunged in.

"You leaving me on my own, sir? Heading on to greener pastures like you said?"

His grin faded. He reached for his tea but didn't drink it. A long silence fell, during which Rachel could hear herself chewing. But the poutine had lost its greasy appeal; she pushed it aside, depressed.

When he still didn't speak, she said on a sigh, "You don't have to apologize." She waved her plastic fork, meaning to indicate all of Saint-Isidore. "After what happened here, I get it. I mean, I get what I can never get—God, I'm not making any sense." She cleared her throat and tried again, liking the way his eyes warmed up at her efforts. "I'm not you; I can't walk in your shoes. I don't know what it's like to sit in a room full of senior officers and hear them talk about 'anti-Muslim activists.' Would we say 'anti-Jewish activists' and think that was okay? Or 'anti-Québécois'?" She shook her head wisely. "We'd never say that—we'd think it was a crime." Her fork clattered to the table. "So I get why you have to go. You have bigger battles to fight."

She blinked back sudden tears. "I'll just miss you, is all." And then more brashly, to make up for her tears, "Here's a compliment for you, sir: I can't say you slowed me down."

He laughed again, the sound gentler, warmer. Then he reached across the table for one of her hands. He cupped his hand around hers and Rachel swallowed.

"You *do* deserve a promotion," he said, "but it won't be at my expense. Superintendent Killiam has decided to expand my role, to allow me greater latitude in investigations like these. I won't be as constrained, and I *will* be allowed to say whatever is on my mind. I'll be acting as an advisor on the threat posed by groups like the Wolf Allegiance. But my bread and butter—my *first* love—" he said with the warmest smile and a quick squeeze of her hand, "will still be working with you. If you won't mind those times you find me slow to catch on."

She gripped his hand with hers, grinning at him like a fool.

In an offhand voice, she said, "I'll do what I can, sir. One of these days, you'll catch up."

They smiled at each other like the old and steadfast friends that they were. Then Khattak reached into his pocket and drew out the envelope Rachel had given him.

He passed the envelope back to her. She nodded, knowing where this was going.

"Tom Paley," she said. "We weren't able to sort out why his photograph was included with the rest. And if this isn't about Isabelle and everything that happened here, we need to take another look at how Paley died, and whether there's something more to it."

Khattak nodded, too. "Yes, agreed. But there's something else as well."

Rachel sifted through the photographs again, concentrating. "What's that, sir?"

His long fingers drew out the photograph that still embarrassed Rachel. The photograph from Algonquin, where she'd lain on the ice in his arms.

"I want you to keep this photograph of us."

She looked up at him with a blush, but his gaze was steady and sure. "Yeah?"

"Yes," he said firmly. "With everything that's happened—everything that *could* happen—I want you to remember. I want you to know that every moment was worth it."

This time when her tears fell, Rachel really didn't give a damn. She didn't even bother to wipe her tears away.

She looked at him and said, "You need to know something, too."

He waited, watching her with that look—amazement, appreciation, gratitude—the way no one else had ever looked at her.

She slipped the photograph into her pocket and leaned closer to kiss him on the cheek.

She murmured into his ear, "You're the best friend I've ever had."

Epilogue

Sehr reached out to snag the envelope that was wedged under the screen door of her home in Toronto. It was handstitched on exquisitely marbled paper, her name typed on its surface in a sophisticated font. She took it inside and placed it on the writing desk in the hallway. The envelope was so delicate, it couldn't be torn across. She used a letter opener to slice it at the seam instead.

At first she thought the envelope was empty, but when she shook it lightly a photograph came loose. It fell onto her desk. Curious, she flipped it over.

The photograph was of Esa.

Alizah was wrapped in his arms, her face half-hidden in his chest.

His face was turned toward the camera, and on it was an expression that Sehr had never seen. A fierce kind of tenderness, and something deeper still.

For a moment, she clutched at the desk.

She still hadn't gathered herself when a hand knocked at her door. She could see Esa's silhouette through the glass, but she couldn't force herself to move.

"Sehr?"

Esa called to her. She knew he could see her. When she didn't speak, he said her name again, this time his voice grave and deep. Puzzled. And a little afraid.

But Sehr didn't answer. She left him waiting at the door.

Esa took out his phone to call her. A message appeared on the screen, accompanied by a photograph of him standing at Sehr's door. He flattened himself against the door, his sharp eyes canvasing the street. The leafy Toronto neighborhood was quiet, but the menace that had begun in Saint-Isidore had reached out to touch him again.

Someone was still following him, close enough to observe his every action. Close enough to take out a camera and point it at him like a gun.

He skipped over the photograph to read the message again, the sour taste of fear in his mouth.

I hope you enjoyed the first Act.

Author's Note

On January 29, 2017, a young man by the name of Alexandre Bissonnette opened fire after evening prayers inside a mosque in the Sainte-Foy neighborhood of Québec City in Québec. He killed six people and injured nineteen more. He was later charged with six counts of first-degree murder and would eventually plead guilty on all counts.

Though in initial statements the prime minister of Canada and the premier of Québec both called the shooting a terrorist incident, Bissonnette was not charged with a terrorism offense. Under the Canadian Criminal Code, terrorism is defined as an act committed "for a political, religious or ideological purpose, objective or cause" that has "the intention of intimidating the public, or a segment of the public, with regard to its security." To charge Bissonnette with an act of terrorism, prosecutors would have had to prove these elements beyond a reasonable doubt when it came to the motive for Bissonnette's attack on the worshipers at the mosque. They would also have had to establish the participation or support of a terrorist group, rather than the act of a person acting alone or simply "inspired" by terrorist materials.

Yet in discussions with interrogators, several critical factors about Bissonnette's views came to light. He was fascinated by mass shootings, and he had a distinct anti-feminist, anti-Muslim, and anti-immigrant animus. A friend described his ideology as that of the "extreme far right." He was obsessed with President Trump's iterations of the Muslim ban, particularly in the days leading up to the shooting. Though not explicitly linked to far-right groups, Bissonnette paid close attention to positions taken by the far right on immigration and on Muslims in Québec. In the weeks prior to the attack, he consulted this material more frequently, particularly as espoused by conspiracy theorists, neo-Nazis, and white supremacists. American commentators also held a unique fascination for Bissonnette. Among the Twitter accounts he searched along with President Trump's were those of Fox News anchors Tucker Carlson and Laura Ingraham, the former Ku Klux Klan leader David Duke, Alex Jones of InfoWars, and Richard Spencer, the notorious white nationalist. In the month before the shooting, Bissonnette checked the Twitter account of Ben Shapiro, editor of the conservative Daily Wire, ninety-three times.

In the aftermath of the shooting, Bissonnette would tell interrogators that he snapped on January 29, 2017, after reading Prime Minister Trudeau's statement welcoming refugees to Canada. Bissonnette decided to act against the threat he perceived, a perception stoked by his online consumption of radical white nationalist views, the target his local Muslim neighbors. Later he would tell a social worker that he wished he had killed more people at the mosque that night, as they would be going to heaven, while he was living through hell. Yet when he chose to plead guilty to his crimes, he said this in his Statement of Guilt: "I do not know why I committed such a senseless act. And to this day, I have a hard time believing it. In spite of what has been said about me, I am not a terrorist, nor an Islamophobe, rather a person who was carried away by fear, negative thoughts and a horrible form of despair."

Researching this book, I considered the process of radicalization Bissonnette had undergone—the American and Canadian sources he'd relied upon to form his world view, the targets he'd chosen to blame rather than exploring the appropriate means to cope with his serious personal issues. My research pointed to two troubling conclusions. There has been a surge in the participation of white men in white nationalist movements, alongside a growth in the number of these movements, whose radical and violent agendas are currently understudied. Some of these groups specifically identify Muslims and Muslim communities as a threat that must be confronted with violence, though their speech and manifestos additionally target communities of color, women, Jews, and other marginalized groups, including all points of intersection. Writing this book, I considered whether these ideologies were gaining traction and whether these activities were on the rise mainly as a matter of coincidence or whether they reflected the populist, reactionary politics currently sweeping the West.

My research into hate speech and acts of violence against Muslims and Muslim communities indicated that a marked increase in hate speech and hate crimes could not be satisfactorily explained by happenstance. In the United States and Canada and in many European countries, fear, suspicion, and hate are cultivated and promoted through effective and well-funded channels: far-right news media, online commentary (particularly in online subcultures), political actors and lobbyists, and popular demagogic personalities, all of whom are able to capitalize on terror attacks that occur against Western targets to assign collective guilt to a perceived "Islamic threat" at home. This perceived threat includes vulnerable and innocent targets such as the members of the congregation who were murdered at the mosque in Sainte-Foy. The victims of the Sainte-Foy attack were notably Canadian Muslims of West African or North African descent, similar to the characters in this book.

I wrote this book because I have long studied the incipient and incremental nature of hate and the fatal places hate often takes us. I wrote it to illuminate the connections between rhetoric, polemics, and action. To suggest that the nature of our speech should be as thoughtful, as peaceable, and as well-informed as our actions. The things that we choose to turn a blind eye to because we assess their impact as negligible on our lives—especially when we are not members of any vulnerable group—have the power to harm us all more deeply than we know.

RECOMMENDED READING

For general reading on the subject of what constitutes Islamophobia and how it achieves traction in public and private life, I recommend: *Fear, Inc. 2.0: The Islamophobia Network's Efforts to Manufacture Hate in America,* by Matthew Duss, et al.; *American Islamophobia: Understanding the Roots and Rise of Fear,* by Khaled A. Beydoun; *The Islamophobia Industry: How the Right Manufactures Hatred of Muslims,* by Nathan Lean; and *Islamophobia: The Challenge of Pluralism in the 21st Century,* by John L. Esposito and Ibrahim Kalin.

To have a deeper sense of where the trends in Canada and the United States may be heading, I recommend reading the *European Islamophobia Report 2017,* available here: http://www.islamophobiaeurope.com. And compare the rise of hate speech in Canada: https://www.macleans .ca/politics/online-hate-speech-in-canada-is-up-600-percent-what -can-be-done.

For more information on the rise of white nationalism, please visit the website of the SPLC, or Southern Poverty Law Center: www .splcenter.org/fighting-hate/extremist-files/ideology/white -nationalist. For further reading on the FBI's monitoring of white supremacist organizations, see https://foreignpolicy.com/2017/08/14 /fbi-and-dhs-warned-of-growing-threat-from-white-supremacists -months-ago, and on the infiltration of law enforcement by white supremacist elements, see *PBS NewsHour* at www.pbs.org/newshour /nation/fbi-white-supremacists-in-law-enforcement.

And finally, on Alexandre Bissonnette and the Québec mosque shooting, see general reporting in the *Washington Post* and the *Montreal Gazette,* including Andy Riga's profile on Bissonnette at https:// montrealgazette.com/news/local-news/alexandre-bissonnette-inside -the-life-of-a-mass-murderer.

Acknowledgments

Another step on Esa and Rachel's journey and I have so many people to thank. Everyone at Minotaur who shepherded this book into becoming what it is, and the wondrous people in my life who shared their insights to help me tell this story I wanted to tell for so long.

I have a trio of guardian angels—Elizabeth, Danielle, and Catherine, who took on Esa's story and helped him make it to the page. Elizabeth, after me, Esa belongs to you. Thank you for bringing him to life. Danielle, I can't find the words—I'm just so grateful to have you on this journey. Catherine, thank you especially for *this* book and for your brilliance in taking on Esa's mantle and making his story shine. And to my UK family at No Exit Press/Oldcastle Books, thank you for your unstinting support, especially dear Katherine and Clare.

As always, I am deeply grateful to my amazing family and friends and to my community of writers and readers for caring so much about my books. This work is work we're doing together and every one of you inspires me. Uzmi and Sajidah—this was *our* book, born of our pain. Thank you, my sisters—both of the pen and of the heart.

I'd especially like to thank two people I've been speaking to this past year in some depth about the impact of the new *laicité* controversies in Québec and France. Émilie Gascon-Léger, your personal story and your love of Québec helped me find the heart of this book. Thank you for showing me such generosity and kindness—any mistakes are mine. Rim-Sarah Alouane, your courage in speaking out and your brilliant, dedicated scholarship helped me to appreciate what's truly at stake in debates about identity and belonging. Thank you for educating me.

Thank you to the amazing journalist Tabassum Siddiqui for your thorough tutorial on campus and talk radio. Nothing was more helpful than seeing those rooms through your eyes.

My deepest gratitude to the National Council of Canadian Muslims for your unparalleled leadership on civil liberties and for taking on hate on behalf of our communities. Ihsaan and Amira, I don't have a lot of heroes, but you two are certainly among them. God keep you and grant you strength—may our days be brighter ahead.

For Nader, who gives me everything in this life, and who I claim in the Hereafter, my always and only love: thank you, light of my eyes.

And for my brothers and sisters who think their pain and loss is unseen, know that I remember, and hold you in my heart.